Amish Brides

Center Point
Large Print

| Books are produced in the United States using U.S.-based materials | Books are printed using a revolutionary new process called THINKtech™ that lowers energy usage by 70% and increases overall quality | Books are durable and flexible because of smythe-sewing | Paper is sourced using environmentally responsible foresting methods and the paper is acid-free |

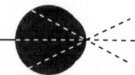

This Large Print Book carries the Seal of Approval of N.A.V.H.

Amish Brides

Jennifer Beckstrand
Molly Jebber
Amy Lillard

CENTER POINT LARGE PRINT
THORNDIKE, MAINE

This Center Point Large Print edition is published
in the year 2017 by arrangement with
Kensington Publishing Corp.

Compilation copyright © 2017
by Kensington Publishing Corp.
"The Reluctant Groom" © 2017 by Jennifer Beckstrand.
"Joshua's Bride" © 2017 by Molly Jebber.
"A Summer Wedding in Paradise"
© 2017 by Amy Lillard.

The text of this Large Print edition is unabridged.
In other aspects, this book may vary from the original edition.
Printed in the United States of America on permanent paper.
Set in 16-point Times New Roman type.

ISBN: 978-1-68324-447-9

Library of Congress Cataloging-in-Publication Data

Names: Beckstrand, Jennifer. Reluctant groom. | Jebber, Molly.
Joshua's bride. | Lillard, Amy. Summer wedding in paradise.
Title: Amish brides / Jennifer Beckstrand, Molly Jebber, Amy Lillard.
Description: Center Point Large Print edition. | Thorndike, Maine :
Center Point Large Print, 2017.
Identifiers: LCCN 2017016723 | ISBN 9781683244479
      (hardcover : alk. paper)
Subjects: LCSH: Amish—Fiction. | Weddings—Fiction. | Christian
fiction, American. | Romance fiction, American. | Large type books.
Classification: LCC PS648.A45 A27 2017 | DDC 813/.01083823—
dc23
LC record available at https://lccn.loc.gov/2017016723

Contents

THE RELUCTANT GROOM

Jennifer Beckstrand

For my dear friend,
Tonya Robinette,
who literally prayed me
through this story

Acknowledgments

I want to thank my agent, Nicole Resciniti, and my editor, John Scognamiglio. Nicole's instincts are spot-on, and John's eye for a good story never ceases to amaze me. I must also thank my husband, Gary, who is my biggest fan, my biggest supporter, and the prototype for all my heroes.

Chapter 1

Amish *fraas* were supposed to butt into their children's lives—not the other way around. But Anna Helmuth's daughter Esther passed out advice like most Amish *mammis* handed out cookies. And Esther had real trouble taking no for an answer.

"Mamm," Esther said, stuffing her yarn into her jumbo-size canvas bag. "Your hands are going to shrivel up like chicken feet if you insist on crocheting a dishrag for every unmarried boy and girl in the district. You don't want to be a cripple, do you?"

"I'd rather not be a cripple." Anna purposefully doubled her speed with the crochet hook. Esther meant well, but she knew nothing about crochet or cripples. Anna's hands were sure to shrivel up with arthritis if she didn't keep them limber with her handicrafts. And there were so many of *die youngie* who still needed a dishrag. How was she supposed to get two young people together without a crocheted gift to soften them up?

"You're working too hard, Mamm," Esther said. "A woman your age shouldn't be flitting about town making matches for all the unmarrieds. It's not *gute* for your health, and it's not exactly respectable, either. Mary Eicher

11

says you encourage young people to kiss. *Before* they're married."

Poor Esther. She was always so worried about what other people thought.

Felty, Anna's husband of sixty-six years, glanced up from his newspaper. "When you're in love, it doesn't hurt to do a little spooning to see if you like it."

Esther fastened her most serious frown on her face. "Cassie told me that Dr. Reynolds kissed her for the first time in your barn. And there are rumors that Titus kissed Katie Rose Gingerich right here in your kitchen in front of their parents and you." She waved her hands in Anna and Felty's direction.

Felty grinned, even though he seemed to be paying rapt attention to his reading.

Anna couldn't keep a smile from her face either. "Isn't it *wunderbarr* that Titus found love right here in our kitchen? It didn't even matter that both his goats pooped on my rug."

Esther grunted. "I'm glad Titus found Katie. I was sure no girl would ever fall in love with him. But that's no excuse for letting him kiss her right out in the open like that."

Anna reached out and patted Esther's hand. "Now, Esther. I don't make a habit of encouraging *die youngie* to kiss. They might think it strange that a middle-aged woman was so concerned about their lips."

"But you *do* encourage matches," Esther said.

"Of course," Anna said. "All young men should be married before they make nuisances of themselves. Bachelors and fish stink after three days, you know."

Esther grunted when she didn't agree with something Anna said. She was doing a lot of grunting today. She sounded like a bear who'd missed her breakfast. "It's not your responsibility, Mamm."

Anna snipped her yarn and tied a knot. "I don't know who else would make the matches if I didn't."

Felty always stood up for her. She loved that about him. "If it weren't for your *mater*, half the population of Bonduel would still be single."

Anna smiled at her husband. "I wouldn't dream of quitting. *Die youngie* need my help."

Esther did the grunting thing again and zipped up her canvas bag. "Well, you could at least charge people money for your matchmaking. It would help pay for all that yarn."

Anna tried hard to keep her patience. Esther was her very own daughter. Hadn't she taught Esther better than to think she could put a price on true love? "I wouldn't dream of charging money. Seeing two people fall in love is payment enough."

Esther scrunched her lips together as if she held a pickle between her teeth. "Yarn doesn't grow on trees."

Anna simply gave her daughter a sweet smile. Esther was sixty-eight years old and a strong, determined widow. Anna had done her best to raise her, and she'd turned out quite well, even if she did have misguided notions about yarn and kissing. "Will we see you for Sunday dinner?"

Esther slung her bag over her shoulder, and the weight of it made her stoop. "I'll bring pies and rolls. Do you want me to roast a chicken?"

"*Nae.* I'm trying out a new recipe. Gouda-and-raisin-stuffed hamburgers."

Esther's right eye twitched. "I'll roast three chickens."

Someone tapped firmly on the front door, and Esther opened it since she was on her way out. Suvie Newswenger stood on the porch, nibbling the nail on her index finger and holding a small brown paper bag. She smiled—Anna had rarely seen Suvie without a smile—and threw her arms around Esther as if she were her long-lost sister. "Esther! *Gute maiya.*"

Esther did not take kindly to affection, but she stood patiently until Suvie released her grip. Suvie was like that. Everybody in the community had mostly gotten used to it. When the hug finally came to an end, Esther took a giant step away from Suvie and ushered her into the great room that served as both a kitchen and living room.

"*Cum reu,* Suvie," Anna said, jumping to her feet—well, not exactly jumping. Anna hadn't

14

executed a good jump for probably twenty years. "How *wunderbarr* to see you."

Suvie laughed and reached her arms out for Anna. "I'm sorry to bother you, but I need your help."

Esther raised her eyebrows and gave Anna one of her I-told-you-so looks. "Remember what I said about the yarn."

Felty rested his paper in his lap. "We love you, Esther. Travel home safely and give the *kinner* our love."

Esther transferred her bag to the other shoulder, marched out the door, and closed it a little harder than she needed to.

"*Cum* and sit, Suvie," Anna said. "And tell us what we can do for you."

Suvie waved in Felty's direction. "*Wie geht?*"

Felty folded his paper in his lap. "It's wonderful-*gute* to see you, Suvie. How is your *dat* getting along with that new heifer?"

Suvie plopped onto the sofa, set her brown bag beside her, and took off her bonnet. "My *dat* got a new heifer?"

"Last week."

Suvie giggled and leaned toward Felty as if sharing a great secret. "I hope he hasn't named it yet. He named our last milk cow Fred. I told him not to name another animal on the farm without consulting me."

Felty grimaced. "He named her Rocky."

Suvie laughed harder. "I guess that's better than Fred. We'll just hope that Rocky doesn't give lumpy milk."

Suvie had a round, sensible face and especially intelligent eyes, as if she hadn't forgotten a thing she'd been taught since first grade. The smile lines curved naturally around her mouth, and they'd probably been there since the day she was born.

A more cheerful girl had never been seen in Bonduel.

Did she need help finding a husband?

Surely that couldn't be what she wanted from Anna and Felty. Suvie had been seeing Vernon Schmucker for several months.

"I need your help finding a husband," Suvie said.

Well. You never knew with some people.

Suvie turned to Anna. "It's no secret that you've been successful finding matches for many of your grandchildren, and I am hoping you can do the same for me." She picked up her brown paper bag and unrolled the top. "I brought some cookies to butter you up."

She pulled two blobs from the bag that were probably cookies, even though they looked like lumpy gray pebbles, and handed one each to Felty and Anna.

Anna plastered an excessively cheerful smile on her face, just to prove she wasn't afraid, and took a bite. The cookie crumbled to dust in her mouth.

If she accidentally breathed in, she'd die of smoke inhalation. Stifling a cough, Anna swallowed as best she could. "Would anybody like some milk?"

Felty took a hearty bite. He wasn't shy about strange food. "Delicious," he said. "Peanut butter?"

Suvie's face fell. "Coconut and lemon." She sighed the air from her lungs. "This is one of the reasons I need your help. I can't cook, and a man wants a wife who can cook."

Anna was immediately sympathetic. Not everyone had the talents in the kitchen that Anna had been blessed with. Suvie was a wonderful-*gute* girl. Her lack of cooking skills shouldn't doom her to spinsterhood. "But, dear, why do you need us to help you find a husband? I thought you and Vernon Schmucker were serious."

Suvie sighed again. Long and loud. She must have very deep lungs. "Vernon and I saw each other for six months, and I tried. For sure and certain, I tried. This is nothing against Vernon, but I'd rather be an old maid."

Anna nodded. "I don't blame you." Vernon could do that to a girl.

"He asked me to marry him, and I feel terrible that I might have made him believe that marriage was even a possibility. He didn't take it well, and Clara Yutzy told me he's gained ten pounds in the last month."

"Vernon never had trouble drowning his sorrows in a Big Mac."

"My sister Hannah told everyone that we were practically engaged. She's more frantic to see me married than I am."

"Sisters can be that way sometimes," Felty said.

Suvie shifted in her seat as if she couldn't get comfortable. "I think I should tell you that I have had three marriage proposals. Vernon, Adam Wengerd, and Lee Zook. Lee has assured me that he will still marry me if I can't find anyone else. He feels sorry for me, but I don't feel sorry for myself. I won't marry someone I don't love or someone who makes me cringe whenever we're in the same room. I don't want you to think I'm flighty."

"Of course not, dear," Anna said. "You can't talk yourself into loving someone, though some folks have tried."

"After I turned twenty-four and the marriage prospects began to fade, I decided I was perfectly content to be an old maid."

Anna smiled. Suvie was no shrinking violet. "You bought your own house."

"*Jah*. With the money I earned from working at the feed store. My brothers built that greenhouse for me so I could start my own business." The soft line of Suvie's lips melted into a grin. "I'm twenty-eight years old, and I don't want to be an old maid anymore. There's someone I really like."

Anna leaned forward, mostly to try to clear cookie dust from her throat. "Someone?"

Suvie laughed. "There's a man who bought a shoat this spring, and he's been coming into the feed store almost every week for three months." She smiled sheepishly. "I'm in love with him, and I'm determined to make him fall in love with me. He's tall and handsome and wonderful polite, and he mopes and sulks and broods like a gathering storm. Hardly says a word."

Anna furrowed her brow until she felt her wrinkles crash into each other. "He sounds like a dud. Are you sure you want him?"

Suvie nodded, her eyes wide with eagerness. "I'm sure. He's your great-grandson Aaron Beachy. You don't think your own relative is a dud, do you?"

Felty smoothed his beard with his fingers. "Some of our relatives are duds, but Aaron isn't one of them."

It only took a split second for Anna to realize what a perfect match Suvie and Aaron would make. Suvie was eternally cheerful, Aaron was as gloomy as a funeral on a rainy day. They'd mix like oil and vinegar, raisins and meatloaf, peanut butter and maple syrup. "Why, Suvie," she said, "what a *wunderbarr* idea! Aaron needs a girl like you. He hasn't smiled for three years."

Felty pressed his lips together and stuffed his newspaper between the cushion and armrest of his chair. "I hate to discourage you, Annie Banannie, but it's too soon to talk about Aaron marrying again. Mary hasn't been gone but a few months."

"*Nae*, Felty," Anna said. "Mary passed on almost three years ago."

Felty's brows inched together. "Three years? Are you sure?"

"*Jah*. She died two months before Beth and Tyler's wedding, and their third anniversary is in September. I never forget an anniversary."

"It seems shorter," Felty said.

"*Jah*," Anna said. "Because Aaron still acts as if it happened yesterday."

Felty got that unsettled look in his eye he always had when something troubled him. "It hit us all wonderful hard. They were only married half a year. It's best to stay an old maid, Suvie. Aaron will never get over Mary."

Suvie fingered one of her *kapp* strings. "I don't expect him to get over her. I'm just hoping he can find room in his heart for me too."

Felty shook his head. "Mary's memory casts a long shadow."

Suvie didn't seem especially distressed by this bad news. "I'm sensible enough to know that I could never replace Mary. But I want to try to win a small piece of Aaron's heart even though it might be hopeless to try. That's why I came to you for help."

Anna didn't think it was as hopeless as all that. In her eighty-five years of experience, she hadn't

20

seen much heartache that romance couldn't cure. And Aaron was going to be her next victim . . . er . . . match.

She went to the junk drawer in the kitchen and pulled out a pencil and her trusty notebook. "You've come to the right place," she said, sitting next to Suvie on the sofa and holding her pencil at the ready. "We are happy to match you up with our great-grandson at no charge. Aren't we, Felty?"

"Of course, Banannie. I don't mind paying for extra yarn, especially when your dishrags help so many people fall in love."

Suvie's smile narrowed. "*Ach, vell.* I don't mind paying."

Anna threw out her hands and very nearly lost her pencil. "Absolutely not. *Gotte* has given us our unique talents to help forlorn and desperate people like you. We wouldn't dream of charging money for it, no matter what Esther says."

Felty nodded. "Our daughter means well, but she thinks yarn doesn't grow on trees."

Anna tapped the eraser side of the pencil against her cheek. "So, Suvie, if we're going to couple you up with Aaron, we need to know what we have to work with. Tell us a little about yourself."

"The most important thing you need to know . . . well, maybe not the most important, but it might be an obstacle. I am three years older than Aaron. Is that bad?"

"My brother was six years younger than his wife," Felty said. "They were very happy."

Anna nibbled on her eraser. "It is a concern, but it's not exactly robbing the cradle."

Suvie settled her back against the sofa and smiled as if all Anna's grandchildren were coming for a visit.

Anna wrote "nice teeth" in her notebook. It was *gute* to keep a record of everything, just in case Aaron needed convincing.

"I'm a hard worker," Suvie said, "and a *gute* cleaner. I can make a linoleum floor shine like it was made of marble." She hesitated and scrunched her lips to one side of her face. "I hope I don't sound like I'm bragging."

Anna shook her head. "There's no pride in telling the whole truth. I need all the facts if I'm going to help you catch Aaron." She wrote "humble" in her notebook.

Suvie giggled. "Okay. I love to work in the garden and to grow plants at my greenhouse. My *mamm* says I have two green thumbs." With her smile in place, she sighed as if one of her plants had just died. "But I don't cook and my sewing skills are lacking, though I know how to make a dress if it's an emergency. My sister says I'm too cheerful and that I laugh too much, but I'd rather laugh than cry since crying makes my eyes puffy. I tend to be bossy, and I chew my fingernails, and I don't like grapes. Dogs make

Suvie's lips twitched, whether in amusement or uncertainty, Aaron couldn't tell. "*Jah*. They're waiting at the front door."

Aaron was getting more and more confused. "You left my grandparents on the porch?"

"They're not in any danger."

"I'm sure they're not in any danger, but why are my grandparents on the front porch?"

"They didn't want to walk all the way around the house to find you. They volunteered to guard the petunias and the casserole from raccoons and stray dogs."

Surely his brows were touching at the middle of his forehead. Suvie had brought Mammi and Dawdi along to hold her petunias?

"Do you want to see them?" Suvie said.

Aaron wasn't sure if she meant his grandparents, the petunias, or the casserole, so he simply nodded and plastered what he hoped passed for a smile on his face.

Suvie practically skipped down the porch steps, and Aaron had no other choice but to follow her. He couldn't very well leave his grandparents to languish on the front porch, even if he had no idea why they were here or why Suvie had brought them.

Or maybe they had brought Suvie.

Dare he ask? "So, what are you doing here?"

Suvie turned and grinned at him. "Well, somebody had to bring the casserole."

27

And why was the casserole here?

It would probably be easiest if he didn't ask.

His house wasn't big. They made it around to the front in ten seconds flat. His great-grandparents stood on his front porch as promised, Mammi holding a white pan in her hands, Dawdi with a flat of petunias.

"Oh, Aaron, how *wunderbarr*," Mammi said, lighting up like a double propane lantern when she saw him. "I just knew you'd be home and looking very handsome. Didn't I tell you, Felty?"

"You're smart as a whip, Banannie."

Mammi wore a bright pink dress under her black apron, which made a very stark contrast with her snow-white hair and twinkly blue eyes. Nobody had the heart to tell her that elderly Amish women were supposed to wear black, or if they were feeling especially daring, charcoal gray.

Aaron cracked a smile. Even though it wasn't a proper color for an old lady, he sort of liked the pink. So many *fraas* dressed as if they were expecting to die soon and wanted to save their families the trouble of dressing them for their funerals.

His smile drooped. Life was so short and so sad. It was a wonder everyone didn't wear black. His *mammi* wore pink because she didn't understand how hard life really was.

Mammi handed the casserole to Suvie and wrapped her arms around Aaron's waist. She was short and sweet and couldn't reach her arms around his neck, even when she stood on her tiptoes. All of the Helmuth grandsons and great-grandsons had inherited their height from Dawdi Felty. "Now, Aaron. We're not going to stay, but we wanted to come with Suvie and make sure you got settled in okay."

Aaron raised an eyebrow. "Settled in?"

Mammi patted Aaron on the arm. "I mean that we always like to keep an eye out for our grandchildren and help wherever we're needed." She took the flat of petunias from Dawdi and handed it to Aaron. "Our work here is done. We'll see you next week at Titus's barn raising."

Aaron stared down at the petunias in his arms, not quite sure what to do with them. "You're leaving already?"

Mammi's eyes glistened like stars. "Don't be sad. Suvie will be here, and we've already overstayed our welcome." She took Felty's arm, and they ambled toward their buggy.

Suvie will be here?

Aaron slowly turned his gaze to Suvie, who clutched the casserole in her hands and smiled at him as if she expected him to tell her a joke or something. She didn't look like she was planning on going anywhere anytime soon, which only increased his confusion and made him a little wary.

A lot wary.

What did she want? Was he supposed to know? Suvie transferred the casserole to one hand and waved to Mammi and Dawdi as they drove away. Then she eyed Aaron like a cow at auction, and her smile got wider. "Let's get started then," she said.

"Get . . . get started with what?"

"I guess I don't mean *us*. I mean *me*. I brought this Spam asparagus casserole for you to eat, and I'm going to plant these petunias in your garden."

He studied the casserole in her hands. Bits of asparagus and Spam swimming in a runny, orange cheese sauce. The petunias looked little better. The few flowers on the stems drooped forlornly, and the plants themselves were about three days from drying up completely and blowing away. He was at a complete loss for words, except for the question on the tip of his tongue. "Why?"

Suvie reached out and plucked a dead flower from one of the petunia stems. "Why what?"

"Why did you bring me this?"

"A widower like you doesn't get a hot meal very often. Bake at 375 for thirty minutes."

"Did you . . . did you grow the petunias yourself?" Suvie had a greenhouse where she raised plants to sell to local gardeners, but if she cooked like she grew flowers, he might be better off just throwing everything in the trash.

"*Nae*. I sold out of my petunias weeks ago. I

30

bought these at Walmart, and they were almost the last ones they had."

Aaron tried for a smile, but he just couldn't muster one. "Why?"

"The season to plant is over. Most people planted their petunias in May. The tenth of June is a little late so most stores are out of flowers."

"But why did you go all the way to Walmart?"

"I needed petunias."

"Why?"

Suvie finally seemed to comprehend what he was asking. She beamed like a sunrise. "*Ach,* I wanted petunias because I remembered that they were one of Mary's favorite flowers."

Aaron's heart felt heavier at the very mention of Mary's name. "How did you know?"

"She told me. Roses and petunias. She loved them both. One fussy flower and a sturdy one. I thought you might enjoy some in your garden in memory of her."

Was it his imagination, or did the clouds part for a few seconds? Somebody else remembered Mary. Someone besides his mother-in-law was willing to say her name out loud. "*Denki.* That is very thoughtful of you. I'll plant them tomorrow."

Suvie raised her eyebrows and shook her head as if he'd just made a grave error in judgment. "These flowers are mere hours from death. I'm going to plant them now so they might have a chance to bloom before September."

"It's going to rain."

She shielded her eyes from the nonexistent sun and gazed up at the sky. "It won't rain for at least another hour. I've got time." She took the flat of petunias from him and gave him the casserole, then turned her back and marched toward the narrow flower bed up against the house.

Aaron frowned. Should he offer to help? He wasn't especially eager to make friends with a girl, and he wasn't especially good at it either. Making conversation took too much work. He didn't need the aggravation or the bother. If Mary were alive, she would have been the one to roll up her sleeves and plant petunias with Suvie Newswenger. "Do you need gloves or anything?"

"I brought my own trowel and gloves and a tin of fertilizer."

"Okay." He stood looking at her for a few seconds before opening his front door and awkwardly strolling into his own house. With the door shut, she couldn't see him, so why did he feel so uncomfortable?

Probably because Suvie wasn't above peeking into other people's windows and making herself right at home. He'd pull the curtains just in case she got tired of planting petunias and snooped around.

He peeled back the plastic wrap from the pan, stuck his finger in the casserole, and took a taste.

It tasted like watery Cheez Whiz with just a hint of Spam. Maybe it wouldn't be so bad for supper. It couldn't be worse than three years of ramen soup.

Suvie had been the teacher's helper in school when Aaron was in fifth grade, and she always held her own with the rowdy boys who tried to give her a hard time. She was three or four years older than Aaron, and he couldn't begin to guess why she wasn't married yet. She had a pretty face and seemed nice enough.

Suvie was always so cheerful, as if she didn't know any other way to be but happy, as if she didn't even care that there was sadness in the world. Aaron couldn't muster that kind of cheerfulness. His world had stopped turning the day Mary died, and it made him sad that other people had gone on with their lives. Only days after the funeral, his own *mamm* had taken a trip to the market and his *dat* had started working in the fields again. Life did not go on. Why were they so determined to pretend it did?

Weeks, months after the funeral, it had been all Aaron could do not to lash out at family members who smiled or laughed or acted as if no one had died. Didn't they know that the world was over? His family had tried to console him, but their words had been empty and meaningless and—although they didn't mean it—cruel. *Gotte* didn't need another angel in heaven, and nobody really knew for sure that Mary was in a better place.

A *ping* sounded against the kitchen window. And then another. And another. In a matter of seconds, the window was streaked with water droplets. He'd told Suvie it was going to rain.

He grabbed his straw hat and opened the front door. Suvie was planting petunias on the small, circular berm in the center of Aaron's yard. He frowned. A tall, spindly, dead rosebush stood in the middle of the berm, and he didn't want Suvie anywhere near it. Pressing his hat onto his head to keep the wind from taking it, he jogged outside yelling Suvie's name. Huge drops of water pelted him in the face, and he squinted to keep from getting rain in his eyes. "*Denki* for coming and for the casserole. I'll finish planting tomorrow."

Suvie laughed and blinked the water from her eyes. "Rain is a gardener's best friend. I can't rest until these flowers have a *gute* home."

Aaron groaned inwardly. He couldn't very well leave Suvie to plant her flowers by herself in the rain. And he couldn't very well risk her disturbing the rosebush. "Okay, then. I'll help you finish."

"No need. I'm already wet."

"I'll go get my gloves and a trowel."

She studied his face and smiled. "Okay. It will be fun."

Fun like a hole in the head. "Do you mind planting those petunias in the bed up against the house? This piece of ground is special."

She raised her eyebrows into a question but didn't argue. "For sure and certain."

Growling all the harder, Aaron ran to his tool-shed for his leather gloves and a trowel. He would be soaked to the skin by the time all those petunias got planted, but it didn't seem right to leave Suvie to do it herself. What would his *mamm* say? He grabbed a shovel on his way out. Maybe he could dig one big hole and bury all the petunias at once.

When he returned, Suvie had moved herself and the petunias to the flower bed right under the front window. Unfortunately, he hadn't pulled the weeds there for three years, and it was a mess. "Are you sure I shouldn't just do this tomorrow?" he said, knowing what her answer would be before he even asked. Suvie seemed like the determined type. If she wanted those flowers planted, they were going to get planted, come high water or pouring rain.

With both hands, Suvie tugged at a tall, leafy weed. It released its hold on the soil, and she was catapulted to the ground and onto her back-side.

"Are you okay?"

She smiled even though she was now sitting in the mud. Water dripped like rain off the brim of her black bonnet. "Cocklebur. Those things are persistent."

"Let me." With his shovel, Aaron made quick

work of the other two cockleburs, and Suvie smiled at him as if he'd invented petunias.

He suddenly found it hard to breathe, as if her grin had paralyzed his lungs. Either that or the rain dripping down his face made it hard to catch a breath.

Ignoring his breathing problems, Aaron worked his shovel along the edge to loosen the thick weave of grass that had encroached on the flower bed. Once he had gone around the perimeter of the flower bed, Suvie pulled up the loosened mounds of grass and tossed them onto her growing pile of weeds. They finished pulling weeds together, and Aaron worked the soil with his shovel. Of course, it wasn't really soil anymore—more like a giant mud puddle, and the water was rising.

Suvie pinched a petunia from the container and tried to dig a hole with her trowel. Mud immediately oozed into her hole, and she smiled wryly at Aaron. "It's like planting flowers in a bowl of pudding."

Aaron swiped his hand across his face to clear the water from his eyes. "Maybe we should try tomorrow."

She cocked an eyebrow and laughed. "You keep saying that. I'm beginning to suspect you're not having fun."

Was he having fun? He didn't know if *fun* was the right word, but he hadn't been having a completely unpleasant time. "I haven't played in the mud since I was ten. But planting flowers seems futile. What if they wash away?"

Suvie's smile grew even brighter, though he couldn't guess why. "You're right, of course. This is no time to plant flowers."

Aaron heard a crack and a whoosh and looked up just in time to see his rain gutter burst at the seam directly over his head. A gush of water slapped him in the face and chest, then bounced off him and hit Suvie smack on top of her head. She sucked in her breath and released a high-pitched squeak as rainwater cascaded from the broken gutter and soaked her clear to the skin.

Aaron reached up and tried to push the section of rain gutter back into place, but it gave a loud groan and broke off completely. It thudded to the ground, missing Suvie only because he grabbed her wrist and yanked her out of the way before it could conk her in the head.

With heart going a mile a minute, he took a step back. "Are you okay?"

She didn't look okay. She looked like a drowned rat. One side of her mouth curled upward as she propped her hand on her hip. "You haven't cleaned those rain gutters out lately, have you?"

Not for three years. "Sorry. I'm afraid of heights."

She started laughing. Suvie laughed a lot, but considering she was soaked to the bone and her chin was quivering, he wouldn't have expected her to laugh at that particular moment. "Don't apologize. The look on your face was worth a whole garden of broccoli."

He didn't like broccoli.

But did it matter? Suvie's smile had him so *ferhoodled*, he couldn't begin to make sense of his scattered thoughts. All he knew was that the look on *her* face was worth a strawberry rhubarb pie. With whipped cream.

She pulled her bonnet off her head and wrung it out like a dishrag, but the scarf under the bonnet was just as wet. She looked so soggy yet so positively, adorably bubbly with water dripping from the end of her nose, he couldn't help it. A chuckle started from deep within his throat and flew out of his mouth. Suvie eyed him in surprise and then joined him. He laughed until his tears mingled with the rain running down his face.

Suvie tried to catch her breath and did her best to look indignant. "Are you laughing at me?"

"*Jah*," he said.

She smiled so wide, he could see most of her teeth. She had very nice teeth. "Afraid of heights. A likely story."

Aaron couldn't remember the last time he'd laughed so hard. Come to think of it, he couldn't remember if he'd laughed in the three years since Mary's passing.

Guilt tugged at him like a bucket of cement

hanging around his neck. He shouldn't be laughing. What was there to be happy about? Mary was dead. Mary would never have a chance to share a laugh with anybody again.

Suvie wiped her cheek with her damp bonnet and studied Aaron's face. "Are you okay? Your hat won't sag like that once it's dry."

Aaron tried to hide his frown. Suvie didn't need to know how much it hurt him that other people were happy. The sooner she went away, the better. "Don't worry about the petunias. I'll plant them tomorrow. Lord willing, it will be dry."

Suvie hesitated as doubt traveled across her face. "Oh. *Jah*. I won't worry. I know they're in *gute* hands."

"I won't let them die."

Another long pause. "Okay." She bent over and extracted her trowel from the mud. "Maybe I will see you at the feed store sometime."

She turned and took three steps toward her buggy when his conscience practically screamed at him. His conscience sounded a lot like his mother, and she wasn't about to let him send Suvie off like that. The scarf covering her hair drooped precariously over her ears and her mint green dress looked as if it had been weighted down with rocks. "Suvie, wait."

She hesitated.

"Why don't you come in and dry off?"

She gazed up at the sky, which was still dripping with rain. A slow smile formed on her lips. "It might not do any good."

"I have an umbrella."

She took off her gloves and smoothed a piece of soggy hair from her neck. "Do you have enough towels?"

He thought hard about that. "I have two."

That must have been the right answer. She nodded and slogged her way to the front door. Aaron followed, opened the door for her, and winced. It was the right thing to do, inviting Suvie in to dry off, but he wasn't much of a housekeeper and the kitchen was a mess. Mary had always kept the house so tidy, and when she died, polishing the furniture and shining the chrome had seemed unimportant compared to nursing his broken heart.

Suvie sat down right inside the door and took off her shoes. Gritty, muddy water dripped from her socks, which she also removed and stuffed inside her shoes. Aaron pried his boots off his feet and set them on the mat by the front door. He pulled Suvie to her feet, and she followed him into the kitchen.

The cheesy, watery casserole sat on the table. "Did you make that?" he said.

She turned a dark shade of pink. "I wanted to impress you, but I'm not a cook. Your *mammi* Anna made it. I hope you don't mind."

"Have you ever tasted Mammi's cooking?"

"*Nae.*"

He cracked a smile. "There are probably better ways to impress me."

She bloomed into a smile. "Oh, *sis yuscht.* I was a little unsure when I saw the floating chunks of Spam."

"It doesn't matter. I always eat Mammi's cooking, no matter how bad it is."

"We must all make sacrifices yet."

She smiled at him and he smiled at her, and they came to an unspoken understanding about Mammi's cooking. "I'll get a towel," he said, hoping she didn't notice the dirty dishes in the sink or the garbage piling up in his trash can.

Suvie squeezed water from her apron into the sink. "I'll wait here."

Aaron's stockings squished all the way up the stairs. He sat on the floor so he wouldn't get his bed wet and took them off. With lightning speed, he dried off and changed his trousers and shirt, feeling more and more awkward the longer he left Suvie downstairs by herself dripping on his dirty kitchen floor.

Mary would never have let herself get caught in the rain like that. She would have been sensible and waited for a dry day so her hands wouldn't have gotten muddy. She never allowed a hair out of place or tolerated a wrinkle in her dress.

It wasn't a bad quality to dive into a project like Suvie seemed to prefer. Weeding and planting

41

in the rain had been like an adventure. Almost getting smacked in the head with a rain gutter was definitely exciting. He banished that idea from his brain. Mary was dead. He wouldn't let himself have an adventure. She wasn't there to share it with him.

Aaron retrieved his only other bath towel from the closet and practically ran down the stairs. "Sorry it took so long. I dried off."

She straightened the scarf on her head, and she must have wrung out the hem of her dress in the sink because it was no longer dripping on the floor. She stood staring at his sink with an almost woeful look on her face.

He really should have done those dishes yesterday. And the day before. "Is everything okay?"

"This sink is atrocious."

He didn't know what *atrocious* meant, but it didn't sound good.

She slid a stack of dirty plates to one side of the sink. "Don't you ever clean it? It's a travesty to have such a beautiful stainless steel sink and keep it hidden under all this dirt."

He didn't know what *travesty* meant either, but it sounded like she was lecturing him. Didn't she know how hard it was just to get up in the morning? He slumped his shoulders. "I don't have the heart to do things around the house. Everything reminds me of Mary." Why had he told her that? Suvie didn't care about his broken heart.

She either didn't recognize the sadness in his voice or decided to ignore it. "*Ach*, that's just an excuse." She smiled as if she didn't even feel sorry for him. "A sink like this needs to be cherished. Mary probably picked out this sink."

Aaron furrowed his brow. Mary *had* picked it out when they were building the house. How did Suvie know such things?

Her smile got wider. "Stainless steel is practical and pretty. Mary was always smart about things like that. I love how she could take scraps of fabric that didn't seem to match at all and make a beautiful quilt or a pillow. Do you remember that quilt she made that sold for six hundred dollars at auction? I've never seen anything like it."

Aaron took a deep breath as ribbons of warmth traveled up his arms. Nobody seemed to feel comfortable talking about Mary anymore, and yet here was Suvie Newswenger standing in his kitchen praising Mary's sink and her quilting.

"*Jah*," he murmured. "Mary was always sewing or quilting something."

"Or cooking. Her pretzels were like manna from heaven, and I confess I envied them. The best I could ever do was a decent loaf of bread." She took the towel from his hand, removed her scarf, and scrubbed the towel against her hair like a piece of sandpaper on wood. "My family ate a lot of doughy bread before I managed to bake it right. Once my *mamm* sliced my bread and put the whole loaf, slice by slice, in the frying pan to finish cooking. We drizzled olive oil on it and made excellent toast."

Suvie deftly wrapped her hair back into a bun and secured the scarf at the nape of her neck. Her fingers were long and graceful, and Aaron had a hard time pulling his gaze from her chestnut brown hair that caught the light from the window.

He lowered his eyes, mostly so the warm glow of her hair wouldn't distract him. "You're right. I should have taken better care of Mary's sink."

While she dabbed at her arms with a towel, she glanced in his direction and laughed. "It's not as bad as all that. You're not in trouble. And it will only take me five minutes to get this sink back in shape. The floor will take a little longer."

"The floor?"

"The wood is beautiful. It needs a good clean and polish. The *gute* news is that I planned on being here all morning planting petunias. I don't have to be to work until one."

"You . . . want to mop my floor?"

Her lips twitched in amusement. "There are three Froot Loops stuck to one of the floor-boards, and a Christmas peppermint drop in the corner that won't budge without a chisel."

"I hadn't noticed."

Suvie draped her towel over one of his kitchen chairs. She didn't look much drier, but at least she wasn't dripping on his floor, which he

44

apparently hadn't swept since Christmas. "I don't want to alarm you, but your dust bunnies are so big they're reproducing." She took the dirty plates out of the sink. "You can do dishes while I mop."

Aaron widened his eyes. "Can I?"

Suvie's laughter proved she wasn't annoyed with him. Did she ever get her feathers ruffled? "One thing you need to know about me is that I'm bossy. Kick me out anytime you want."

"Well, I would, but I really need my floor mopped."

Without asking, she searched his broom closet until she found the mop and a bucket, which had been pushed clear to the back. The broom was a little closer to the front. He'd dropped a mug sometime around Easter and had to sweep up the broken glass.

Suvie had the nerve to rifle through his cupboards until she found some detergent to clean the floor and an old bottle of wax. "I'll bet Mary loved this kitchen," Suvie said. "The window lets in so much light."

Suvie swept and mopped while Aaron washed up the dishes and wiped down the counters. They talked about Mary and how she liked things tidy and how their first fight as a married couple happened because Aaron didn't pick up his stockings. Suvie told him about her greenhouse and her sister who loved dogs but was allergic to them and her brother who had lost the hearing

45

in one ear after a long illness. She laughed at his story of his nephew who refused to eat anything but bread, peanut butter, and potato chips, and his *mamm*, who thought apple cider vinegar cured everything.

Suvie was loud and funny and not afraid to tell him about the time she'd stolen a pie her mother had made and had eaten the whole thing, or the time she had painted red spots on her face to get out of going to school on the day of the spelling bee. She couldn't have been more different from Mary, who was so prim and proper she was worried about singing too loud in church. Mary would never have worn a mint green dress. She would have been mortified to be accused of being a peacock. But the color suited Suvie. It brought out the blue of her eyes.

Maybe Mary had been overly concerned. There didn't seem to be anything wrong with mint green.

Suvie did most of the talking as she scrubbed the sink until it looked as new as the day Mary had picked it out, then shooed Aaron out of the kitchen and waxed the floor until it was so bright he had to squint when the light reflected off it.

He didn't mind that she talked so much. He liked the sound of her voice, and he didn't feel the uncomfortable need to come up with clever things to say to her. He could just listen and talk when he felt like it. And Suvie wasn't one of those girls who wouldn't let him get a word in edgewise. She seemed to sense when he wanted to say some-thing and when he didn't and was happy to fill in the awkward silences with her own stories.

Suvie tiptoed to the closet and stowed the mop and bucket, retrieved her bonnet, trowel, and gloves from the table, and gave Aaron a smile. His heart pressed against his ribs until he almost couldn't breathe.

For sure and certain he loved a shiny sink.

"I'm coming tomorrow to finish planting petunias," she said. "And then I'll help you take out that dead rosebush yet."

Aaron clenched his teeth, took a deep breath, and tried to remember that Suvie couldn't begin to understand what he and Mary had shared. "That rosebush is wonderful important to me. I like it just the way it is."

Suvie grinned. "But it's dead. I don't wonder that it scares folks away when they drive past your house. If people find out about the rain gutter, you'll never have another visitor again."

It felt as if his horse, Coke, had galloped into the room and parked a hoof on his rib cage. "Mary planted that rosebush the week before we were married. It is a remembrance of our love for each other. I don't want it moved." His voice cracked, but he didn't lose his composure. So what if his eyes stung? Suvie would never notice.

Suvie leaned toward him and suddenly seemed

five feet closer. "*Ach, du lieva,*" she said. "Why didn't you say so in the first place? Of course we can't pull it out. If you'd told me that earlier, I wouldn't have been so insistent. I'm sorry I insulted your rosebush."

Her lips parted in a slight smile, but he could tell she wasn't poking fun or feeling sorry for him, almost as if she didn't think less of him for wanting a dead rosebush in his yard. "Don't worry. My *mamm* and *dat* insult the bush all the time. They want me to move on."

Suvie tilted her head to the side as if to get a better look at him. "Maybe you don't need to move on as much as expand."

"Expand?"

Her eyes sparkled as she bent over and picked up her soggy shoes and stockings. "I don't know. Sometimes I can't even understand myself." She opened the door, stuck her head out, and looked to the sky. "Still raining."

"Do you want my umbrella?"

"*Nae,* I'll make a run for it. I'll be back tomorrow unless it's still raining, in which case I'll come the day after that or the day after that. The first dry day, unless it's Sunday, in which case I'll come the day after that."

Her smile was as bright and warm as a roaring fire in the hearth, and he found himself hoping there wouldn't be a cloud in the sky tomorrow.

Chapter 3

"It's a wonderful nice day to plant flowers," Anna said as Felty drove the buggy down the lane. "Aaron desperately needs petunias. People think a grumpy old man lives at his house when they see the dead rosebush. Maybe we should tie some ribbons around it."

"Ribbons would look very pretty, Annie Banannie," Felty said. "But I don't think Aaron wants anyone touching his beloved rosebush."

Suvie sighed. Poor Aaron. He must be very sad indeed if the dead rosebush was all he had to remind him of Mary.

It had rained for three days straight, and if the rain had lasted any longer, Suvie would have marched over to Aaron's house, planted the petunias in his mud puddle, and not even have cared if they died. Anna was right. Aaron needed flowers in his life. Suvie hoped he realized he needed her too.

Thank the *gute* Lord, the rain had stopped sometime after midnight last night, and Suvie was up before the sun, unable to sleep with the butterflies making quite a fuss in her stomach. She had walked up Huckleberry Hill to Anna and Felty's house, and Anna had whipped up a quick batch of butternut squash and raisin soup for

Aaron before the three of them piled into the buggy and drove to Aaron's house.

Suvie had nearly come by herself instead of imposing on Anna and Felty to come with her, but she was smart enough to know that Aaron would be less likely to reject her if she brought his grandparents along. He might not have any interest in Suvie, but he loved his *mammi* and *dawdi* and wouldn't purposefully do anything to disappoint them.

Besides, Anna and Felty were experienced matchmakers. They knew exactly what had to be done to win Aaron's heart.

Anna reached back and patted Suvie's arm. "This soup is going to make Aaron fall in love with you, for sure and certain. And if that doesn't work, the dishrags will. No boy can resist a dishrag."

Suvie's heart sped up when they came around a bend in the road and Aaron's dead rosebush came into sight. Four days ago, Aaron had smiled at her. He'd laughed at her jokes and helped her pull weeds. He'd been impressed by the shiny sink. Maybe he'd think about maybe giving her a chance.

Suvie would have jumped out of the buggy and up Aaron's porch steps, but she was in the back seat, and it would have been rude to vault over Anna to get out. Anna was in her eighties, and Suvie wouldn't dream of rushing her, even if it meant she'd have to wait a few extra minutes to see Aaron.

When they finally made it out of the buggy, Suvie raced to the porch and knocked on the door. She could only be so patient.

Anna caught up with her and clucked her tongue. "I'm afraid you're going to have to bury those petunias instead of plant them."

Suvie glanced over at the flat of petunias that was still sitting in the muddy flower bed. A gasp sort of oozed from between her lips. Her petunias had been reduced to slimy, wilted green stems by four days of heavy rain.

They were definitely dead.

Had her chances with Aaron died with the petunias?

Anna patted the bowl she held tightly in her arms. "Don't worry, dear. We don't need petunias to catch Aaron's heart. My soup will do the trick."

Suvie cracked a smile and then couldn't help the giggle that escaped. She and Aaron were equally unenthusiastic about Anna's cooking. They had at least one thing in common. "You're right, Anna," she whispered, just in case Aaron was listening on the other side of the door. "Your soup could very well bring us together."

When Aaron didn't answer, Suvie knocked again—louder, just in case he hadn't heard her pounding the first time.

Anna smiled her most patient grandmotherly

smile and shrugged. "I think you're going to have to sneak around the back again and peek in his window."

"Lord willing, he's not in his underwear," Felty said.

Anna widened her eyes with a scold. "Now, Felty. You shouldn't talk about our grandson that way."

"Well, he wears underwear, doesn't he?"

Suvie laughed and turned bright red at the same time. Did Anna and Felty ever behave like normal old people? "Maybe you should come with me just in case."

Aaron's grandparents glided down the porch steps like seventy-year-olds while Suvie almost tripped, she was so nervous. She was still the fastest of the three of them and led the way around the house to Aaron's back yard. Aaron was standing next to that strange pile of rocks sitting in the middle of his lawn. He tossed a fist-size rock on top of the pile and dusted his hands on his trousers.

He looked up, gave Suvie a dazzling smile, and just as quickly averted his eyes and stared at Anna as if he were determined not to make eye contact with Suvie. She did her best not to let frustration choke her even though it was clear that Aaron was infinitely more interested in his *mammi* than he was in Suvie. Too bad he was so handsome. It only made the torture worse.

"Aaron, dear," Anna said, handing her bowl of soup to Suvie and giving Aaron a pat on the cheek. "We thought it would never stop raining."

Suvie swallowed her disappointment and gave Aaron a wry smile. "Don't you ever answer your front door?"

He seemed to reluctantly turn his eyes to her. But his grin gave her a little hope. "Don't you ever knock?"

She raised her eyebrows. "All the time. And loud. My knuckles are sore from knocking so hard. I've been reduced to spying into windows."

"I . . . I like the baby blue," he said, and it took Suvie a moment to realize he was talking about her dress.

He liked her dress? She'd wear it every day.

He hesitated before fixing his eyes on his *mammi* again. "I really like your purple dress too, Mammi."

Anna waved the compliment away. "*Ach*, don't pay any attention to me."

"You have quite a rock pile here," Felty said.

Aaron lifted his chin as if daring his *dawdi* to argue with him. "I'm faithful about it."

Suvie stared at her hands and tried to look completely uninterested in the conversation, though she was wonderful curious about why Aaron had a pile of rocks in the middle of his yard. She suspected it had something to do with Mary, but she was too polite to ask.

"Mary would be pleased to know that her memory is still alive on your lawn," Anna said, giving Aaron a second pat on the cheek.

Mary's memory? Suvie was pretty sure that when she died, she wouldn't want to be remembered as a pile of rocks, but if it made Aaron feel better, then who was she to judge? Her *aendi* Ruth had told her that even though everybody felt sadness, people were sad in different ways. Maybe the rocks were Aaron's pile of sadness.

Anna took the bowl of soup from Suvie and passed it to Aaron. "We just came to make sure you get settled in."

Aaron frowned. "Settled in?"

"*Jah*, and to give you this soup and"—she reached into her apron pocket and pulled out three colorful handfuls of yarn—"these dishrags." She turned and winked at Suvie, as if all her problems were now solved. Suvie truly hoped that those dishrags were as powerful as Anna claimed. "Felty and I need to go. I've got to make peanut butter spread for the fellowship supper on Sunday, and you know how hard it is to stir. But Suvie is staying. I know you'll enjoy that."

Aaron glanced from Anna to Suvie and back again, frowning like a little boy whose *mamm* was leaving him with a mean babysitter. "I don't mind planting the petunias myself. It's no trouble."

If Suvie hadn't been so in love with Aaron, she

might have worked herself up to a stomachache and gone home with her tail between her legs. But she wasn't about to give up, even though Aaron was looking at her like he wished she'd leave. Anna had knitted dishrags and made casserole and soup. Suvie had searched four stores in Shawano for petunias and spent an hour getting the mud stains out of her mint-green dress.

She wouldn't quit, even though Aaron so obviously wanted her to. She and Anna had gone to too much work already to let go now. And most of all, Aaron, no matter how immovable, was definitely worth the effort. He was handsome and smart, hardworking and godly, and she liked the way his lively eyes studied her face as if he were trying to understand all her hopes and dreams with one glance. He was a *wunderbarr* grandson, and she loved how devoted he had been to Mary. Few men treated their wives with that much affection, and Suvie wanted that in her life. She wouldn't let an uncertain look from Aaron or a flat of dead petunias stop her.

"Now, Aaron," Anna said, "I've had quite enough of your unselfishness. You're going to need help with those petunias, and no one knows how to plant a flower like Suvie. Her thumbs are so green, she could probably even bring flowers back from the dead." Anna turned her back on Aaron and raised a doubtful eyebrow at Suvie. Anna had done all she could to help, but Suvie was going to have to be creative if she wanted to spend any amount of time with Aaron today. Those petunias were not coming back.

Felty turned back and smiled at Aaron. "We came for no *gute* reason and now we're leaving you two alone together for no *gute* reason. I'm glad you're not the suspicious type."

"Now, Felty," Anna said, hooking her arm around his elbow and pulling him away. "We don't need a reason to see our grandson."

"No, we don't," Felty said.

Anna and Felty disappeared around the side of the house, and Aaron stood staring at his boots. If Suvie waited for Aaron to decide he loved her, she'd be waiting a long time. She'd have to make her own hay.

She pasted on the most radiant smile she could muster. "I have bad news."

He raised his gaze to her face, and her heart sank even lower. "What's wrong?"

What was wrong? Too many things—like the fact that he didn't want her here and that his eyes were full of resentment. She took a deep breath and widened her hopefully convincing smile. Maybe it wasn't resentment. Maybe Aaron felt cautious. And suspicious. Felty had practically warned him to be suspicious. Suspicion was better than resentment. Her determination wouldn't fail her if she pretended he was suspicious instead of resentful.

"The petunias are dead," she said.

He nodded. "They looked wonderful soggy last night. I should have brought them in the house."

She cleared her throat. Twice. "Speedy Weaver might have a few leftovers at his greenhouse. Should we go find out?"

He wrapped his hand around the back of his neck as if he were trying to loosen a noose. Suvie's heart fell so far, it was probably six feet underground. "*Ach, vell*, maybe you should go by yourself," he said. "I have a field to plow."

She was smiling so hard, her lips would probably permanently stick to her teeth. "Okay. Can I borrow your buggy? Anna and Felty drove me here."

He wilted like a leaky tire. "*Ach*. I suppose I should drive you."

"Not at all. I can go myself." She brushed an imaginary thread off her sleeve just to remind him that she was wearing a blue dress and that he liked it. "I'm a very *gute* driver, except for that one time I drove Judy off the road and into a ditch. Or the time I hitched her up wrong and she left without me. Or that one day when I lost the reins and she went three miles in the wrong direction before she tired out."

Aaron curled one side of his mouth. And then the other. Her heart did a little jump. "You always say something I don't expect."

"Is that a *gute* thing or a bad thing?"

"I don't know. But I do know I'm driving to Speedy Weaver's house."

Suvie didn't have to fake that smile anymore. Aaron's resistance was all but gone. "Well, okay, but don't blame me if your field doesn't get plowed."

"It's too muddy anyway."

He put Mammi's soup in the house, and she followed him out to the barn to hitch up his horse to the two-seater, open-air buggy. They climbed in, and Aaron guided the horse down the lane.

"I see you fixed your rain gutter," Suvie said as they turned onto the road in front of Aaron's house.

"In the dark with a flashlight. I didn't want my foundation to sink."

"You really need to clean out your gutters. Your house could float away in the next storm."

He studied her face. "You really are bossy."

Suvie smiled and batted her eyelashes. "*Jah*, I am. You'd better clean them out before your *dawdi* decides to do it for you. He was talking about it this morning. A ladder is no place for an eighty-seven-year-old."

"You'll have to convince him not to try it," Aaron said.

"Me? I couldn't even talk your *mammi* out of making you a batch of butternut squash and raisin soup—though I didn't try very hard. It makes her so happy to feed her grandchildren, and she thinks you're too skinny. You should gain some weight if you don't want a plate of your *mammi*'s treats every day."

He cocked an eyebrow. "Do you think I'm too skinny?"

Suvie laughed at the look of mock distress on his face. "When you were in the feed store last week, Melvin called you a tall glass of water, but I don't know if that means you're too skinny. Your *mammi* thinks you are."

"I've lost some weight since Mary died. I eat because I have to, not because I find any pleasure in it. Everything tastes like cardboard."

She let her mouth fall open. "That is the most unbelievable thing I've ever heard. Have you tasted Clara Yutzy's peanut butter chocolate drops?"

His lips twitched as if he were trying not to smile. "I can't say that I have."

"Or what about Lia Zimmerman's dinner rolls? Or Moses Zimmerman's cheese? Have you gone to Nelson's bakery right after she takes a peach pie out of the oven?"

"*Nae*," he said.

"Aaron Beachy, I'm ashamed of you. So many *gute* things to eat, and you can't do any better than bran flakes? Don't try to deny it, I saw them on your counter the other day. I almost threw them away, I was so offended."

"I don't want to get fat."

59

She threw back her head and huffed her displeasure to the sky. "You're a long way from fat, Aaron Beachy, but if I have anything to say about it, you're going to gain a few pounds. I'm shocked at how much *appeditlich* food you've missed out on."

"Have I told you how bossy you are yet?"

"*Denki.* It's one of my best qualities."

The rain had left small puddles everywhere on the dirt roads, and Aaron sped up whenever they came to one. The horse and buggy splashed its way over the long country road, with Aaron whooping whenever the water splattered higher than a few inches. Up ahead, a puddle at least eight feet wide covered the whole road. Aaron prodded the horse to go faster. "I love a good puddle." Just as quickly, he slowed the horse to a walk and furrowed his brow. "Unless you're afraid you'll get your dress dirty."

Suvie beamed at him and wrapped her fingers around the edges of her seat. "I know how to do laundry yet."

Grinning like a tomcat, Aaron flicked the reins, and the horse broke into a trot. Suvie held her breath as the cool, humid air whipped past her face and tried to tug her bonnet off her head.

With a whoosh, the buggy wheels rolled into the water, but the puddle was deeper, much deeper, than either of them had anticipated. Suvie had barely enough time to let out a dismayed squeak when the buggy tilted wildly to the side. Her tight grip on the seat didn't help her as the buggy lurched and threw her into the water.

The water couldn't have been more than ankle deep, but the splash sounded tremendous in her ears, and she landed face-first so that pretty much every inch of her front got soaked. *Oy*, anyhow! She hoped Aaron liked *muddy* baby-blue dresses.

Her eyes must have been playing tricks on her. She thought she saw four, maybe five little boys jump up from behind the tall weeds by the side of the road and run away.

"Are you okay?"

Suvie pushed herself to a sitting position, which got her chin out of the mud but completely soaked her backside. She could feel the water seeping up her back. She wiped her eyes with a mud-caked hand and looked up to see Aaron standing over her, holding his hand out to her and looking much more serious than he needed to.

A giggle tripped from her lips, as did a small pebble that she must have eaten when she went face-first into the puddle. She took Aaron's hand, and he pulled her and about ten pounds of water to her feet. "I wish I had known that this is what you meant by *getting my dress dirty*." The giggle turned into a throaty laugh that she couldn't control.

He looked at her as if maybe he thought she'd hit her head. "Do you need a doctor?"

"And I thought *I* was a bad driver."

He gave her a reluctant smile. "I'm a *gute* driver. You should have held on tighter." He took her arm and tugged her to dry ground.

"You're a bad driver, and that was worse than the roller coaster at Wisconsin Dells."

Still laughing, she bent down, gathered the hem of her dress in her fists, and tried to wring it out. It was like trying to squeeze water out of a handful of beach sand. "It's no use. I'm going to have to stand here until I air dry."

Aaron chuckled and turned his face away.

"What?" she said.

She could tell he was trying to wipe the smile off his face and couldn't quite manage to look concerned or contrite. "You look like a mud toad. A blue mud toad."

Suvie quit laughing long enough to grunt her indignation. Bending over, she scooped up a handful of mud and flicked it in Aaron's direction. It hit him on the shoulder and one drop splashed onto his cheek. He half-growled, half-laughed, swiped the glob of mud from his face and smeared it down Suvie's forearm. Then he quickly scooped up his own handful of mud and cocked his arm, ready to throw.

Suvie backed away, giggling uncontrollably. "Now, Aaron, don't forget it's your fault I'm wet. You should have let me drive the buggy."

Aaron showed all his teeth when he smiled.

They looked extra white next to the dark smear of mud down the side of his face. "That pretty blue dress needs some dots."

She turned and ran a few steps away from him, when he released his ball of mud and it hit her in the back of the head. It was a pebble-size ball of mud and she barely felt it, but she couldn't resist teasing him. She made a face and pressed her palm to the back of her head. "Ouch, Aaron. Ouch."

She drew out the syllables convincingly enough that Aaron immediately came to her side. "I'm sorry. I'm really sorry. Did that hurt?"

Stifling a smile, she took the mud he'd just thrown at her, leaned close to him, and smeared it down his other cheek.

He growled and grabbed her wrist. "You're tricky," he said, but certainly didn't seem too put out about it.

Where he touched her, her skin seemed to burn and tingle and melt all at the same time. Was that normal? Were the sudden heart somersaults and tightening of her throat normal too?

He stared at her with something akin to surprise on his face.

Nope. He didn't think it was normal either, but he didn't seem inclined to step away.

Suvie wasn't a fussy type of girl, but if he looked at her like that much longer, she might faint. She slowly withdrew her wrist from his hand and squeezed some water out of her sleeve. It dribbled onto his boots.

"*Ach*," he groaned. "I just bought these boots."

They laughed until Suvie thought her ribs might explode. She hadn't expected Aaron to be so much fun.

Suvie led Aaron's horse out of the puddle while Aaron pushed the buggy from the back, soaking his already-damp boots.

"There's a deep hole on one side here," Aaron said. "It's a *gute* thing Coke didn't step in it. He might have broken his leg."

"I'm happy I could sacrifice my blue dress to save Coke."

Aaron smiled. "I used to really like that blue dress."

Once the buggy was upright, Aaron walked around the perimeter of the puddle. Something caught his eye, and he called out. "Who is this little spy?"

All Suvie saw was a straw hat and a backside retreating as fast as they could go.

"Come back here," Aaron called.

The little boy didn't stop. He was scared out of his wits for sure and certain, even though Suvie couldn't see that he'd done anything wrong.

"Toby Byler, I know where you live," Aaron yelled. "Would you rather I come to your house and talk to your *dat*?"

Toby stumbled to a stop, slumped his shoulders,

and turned around. He shoved his hands in his pockets and started back toward them.

Suvie drew her brows together. "Is he in trouble?"

Aaron surprised her by grinning. At least he wasn't angry. "A boy running away that fast has been up to some sort of mischief. A guilty conscience puts wings on your feet."

Toby Byler couldn't have been more than seven years old. His *dat* trained horses and kept goats. His *mamm* had been just a year ahead of Suvie in school, and their family was in Suvie's district. She saw them every other Sunday at *gmay*.

"*Cum*, Toby," Aaron said, when Toby seemed content to keep about twenty feet back.

Toby gritted his teeth, hung his head, and took the last few brave and dreaded steps toward Aaron. He had adorable, chubby cheeks, long, dark eyelashes, and a tooth missing on top.

Aaron laid a hand on Toby's shoulder and got down on one knee to look the little boy in the eye. "Toby," he said, so gently it made Suvie's heart melt. "Why were you hiding in the bushes?"

That was all it took to reduce Toby to crying. He screwed up his face as plump tears rolled down his cheeks. "They left me, and then I got scared and couldn't run."

"Who left you?"

Toby pressed his palm over his eye to rub the tears away. "Johnny and them. We was waiting for

Reuben Schmucker." Toby became more upset with every word. His nose began to run furiously.

Aaron pulled a handkerchief out of his pocket and handed it to Toby. "Why were you waiting for Reuben Schmucker?"

Toby swiped the handkerchief across his face, leaving a very gooey trail of mucus along his cheek. Aaron took the handkerchief from Toby and wiped up the mess.

"Reuben always brags about his fancy bike. Me and Johnny and them dug a hole under the water so Reuben would fall in and get his bike dirty. Nobody can see how deep it is because the water covers it."

"You dug a hole?"

Toby nodded and sniffed. "With buckets and shovels and stuff. We finished right before you came. I didn't mean for Suvie to get hurt."

Suvie knelt beside Aaron and took Toby's hand. 'I know you didn't. Don't cry. I'm okay."

Her compassion seemed to make Toby feel worse. He sobbed and pressed his fists to his eyes. "Johnny said Reuben was coming right now and nobody else. I didn't want your horse to break his leg."

"My horse is okay," Aaron said, "but he might have been seriously hurt."

Toby cried even louder. "But Reuben made me eat a worm," he said, as if that explained everything.

Aaron gave Suvie a quick smile. She lost the ability to breathe.

Four other boys came tromping across the pasture. *Johnny and them,* as Toby had described his friends. They must have gathered up enough courage to own up to their own sins. Either that or they wanted to be sure Toby wasn't tattling on them.

All of the boys were in Suvie's *gmayna.* Johnny Wengerd and his brother Perry were Aaron's closest neighbors. Max Zook had to be about the same age as Toby, and Jethro Glick was probably the oldest of the five, though no more than eleven or twelve. He lived with his grandparents and made deliveries in his pony cart for the *Englischer* at the gas station.

Aaron focused his gaze squarely on Johnny. "So you were trying to sink Reuben Schmucker's bike?"

Johnny puckered his lips as if he'd just sucked on a lemon. "I told you Toby was a tattletale."

"Reuben made Toby eat a worm," Max said.

"And he lit a whole row of firecrackers on our porch," Perry said.

"He brags about his bike when everybody knows he found it in the park and took it home without asking."

Aaron held up his hand to stop the protests. "It doesn't matter what Reuben has done. What does Jesus say about it?" When his question was met with silence, he tilted his head and looked Toby in the eye. "Toby, how does Jesus say we should treat those who despitefully use us?"

"To turn the other cheek," Toby mumbled.

"That's right," Aaron said. "And what else, Johnny?"

"We have to forgive people."

Toby started crying all over again. "But he made me eat a worm." Forgiveness seemed a tall order when compared to something as terrible as worms.

"He threw eggs at my sister."

Reuben's list of sins was getting longer and longer.

Aaron stood up. His height lent him a great deal of authority. "It doesn't matter what Reuben did. Do you know what could have happened? An *Englischer* driving down this road in a car might have gotten in an accident. My horse could have broken her leg or Suvie could have drowned. Look what you did to her." He motioned toward Suvie, who stood up and let them see her in all her drenched glory. Jethro bit his bottom lip. Perry averted his eyes and blinked rapidly. Was he fighting tears? She must truly look a sight.

Well, *gute*. It was for a greater cause.

"I'm sorry," Max said.

Toby's sobs got louder. "I'm sorry too."

"Me too," said Perry and Jethro together.

"What about you, Johnny?" Aaron asked.

Johnny lifted his chin and pressed his lips into a hard line. "I suppose I'm sorry too, about Suvie. But Reuben isn't sorry about making Toby eat a worm."

Toby nodded vigorously. "I threw up."

"The important thing is that you forgive Reuben in your hearts." Aaron patted Toby on top of his head. "Even if you threw up."

Toby looked up at Aaron and wiped his eyes. "Are you gonna give me the willow switch?"

Surprise, then pity, then compassion traveled across Aaron's face. He got on one knee and lifted Toby to sit on his bent leg. "I would never give a fine boy like you the switch. Or any boy, even Reuben Schmucker."

"But Suvie almost drowned."

Aaron took out a second handkerchief and held it to Toby's nose. Toby obediently blew. "*Gotte* doesn't like it when we sin, but Jesus loves us so much that he took the switch for us. Our job is to make things right and ask *Gotte* to forgive us."

Toby's bottom lip quivered, and he gave Aaron a tentative smile. Not getting the switch was *gute* news indeed.

Aaron nudged Toby off his leg and stood. He folded his arms and looked at the boys as if he were having a man-to-man conversation. "So what do you need to do now?"

Jethro let out a long sigh and pushed his lips to one side of his face. "It wonders me if we shouldn't fill in the hole."

Aaron nodded and gave them a manly look of approval. Suvie did her best to hide a grin. "You got shovels?"

Johnny poked his thumb in the direction of the tall weeds. "Over there. It's where we put all the dirt too."

Aaron, Suvie, and the boys walked over to the weeds. There were three shovels, four plastic buckets, and a whole pile of garden trowels, plus a rather substantial hill of mud. They'd gone to a lot of work for Reuben Schmucker, even though he'd never truly appreciate it.

"Okay, then," Aaron said. "Let's fill up that hole."

Suvie grabbed a large plastic bucket, filled it with mud, and starting dragging it to the puddle. Aaron, with a shovel in his hand, took the bucket from her. "Mud is wonderful heavy," he said, grinning from ear to ear and turning her knees to pudding. Butterscotch chocolate pudding, which was why she had trouble keeping up with his long strides as he carried the bucket the rest of the way to the puddle.

"I can carry my own bucket," she said, making no attempt to take it from him. She liked seeing the muscles flex beneath his shirt. "You forget I keep a greenhouse and move dirt around all the time."

He set the bucket at the edge of the puddle. "You nearly drowned. You shouldn't exert yourself."

"I didn't nearly drown."

Her knees almost gave out altogether when he leaned close to her ear and whispered. "These boys think you did. They've got to understand that foolish actions have serious consequences."

"Okay. You're right," she said, hoping he wouldn't hear how loud her heart was beating. If he would quit looking at her that way, she could at least try for some composure. "But I can still carry my own bucket."

His intense gaze stayed locked on her face, and he seemed to loom closer without even moving. "I know you can." He reached out and brushed his thumb across her cheek. "You have a spot of mud right there," he said, his voice as low and silky as chocolate milk.

"I . . . I've got spots everywhere," she mumbled.

"I like them."

Her pulse might have broken some sort of speed record. "I need a bath."

"*Jah*. You smell." He pulled a third handkerchief from his pocket and handed it to her. "You can use this for the spots."

Suvie sighed even as a giggle tripped from her lips. Leave it to Aaron to send her to the moon with one look and then pull her down to earth with one word.

He shook his head. "I'd get a lot more done if you stopped doing that."

"Stopped doing what?"

He shrugged and tapped his shovel into the dirt. "That smiling thing. It's distracting."

"You like when I smile?"

"*Jah*. You have *gute* teeth."

She arched an eyebrow and tried not to take it as a compliment. She shouldn't get her hopes up like that. "Well, what about you and that handkerchief trick? How many have you got in that pocket?"

Aaron's eyes quit dancing. "Mary liked me to carry extras. She pressed three for me every morning. It's a way to keep her close to me every day."

Suvie smiled and touched his arm. "Of course it is. They really come in handy. Mary was always so thoughtful like that."

Aaron studied her face, and the light behind his eyes grew brighter. "Whatever you do, don't start crying, because I'm out of handkerchiefs."

"I can use Toby's old one."

He made a face. "If you really want to."

Toby muscled his way between Suvie and Aaron with a garden trowel full of dirt. About half a cup or so. At this rate, they'd be fortunate to fill the hole before school started in the fall. "Are you going to help us or what?"

Suvie grinned at Aaron, picked up her bucket, and dumped it into the puddle.

He smiled back and nearly blinded her, and she thought there was no better way to spend a bright June day.

Unless it was in dry clothes.

With no sand in her ears.

Chapter 4

Suvie and Aaron walked out of Weaver's greenhouse together.

"*Ach, vell*," Suvie said, hopping into the buggy and settling in. "I know what I'm going to grow more of next year. I had no idea petunias were so popular."

She was wearing a lavender dress today, and it was just as pretty as the baby-blue one. Everything seemed to accent her deep blue eyes.

"Maybe Mary's garden won't get petunias this year," Aaron said, though it wasn't the end of the world. That had already happened. Mary's garden didn't have petunias last year either. They'd already been to three other places. It appeared that petunias were as rare as hen's teeth.

Still, he'd be disappointed to have to cut their trip short and go home. Aaron was sort of enjoying searching for petunias with Suvie. She liked to laugh and she liked to boss him around, and he didn't mind being bossed. She always had something interesting up her sleeve.

Suvie unwound the reins and handed them to Aaron. "Let's go. I'm not giving up yet. There's a greenhouse in Wautoma that might have some petunias."

"Wautoma is an hour away by car."

She grinned. "It might be a fun adventure."

It just might be with Suvie. She even made shoveling mud seem fun.

After they'd filled that hole in the puddle last week, they had both decided that Suvie was too soggy for a petunia-hunting trip, so he'd reluctantly taken her home with a promise to return. This morning, Aaron had popped out of bed an hour earlier than usual and scrubbed his stainless steel sink for good measure. His bran flakes had seemed crunchier, and he'd put an extra spoonful of sugar in his *kaffee*.

Mary would never have let herself fall into a mud puddle like that. She didn't like mud, and she couldn't stand being dirty. If she had fallen in, she would have gone straight home, showered, and done three batches of laundry.

But Aaron didn't mind the sight of Suvie slogging around in her filthy dress, bailing water out of the puddle and bringing fresh dirt to fill the hole. It was nice to have a friend to do things with. It had been her suggestion to buy the boys ice cream. Aaron had bought her a cone too, though she ate it out behind the store so she wouldn't shock passersby.

"Much as I'd like an adventure, I don't think Coke could make it all the way to Wautoma and back today," Aaron said.

Suvie slowly expelled all the air from her lungs. "You're right." A light turned on behind her eyes, and she sat up straight. "I'm giving up."

"You just said you'd never give up."

There was so much enthusiasm behind her smile that he couldn't help but smile back. "*Ach*, we'll find petunias somewhere, but I'm going to have to go to the bishop's dairy and make some calls." She snatched the reins from his hands and jiggled them to get the horse moving. "Enough of this lollygagging. I know exactly where I want to take you."

He gave her a look of righteous indignation and took back his reins. "My buggy. I drive."

"The last time you drove, I ended up in a mud puddle."

"The last time you drove, you ended up in a ditch."

She huffed in protest as if he'd insulted her entire family. "That was a year ago, I'll have you know, smarty-pants."

"Let's not take our chances." Aaron guided Coke to the main road. "Which way?"

"Go left, then left, then straight, then right."

He chuckled. "Do you think you could give those directions one at a time?"

They rolled down the main road for two miles, then turned left and then right onto a road Aaron knew well. "Why are we going to my cousin Moses's place?"

Suvie nibbled on her fingernail. "You need to have some of his cheese."

"I've had his cheese before."

Suvie leaned over and nudged him with her elbow. "That loaf of bread sitting on your table is the only thing waiting for you at home. I've got to fatten you up."

When Suvie had come this morning, she had brought a loaf of Mammi's famous jalapeño banana bread, and it was famous for a reason. Aaron shuddered. Moses's cheese would taste wonderful-*gute*.

Moses owned a cheese factory where he and four or five of Aaron's cousins made cheddar and baby Swiss cheese. Moses and his wife, Lia, ran a small store at the side of the factory where they sold their cheese and some of Lia's baked goods.

The bell above the door tinkled as Suvie and Aaron entered the shop. Moses and Lia's little boy, Crist, played on the floor with some marbles while Lia sat on a stool studying a notebook and twirling a pencil in her fingers. She looked up and bloomed into a smile. "*Ach, du lieva*, Aaron. How *wunderbarr* to see you. You haven't set foot in this shop for three years. Are you allergic to cheese?"

"I see you at family gatherings," Aaron protested.

Lia curled one side of her mouth. "You've missed the last three. Besides, when a hundred or so of us get together, I hardly see my own shadow."

Aaron gave her a reluctant smile and massaged the back of his neck. "I haven't felt much like getting out."

Lia smiled at him as if she were in on a secret. "Well, I'm glad you're getting out now, and with Suvie, no less. How are you, Suvie? I'm wonderful glad you let Aaron tag along with you. Gideon says he saw you buying ice cream together yesterday."

Suvie winced. "I hope he didn't see me. I looked quite a sight. Aaron accidentally dumped me into a puddle."

Lia's eyes twinkled. "He didn't say what you looked like, just that you and Aaron were together. I was happy to hear it. Aaron needs to get out of his house more often."

Suvie gave Lia's hand a squeeze. "How are you feeling with the new baby on the way?"

Aaron turned his head and tried to look interested in the assortment of cheese curds in the small cooler next to the counter. Talk of pregnancy and babies always made him upset. Mary would never get to be a mother.

Lia placed her hands over her growing abdomen. "*Ach*, I can't seem to get enough to eat, but other than that, I'm fine. Aaron's *mater* is going to deliver my baby."

Aaron swallowed the lump in his throat. His mother was a midwife, but all the doctors and midwives and prayer in the world hadn't been able to save Mary. No wonder he stayed away from family gatherings. There was always too much talk of babies and such.

He picked up a restaurant supply catalog that sat on the counter and started leafing through it while Suvie and Lia talked about babies. He wanted no part in the conversation.

"I want to buy Aaron some cheese and some of your delicious rolls," Suvie said. "I'm trying to fatten him up."

Aaron looked up when Suvie said his name.

"If anybody can do it, you can," Lia said.

Suvie grinned. "Everybody knows how bossy I am."

Aaron didn't like the smug way Lia was looking at him, as if she knew more about his life than he did. His whole family was eager for him to remarry, even though they knew how devoted he was to Mary's memory. It was almost as if none of them understood the strength of love.

He clenched his teeth. He and Suvie were just friends. He never planned on marrying again, and Suvie was three years older than him. If they were dating, as Lia seemed to hope they were, they'd only be allowed to see each other once every two weeks. They'd already seen each other two days in a row. They weren't dating.

Aaron was pretending to be fascinated with eight different kinds of salt shaker when Suvie nudged him quite forcefully from behind. He glanced up from the catalog. She was holding five bags of cheese curds and three substantial blocks of cheddar. "A cheese store is no place for a frown. Are you gloomy because I'm so bossy or are you annoyed that I want to fatten you up?"

Neither. And he didn't know what to tell her. "That's a lot of cheddar."

She pressed her lips together in a wrinkly pucker. "Too much? You're right. Probably too much."

"We have some jalapeño cheese curds," Lia said. "A new recipe."

Suvie's face lit up. "To go with Anna's jalapeño banana bread." She slid open the glass door on the refrigerated case, put back all the cheddar and four bags of curds, and grabbed a bag of the jalapeño stuff. "What kind of cheese was Mary's favorite?"

The unexpected question made Aaron catch his breath. His family was trying to convince him to forget Mary, but Suvie seemed intent on reminding him. Warmth spread through his chest and down his spine. Suvie cared. Suvie understood. Mary's memory was what really mattered.

He could have hugged her.

Well. *Nae.*

Not hugged her. It wouldn't be appropriate to hug her. But he was more than grateful that she wasn't like everyone else.

When he didn't answer, she interrupted her search through the refrigerator case to turn and look at him. "Don't remember?"

Nae. He remembered everything. "She loved Swiss."

Suvie nodded. "We'll buy some Swiss in honor of Mary. But you'll have to eat it yourself. I hate Swiss."

Suvie cared about Mary. She cared that he was grieving, and she didn't seem inclined to talk him out of it. The thought made him feel lighter. He grunted in Suvie's direction. "Don't like Swiss cheese? What's wrong with you? You haven't lived until you've eaten fried Swiss cheese."

Suvie pulled a small block of Swiss cheese from the refrigerator and a bigger one of cheddar. "And you need to try cheddar on a stick. We'll take both. Do you have rolls, Lia?"

"One package left." Lia stepped around Crist and pulled a plastic bag of golden-brown dinner rolls from one of the shelves. "I've got to teach Moses how to make rolls, because I won't have much time to stock his shelves after the baby comes."

Suvie placed her armload of cheese on the counter. "Aaron's *mammi* has been giving me some pointers on cooking."

Aaron pressed his lips together and made a mental note never to try any of Suvie's cooking.

The look of alarm on Lia's face almost made him laugh. "*Ach,* Anna is a dear, dear woman, but she's getting on in years and doesn't have the energy she used to. Come here, and I will show you how to make rolls."

"That's very kind of you," Suvie said.

Lia gave her a weak smile. "Anything to ease Anna's burden."

"One more thing," Suvie said. "Do you have any extra petunias? We're asking everybody."

Lia thought about it for a minute and shook her head. "I've got raspberry starts and some volunteer tomato plants, but no petunias."

"That's okay. We've still got a few places to look."

Lia rang up two blocks of cheese, the jalapeño cheese curds, and the rolls. Suvie took Aaron by surprise when she pulled some money out of the small coin purse she kept in her canvas bag.

"I can pay," Aaron said, stepping up to the counter and reaching for his pocket.

Suvie nudged him to the side. "My treat. You'll eat more if you feel guilty about all the money I spent."

He chuckled. "You're wonderful eager to fatten me up. Are you ashamed to be seen with someone so scrawny?"

A smile crept onto her lips and her cheeks turned a soft shade of pink. "You're anything but scrawny." He expected her to say something bossy like, *You have to eat all this cheese,* or *Don't think being scrawny will get you out of planting petunias,* but she looked down and seemed to concentrate very hard on the money in her hand.

Lia counted out her change. "I hope the cheese works out for you," she said, giving Suvie an encouraging smile.

Suvie glanced at Aaron and then back at Lia. "*Denki*. I hope so too. If the cheese doesn't, for sure and certain the rolls will, though I'm going to buy some chocolate just in case." Suvie sighed as if she'd been holding it in for a long time and gave Aaron a grin that almost knocked him over. How did her smiles always seem to catch him so unprepared? "I paid, so you have to carry the bag." *There* was her bossy side. He kind of liked it. At least he didn't have to guess what she was thinking.

He drove the buggy to a small park by the side of the road, which was basically a picnic table sitting next to a flower box full of weeds. They sat at the table, and Suvie pulled everything out of the bag. "I hope you have a pocketknife."

He did. She directed him to cut open both the Swiss and cheddar while she untied the wire from around the rolls and the cheese curds. "Cut ten slices of each," she said.

"You're planning on eating twenty slices of cheese?"

"*Nae*, you're eating twenty slices of cheese, Skinny Boy."

He obediently sliced cheese onto a napkin while

she laid two napkins on the table and placed a roll on top of each.

"Mary made wonderful-*gute* rolls," Suvie said. "Her crescents were always rolled perfectly."

"Mary made her rolls with about a pound of butter." He put a slice of Swiss cheese inside his roll and took a bite. "Lia's rolls are delicious too, especially with Swiss cheese."

"Her baby is coming soon. It will be busy with two little ones and the store to mind." Suvie glanced in his direction and broke off a piece of her roll. "Does it make you anxious when you see someone like Lia?"

"Someone who is about to have a baby?"

She took a bite of her roll and nodded as if it were the most normal question in the world. Did Suvie ever tiptoe around anything? He studied her face. She hadn't been afraid to talk about Mary, and she hadn't once lectured him about getting over her. Maybe she truly just wanted to know how he felt.

He balled his fist under the table. "I usually don't know a woman is going to have a baby until she's far along enough to show. By then the danger of an ectopic pregnancy is over, and there's no need to worry."

"I'm sorry that you lost her. She was a wonderful-*gute* woman."

He fingered the edge of his napkin. "She was everything to me. My family doesn't understand that I can never be happy again because Mary will never be happy again. She'll never eat fried Swiss cheese or crescent rolls or see the petunias bloom in our garden."

"You might never see that either."

One side of his mouth curled upward. "I suppose not." He crumpled the napkin in his hand. "I feel guilty even enjoying this cheese because Mary can't."

She drew her brows together as if she were pondering his every word. "So you have to be miserable because you think Mary's miserable?"

A question like that would usually have irritated him, but Suvie didn't seem to be accusing him or implying that he should change his mind. She was just asking. How long had it been since someone really cared how he was feeling? "*Jah.* She's dead. You can't get any more miserable than that."

Suvie scrunched her lips to one side of her face as if he'd just said something dumb. "Are you sure? I mean, you could be right. I don't know what it's like to be dead, but heaven sounds like a pretty *wunderbarr* place, at least in the Bible. I imagine you can eat anything you want and never get fat. I would eat four cheesecakes every day and whole-wheat pancakes with butter and maple syrup and ten ears of corn on the cob. And this cheese curd. It's delicious."

Aaron chuckled. "Good thing you can't get fat in heaven."

"And maybe a pound of bacon. Or maybe I should save that for special occasions. Would it be possible to get tired of bacon?" She took another roll from the bag. "Or these rolls?"

"I thought you bought those rolls for me."

"I did."

Aaron pointed to the one in her hand. "You've eaten three already."

"You've got to learn to eat faster, Aaron Beachy. I have four older brothers and if I didn't eat fast at the dinner table, I got nothing. I started taking my second helpings first just in case." She stuffed her fourth roll into her mouth.

Mary ate like a bird. Suvie had a hearty appetite. Aaron didn't mind. It made him smile to see her enjoy her food.

Suvie ate four cheddar slices and none of the Swiss, four rolls, and half the cheese curds. "*Cum*," she said. "We've got four more places to get to yet."

"Four? Where are we going?"

"To fatten you up," she said, smiling at him like it was a great secret. It was *gute* he'd finished all his chores this morning.

She took him to Sarah Nelson's bakery, where they bought an apple pie right out of the oven and ate the whole thing out of the tin with two forks.

"Three more places," she said.

"I'm going to burst," he protested, even though he didn't really want to stop.

They went to Lark Country Store, where she bought firewood—who bought firewood?—graham crackers, and marshmallows, but was very bossy about the fact that they didn't need chocolate.

Aaron couldn't ignore the looks he and Suvie got from people shopping at the store. Mattie and Ruth Petersheim whispered behind their hands in the candy aisle and Elmer Lee Kanagy beamed at him as if he'd invented indoor plumbing. "Glad to see you out," he'd said, as if Aaron had been hibernating for the winter.

He wanted to climb on the check-out counter and announce that he and Suvie were just friends, but it wouldn't have done any good. The Amish loved to gossip almost as much as they loved breathing. They would say whatever they wanted to about Aaron and Suvie, no matter how much Aaron protested. He tried not to let it bother him. No one else knew how deeply loyal he was to Mary, and he couldn't make them understand even if he talked until he was blue in the face.

They left Lark Country Store and, as usual, Suvie directed him where to drive the buggy. It made him smile to see how happy it made her to boss him around, and he could tell she loved being sneaky about it.

Suvie directed Aaron to drive the buggy down a dead-end road. "We're going to Yutzy's candy shop?" he said.

"You really have to try their chocolate drops. They have seven different flavors."

Aaron groaned. "I know you want to fatten me up, but I didn't think you were going to try to do it all in one day. After that pie, I don't think I could eat another bite of anything."

Her eyes sparkled with a tease. "There's always room for chocolate. Hasn't anyone ever told you that?"

"You're making that up to get me fat. If I eat any more, you're going to have to roll me out the door."

She smiled sympathetically. "Don't you worry. I lift bags of dirt for a living. I don't mind rolling you all around town."

Aaron chuckled as he tied the reins and jumped from the buggy. Suvie didn't seem like the type to take no for an answer, and he didn't really want her to. It was sort of fun having apple pie and chocolate drops for dinner. Mary would have raised an eyebrow at such an unhealthy diet, but it was better than bran flakes or even ramen soup. Or Mammi Anna's Spam and asparagus casserole.

The sign on a hook by the door read, OPEN. IF NO ONE IS HERE, KNOCK ON THE FRONT DOOR.

Suvie strolled into the shop. There was a small, open window in the wall between the shop and a kitchen where, like as not, they made the candy. Suvie stuck her head through the window and yelled. "Clara? Carolyn? You have some customers."

The walls of the candy shop were lined with shelves filled with all sorts of candy and cookies and bread. A butcher-block table sat in the middle of the room piled high with plastic tubs of chocolate drops, peanut clusters, and chocolate-covered raisins. The apple pie became a distant memory.

Maybe he had a little room left for some coconut-chocolate crunchies.

Suvie pointed to the tubs of chocolate on the table. "We have to get at least three flavors of chocolate drops and some turtles. They taste like they're straight from heaven."

"I want the coconut ones," he said, not even trying to hide his enthusiasm.

She smiled at him, and his heart skipped around his chest like a trotting pony. "I like coconut too. A lot."

One of the Yutzy sisters appeared in the kitchen and opened the door that led from the kitchen to the shop. The Yutzy sisters were twins, and Aaron hadn't ever been able to tell them apart, even in school, when Clara had sat next to him for a whole year.

"Suvie!" Clara—or Carolyn—said. She gave Suvie a quick hug before turning her eyes to Aaron. "Aaron Beachy, it's *gute* to see you. I don't think you've ever set foot in our shop before."

Suvie nodded so vigorously, she fanned up a breeze. "Can you believe it, Clara?"

Clara.

"Aaron has never tasted your peanut butter chocolate drops," Suvie said. "Or your turtles. Or your macaroons. I've scolded him sharply for it. Think of all the happiness your candy could have brought him."

Clara gave Suvie another quick hug. *"Ach, denki.* You've always been one of our best customers."

Suvie laughed. "It wonders me that I don't weigh three hundred pounds yet."

Aaron glanced at Suvie out of the corner of his eye. She wasn't fat, but she wasn't petite like Mary. She looked like someone who did a lot of hard work and never complained about it—wiry and tall, strong and pretty. She wasn't dainty or fragile like Mary, but she radiated quiet strength. *Ach, vell,* maybe not so quiet—but he didn't mind that Suvie liked to talk. He'd been swimming in silence for three long years.

He pried his eyes from the table of goodies. Clara stared at him as if she were trying to see down to his bones. "I hope you'll be coming around a lot more." She raised her eyebrows and gave him a small nod. "With Suvie."

"I hope so too," Suvie said. "It would be a pity to miss out on all these *appeditlich* treats."

Aaron clenched his teeth. He didn't like the way Clara eyed him, as if she suspected something. "Suvie and I are *just* friends," he blurted out—emphasizing the *just*. It was about the most *deerich* thing he'd ever said, because no one had even asked.

Clara pressed her lips together. "Okay."

Suvie smiled at him as if they were standing in his kitchen sharing a silly joke. "We *are* friends, and that's why I'm making him try the peanut butter chocolate drops and the mint ones. And he wants coconut too."

If Aaron had been uneasy about Suvie's expectations, her reaction put all those worries to rest. It was plain from the unconcerned look on her face that she didn't expect anything more than friendship from him. He didn't want to have to hurt Suvie's feelings when he told her that he would never stop loving Mary and that he would spend the rest of his life mourning for her.

He should have been relieved that Suvie felt that way about him, but disappointment tasted like soggy bran flakes in his mouth. Maybe it would be nice to have a girl take some interest in him, even if he could never return her love. But why should he be disappointed? This was exactly the kind of relationship he wanted with Suvie—with any girl now that Mary was dead.

Suvie picked up the peanut butter chocolate drops as well as the coconut chocolate crunchies, the mint chocolate pieces, and a tub of macaroons for *gute* measure.

When Suvie reached for her coin purse, Aaron yanked a twenty-dollar bill from his wallet and handed it to Clara. "I'm paying for this one."

"But I made you come," Suvie said.

"There were times when I could have come here for candy, and I was too lazy to do it. The stain of that shame follows me everywhere."

Suvie stuffed her coin purse back into her bag. "I'm happy I can help you clear your conscience."

"That, and I want to take home the leftovers," he said.

Suvie laughed. "I knew you were sneaky."

Clara gave Aaron a crooked smile. "It's nice to see two friends who have such a *gute* time together."

Suvie grabbed the sack of goodies from Aaron's hand and waved as she blew out the door like a warm spring breeze. "*Denki*, Clara. For sure and certain, we'll be back."

There was nothing Aaron could do but follow. Suvie had a way of taking charge that was impossible to resist.

He cupped his hand over Suvie's elbow to help her into the buggy and climbed up beside her. "Okay. Hand me a macaroon."

"Not yet."

"Not yet? What do you mean, not yet?"

"Well, you have to give the apple pie more time to digest, and there's a special place we have to go to eat the chocolate."

91

"Why do we have to eat the chocolate at a special place?"

She motioned for him to get the buggy moving. "Don't ask questions."

"This buggy is a special place. I want a macaroon."

She giggled. "You have to be patient."

"But what if you sneak the macaroons while I'm driving? You've been known to eat more than your fair share."

"I promise I won't eat any macaroons until we get there."

"What about the peanut butter chocolate drops?"

"I'll save you at least one," Suvie said, with that mischievous glint in her eye and laughter tripping from her lips. Was she ever sad?

After twenty minutes of her giving him directions, he figured out where they were going. She directed him to drive almost halfway around the lake before she found a spot that satisfied her. "Stop here," she said. "It has a fire pit."

Aaron smirked. "We passed at least ten other spots exactly like this one, and they were a lot closer to home."

Suvie flashed a smile. "But this way we can watch the sunset over the lake."

"The sun is behind us."

She widened her eyes and shaped her mouth into an O. "We still have time to drive to the other side of the lake."

Aaron stifled a smile, jumped from the buggy, and pretended not to hear her. "Do you want me to build a fire?"

"*Jah*. On the other side of the lake."

He walked around the back of the buggy, took Suvie's hand, and helped her down. "This will have to do. If we wait any longer, all those peanut butter chocolate drops will be gone."

Her mouth fell open in mock indignation. "There's nearly half left."

Aaron built a fire while Suvie spread out the plastic grocery bag and laid the tubs of peanut butter, mint, and coconut chocolates on it. Then she opened the graham crackers and marshmallows and placed them next to the chocolate drops. "Now," she said, wiping her hands down her apron, "this is how you do it. You roast a marshmallow—but don't burn it—then stack four chocolate drops, whatever flavor you want, on your graham cracker, and put the marshmallow on top of it."

"What if I like burned marshmallows?"

"Nobody likes burned marshmallows. You only pretend to like burned marshmallows because you're ashamed that you don't know how to properly roast one."

Aaron chuckled. "That's not true. I like the ashy taste in my mouth."

"I don't believe you, and I can see I'm going to have to roast marshmallows for both of us."

He threw one more piece of wood into the flames, unable to ignore the way Suvie's already-bright eyes reflected the fire's glow and sent warmth coursing through his veins. If he'd been a peanut butter chocolate drop, he would have melted into a puddle already.

She threw a dried leaf into the fire and turned her eyes to him, then immediately looked away as an attractive blush tinted her cheeks. "What are you thinking about?" she said.

He cleared his throat. He had no idea what he'd been thinking. The light from Suvie's stunning blue eyes had overtaken every thought in his head. But he couldn't very well tell her that. "It wonders me why anyone would buy firewood at the store."

She curved one side of her mouth. "Where else would you buy it?"

"I cut my own."

"*Now* you tell me! I could have saved three dollars."

While they waited for the fire to burn down to coals, they talked about firewood and her fear of chain saws and how she used a pellet stove to heat her tiny house and how one of her brothers checked on her every day. She gave him the whole tub of macaroons, and he ate three before she even had time to raise an eyebrow.

With a little searching around their fire, he found two *gute* sticks and whittled points on them with his pocketknife. He handed the longest one to Suvie, and she skewered two marshmallows. "I'll do one for you."

He shoved two marshmallows onto his own stick. "I can do my own and make an extra for you. You're going to love the smoky, burned flavor."

"I won't have you burning my valuable marshmallows."

"I like them burned," he said.

She made a face and huffed out her displeasure in one drawn-out breath. That girl must have deep lungs. Her sigh lasted long after Aaron thought she would run out of air. He laughed and made her laugh while sighing, and the rest of her breath came out like a stuttering engine. If he'd known it was this much fun to contradict her, he would have been doing it all day.

"You only think you like them burned," she said, when she stopped laughing.

"We'll see."

Mary hadn't been much for the outdoors. It was too easy to get dirty. She never would have sat on the ground without a blanket underneath. But there wasn't a bench or even a good-sized rock to sit on, so Aaron surrendered and knelt in the dirt to roast his marshmallows. Suvie held her stick near the coals and scooted close to Aaron on the side where the smoke didn't blow in their faces. Her sleeve brushed against his and that familiar warmth threaded its way up his arm and down his spine.

He liked Suvie, and it was nice to have a friend to eat pie and go to the lake with, especially on days when he felt extra lonely—which had been every day for the last three years.

His marshmallows caught on fire, and he let them burn for a few seconds before blowing them out.

Suvie groaned. "There go two perfectly *gute* marshmallows." She reached back for a graham cracker and a tub of chocolate. "What kind of chocolate do you want with your ash cake?"

He didn't even flinch. "Coconut, please."

She placed the coconut crunchies on the graham cracker, and Aaron slid one of his marshmallows between the crackers. He plucked the other marshmallow off the stick and shoved it in Suvie's direction. "Try this." She wrinkled her nose and made a horrified face that prompted Aaron to laugh. "Okay," he said. "I'll eat it myself." He popped it into his mouth. "Hmm. So *gute.*"

Suvie made another face. "A mouthful of ashes."

He ate his burned s'more with great relish even though it didn't taste all that good. He enjoyed watching her pretend to gag every time he took a bite.

She finished roasting her marshmallows to a beautiful golden brown and carefully constructed two peanut butter chocolate s'mores. She flashed that breathtaking smile and handed one to him. "You at least have to try it."

Silky chocolate oozed from between the crackers, and he really couldn't resist, no matter how much he liked to tease her. He took a big bite, savoring every bit of chocolate, peanut butter, and marshmallow.

"I have to admit it was a little better than mine."

Smug satisfaction twitched at the edges of her grin. "I like a man who's not afraid to admit when he's wrong."

He grunted. "Wrong? I'm not wrong. I only said it was a little bit better than mine."

A laugh escaped from between her lips. "I can see we still have some work to do on the *admitting you're wrong* part. But I won't gloat about it. Do you want another one?"

"*Jah*, if you don't mind."

Her eyes sparkled like two brilliant stars. "It would be my pleasure."

He sat back and let her roast him marshmallow after marshmallow until he truly couldn't eat another thing.

"I don't think I've ever had s'mores for dinner before," he said. "Next time, I'll bring a couple of steaks from my *dat*, and we can grill them over the fire."

Suvie cocked an eyebrow. "It wonders me if you cook steaks the way you cook marshmallows."

"Of course."

She giggled and poked at the fire with her roasting stick. "How many beef cattle does your *dat* raise every year?"

"Only three or four head. He doesn't have the land for more."

"Will you raise beef too?"

"*Nae.* At one time, I wanted to start a dairy."

"But not anymore?"

"I haven't felt like doing much of anything since Mary died." The dairy was a forgotten dream. He supported himself—just barely—by planting corn on some of his land and leasing out the rest. He was too miserable to do anything but survive.

"Maybe it's not too late." She hissed as a stray piece of ash from the fire landed in her eye. "Ouch." She blinked rapidly and then covered her eye with her hand.

"Here. Let me see." He rose on his haunches, nudged her arm, and turned her toward him. "Open up." He steadied the back of her head with one hand and pulled her fingers from her face with the other, then he gently pried her eyelid open. "Blink. Look to your left. Look up."

"I think a dairy is a wonderful-*gute* idea," Suvie said, as he studied her eye. "You're smart and a hard worker, and there's plenty of room to expand your barn."

"Look to the right."

"And you're wonderful handsome," she said.

98

She thought he was handsome? Was he sure that was what she had said?

He didn't know if he was handsome, but he knew one thing. In the gathering darkness by the light of the fire, Suvie was about the prettiest thing he'd ever laid eyes on.

He drew air into his lungs, and the world seemed to stand still, or at least their little section of the lakeshore stood still. He was suddenly acutely aware of the caress of her breath against his cheek and the heady scent of flowers that she seemed to carry with her wherever she went. His gaze traveled to her full, smiling, probably-soft-as-rose-petal lips, and the urge to kiss her seized him like a steel trap.

He traced his fingers along the soft contours of her throat and around to the back of her neck. All he could hear was the sound of his heart clanging in his ears as he pulled her closer and brought his lips down on hers. He'd been right. Her lips *were* as soft as rose petals, and he wanted to drink her in.

The kiss wasn't near long enough, but he pulled away to come up for air.

Suvie never took her gaze from his mouth as a sigh parted her lips, sending a tremor through his entire body. He felt her tremble too, as if an earthquake had rocked both of them.

"My eye feels better," she whispered, "but I think I'm going to faint."

"I think I'm going to kiss you again."

Which he did. And it was just as *wunderbarr* as the first time.

He was starting to like this whole friendship thing.

Chapter 5

Aaron studied the pancakes on his plate. He'd forgotten to oil the skillet before pouring the batter, so the pancakes were in shreds, but they smelled good just the same. He'd never actually made pancakes before, so he was pleased with his first attempt. While they were still hot, he spread them with butter, sprinkled the last of the peanut butter chocolate drops over the top, and doused his whole plate with syrup. He cut a triangular slice and took a bite. Probably the best breakfast he'd eaten in three years, if you didn't count the benefit breakfasts that the district sometimes put on.

The pancakes tasted like little slices of heaven, but he probably should have settled for his bowl of bran flakes. If he kept eating like this, Suvie would have her wish. He'd fatten up like a Christmas hog.

He took another bite and smiled to himself. He loved that look Suvie got on her face when she bossed him around, as if she truly thought she could make him do what she wanted simply by giving him orders. He looked forward to proving her wrong. For sure and certain, he'd make her laugh with his stubbornness.

Just thinking about Suvie made him feel ten pounds lighter, as if they'd eaten air for dinner instead of cheese and pie and s'mores. There were so few things that had made him happy in the last three years that he felt like a different person. He was sitting in his kitchen eating pancakes, thinking about Suvie Newswenger, and smiling. Maybe he *was* a different person.

He took another bite. But maybe he shouldn't have kissed her. He'd enjoyed the kiss, but he and Suvie were just friends. Had he been disloyal to Mary? He took a swig of milk and put that thought out of his mind. He didn't want to think about guilt or shame during breakfast, especially when he was enjoying his homemade pancakes so much.

His heart raced when he heard a knock on the door. Suvie was planning on another outing to look for petunias today, but he wasn't expecting her so early. The knock was rather weak compared to the banging Suvie usually gave the door. Maybe it wasn't her. He took another bite before hurrying to the door. If Suvie was on the other side, he didn't want to keep her waiting.

Lydia Schrock, Mary's mother, stood on his porch, leaning on her cane and frowning like a walleye pike. Aaron felt a little guilty that his heart sank. He usually welcomed Lydia's visits because she was the only one who understood his grief over Mary. Lydia's heart was broken too.

She was dressed in black from head to toe, including the black bonnet on her head. Lydia hadn't stopped wearing black since the day Mary died. Aaron had always thought that Mary looked like her mother: petite, pretty, with a good-natured face and good sense in her eyes. All that had changed when Mary died. Lydia was only forty-six, but she looked twenty years older. She hunched over her cane as if it pained her to stand up straight, her face was gaunt and worn, her chestnut hair laced with abundant strands of gray.

Aaron glanced across the yard. Mary's brother Freeman leaned against Lydia's buggy and glared in Aaron's direction. He often drove Lydia places because she didn't drive herself anywhere anymore. Aaron waved to him, but Freeman folded his arms and turned his face away.

"Lydia," he said, shaking off his disappointment that Lydia wasn't Suvie. "*Cum reu.*"

Lydia hobbled into the hall and pulled off her bonnet. Her ashen features blended unpleasantly with her white *kapp*.

"Do you want to sit down?"

"*Jah*," she said, panting as if she'd run all the way from her house. "I get so out of breath anymore." She sat on the small love seat in his tiny front room and motioned for him to sit next to her. When he sat, she reached up and patted his cheek affectionately. "No one but you, Aaron. No one but you understands what I suffer because of Mary's death. Menno won't sleep in the same room with me anymore because he can't stand to listen to me cry at night. I told him right out that I can't stand listening to his silence. He acts as if Mary doesn't deserve his tears anymore. None of them will listen to me, and they only care about themselves, the whole lot of them. Freeman started smoking. Dinah does nothing but stare at her phone all day. Joe left the church and went to live with his girlfriend in Stevens Point."

"I'd heard that. I'm very sorry."

"He might as well have stabbed a knife into my heart, for all he cares." She took his hand. "You would never do that to me, would you, Aaron? You'd never forget Mary like that."

"Of course not," he said, his voice full of conviction. Lydia should never doubt his faithfulness.

"They've all stopped mourning for her, even Menno. His smiles break my heart. He's forgotten her. They've all forgotten her. Everyone except you and me."

Aaron nodded. "My mom says I need to get over it and move on, but I loved her more than that."

Lydia's chin quivered. "Menno plowed a field the day after the funeral. They don't even try to understand."

Aaron slipped his hand over Lydia's. "I promise I will never forget Mary."

Lydia sandwiched his hand between her own. "I have heard some terrible rumors, and I came to you so you could put them to rest. I haven't been able to sleep."

Aaron stiffened. He knew what rumors Lydia was talking about even before she told him. He'd seen the looks at the market, the whispering behind the hands. "What rumors?"

She stood up and paced the small room, her agitation evident in the way her hand gripped her cane. "I know it can't be true. You love Mary and no one else, but Lorena Yoder tells me that you are dating someone."

Aaron's throat was so dry he couldn't swallow. "Suvie and I are just friends." He was telling the truth, but it felt like a lie when he thought of that kiss.

Lydia stopped pacing and pinned him with a suspicious glare. "Friends? Aaron, that's how bad things start. It's a dangerous path, and it smacks of disloyalty to my poor daughter."

Aaron wanted to argue with her, to tell her he would never love anyone but Mary, but he'd be fooling himself if he didn't admit that some-thing had stirred within him when he'd kissed

Suvie. *Ach.* Something had stirred long before the kiss or he wouldn't have been tempted. He had wanted to ignore his conscience because it was easier to pretend that he saw Suvie only as a friend instead of feeling guilty about his growing feelings for her.

Suvie was eager and fun and wonderful bossy. Her smile could have charmed the scales off a snake, and he'd brave a dozen rainstorms just to hear that laugh. She wasn't reserved or particular like Mary, and she couldn't cook or sew, but he didn't mind that Suvie was different. Suvie was herself, and he liked that she didn't tiptoe around him or try to be someone she wasn't.

He liked Suvie. A lot.

And every thought in Suvie's direction was a step away from Mary.

How had he let it go this far?

He hung his head and buried his face in his hands. "*Ach*, how could I have been so blind?"

"I don't think I could bear it if you forgot Mary too."

Aaron squeezed the bridge of his nose to keep the tears from flowing, but it did no good. "Suvie came to plant petunias, and I had no thought that anything would come of it." A sob escaped his lips. "I came very close to forgetting how much I love Mary."

Lydia sat next to Aaron and tapped her cane on the floor. "Don't ever forget. She's not really dead as long as the two of us refuse to let her go."

Aaron blew a deep breath out of his lungs. "I'll never let go. I promised Mary a long time ago."

"She loved you very much."

"And I love her." Aaron wiped his eyes with one of his three handkerchiefs and tried to smile at his mother-in-law. "You raised a *gute* daughter."

"She was my joy. There will never be anyone like her ever again." A tear trickled down Lydia's face. "Let's put a stone on Mary's pile together today. It would mean so much to her."

Aaron nodded. Three days after Mary's funeral, he'd found a smooth, round rock the size of his fist sitting in the middle of his lawn, and the idea had come to him to build a sort of monument to his late wife—a monument to mark the number of days he spent without her and the weight of his grief at her passing.

Mary would stay forever in his heart, no matter how many Suvies tried to replace her.

Suvie couldn't concentrate on anything with so many questions running about in her head. Did every first kiss feel so good?

Did every girl squeal with delight as soon as the boy took her home from her first kiss? Or hug herself and do a little dance around her kitchen? Did every girl feel like flying and singing and laughing until her sides hurt? Suvie hadn't been able to sleep a wink last night, but she didn't even feel a bit tired this morning.

"What excuse are we going to give Aaron for coming today?" Anna said as Felty pulled his buggy in front of Aaron's house. "We can only help Suvie get settled in so many times before Aaron gets suspicious."

Suvie was so giddy, the laughter flowed from her mouth with the least excuse. "You made some of your famous ginger snaps. Aaron can't get suspicious about those."

Well, he *could*. If he weren't cautious, he'd break a tooth biting into one.

Anna's eyes twinkled merrily. "That's true. He loves my ginger snaps, but it wonders me why you wanted us to come with you today. Things with Aaron seem to be going so well."

Suvie didn't want to worry Aaron's grand-parents by telling them about the doubt that had been dogging her all morning. Aaron had kissed her last night. He was bound to be having second thoughts this morning. After all, Suvie was a twenty-eight-year-old, bossy spinster who wasn't the cream of the crop like Mary had been. Boys weren't prone to swoon when she was around, and Aaron wasn't prone to swoon at all. Anna and Felty were sort of protection—and maybe comfort —in case Aaron got smart and decided he wasn't really interested in plain Suvie Newswenger.

Suvie knocked on Aaron's door with a little less forceful enthusiasm than she usually had. She just couldn't be sure that Aaron had enjoyed the kiss as much as she had. Maybe he'd lost his balance and his lips had accidentally fallen onto hers. Maybe he hadn't meant to kiss her at all.

She hadn't expected him to answer. Sighing, she gave Anna and Felty a bright smile so neither of them would have anything to worry about. "I'll go around to the back and see if he's home." He should be home. They had agreed to go searching for petunias one more time this morning. Of course, that was before he'd kissed her . . . or accidentally fallen onto her lips with his face.

Anna looked up at the sky as little drops of water appeared on Aaron's sidewalk. "Oh, dear. It's starting to rain. We'll wait on the porch where it's dry."

Felty lifted the tinfoil that covered Aaron's plate of ginger snaps. "Do you think Aaron will mind if I have one of his cookies?"

"I can't see that he should, Felty dear. There will still be plenty for him."

Suvie could hear Felty's teeth scrape against a ginger snap even as she strolled around the corner of the house. A drop of water landed on her cheek and another kissed her lips. *Oy,* anyhow. She was going to think about nothing but kissing for days.

At first she didn't see him. He stood as still as a post with his back to her, staring at the strange heap of rocks that sat in the middle of his lawn. The rain started to fall harder as Suvie trekked across the lawn toward him. "Don't you ever answer your door? Your grandparents are waiting on the porch." When he didn't answer, she said, "Those rocks would make an adorable little wall around your property. You wouldn't even need cement, and you could plant petunias all around the base."

He didn't move, didn't speak, didn't turn around and flash one of his hesitant smiles at her. He often smiled as if he were unsure whether he should be happy or not. It was a very endearing expression. But today, he was having none of it. He didn't even try to shield himself from the increasingly heavy rainfall. Her heart sank. For sure and certain, he regretted that kiss. She chewed on her fingernail and steeled herself for what she feared was coming.

"My garden doesn't need petunias," he said. "I don't want to waste any more time looking for them. You can go home and quit worrying about it."

Suvie swallowed the lump in her throat. She was just *deerich*, foolish, enough to be persistent. "But you've got to have petunias. What would Mary say about your front yard? She loved flowers."

Aaron spun around as if preparing to defend

himself from an attack. "Don't talk about Mary like you knew her."

Suvie pretended his sudden resentment hadn't smacked her upside the head. "I *did* know her. I was the teacher's helper when she was in school. We met often at quilt frolics and canning parties. Mary and her *mamm* brought me chicken soup once when I was sick. She was a *wunderbarr* cook and my friend."

"Then why aren't you sad when you talk about her?"

Suvie tilted her head to one side and furrowed her brow. "Why should I let her memory afflict me? I'm happy I knew her."

Frowning with his whole face, Aaron picked up a small rock from his pile. "You don't seem sorry she's gone."

Suvie blew air from between her lips in exasperation. "Of course I'm sorry she's gone, but what good does it do to wallow in grief?"

Aaron widened his eyes and tossed the rock back onto the pile. "What good does it do? It keeps Mary fresh in my mind. It is a sign that I haven't forgotten her. If you still remembered her like I do, you wouldn't find it so easy to smile. You've forgotten. Everyone has forgotten." He crossed his arms over his chest. "I refuse to forget."

"I don't want you to forget, Aaron. I want you to have happy memories of Mary and let yourself be happy again."

"I'll never be happy again. And that's how it should be. For Mary's sake, I'll not be looking for petunias today. Or ever. And I'll not be spending any more pleasant days with you, Suvie Newswenger. Your s'mores and peanut butter chocolate drops and petunias almost made me forget, and I can't let myself forget."

Suvie didn't know how to argue with something that made no sense to her. She didn't want to argue at all, especially with the gaping hole in her chest where her heart used to be. "I . . . I see," she stammered, trying not to let her voice betray her. If she didn't get away right now, she'd burst into tears, and she'd rather not give Aaron one more bad memory to live with. "Okay then. Maybe we will see you at the feed store sometime. Be sure to get plenty to eat so you don't waste away."

Get plenty to eat?

Every word that came out of her mouth sounded bossy. No wonder Aaron wanted nothing to do with her.

She turned on her heels and made a beeline around the side of the house. Anna and Felty would know something was wrong when she asked them to drive her home.

She stopped when she was out of Aaron's sight, balled her hands into fists, and blinked back her tears. It had been silly and reckless of her to think that she could ever measure up to Mary Schrock. Mary had been pretty and petite, quiet and appealing. Suvie laughed too loud and bossed people around like a fussy Amish *fraa*.

Still, Aaron had given her some hope, and hope was a wonderful powerful emotion. She'd let it run away with her heart.

A drop of rain trickled down her back. She needed to get Anna and Felty out of the coming storm. Old people always took sick when they got wet.

Aaron's grandparents were eating ginger snaps under the eaves that sheltered Aaron's porch. The plate was less than half full. Had she been gone that long? She bent her head against the rain and marched to the porch.

"Suvie," Anna said, as if she were surprised and delighted to see her at Aaron's house. "It's so pleasant here on Aaron's porch, even if he has a dead rosebush in his yard. But I'm afraid we ate more cookies than we intended."

Suvie giggled in spite of herself, hoping they wouldn't notice the tears mingling with the rainwater on her face. She had a feeling Aaron wouldn't mind if they ate all of his cookies. At least they brought pleasure to someone.

"Where's Aaron?" Felty said, studying her face with a perceptive gleam in his eye, like he could tell the difference between tears and rain. "Is he out nursing his rock pile?"

Suvie didn't know what to say. She was probably their first matchmaking failure, and they'd feel bad about it, even if it wasn't their fault. They'd been given so little to work with. "He, uh, he doesn't want to look for petunias."

Anna frowned and got the same gleam in her eye that Felty had. "What has he done now?"

Suvie couldn't keep the hitch from her voice, no matter how hard she tried. "Nothing." Except leave her standing in the rain with nothing to show for it but a thoroughly broken heart and an unfinished box of graham crackers.

Anna clucked her tongue. "Did he try to share his bran flakes with you? That's enough to scare any girl off. What good are bran flakes except to keep him regular?"

"Maybe he likes that they keep him regular," Felty said. "No girl wants a boy who isn't regular."

Anna huffed out an impatient breath. "What's romantic about being regular?"

Felty took off his hat and scratched his head. "I don't know. I prefer prunes."

The wrinkles puckered around Anna's mouth. "That boy is determined to scare girls off with his breakfast cereal."

Suvie gave Anna a sad smile. "I didn't see any bran flakes this morning."

Felty stroked his beard. "But he doesn't want petunias."

Suvie lowered her eyes. "No petunias."

Anna clucked her tongue again. "That poor boy is so concerned about being regular that he can't see how much he needs petunias."

113

Suvie shook her head, unable to give voice to her shattered hopes.

"Oh, my dear girl." Anna pulled a bright pink dishrag from her pocket and handed it to Suvie. Then, almost defiantly, she took one of Aaron's cookies off the plate and gave it to Suvie as well.

Suvie tried to take a bite to make Anna happy. She managed to etch a tooth mark into the cookie.

Anna tightened the tinfoil around the plate and what was left of Aaron's cookies and set the plate on the porch. "Even though I'm quite put out with my great-grandson right now, I still love him and he still deserves a plate of goodies. It's his own fault if they're halfway gone." Felty took Anna's hand, and they tromped down the porch steps together, heedless of the rain that fell on them as soon as they left the shelter of the porch. "I'm going to have a talk with that boy and set him straight," Anna said.

Suvie sighed. "Please don't. Aaron can live his life any way he sees fit. He never asked me to plant petunias."

"Well, he's not going to catch a wife with bran flakes. Somebody needs to tell him that being regular is not the least bit romantic." Anna let Felty help her into the buggy. "*Ach*, Felty. Sometimes I think nobody would get married without our help. *Die youngie* are so thick sometimes."

Chapter 6

Aaron stood and brushed the dirt off his hands. He came here often enough that the grass around Mary's headstone never got very high. He'd chosen a two-foot-tall vertical headstone so Mary's grave would be visible from the dirt road that ran alongside the secluded cemetery. Her name, along with the dates she had lived, was etched into the homemade concrete stone. Her life had been so short. Sometimes, *Gotte*'s will was painfully hard to accept.

Aaron didn't even look up when he heard a buggy coming up the road, its wheels crunching over the dirt. The people who came to visit the dead wanted to be alone with their grief. Aaron would give whoever it was what privacy he could.

"I thought I'd find you here."

Aaron turned around. Dawdi climbed down from his buggy like a much younger man and tromped toward Aaron with a grocery bag in his hand and a deep furrow between his brows.

Aaron pressed his lips into a hard line. He didn't have to guess very hard why Dawdi was here. Aaron had put Suvie off but good this morning. He'd been upset and unsettled by Lydia's visit, and he hadn't tempered his tongue. He could be man enough to admit that he hadn't been very nice to Suvie, and Dawdi didn't like it when his grandchildren behaved badly. Aaron tried to steel himself for what was to come. Could he could bear another lecture today?

"You don't have to say a word, Dawdi," Aaron said, slipping his hands into his pockets and kicking at the grass at his feet. "I'll apologize to Suvie first thing tomorrow morning."

The furrow creasing Dawdi's brow gathered into a pile of wrinkles, and he smiled the grandfatherly smile that always warmed Aaron from the inside. "I'm not here to tell you anything. I came because Anna asked me to bring you some presents."

Aaron frowned. "To the cemetery?"

Dawdi pulled two bright blue, knitted blobs from the plastic bag. "A potholder and a dishrag," he said, handing them to Aaron. "Only the most challenging grandchildren get both."

"I'm one of your most challenging grand-children?"

The corners of Dawdi's mouth curled upward. "I think it's because your *mammi* doesn't like bran flakes."

"Bran flakes?"

Dawdi reached into his bag and retrieved two boxes of breakfast cereal. "Your *mammi* wants you to try these."

Aaron stuffed his dishrag and potholder into his pocket and took the boxes. "Cap'n Crunch and Froot Loops?"

"Cap'n Crunch peanut butter. They're the most romantic cereals she could find on short notice."

The other thing in Dawdi's bag was a tub of cheese curds. "Your *mammi* says these will plug you right up. That's all I have to say about that."

Dawdi had tracked him all the way to the cemetery to give him cheese curds and two strange boxes of cereal? He couldn't quite figure out what his grandparents were up to, although this was nothing new.

Dawdi wadded up his plastic bag and slid it into his pocket. "I'm sorry to interrupt your visit with Mary."

Aaron glanced at the headstone. "I was just leaving."

"When I was younger, I used to go to my *dat*'s grave and tell him all my problems. It was *gute* to talk things out, even though my *dat* never answered back. What do you say to Mary when you come?"

Aaron shifted his feet and hugged the peanut butter Cap'n Crunch to his chest. "*Ach*. Lots of things."

"Do you tell her you love her?"

"*Jah*. Of course. And that I miss her."

Dawdi nodded. "I can tell you miss her very much."

Aaron tensed. "There's nothing wrong with that, Dawdi." He thought he might turn and walk away if Dawdi started in on how he should

117

"get over" Mary. He'd heard it from Mamm and Dat and his siblings and cousins and everyone else. He didn't want to hear it anymore.

"Of course there's nothing wrong with missing Mary," Dawdi said. "You're going to miss her for the rest of your life."

Ach. Maybe Dawdi wasn't going to give him a lecture. "My *dat* says I should get over her."

Dawdi looked at Aaron, his eyes alight with eighty-seven years of wisdom. "You'll never get over Mary, but maybe it's time to find another way to be true to her memory."

Aaron expelled a deep breath. "That just another way of saying I need to get over her. If I truly loved her, she should always be fresh in my mind, even if she's not with me anymore."

"That's why you have the dead rosebush and the rock pile."

Aaron nodded, aching for Dawdi to understand. "I put a rock on it for Mary every day. It's a monument to her. And don't tell me that it is a graven image. Samuel the prophet built a stone altar in remembrance of *Gotte.*"

"Aaron, you *have* built an altar to Mary, but it's not that pile of stones in your back yard. Your grief is your altar." Dawdi laid a firm hand on Aaron's shoulder and gazed at him so intently that Aaron had to look away. "Do you think that Mary would like to be remembered for the misery she brought into your life?"

"She brought me nothing but happiness."

"When she was alive she did, but now every memory makes you sad. You are weighed down with despair every time you think of her. Her whole life was about love and happiness, and I don't think she would be glad to know she caused you such paralyzing grief in her death."

Aaron's chest was so tight he couldn't breathe properly. Dawdi didn't know what he was talking about. "I honor Mary with my grief. Everyone knows how loyal I am."

"What good do your tears do? What good do they do Mary? I'm not Mary, but I'll be dead soon enough, and I know that this is not how Mary would have liked to be remembered. When people remember me, I want them to laugh at a joke I told or smile at my collection of license plates. I don't want Anna to mope around all day because I'm gone. I want her to be happy she knew me, even if she misses me. Is this the way you would have wanted Mary to behave at your passing?"

"I don't know."

"Don't you?" Dawdi raised an eyebrow. "What would she say to you if she were here?"

Aaron lifted his chin. "She'd thank me for not forgetting her."

"And then chastise you for using her as an excuse to be miserable. What good is your life if you spend it longing for the dead? You've betrayed her memory by closing your heart."

Tears burned the corners of his eyes. "But, Dawdi, I'm can't help being sad she's gone."

Dawdi took the boxes from Aaron's arms, set them on the ground, then gathered Aaron into a stiff embrace. "You wear your grief like a badge. Like a dead rosebush sitting in your front yard. Life is a choice, Aaron. Happiness is a choice."

Aaron sobbed into Dawdi's shoulder. "I don't know how to be different. I can't be different. Ask Mary's *mater*. She understands."

"But does Lydia bring you comfort or try to make you feel worse?"

"The worse we feel, the better we loved Mary." He winced. He sounded stubborn and petulant, like someone who knew he was wrong but couldn't bring himself to admit it. Lydia believed it, but he couldn't say for sure and certain if he believed it himself.

Dawdi nudged himself away from Aaron. "Maybe Freeman loved Mary more than anybody."

"Freeman?"

Dawdi gave a short whistle, and Freeman Schrock emerged from Dawdi's buggy. His tortured expression spoke of pain but not anger, as if it hurt too much to be mad at life anymore. He slid a pack of cigarettes from his pocket, tapped one from the pack, and lit it. Smoke seeped from his mouth like fog from a cave. He trudged toward Aaron and Dawdi as if it were

120

painful to walk. When he was a few feet from Aaron, he stopped and took another puff.

"Hello, Freeman."

"Aaron." Freeman's long bangs covered half his face, and he slouched as if two giant hands pressed down on his shoulders. He looked so sad yet so painfully innocent that Aaron had the almost overpowering urge to pull the kid in for a hug.

"Did Dawdi bring you to visit Mary's grave?"

Freeman took another puff on his cigarette. "He asked me to come talk to you, but I don't know what I'm doing here. It won't do any good."

Dawdi wrapped his arm around Freeman's neck, which brought him close to the smelly cigarette. Dawdi didn't seem to mind. "You two have more in common than you think. I wanted you to talk to him instead of glaring at Aaron from a distance."

Freeman tossed his cigarette butt to the ground and stepped on it with his boot. "I've only got a few minutes. My friends are waiting."

Aaron hated to see what Mary's little *bruder* had become. He was only eighteen and still in *rumschpringe*, but he'd thrown his hat in with the wrong crowd. Word was that Freeman had not only taken up smoking, but he been seen drunk on more than one occasion.

Aaron couldn't resist asking. "What friends?"

Freeman nudged his discarded cigarette butt with his toe. "Nobody in particular."

Aaron had a soft spot for boys like Freeman. Their lives could so easily turn on the pivot of one or two bad choices. And Freeman was Mary's *bruder*. Aaron had a deep obligation to help him, for Mary's sake. Why hadn't he realized it until now? He'd been too wrapped up in his own problems to notice that Freeman needed help.

Had he truly been that selfish for three years? He couldn't stand by and let Freeman destroy himself and his future. Freeman shouldn't live like this. He was an orphan as sure as any child who'd lost his parents.

Aaron pointed to a bench under one of the few trees in the cemetery. "Will you sit?"

Freeman pressed his lips together resentfully, but he nodded and let Aaron lead the way to the bench. Dawdi sat on one side, Aaron on the other, with Freeman in the middle.

Aaron leaned back and folded his arms. "Freeman, you're man enough to hear the hard truth, and I'm going to give it to you. You are throwing away your life for a pack of cigarettes and a beer bottle. You get drunk, you smoke, and you scowl at everyone. Is this the kind of person you want to be?"

"What do you care?" Freeman said. "You've worked so hard to make sure everyone sees how much you are suffering. When have you ever cared about anything but your own grief?"

Aaron's stomach twisted into a knot. "Despite how I've acted, I do care yet."

"You care even less than Mamm does. The day Mary died, it was like all her other children died too, or might as well have. She's hardly gotten out of bed for three years. She loved Mary so much that there's no room left for the rest of us. She can't spare any kindness for her other children."

"She's grieving for Mary."

"Well, she should grieve the rest of her children too, because we're dead to her."

Aaron propped his elbows on his knees and stared at the ground. Had this been his doing or Lydia's? Freeman not only lost a sister that day, he'd lost a *mater* and a brother-in-law who were too wrapped up in proving how sad they were to see that they were hurting others.

Aaron clamped his mouth shut and stifled a sob. Dawdi was right too. Mary would be horrified to think that the memory her life had brought him so much pain. He'd been irritated with Suvie because she hadn't seemed sad enough that Mary was gone, but she was the one who had it right. *Why should I let Mary's memory afflict me?* Suvie had said. *I'm happy I knew her.*

All Aaron had to show for his grief was a dead rosebush and a pile of rocks, when he might have been able to help Lydia heal and give Freeman the direction he so desperately needed.

And then there was Suvie.

He had pushed Suvie away when she had been nothing but patient and long-suffering and eager.

And *wunderbarr*.

Suvie, with her loud, unapologetic laugh and her muddy dresses and her waterlogged petunias, was *wunderbarr* beyond words.

And. He. Loved. Her.

His heart leaped inside his chest and pulled him to his feet.

He loved Suvie Newswenger!

Feeling as if a three-year pile of rocks had suddenly fallen off his chest, he staggered to one of the trees and leaned against the trunk to catch his breath. His heart was pounding as if he'd just run a race or seen a stunning sunrise or escaped an angry badger. He loved Suvie, and when he thought of her, he wondered if he might just be able to remember Mary with love rather than with pain and honor her memory instead of dragging it around like an anvil on a chain.

The thought liberated and terrified him at the same time. What did he have to hold on to if not the pain?

Maybe he just needed to hold on to Suvie.

Freeman pursed his lips and pulled another cigarette from his pocket, as if trying to care as little as he thought Aaron did. Aaron swiped the cigarette from Freeman's mouth with a wave of his hand, and it fell to the ground. "Not here, Freeman. You stink to high heaven."

"I do not."

"*Jah*," Dawdi said. "You smell very bad, especially your breath."

Freeman plucked his cigarette from the ground and resentfully slipped it back into his pocket. "Nobody's ever told me that before," he mumbled, his voice laced with resentment and maybe just a little embarrassment. He probably realized it had gotten very bad if Felty Helmuth had something to say about his body odor.

"Your Amish friends are too polite to say anything, and your *Englisch* friends don't notice because they smell worse than you do," Dawdi said.

"Politeness didn't stop you," Freeman said.

Dawdi put his arm around Freeman. "There comes a point where being honest is more important that sparing someone's feelings, especially when I can see there's going to be trouble down the road, like with you and the smoking." Dawdi nodded at Aaron. "Like with Aaron here. You've told him what he needs to hear, even if he doesn't like hearing it."

Aaron sat down, pressed his fingers to his forehead, and huffed out a breath. "Freeman, I hate to say this because you're Mary's little *bruder*, but I think . . . I think you're right."

Freeman narrowed his eyes. "About what?"

"I haven't cared about much of anything but my own grief these past three years."

"I shouldn't have said that. Mary was your wife."

Aaron shook his head. "You are right, and so is Dawdi. I've been betraying Mary's memory by choosing to nurse my grief. But I want to change that. Can you help me?"

"*Nae,*" Freeman said. "I'm only eighteen. What do I know? I'm addicted to cigarettes, and my *mamm* doesn't love me anymore. I've got my own bucket of problems."

"Can we just be friends then?"

"I don't know," Freeman said. "You're kind of old."

Aaron gave him a genuine smile. He might be old, but he hadn't felt this young in years. "You've helped me more than you know already."

Freeman shrugged. "Probably. I think I deserve that box of Froot Loops for my trouble."

Aaron cocked an eyebrow. "You can't have my Froot Loops."

"I'm afraid Annie Banannie would never approve," Dawdi said. "The best I can offer you is the cheese curds. They're guaranteed to plug you up."

Aaron came home to a dark and empty house. All he could hear was his own breathing as he fumbled for the matches and lit the mantle on the small propane lantern. The lantern hissed to life as he blew out the match and sat down in his favorite chair, the one that looked out the window to the back yard. He could make out the outline of Mary's rock pile by the sliver of moon in the eastern sky.

An hour ago he thought he might have the strength to do it. Now he wasn't so sure. The grief crushed him. The guilt nearly suffocated him. He buried his face in his hands and sobbed like a child.

Nothing needed to change. He could go on just like he'd been living for three years, eating his bran flakes every morning and putting another rock on his pile every day. He wouldn't have to face the pain of telling Mary goodbye, and he wouldn't have to live with the guilt of falling in love with someone else.

Someone else.

He imagined the sound of Suvie's laughter. She had so much life ahead of her and so much love inside her. He pictured her bright, genuine smile, ignored the ache in his bones, and clawed his way out of the deep pit he'd fallen into.

He would choose to honor Mary's memory with the way he lived and the way he loved. He would take hold of the parts of him that were left and broken and build again. Like the pile of rocks, he would make something new out of his grief and choose to live and cherish the life *Gotte* had given him.

He cried until the moon set in the western sky.

Chapter 7

A bowl of bran flakes was no way to start the day, especially when it was so gloomy outside already. But Aaron seemed to eat a lot of them, so Suvie had bought a box at the store yesterday, just to see what all the fuss was about. She had mistakenly thought that Aaron ate them because they were delicious.

Nae.

Aaron ate them because he wanted to make himself more miserable than he already was.

That was the only thing she could conclude.

Suvie took a deep, shuddering breath. She hadn't shed one tear after Friday, but her heart felt as if she'd been crying for a whole year. She didn't understand why Aaron didn't want to be happy. Happiness was all Suvie had ever wanted. She had thought she could find it with Aaron, but she shouldn't have bothered. Now she felt worse than if she hadn't tried at all.

She made one last attempt at the bran flakes. It was no use. A whole cup of sugar couldn't make those things taste better.

She set her spoon down and chastised herself for being out of sorts. No matter how bad she felt now, she wouldn't have been satisfied if she hadn't tried to win Aaron's heart. She loved him, for goodness sake, and Aaron was worth the heartache, no matter how acute or how long-lasting. For a few glorious days, she had been happier than she had been in her whole life. She had gone to the lake and made s'mores and weeded Aaron's flower bed. She had been thrown out of a buggy, done three times as much laundry as usual, and discovered that Toby Byler ate worms.

Her heart swelled until she almost couldn't breathe. She'd made Aaron laugh and gotten her first kiss. What did she have to cry about? She was no worse off than when she had started three weeks ago, and now she had a pallet full of *gute* memories to hold.

Suvie took a swig of *kaffee* before stepping outside the kitchen door and pouring the rest of her soggy bran flakes into the flowers. Hopefully they wouldn't die.

The wind blew the screen door shut as she stepped back into the house. It looked like another storm. At least the crops would be well-watered, but she would never again hear the rain without thinking of Aaron and his clogged rain gutters.

The look on his face when that gutter came down . . .

That memory would always make her happy. And a little sad.

Someone rapped urgently on Suvie's door, and she hurried to the front room. No one should be forced to wait out in this wind.

Anna and Felty stood on Suvie's front stoop, grinning like two hens with a nest full of eggs. Anna held a colorful box of cereal in her hands, which she immediately handed to Suvie. "Suvie, dear! We have finally discovered the secret, and it's not dishrags after all. It's peanut butter Cap'n Crunch."

At least it wasn't bran flakes.

Suvie felt her lips curl upward. Anna could coax a smile out of a hog on butchering day. "The secret to what?"

"It's an emergency," Felty said, his eyes twinkling like the sun bouncing off a choppy lake.

"We need you and the cereal to come with us immediately," Anna said. "And a rosebush. Do you have a rosebush?"

"A rosebush?"

Anna nodded and clapped her hands together. "*Jah*. In your greenhouse. Do you have a spare rosebush? We'll pay double the price."

Suvie was getting more confused by the second. "You want a rosebush?"

"And we want you to come with us," Felty added, just to be sure she'd heard that part.

"I have three rosebushes—a Horace McFarland, a Mister Lincoln, and a pretty pink variety."

Anna paused with her mouth open, at a sudden loss for words. It didn't take her long to recover. "Well. Bring the pink one. We don't need those other two boys getting in the way."

Anna and Felty seemed to be in such a big rush that Suvie thought it might be rude to delay them with questions. They obviously had some sort of rose emergency, and as a gardener, Suvie was the best one to help them with it. She put on her bonnet and hurried to the greenhouse, where she retrieved the plastic pot that held her last pink rose. How nice that someone would be planting it before autumn time. They'd have beautiful roses next spring.

Anna and Felty were already settled in the buggy when Suvie came back. She squeezed in beside Anna with her arm firmly around the rose pot in her lap. Felty was usually a very cautious, *very* slow driver, but today he snapped his horse into a trot and took off down the road like a crazy teenager.

Once Suvie caught her breath and gathered her wits, she asked the obvious question. "Where are we going?"

"We're just doing the job you hired us for," Anna said. "Although we want no money in return. Isn't that right, Felty?"

"That's right."

The job she hired them for? Suvie couldn't think of what that might be except for matching her with Aaron, and that had turned out badly. Surely they weren't going to try to match her with another one of their grandchildren. Mortified at the possibility, she gave Anna a weak smile. "It looks like rain. Maybe it would be better to try planting my rose on a sunny day."

Anna reached down and lifted another box from the floor of the buggy. Cocoa Pebbles. "Stuff and nonsense. The best day to plant is always today, even in the rain."

It didn't take Suvie long to figure out where they were going, and she nearly opened the buggy door and jumped out, even with Felty racing down the road like a runaway train. It had been a week, and she was not going to try again with Aaron, no matter how insistent Anna and Felty were. Aaron had his pile of rocks and his weed-choked flower beds. He didn't have room in his heart for any-thing or anyone else. She'd rather not make a fool of herself a second time.

Felty pulled into Aaron's driveway.

Anna gripped her cereal box like a long-lost friend. "I hope these Cocoa Pebbles are *gute* enough. They were out of Cap'n Crunch this morning."

The three of them got out of the buggy, and Suvie nudged the rose in Felty's direction. "Please take the rose to Aaron and give him my best. I'll wait in the buggy."

"Now, Suvie dear," Anna said. "Aaron asked us to bring you. It wouldn't do anybody any *gute* to sit in the buggy."

A protest formed on Suvie's lips, but it died as soon as she noticed the dead rosebush—or didn't notice it. The gnarled plant was gone, a good-sized hole in its place. Suvie's mouth fell open. Aaron had dug up Mary's rosebush? Or had one of his family members come in the night and decided to take matters into their own hands?

She gazed around his yard. A row of fist-sized rocks lined the newly weeded flower beds, the berm in the center of his lawn, and the gravel path leading up to his house. There were a lot of rocks. Somebody must have been collecting rocks for years to make such an impressive border.

Suvie held her breath as her heart skipped around in her chest like an agitated bunny rabbit. She would not allow herself to hope. Aaron had made himself very clear.

Numb and a little *ferhoodled*, Suvie let Anna lead her to Aaron's front door, where Felty—who was the only one who didn't have something in his hands—knocked.

Her heart sank to her toes when there was no answer. If Aaron was waiting for her, wouldn't he come to the door? Maybe Anna and Felty were only hoping Aaron was interested in Suvie.

Anna beamed and held her cereal tighter. "You'll have to go around, dear. He really needs to see you."

Suvie glanced at Felty. His arms were empty. Couldn't he go around and let Suvie remain safely on the porch with Anna, the cereal, and the potted rose?

Felty smiled a kindly, grandfatherly, irritating smile. He wasn't going anywhere.

Suvie huffed out a breath and marched around the side of the house. She'd have to hurry. A distant roll of thunder told her that a downpour was only a few minutes away. If she found Aaron, which was looking unlikely, she could hand him the rose, wish him well, and run away before he even said a word. It would be better that way. She didn't need to compound her heartache.

As she expected, Mary's pile of rocks was gone, leaving a patch of dead grass as the only sign it had been there in the first place. More heart palpitations. More holding her breath and scolding herself for being so *deerich*. She would not let her childish hopes get the better of her.

Aaron sat on his back porch with an unopened umbrella next to him. Irritation bubbled up inside her. Aaron didn't want her here. She was only making a pest of herself. "Can't you answer your front door so people don't have to hike all the way around the house?"

His smile might have knocked her over if she hadn't been determined to keep her head. "You brought a rose."

She hastily set the rose on the bottom porch step and stepped away. "It's pink. Plant it soon."

"Will you help me?"

Suvie folded her arms to keep her heart from

jumping out of her chest. "You just have to dig a hole and make sure the roots aren't packed together."

"I know. But will you help me?"

"It's going to rain."

He wrapped his fingers around the umbrella at his side. "I have an umbrella." He stood up and came down the steps toward her. Her heart pounded in her ears and her tongue went numb. Was this unbridled happiness or sheer panic?

Aaron pointed to the corner of the house. "There's something I want to show you."

She lost all ability to think clearly. "I left your grandparents on the porch with a box of cereal."

Smiling that aggravatingly stunning smile, he took her hand—*took her hand*—and tucked it under his elbow. "*Cum.* I want to show you."

Dazed and giddy, Suvie let him lead her around to the side of the house. Ten flats of big, beautiful petunia blooms sat on the grass next to the foundation.

Suvie couldn't help herself. She laughed out loud. "Where did you find these?"

His grin seemed to go all the way to his toes. "I hired a driver. Two Walmarts in Green Bay, then De Pere, Appleton, and Neenah. I wanted a lot."

She almost didn't dare ask the question. The

135

answer held too much hope or too much pain. "Why?"

Thunder clapped, and the rain announced itself with a roar. Aaron opened his umbrella and held it over his head. It was too small to keep more than one person dry.

Suvie gasped as he slid his arm around her and pulled her to him. "You'll have to stand this close if you want to stay dry," he said, with a light in his eyes that sent warmth spreading through her chest. What had happened to him? And was she awake or still in bed dreaming of something that would never be? She felt his breath against her cheek as he studied her face. "Will you help me plant these?"

He was breathlessly close, and under the umbrella, it seemed they were the only two people in the world. She couldn't concentrate on anything else but the feel of his arm around her and unrestrained tenderness in his eyes. "I . . . I don't know. I can't think straight when you're this close. We need a bigger umbrella."

Aaron chuckled. "I brought out a puny one on purpose."

"Well, if your plan was to make me feel like I just fell off a cliff, it's working."

His smile faded, and he tightened his arm around her. An unintentional sigh escaped her lips. She could be quite comfortable in his arms for the rest of her life. "I've been wonderful selfish, Suvie, but I want to make things better. I'm sorry for what I said that might have hurt you."

"You mean when you told me you don't like vanilla ice cream?"

His lips twitched upward. "That and the time I accused you of trying to make me forget Mary or when I said I didn't want to plant petunias with you ever again. Or when I pushed you away out of a sense of loyalty to my deceased wife. I was wrong."

"What about Mary?"

"I will always love Mary, but I can't go on living as if I were already dead. Mary would have wanted me to be happy."

"I think she would have."

He traced his finger down the side of her face. "You make me happy, Suvie. I love you, and I want to plant petunias with you something wonderful. For the rest of my life."

She held her breath as he seemed to get even closer without moving a muscle. She had to be dreaming. Could anything make her feel this giddy in real life? "I think I'd like that too."

He lit up like a whole box of fireworks at a wedding. "You would?"

She nodded. "Even though you like bran flakes and Swiss cheese."

She shivered at the way he gazed at her. "I like you much better than bran flakes." Without warning, he kissed her, making her heart stop altogether and squeezing the breath right out of her lungs.

Oy, anyhow! It just got better and better.

And she was pretty sure it wasn't an accident this time.

Chapter 8

Suvie and Aaron stood before the bishop, facing each other but not daring to actually look up. It was too embarrassing to be in front of all these people, everyone's eyes on no one but him and her.

Suvie's heart hadn't slowed down since Aaron had asked her to marry him while they had planted the ten flats of petunias in every nook and cranny of his yard. She might never feel normal again, which was fine by her. She could get used to this *ferhoodled*, dizzy feeling.

She wore a white apron and white *kapp* and a deep purple dress she'd made especially for the occasion. If the hem was a little crooked, Mamm hadn't said a word. Suvie had always wanted to wear purple when she got married. Her attendants were in purple too, and her wedding plates and glasses were white and purple with green napkins.

Mamm, who had despaired of Suvie ever finding a husband, had insisted on twelve attendants and had tatted a beautiful handkerchief for each of the girls. Suvie was impressed that she had finished all the handkerchiefs on such short notice. Of course, she might have been tatting for years and years in hopes of a wedding for her hopeless daughter.

Suvie kept her eyes downcast, but she could barely contain the emotions swirling inside her. It would be unseemly to cry in the middle of her vows, but her heart was as full as a wagon after the corn harvest.

Thank the *gute* Lord that Amish weddings did not include kissing. It was all she could do to muster the vows. A kiss in front of all these people would have been quite impossible yet.

After the ceremony, Aaron stayed glued to her side as they walked to the giant tent Dat had rented for the wedding supper. She smiled at Aaron. Aaron smiled back. He hadn't stopped smiling since that rainy day under the umbrella.

It was a *gute* thing. Aaron deserved to be happy. Suvie planned to do everything in her power to see that he was always smiling.

Suvie and Aaron sat at the head table, and Freeman, Mary's brother, was one of the first to approach them. He smelled heavily of breath mints, and his smile seemed forced and a little sad, but his open face spoke of deep sincerity. "I am wonderful happy for you," he said, "but sorry my *mamm* couldn't see clear to come."

Aaron had gone to visit Lydia three times after

he and Suvie got published, but Lydia could not be happy and tried her best to make Aaron feel terrible about his choice. Since Lydia refused to hear him, Aaron settled for writing a long letter, giving her the same advice Dawdi and Freeman had given him. But Freeman had told him she'd torn it into little pieces and thrown it into the stove. Suvie prayed every night that Lydia would find some peace, but her grief had defined her life for so long, it would be a hard road back and she would have to choose it herself.

Mamm was almost as giddy as Suvie was. After a supper of chicken, mashed potatoes, corn, and celery dressing, Mamm handed out pens with Suvie and Aaron's names on them, and two of Suvie's brothers lit fireworks even though it was only one o'clock in the afternoon. Mamm's enthusiasm was overflowing.

During supper, Aaron held Suvie's hand under the table when he thought he could get away with it, and while he didn't say much, he was for sure and certain wearing out his cheeks with all the smiling.

After supper, Anna and Felty came to their table, Felty carrying a cardboard box.

"This is part of your wedding present," Anna said, tapping her finger on the box. "There are three more just like it in our buggy."

Aaron squeezed Suvie's hand. "What is it, Mammi?"

"Four boxes of Cocoa Pebbles, twenty peanut butter Cap'n Crunch, five Froot Loops, and one Count Chocula. I'm not sure about that one, but it has a very interesting picture on the front of the package. And no bran flakes." Anna leaned across the table and pinned Aaron with a stern gaze. "Please don't ever buy bran flakes again. You never know what could happen."

Felty shrugged. "Well, Annie. They do keep you regular."

Anna shook her finger at her husband. "Aaron and Suvie do not want regular. They want *wunderbarr*. No more bran flakes for them."

Suvie giggled. "I will try very hard to keep Aaron from eating another bran flake ever again."

Anna seemed satisfied. "*Gute*. There's no use getting off on the wrong foot. Marriage is hard enough."

Felty's eyes widened in surprise. "You think marriage is hard?"

Anna waved away his concern. "Now, Felty. Everyone isn't as perfectly matched as we are, and Suvie doesn't know how to cook. There are bound to be some rough patches."

Suvie laughed. "Especially since I don't know how to cook."

Aaron didn't seem the least bit upset. "We've got plenty of cold cereal to eat for breakfast, supper, and dinner. And I can make pancakes."

"And s'mores," Suvie said. "I know how to make s'mores."

Anna and Felty walked away, and Anna pointed to Aaron's little sister Priscilla and whispered something to Felty.

Aaron leaned close to Suvie's ear. "Do you think they're thinking of another match?"

Suvie giggled. "Priscilla is almost twenty-two. Anna can't resist."

Aaron leaned closer so their arms were touching. "I can't resist you." He squeezed her hand again. "Are you happy?"

The bishop was looking in their direction. Suvie scooted a few inches away from Aaron and grinned. "Happier than I could have ever imagined. *Gotte* is *gute*."

"Lord willing, I'm going to make you happy every day for the rest of your life."

"I'll look forward to it," she said.

"Me too."

JOSHUA'S
BRIDE

Molly Jebber

Patty Campbell, my dear friend,
talented author, and mentor.

And

DJ Welker, my dear friend, talented
author, and wonderful editor.
Thank you both so much for your friendship,
encouragement and support.

Chapter 1

1885—Lancaster, Pennsylvania

Madeline grinned, put a finger to her lips, and pointed to her daed in his plain coat, and snoring on the front porch in his favorite rocking chair with a blanket half covering him. His straw hat sat lopsided on his head, and his brown hair covered his right eye. She pointed to the back door.

Joshua grinned and went outside with her. He clasped her hand. "Let's go behind your daed's shed by the weeping willow trees."

She squinted, shielded her eyes, and shivered. She was tired of cold weather and anxious for spring to arrive. Anytime she was with Joshua, she was happy. He had a lilt in his step, smiled most of the time, and didn't let much get him down. He tackled his problems and had faith they would work out fine with God's help, no matter how long it took. He'd been quiet and fidgety today at the church meal, and he hurried to their shady spot. Something was on his mind, but what?

She stood in the shade. "What's wrong? You're acting odd."

He held both her hands and stared into her eyes. "Everything's fine." He cleared his throat.

147

"Beautiful Madeline, love of my life, will you marry me?"

She clapped her hands and jumped for joy. "Jah! Jah! Jah! I'd love to marry you!" She'd found the perfect husband, and they would be together forever. She'd tuck this eighth day of March in her mind as the day she began planning her future with her fiancé. "I'm so happy, Joshua."

Joshua picked her up and twirled her around. "I love you, Madeline Lehman, soon to be Mrs. Stutzman." He set her on her feet. "Your daed granted me his permission the other night."

Her daed loved Joshua as if he were his son. He'd said so more than once. The two men had become fast friends. Her mamm would've loved Joshua. She could envision her mamm and herself getting ready for the wedding. They'd have planned, cooked, and sewed to prepare for the special day together. Her mamm had been a strong woman of faith and brought so much joy to their lives with her cheerful outlook on life and compassionate heart. She'd been patient with Catherine's quick temper and curiosity about the world. Madeline was glad Mamm hadn't known about Catherine's leaving her Amish life behind for good.

She'd never forget the day she found Mamm on the floor. She'd shaken her to rouse her to no avail. Mamm's body was cool and her eyes blank and wide open. Her older schweschder, Catherine, had screamed and run to fetch their daed. He'd rocked her mamm in his arms and then carried her body to the wagon and driven to Dr. Wilson's office. He came home and said the doctor didn't know what took her life. It'd been over five years ago when they lived in Shipshewana, Indiana. She laid her hands in Joshua's. "I wish Mamm were here to share in the most wonderful day of my life."

"From what you've told me about her, she sounds like a loving and wise mamm. I'm sorry I didn't get to know her." Joshua gently squeezed her fingers.

Two cats a few feet away, meowing and chasing each other, brought a smile to her lips as she gathered her thoughts. She tilted her head and stared at their hands. "Did you tell your parents you were going to ask me to marry you today?"

"I did." He dropped his eyes from hers.

"Please tell me what they said." She frowned and stared at her hands.

"They asked me not to marry you." Joshua gently lifted her chin until her gaze met his. "They're afraid you'll leave Lancaster like Catherine. As time passes, I'm certain my parents will grow to love you."

"Joshua, maybe we should wait to wed."

He swiped sweat from his brow with his shirt sleeve. "You are the fraa for me, Madeline. I won't let them ruin this important time in our lives." He tapped a finger to his chin and stared at the sky for a moment. He smiled. "Let's ask the bishop to schedule a date in June. It's not too far away, but we'd have enough time to invite everyone and plan the day."

She sighed. "Joshua, we have to consider your parents' request we not marry."

He kissed her cheek. "As time goes on, Mamm and Daed will understand we're committed to each other forever and they will regret wrongfully judging you because of Catherine's decisions. I'm hoping Nathaniel will fall in love with a sweet Amish woman someday soon and take his mind off his past with Catherine. Then we can be one happy family."

The love of her life had a positive outlook on problems. She'd be sad to delay their wedding. She'd throw caution to the wind and have faith everything would work out well. It was unfortunate Joshua's bruder, Nathaniel, had fallen in love with Catherine and she'd left without a word to him. Madeline hoped Joshua was right and that his parents would see how much she loved Joshua and understand she wouldn't leave Joshua like Catherine had left Nathaniel.

"I'm going to visit the bishop tomorrow. I'd like to get on his schedule as soon as possible. I'm ready to start building our haus."

Her heart swelled with joy. "You are a good provider. I'm blessed Daed moved us to Lancaster three years ago. I had prayed moving from

Shipshewana, Indiana, and kumming here would be a fresh new start for us. I'm blessed to have met you, and your friendship with Daed has helped him through his grief with Mamm and Catherine's departure from us. I thought her meeting Nathaniel had turned her life around. I'm so sorry she hurt your bruder, Joshua."

"It's not your fault. I'm confident my bruder will recover. He loved her, and he needs time to get over her. He's burly, and because of his large stature, he's mistaken for a hard man, but he's a softie inside."

"His soft voice amazed me the first time he spoke. You two don't look anything alike, but your voices are similar. I'm surprised Nathaniel is two years younger than you. He looks older. Catherine is two years older than I am, but I always felt like the responsible one."

Joshua had average height and a thin frame. Nathaniel towered over Joshua with his broad shoulders and muscular arms.

"You and Catherine couldn't be more opposite. You've got blond hair, and she's got dark red hair. Your eyes match a dark blue sky, and hers match a green pasture. She's always looking for adventure, and you're calm and content and enjoy the simple Amish life. My parents will kumme to realize what a faithful and loving Amish woman you are once we're married and show them we're committed to each other."

"I'm fearful they won't accept me before the wedding. If they don't, we must reconsider. It wouldn't be proper for us to go against their wishes."

He hugged her. "We'll treat them with respect and pray to God to change their minds. At the same time, we'll look forward to our wedding day."

She blushed. "I love you, and I'll be counting the days until my name changes to Mrs. Madeline Stutzman!"

Daed cleared his throat and came around the corner of the shed. "I thought I'd find you two here. By the glow on your face, Madeline, I assume Joshua proposed?" He grinned.

"He did! Oh, Daed, I'm so happy!"

"I'm thrilled for both of you. I couldn't ask for a better man to marry my dochder." He slapped Joshua on the arm and kissed Madeline's cheek. He chuckled. "Joshua, during the bishop's message today, you couldn't sit still. I had an inkling you were on pins and needles to ask Madeline to marry you this afternoon." His eyes twinkled.

She smiled and nodded. "He took several bites of his food at the after-service meal and pushed his plate away. He usually scrapes and devours every last bite of food on his plate at meals. I wondered why he didn't have an appetite."

"I waited a bit for my parents to change their

minds, but I grew impatient and chose this afternoon to propose marriage to you. The minutes dragged by until after the church service and the trip back here to our special spot. Now we can tell everyone."

"You must be hungry, Joshua. You barely touched your sandwich and beets. Kumme with me. I've got ham spread and apple tarts."

Daed rubbed his slightly round stomach. "I wouldn't mind a sandwich."

They went inside, and the men sat and talked while she fetched the food. Setting plates and glasses of water in front of them, she sat at the round oak table next to Joshua. She loved listening to the two men discuss farming and life.

Knock. Knock.

"You two sit. I'll find out who is here." Madeline went to the front room across the wooden floor and opened the door. "Nathaniel, kumme in." Mrs. Isabelle Stutzman often sent Nathaniel to her haus whenever Joshua was here. She concocted some excuse for Joshua to have to return home. It was a ploy to keep them apart.

Nathaniel avoided looking at her. "I'll wait on the porch."

"Would you like a glass of water or cup of coffee?"

He didn't answer right away. She guessed his

mamm wouldn't be happy if he succumbed to stepping inside and accepting her hospitality. "Joshua and Daed are having some and a bite to eat. Join them for a minute." He'd talked to her before Catherine abandoned him, but now he would do his best to avoid any conversation with her. His mamm had a dominating demeanor, but she worked hard and took good care of her family.

"I am thirsty. I'll have to drink it fast." He stepped inside, and they went to the kitchen and nodded at the two men.

"I suppose Mamm sent you like she has many times."

Madeline sighed. Mrs. Stutzman couldn't stand for him and Madeline to grow their relationship. She'd find any excuse to interrupt their free time together. Sending Nathaniel to deliver her message increased the tension between him and his bruder. Nathaniel had made it clear to Joshua he didn't trust Madeline, and he didn't like kumming to the Lehmans' where he'd spent a lot of time with Catherine.

Nathaniel nodded.

Joshua patted his bruder's arm. "In order to not disrespect my parents, we'll leave."

Madeline passed Nathaniel the glass. She stood at the counter and observed the men. Nathaniel remained quiet. Her heart ached for him. *His divided loyalty to family must be a constant battle.*

Nathaniel drank the water until it was gone. He handed her the glass. "Danki."

Joshua stood. "I'm sorry to cut our visit short. Enjoy the rest of your day." He squeezed her hand.

"I understand, Joshua." Her daed waved.

Nathaniel tipped his hat and followed Joshua outside.

She waved, shut the door, and pressed a hand to her heart. Her life had changed today. She'd promised to wed Joshua. One day, God willing, they'd have kinner. Their family would grow. She'd pray and ask God to bring their families together. She glanced out the window. Dark clouds had gathered and the trees swayed. A storm was brewing.

Joshua followed Nathaniel's wagon and headed home. Once there, Nathaniel jumped out of his wagon and ran to open the barn doors wide.

Joshua and Nathaniel separated their horses from the wagons and took them inside the barn. Silent, Joshua and his bruder fed the animals.

"Nathaniel, may we have a word?"

"There's nothing more to say. You are determined to move forward in your relationship with Madeline, despite how I or our parents feel about the matter. Even if she isn't like Catherine, we don't want ties to her family. If Madeline is cut from the same cloth as Catherine, she'll hurt you when you least expect it, like her schweschder did me."

"One day, I anticipate you'll meet a woman and fall in love with her. In time, I pray your anguish over Catherine will diminish. Madeline's not to blame for her schweschder's betrayal of you. You've got to pray for God to give you the grace to forgive Catherine. Don't let her destroy your life by carrying a grudge against her. It's robbing you of the joy you used to have in life. I care about you. It hurts me to watch you suffer."

"I have prayed but, in all honesty, I know I'm holding onto the anger." He took off his hat and raked a hand through his thick, dark brown hair, much like Joshua's. "Joshua, please listen to me before it's too late. Find someone else to marry."

"I'm in love with her, and I trust her. I won't give her up because you and our parents won't let go of the past." He stepped closer to Nathaniel. "I asked her to marry me. I'll schedule a date in June with the bishop tomorrow."

Nathaniel covered his face and shook his head. "How can you do this to us? You're a foolish, selfish, and disloyal bruder. The tension in our family is about to increase because of you." He bristled and walked out the door to the haus.

Joshua sat on the three-legged milking stool with a thud. Listening to the rain pelt the roof, he held his head in his hands. He loved his family, but he didn't understand them. He and Nathaniel had worked together in the fields and garden and constructing furniture. They'd tossed a ball, fished, and swum in the pond. They'd caught big bullfrogs and fixed frogs' legs for supper, discussed serious matters, and hardly ever had a disagreement until Catherine upset their lives.

He didn't want to argue with his family over his decision to marry Madeline. They chose to wallow in their hurt and frustration over Catherine. He was moving forward with his life and with Madeline. He took a deep breath and walked into the kitchen. "Mamm, Nathaniel said you needed something."

Her lips in a grim line, she shook her head. "No, I just thought you'd been over at Madeline's long enough."

His bruder left the room.

"Madeline and I have agreed to wed in June. I'll tell you the date after I've scheduled it with the bishop tomorrow."

Mamm gasped and dropped the plate in her hands. The glass broke in pieces and scattered across the wooden floor. "You go to her and tell her you are not going to marry her. You have no assurance she won't leave you one day. Your love has blinded you."

"You heard your mamm." Daed stood ramrod straight and glared at him.

Joshua grabbed the trash bin and carefully picked up the broken pieces of glass and threw them away. "I love my family and Madeline. I choose both. Please understand. Catherine is gone from here. Madeline and her daed are brokenhearted and frustrated by her lack of compassion. They regret what she's done to our family and to theirs. Please find a way to forgive and forget Catherine. Forgiveness is God's way."

Nathaniel stormed into the room. "I've been listening to you, and your dismissal of our feelings sickens me. We'll be forced to attend your wedding, share meals, and become a part of Madeline's family if she becomes your fraa. And how do you know Madeline won't follow in Catherine's footsteps? No matter what you say, you don't have any assurance she won't."

"Your bruder's right. You're disgracing us. Fix this now!" His mamm knelt across from him. She paused from wiping up the rest of the broken plate.

He thought smoke would escape their nostrils from the fire burning in their eyes. Their reactions didn't surprise him, but their confrontation had put forth demands he wouldn't obey. They hid their grudge against Madeline and her daed for Catherine's faithlessness from the bishop and community by treating the Lehmans cordially in public.

He admired Madeline and her daed, Levi Lehman, for their discretion in not speaking about his parents with anyone. He wished he could enlist the help of the bishop and their friends to talk sense into them. Bringing others into their disagreement could make their family breach worse. The risk was too great at present. "Madeline is my choice for a fraa. In time, my desire is that you will accept her too. She's a faithful, loving, compassionate woman. In spite of your rejection of her, she wants to get to know you."

"I know all I want to about the Lehmans, and none of it is good," his mamm said.

Joshua walked outside to the workshop. Glad the rain had stopped, he noticed the dark clouds still loomed. Picking up his tools with one hand, he dragged over a wooden crate with the other. He carried the crate and wood he'd been saving to the wagon. Tomorrow, he'd start building his and Madeline's new haus.

He worked in the workshop crafting a maple chair. He finished two legs and went inside.

Mamm gestured to a covered plate on the counter. "We finished supper. Yours is on the table." She poured him a glass of water.

"Danki, Mamm." He put his hands on her shoulders. "Please don't be cross with me. I'm not making these choices to hurt you. I'm looking forward to my future with Madeline. Won't you be happy for me?"

"You foolish man. If one dochder has been raised with wild notions, the other one is sure to follow. Your disobedience will lead you to nothing but heartache. I've already stood by and watched one son's heart get shattered by a Lehman woman, I don't want to do the same with you. I want my sons to find good women to wed and enjoy a lifetime of happiness." She left the room.

Through the open doorway, he watched and listened to his daed and Nathaniel talking about the expansion of the new hardware store in town. Uncovering his food, he hung his head. The tension had been building for months. His family must've been holding out hope he'd change his mind. The line had been drawn, separating him from them with his decision to go against their wishes.

On Monday morning Joshua harnessed his horse to the buck wagon and went to Addie and Elijah Mast's haus. Elijah would help him out. They'd been friends for years, and Elijah had never let him down. He scanned the rolling hills and farms with horses and cows grazing in green pastures along the way. Driving down the lane, he admired the freshly painted white haus and big barn. Elijah's workshop wasn't far from the pond. They hadn't built furniture together in a while. He'd have to make time.

Elijah quit hammering a nail in the crate he was putting together and met him at the hitching post. "Joshua, what a pleasant surprise."

He smiled. "I didn't get to talk to you much

Sunday. I was going to tell you my plan." He gave his friend a sheepish grin. "After the church meal, I went to Madeline's and asked her to marry me. She said jah."

"Congratulations!" He put a hand on Joshua's shoulder. "Did your parents give their blessing? What about Nathaniel?"

He didn't want to tell him the bad news. He'd rather deliver the message his family was elated. His disappointment loomed over him. "My family is opposed to our plans. They are furious with me since I announced Madeline has accepted my proposal to marry. I'm anxious to build our new haus. I'd like to have it ready for us to move into after we wed. Would you mind helping me?"

"I'd be happy to. I'll ask our other friends to join us. I'm sorry your parents are still not accepting Madeline. Are you prepared to face a future of resentment about your decision from your family?"

"I'm moving forward with our plans regardless of their disapproval."

"I respect your decision. They are wrong about her. They do treat her and Mr. Lehman just kindly enough in public for our friends not to notice."

"Madeline does her best to win them over with baked goods and trying to talk to them. They are polite but walk away from her as soon as they can find someone else to speak to. She doesn't complain and smiles and keeps being pleasant to them. There's nothing more she or I can do to convince them."

"Whatever you need, Addie and I are here for you. I've got news too."

"What?" Joshua hoped it was good news.

"Addie's with child!"

Joshua's eyes brightened. "I'm thrilled for you both."

Elijah's smile turned serious. "I'm worried. She's been sick each morning." His friend's broad shoulders slumped, and his dark blue eyes saddened.

"I've overheard Mamm talk about women with child having difficulty keeping food in their stomachs while they are carrying the child. She's probably fine."

"We've waited three years. She isn't keeping food down, and she's had bleeding."

This revelation was a different story. Men didn't usually talk about such things, but he and Elijah were close. Now he was concerned. "Has she gone to Dr. Livingston?"

"Jah, he told her the amount of blood wasn't enough to worry about. He said to take it easy and no heavy lifting."

"Do you need help?"

"No. Both sets of our parents are taking over her responsibilities." He chuckled. "A little too much."

Joshua laughed with him. "Parents mean well, but they can be overbearing."

Addie joined them. "You haven't been to visit for a while, Joshua. I suspect a pretty lady named Madeline is the reason." She winked.

"Your best friend is part of the reason. The other is helping my family on the property, and I'm getting ready to build a haus." He smiled. "Elijah told me you're going to have a new addition to the family. Oh, Addie, I'm happy for you."

Her cheeks dimpled. "We're overjoyed!" She gave him a mischievous grin. "A haus for whom?" Addie bounced on her toes.

"I asked Madeline to marry me, and I'm going to the bishop's place next to schedule the date sometime in June."

"Wonderful news! I'll help Madeline with the meal planning. We'll have to let the women know what to bring. This will be fun!"

Joshua loved the Masts. They loved kinner, and he prayed they would have a houseful. Both of them had expressed wanting them. They'd been good to him and Madeline, even through Catherine's leaving, when the gossip was the main topic of conversation in their community. The couple had lifted his mood, and the excitement of a life with Madeline brought a smile back to his face.

"Addie, may I tell Madeline you're with child,

or do you want to tell her? I know the two of you are close, and I don't want to impose."

"You can share our news with her. My parents and in-laws are spreading the news. I want her to find out before our other friends do. We'll both have joyous occasions to look forward to this year."

Joshua couldn't wait to talk to Madeline about the Masts' having a boppli. She'd drag out her knitting needles and yarn the minute he told her, to make something for the little one. He hoped she'd stitch her dress first. She would rather have had her mamm stitch the dress. Too bad his mamm wouldn't offer to lend a hand. He pushed the problem out of his mind. He would bask in the thrill of Madeline saying jah to his marriage proposal and to Elijah and Addie's boppli announcement.

The Masts' built their haus with extra rooms, expecting to have them filled with kinner by now. He prayed this boppli would be healthy and the first of many for Addie and Elijah. He loved kinner and looked forward to them one day. Girls or boys, it didn't matter to him. Madeline spoke about wanting a boppli, but they hadn't discussed how many. He'd have to ask her. "If there is anything you need, you don't hesitate to ask."

"I would love a cradle."

Elijah squeezed her shoulders. "Joshua is in a

hurry to build his and Madeline's haus before the wedding. As soon as it's finished, I'll build you a cradle."

She pressed her hands to her cheeks. "Danki. Joshua, would you like to kumme in? Are you hungry?"

"I'd love to stay, but I'm anxious to speak with Bishop Kauffman."

Elijah said, "I understand. Let us know what date you settle on. We'll look forward to it. I'll head over to your property early tomorrow morning to get started. I've got some wood I can load and haul over there for you."

"Appreciate it, Elijah. Danki. I should be there around seven."

He bid them farewell and left. He wondered who Elijah and Addie's boppli would resemble. Elijah had dark hair, a stout build, and solid, rock-hard arms and legs. Addie was short, round, and had beautiful honey-blond hair and hazel eyes. He'd consider himself Uncle Joshua to the child. He'd spoil him or her while he waited until he and Madeline were blessed with a boppli.

He traveled to the bishop's haus. The gray-haired man answered the door. "Joshua, kumme in. Are you interested in an oatmeal cookie and something to drink?"

"No, danki. I won't keep you long."

"Something on your mind, son?"

Joshua grinned. "I asked Madeline Lehman to

marry me. She said jah, and I've kumme to ask when you can marry us."

"Congratulations! I'm thrilled for both of you. Do you have a date in mind?"

"Does Thursday, June eighteenth, suit you?" Thankful the bishop hadn't asked him about his parents' reaction to his proposal to Madeline, he would await the bishop's answer and not stay any longer than necessary. His parents had done a good job of hiding their objections to his interest in Madeline, and he didn't want to make excuses for them to the bishop.

"June eighteenth will work out fine." He cocked his head. "Is your family supportive of your decision to marry Madeline? It's no secret Nathaniel suffered heartache after Catherine's departure."

Joshua swallowed around the lump in his throat. "Nathaniel and my parents are cordial to Madeline and her daed. Catherine's abrupt parting is still fresh in their minds. After Madeline and I show them how in love and committed to each other we are as a married couple, I'm certain they'll fall in love with her."

He darted a glance at Bishop Kauffman and hoped the man wouldn't ask him to put off his marriage to Madeline. He couldn't imagine life without her, and he wasn't willing to delay their future together. He wiped the sweat from his forehead. The perspiration formed more from dreaded anticipation than from the flickering flames in the fireplace.

"On Sundays, during our mealtime, I've noticed your parents don't join you and the Lehmans. They do avoid them. I suspected it was because of Catherine. Do you want me to speak to them?"

"Oh, no! Please don't. They are upset with me enough. They'd be really angry if they thought I put you up to discussing this with them. I have faith they will be fine with Madeline given time."

"She's a lovely woman. Nothing like her schweschder, as far as I have observed. She shouldn't be punished for Catherine's bad choices. I pray God will intervene on your and Madeline's behalf."

"Danki, Bishop Kauffman." He stood and shook the man's hand.

"Give Madeline my best."

He smiled, waved, and headed home. He'd not mention his conversation with the bishop about his parents. If the bishop changed his mind and spoke to his parents on his behalf, they might never speak to him again. They'd painstakingly done their best to hide their misgivings about Madeline. They had no idea they hadn't done a good enough job hiding their feelings about her. He grimaced. Would the bishop speak to his parents anyway? The man might think he was doing them a favor.

Chapter 2

Madeline held up the pattern for her wedding dress. She frowned. Her edges were a little crooked. Not like Mamm's, straight and perfect. Joshua's enthusiasm that his family would change their minds about her was infectious. Optimism filled her heart that, given time, they would wilkom her into their lives. She sighed and put her things away.

She glanced out the window. A sow had escaped the pen. Daed was herding her back to the fenced-in area. *Hooray!* Her daed had succeeded. A wagon was headed toward the haus. She jumped up. Joshua was kumming down the lane. Tossing her fabric to the side, she stuck her threaded needle in the small metal box where she kept her needles and dropped it in the basket.

She shrugged into her cloak and ran outside. Today she'd find out her wedding date! "Joshua, did you visit Bishop Kauffman yesterday?"

"Jah! The date is June eighteenth."

Her daed came up behind Joshua and slapped him on the back. "Not far away. Will you have time to finish your haus?"

"I've started it. I met Elijah at the property early this morning, and he's still there. I left him to kumme here and tell Madeline the wedding date and that Addie is with child."

Hands to her cheeks, Madeline yelped. "They must be over the moon thrilled."

Daed smiled. "I'm glad for them."

Joshua held the reins to his horse. "Go visit her. I'm sure she'd love to talk to you. You both have a lot to discuss."

"I'll make cookies and take them to her tomorrow."

"I'd better get back. I've got a haus to build." He grinned.

Daed petted Joshua's horse. "Do you mind if I help you? I can spare some time."

"Jah! You're wilkom to kumme anytime. I appreciate the extra muscle."

"I'll grab tools and be right behind you." He headed for the workshop.

Joshua kissed Madeline's cheek. "You better get busy on your wedding dress."

"I have the pattern cut out."

"You're off to a good start." He grinned, tipped his hat, and guided his horse toward the main road.

She waited outside until her daed left. She'd call Joshua her husband in a few months. When would Boppli Mast make his or her appearance? What a blessing! She couldn't wait to sit and chat with Addie. What would she knit for the child?

How fortunate they were both twenty-two.

Joshua and Elijah were twenty-three. It was good for her and Joshua to share a close friendship with a couple their age. The woman had befriended her at the first church service she attended. *Vibrant* and *cheerful* came to mind when she thought of her friend. Never giving up hope, Addie had believed she'd be a mamm someday. Her treasured friend had been right.

Two deer darted out from the dense woods across the road. A shot rang out. She caught a glimpse of the hunter. She breathed a sigh of relief. The deer bounded away down the road. She lost sight of them. The deer hiding in the woods resembled her hiding her hurt each time she overheard gossipers whisper Catherine's name and stare at her. She'd fled and hurried home. The last couple of months, the chatter about Catherine had died down. The women in the community were friendlier. She suspected they realized she was staying in Lancaster and taking care of her daed, unlike her schweschder. Her future looked bright.

Madeline baked Addie's favorite ginger cookies and drove the buggy to her friend's haus the next morning. She tied her horse to the post, snatched her basket, and joined her friend. "Good morning."

Addie stood at the outside pump with a small porcelain bucket. "Madeline, I'm glad you're here. Congratulations! You're getting married! I'm tickled for you."

Madeline hugged her. "And I'm overjoyed you're having a boppli! Do you have any idea when you'll give birth?"

Addie patted her protruding stomach. "It's hard to tell since I'm naturally thick around the middle. Dr. Livingston is guessing I'm around three months. I was hoping I was with child, but too afraid to get my hopes up. That's why I hadn't mentioned it." She motioned to the front door. "Let's go inside. It's too cold out here for me. I have warm coffee inside."

Madeline followed her to the kitchen. She took off her cloak and set it on the chair next to her. Addie set the water she'd fetched on the counter and poured coffee into two mugs.

Madeline accepted a mug of coffee. "How are you and the boppli?"

Addie sat across from her. "I have no desire for food in the mornings. Each day, my rolling stomach settles around dinnertime. By supper, I'm ready to eat anything in sight." She wrung her hands. "I'm scared, Madeline. I've had spots of blood each day."

Madeline fought to hide the worry in her expression. To lose this boppli would scar her friend forever. She couldn't bear the thought. "Have you told Dr. Livingston?"

"He said to take it easy and not to worry."

There must be something she could do for Addie. "What can I do for you? Should you put your feet up?"

"No, it's not necessary. Dr. Livingston told me I can do light work but not to lift anything heavy. Talking with me about it is what I need. I can tell you anything."

Madeline squeezed Addie's fingers. "I feel the same."

A hard rap interrupted them. "You sit. I'll go to the door." Madeline walked to the front room and opened the door. *Joshua's mamm.* She swallowed. "Please kumme in."

"I didn't know it was your buggy outside." Mrs. Stutzman wrinkled her nose. "I have shoofly pie for Addie and Elijah. You can take the dish to her and give her my best wishes. I won't stay." She shoved the dish into Madeline's hands.

Addie appeared. "Please join us in the kitchen for some of Madeline's delicious cookies and coffee." She gestured. "I won't take no for an answer. Let me have your cloak."

Red-faced, Mrs. Stutzman smiled, brushed past Madeline, and followed Addie to the kitchen. "I won't be here long. I'll just keep my cloak on. How are you? Is there anything you need?"

Madeline sighed. Joshua's mamm turned on the charm the minute Addie joined them. The woman was exasperating. She was a different woman around her sons and friends. All smiles. Madeline had observed her softer side with them. Why couldn't she bestow kindness on Madeline?

"I'm fine. My parents and in-laws are over here most of the time to help, but today they're working at their own places. They'll be here with supper later." Addie served the ginger cookies and coffee. "Madeline, these are scrumptious. Don't you agree, Mrs. Stutzman?"

Madeline glimpsed at the woman. The last thing Joshua's mamm wanted to do was compliment her.

Mrs. Stutzman wiped a crumb from her mouth. "They are quite tasty, but more sugar would add a little needed flavor."

"I'll take your advice and add more sugar next time." Madeline sipped her coffee. She'd be polite. It was important Joshua's mamm understood she wanted to win her friendship.

Addie patted the woman's hand. "Aren't you tickled Madeline and Joshua are getting married? I can't wait to stitch them a gift and choose the food I'll cook and bring for the wedding meal."

Joshua's mamm had taken a sip of coffee and choked. She put the napkin to her lips and recovered. "Madeline and Joshua are not getting married until June. We've got plenty of time to prepare. A lot can happen. We shouldn't rush into doing anything just yet. Don't you agree, Madeline?"

Madeline clutched her skirt, her knuckles

turning white. Mrs. Stutzman counted on the wedding not taking place. It was evident.

"I don't anticipate anything changing our plans. We love each other very much. We would like you to share in our joy." She gently squeezed the woman's hand. She longed for this woman to understand she was sincere.

Mrs. Stutzman stood. "Look at the time. I've got to get home and do a little cleaning. Addie, I'm available if you need anything done." She gave a curt nod to Madeline and left.

Addie scowled. "Mrs. Stutzman doesn't even attempt to engage you in pleasant conversation. Her attitude is appalling. The suggestion for added sugar to the cookies was an insult, as well as her comment the wedding is a ways off and a lot can happen. How rude. I had a hard time not speaking my mind to her about her treatment of you."

"You're a true friend." Madeline sat back. "You did your best to coax her to compliment me and to show your support for Joshua and me. I'll keep trying with her. We all just have to pray that God will change her attitude toward me."

She didn't want the conversation to center around her problems. She came to celebrate Addie being with child. "Addie, let's talk about your boppli. Please don't lift anything heavy and get plenty of rest. May I do laundry? Cook? Anything?"

"No, my parents and in-laws are thrilled to have excuses to kumme and help. We're fine. I'll behave. Speaking of family, have you received word from Catherine?"

Madeline could speak about Catherine without reservation to Addie and not worry she'd be judged. Whatever she told her best friend stayed between them. "No, nothing. In spite of her abrupt departure and bad choices in life, I love and miss her. We didn't agree most of the time about our Amish lifestyle. We found common ground doing the things we loved, like baking, taking walks, and sharing what's on our hearts. I pray she is healthy and safe."

Madeline chatted with Addie another hour. "I've got to go." She hugged her friend. "I'm glad we had time to catch up on our news. We've both got big events to look forward to. The kind which will create wonderful memories." She grabbed her cloak and put it on.

"I'm glad for both of us." Addie hooked her arm through Madeline's.

They went outside. Madeline untied her horse, waved, and got in the buggy. She headed home and held tight to the reins as a mangy dog darted across the road. Her horse reared and she struggled to pull back on the reins and control him. The dog ran away from them. The horse calmed. She relaxed. Life was full of surprises, and not always good ones.

Joshua hammered a nail into a two-by-four alongside Elijah as they built studs for the wall frame. He set his hammer on the ground and flexed his hand. "I'm ready for a break. Are you?"

Elijah dropped his nails into the small pouch attached to his tool belt. "My throat is as dry as paper. I need some water." He hoisted two canteens out of his wagon and handed one to Joshua. "Addie filled these for us. She packed chicken spread sandwiches for us." He pulled two from a basket in back of the wagon and handed one to Joshua.

"You chose a thoughtful and kind fraa. I suspect she'll be a wonderful mamm."

"She's the best." He backed up to the old oak tree. "My parents and in-laws have been supportive in every way. I'm sorry your parents won't be the same."

"There's a buggy kumming. It's Mamm. I wonder if something has happened." He ran to greet her. "Mamm, is everything all right?"

Elijah helped her out of the buggy. "Good to see you, Mrs. Stutzman."

"It's always a pleasure, Elijah. Do you mind if I have a private word with my son?"

"No, of course not." He smiled and walked away.

"Joshua, I visited Addie, and Madeline was there. She's told Addie about the wedding. You and Madeline aren't getting married until June. Why are you telling your friends this early? You don't know what will happen. I urge you to wait to tell others."

Heat rose to his cheeks. She would do anything to rob them of the joy of this time in their lives. Telling their friends about their wedding day was thrilling. Most people were happy for them. He was afraid his mamm would find a way to drive them apart. "I don't foresee anything hindering my marrying Madeline. Therefore, we have no reason to wait to tell our friends we're getting married. I wish you were spreading the news with us."

Mrs. Stutzman crossed her arms and narrowed her big, light brown eyes. "Why are you choosing her over us?" She wrinkled her pointed nose.

"You're the one choosing to shun her, instead of taking her under your wing. She'd love it if you would love her, teach her your recipes, and spend time with her. Mrs. Lehman's passing has left a hole in her heart. She needs you, Mamm. Won't you be a nurturing mamm-in-law to her?"

"No, I won't. She'll move into your haus, get bored with you, and leave you and your kinner one day. You'll embarrass us all over again in this community because of her family's disregard for values of integrity."

He sucked in his upper lip and counted to ten. He thought of Proverbs in the Bible, Chapter

Fifteen, Verse One: "A soft answer turneth away wrath: but grievous words stir up anger." He'd repeated this verse numerous times since his parents started nagging him about Madeline. "Mr. Lehman and Madeline are two of the most congenial and thoughtful people in our community. You haven't taken the time to talk with either of them. Your judgment about them disappoints me."

"Your daed and bruder agree with me. You've been raised in a home where your parents have taught you good morals, honor, and loyalty, I'm sick you've turned your back on us."

"I've not turned my back on you, Daed, or Nathaniel. Mamm, do you think God would honor your attitude toward Madeline?"

"He doesn't honor you disrespecting your parents. We have your best interest at heart. It's our responsibility to protect you."

"I don't mean any disrespect. I'm being sincere."

She huffed and turned on her heel, climbed in the buggy, and left.

From the reception he'd just gotten from his mamm, he suspected Madeline's visit at Addie's wasn't any better. She had thick skin to put up with his family's ridicule. He'd stop at Madeline's on his way home to inquire if she was all right.

Elijah came alongside him. "Here's your sandwich. I put it back in the basket, away from the flies. I take it your conversation didn't go well by the way your mamm stormed out of here."

"You're correct. I'm at a loss as to what to say to her objections about Madeline. She repeats the same words over and over, and I do the same. I don't know how to convince her she's mistaken."

"Surely she'll kumme around when you and Madeline have kinner."

"She's a stubborn woman. I love her, but she rules with an implacable iron fist. Daed supports her in every way. If she would back down, he would too. Nathaniel loves kinner. I'd be shocked if he didn't warm up to his niece or nephew when the time kummes."

They worked for a few more hours. "It's almost time for supper. Why don't you head home to Addie, and I'll stop by Madeline's and ask how her visit went at your haus with Mamm. I don't want her having second thoughts due to Mamm's negative attitude. Danki for your help today, friend."

"Glad to lend a hand." They bid farewell and left in their wagons.

Joshua passed Englischers on horseback and tipped his hat. They acknowledged him and waved back. He'd found the Englischers friendly and polite when in town or in passing them on the road. His parents had preconceived notions against them. He and many others in the Amish community didn't feel the same.

His mamm cooked and baked for elderly widows, and his daed participated in group barn raisings and building additions to homes in the community. They'd been good parents to him and his bruder. He'd always envisioned his parents getting along with his future in-laws. He wanted his and Madeline's families to join them for supper now and then. It saddened him this prob-ably wouldn't happen. The older his parents had gotten, the more stubborn they'd become. Nathaniel's unfortunate experience with Catherine had hardened their hearts. He didn't like the growing tension between him and his parents. He missed the relaxed atmosphere at home, at meals, and in conversations.

He arrived at Madeline's.

She smiled and ran out the door in her cloak to greet him. "I didn't expect you. What a pleasant surprise."

Horse tied to the post, he turned to her. "Mamm sought me out at our property. She told me you were at Addie's when she went there."

She grinned. "Addie praised me for my cookies and expressed her happiness about our wedding plans." She cast her eyes to the ground. "Your mamm said we shouldn't rush to plan. The date is far away and something could change. She desires for us to part. I'm the last woman on earth she wants you to marry."

"I apologize. My parents are digging their feet

in the soil and not moving where we are concerned. I'll finish the haus, move in, and invite them to visit. Maybe then they'll understand this is happening, despite them, and accept you as my fraa."

Madeline rolled her shoe over a small stone. "Don't apologize for them, but please understand I don't want to cause dissention between you and your family. I promise to treat them with love and kindness. My hope is they'll understand how much I love you and see my motives are pure before our wedding takes place. Like I mentioned before, I'm not sure we shouldn't wait."

This sweet woman hadn't said one negative word about his mamm. She'd treated his mamm with respect and was determined to win her over. He admired her more for it. "I don't want to wait. No one can change my mind about you." He kissed her softly.

Blushing, she hugged him. "You're the only man for me, Joshua."

"I'd better get home to supper. Mamm's not happy with me already. I'll not add being late to the kitchen table to the list. I don't know what I'm facing with Daed. I'm sure she told him what transpired today. Danki for understanding and sticking by me." He kissed her again, got in his wagon, and departed.

On the way home, he passed through town. The blacksmith was locking up, and so was the postmaster of the post office, general store, Sally's Restaurant, and apothecary. Two Englischers in fancy gray wool overcoats and black hats lounged on a bench, smoking cigars. Their sleek leather shoes were heeled and narrow. A cluster of women chatted on the corner in their colorful cloaks. He had to admit the women with their, fancy decorated bustle dresses and the men with their straight pants and double-breasted suit jackets in the spring and summer without winter coats and cloaks painted a lively picture. These worldly things didn't appeal to him. He'd stick with his simple clothing. There wasn't any English dress that would make Madeline more beautiful to him than her Amish ones.

He guided his horse to the barn. Daed slung an ax over his shoulder not far away. He struck the wood just right and split it down the middle. No wave, no acknowledgement. Not a good sign. Mamm must've talked to him about their exchange earlier today.

He took care of his horse, walked outside, and approached Daed. "How was your day?"

Daed buried the ax in the main stump he used to balance his wood. "Terrible. Your mamm told me how you upset her. She has your best interest at heart, but you won't listen. I agree you shouldn't be announcing your wedding date to anyone until it's closer. Save yourself the embar-rassment of having to cancel your big day.

Nathaniel wishes he'd never met Catherine. In time, I'm sure you'll feel the same about Madeline."

"The marriage has already been announced. Your judgment about her frustrates me. In spite of Mamm's cold reception today, Madeline was forgiving and gracious. My haus will have a roof, walls, and doors soon. I'll move into it in a few days. I've been working hard on it, and Elijah has helped me. I want to move in and work on the inside so it will be ready for Madeline to join me after our wedding. You're wilkom to visit anytime, and I'll continue to stop by here."

Joshua wanted his family to understand he wasn't abandoning them, just moving on with his plans. He wanted them to be a part of his life and once they were married, Madeline's.

"Maybe it's good you're moving into your haus early. I'm exhausted from endless conversations to convince you to kumme to your senses about her. If you plan to sit at our table for meals after your mule-headed determination, forget it. You fend for yourself, since you insist on being stubborn and disobedient."

"Daed, please. I don't want to miss our chats about our workday, what's happening in the community, farming, and taking care of the animals. We share wonderful memories fishing, hunting, and just sitting on the porch and talking. I'm sad about the dissention between us."

"Apologize to your mamm. You chose this path

for your life. We won't condone it." He gripped the ax, pulled it free out of the wood, and didn't look up.

To say another word would've frustrated his daed further. He'd learned as a child when Daed went back to his task, he was done with the discussion. Where was his bruder? He went inside and found Nathaniel at the cook-stove heating a pot of water. "Are you cooking?"

His bruder had been known to fry an egg or two, but he'd never cooked a full meal.

"You've made a mess of things around here. Mamm's been in the garden jerking weeds out and scowling all afternoon. She ran into Madeline at Addie's. What did that Lehman woman do to upset her?"

"She's angry we're telling our friends about the wedding."

"Are you mad? You should keep the date a secret until it's near."

"I've heard this from all of you. I don't agree. I'm sorry you and our parents are upset, but I won't be here much longer. I'm moving to the new haus I'm building and going forward with my plans for a future with Madeline."

"Running away won't change things."

"I'm not running away. I don't want separation. My goal is to have the haus complete and in good shape before the wedding. If I'm there, I can build the haus and work on the property. If you need me for anything here, all you have to do is ask. I want us to reunite as one big happy family."

"Stop being a young fool. Would you want the Lehmans becoming part of our family if you were in my position? Your head is in the clouds."

"I could say the same about all of you. Madeline doesn't deserve to be shunned by you for the sins of her schweschder." The Bible verse about a soft answer turning away wrath came to mind. He took a calming breath. "Listen, Nathaniel. It's not my intention to hurt you. Let's put our differences aside and enjoy the friendship we've always had."

"Not possible until you clear the dust from your eyes and let her go." He grabbed potholders and lifted the hot pot.

Joshua opened the door for him. He watched his bruder take the pot to their mamm. She had two dresses and lye soap. She must have been planning to take stains out of the garments in the laundry shed. He'd observed her doing this many times. He'd miss being with his family, taking part in their daily rituals in his childhood home. She'd taught her sons to clean haus, wash laundry, cook meals, and bake treats. They'd created a lifetime of fond memories together.

He'd cook supper tonight. Unhooking a pan from the wall, he set it on the hot stove. The fire underneath was going strong. Eggs, bacon, boiled potatoes, and ham slices had been set aside in covered bowls. He cracked the eggs and put them in one skillet and set the meat and potatoes in the other. He rushed to the back door and yelled, "I'm making supper. Won't take long. You might want to wash your hands and kumme inside."

Nathaniel waved, and Mamm gave him a curt nod.

He slid the eggs onto plates with bacon and ham for each of them. He sliced Mamm's fresh peach bread and placed it in a basket on the table next to a crock of country butter. He set the plates at their customary seats.

His family came inside and avoided eye contact.

This should be an interesting supper.

They sat and Daed prayed thanks to God for the food.

With a knot in his stomach, Joshua said, "Mamm, can we reconcile? I don't want you upset."

She wiped tears from her eyes. "I'll be upset until you kumme to your senses about *her*." She softened. "Joshua, we're being hard on you because we want you to understand the mistake you're making. It's our job to protect you. We love you."

"I love you too." He covered her hand with his. "I don't need your protection in this case. I know what I'm doing." He'd move out of his family home tonight. The weather was cold, but the snow showers had slowed and formed no accumulation. He hoped not to see another snowflake and was ready for warmer weather. He had enough blankets to make a bed. The house was enclosed, but it still needed work. He didn't mind. A wood fire would be sufficient for rudimentary cooking and keeping warm until he could get into town and purchase a sturdy iron stove. The tension had grown unbearable for them and for him. Removing himself would give them time to reflect. "I'm packing a bag and moving to the new haus after supper. I'll miss you. I want nothing more than for us to heal and restore our relationship."

He shoveled food in his mouth and waited for them to respond.

They didn't.

He carried his plate to the sink, filled a pot with hot water for the dishes, then placed it on the stove and wiped his watery eyes. He never thought the day would kumme when his family would distance themselves from him.

Mamm shocked him and pulled him close. "Amidst my anger, it's important to me you understand I love you." She stepped away and wiped tears from her eyes. "I'll do the dishes. Go pack your things."

He wrapped his arms around her waist and hugged her tight. "I love you, Mamm."

Daed raised his head. "Son, you don't have to move. We're just protecting you because we care."

"Stay, Joshua." Nathaniel didn't look up.

"I'm not leaving in anger, but in sadness. Please search your hearts and trust me to make my own decisions. Please keep in touch." Joshua went to his room and filled a clean sack cloth bag he kept for traveling, his heart heavy.

Chapter 3

The last two weeks had flown by, and the weather had been a bit warmer, with sunshine for church service this past Sunday. Here it was Wednesday already. The week was half gone. Madeline rubbed her temples and peeked out the front window. Joshua had been camping at the new haus and his parents hadn't kumme to see it. He'd joined his family for meals, and they'd shared laughs and talked about anything but Madeline, according to Joshua. She pressured him to tell her how his parents had treated him. They had been good to him, as long as her name wasn't mentioned.

At church, the Stutzmans smiled at her and her daed for show in front of their friends. No conversation. This reinforced her doubt about their getting married. Was this God's will for their lives? Family harmony was important. *Necessary.*

Would Daed remember her request for flour while he was in town? She raised her brows and cocked her head. Was a boppli crying outside her door? *Surely not.* Opening the door, she gasped and bent to peek at a child. Who would leave a boppli on a porch for even a second? She stood and scanned the property. *Catherine.* Her schweschder was running to her buggy.

Madeline picked up the child swaddled in a heavy knit blanket, ran, and yelled, "Catherine, wait!" She reached her.

"Let me go, Madeline." She pinched her lips and yanked her arm from Madeline's hand. "I wrote everything I had to say in the note in the crate with the child."

"Is this boppli yours?"

She refused to glance at the infant. "Yes, it's a girl. I haven't named her. I didn't want to get attached. I want to travel and maybe marry one day. Another man won't want to raise a baby that's not his. A child would be a nuisance for my way of life."

"Kumme inside," Madeline pleaded. "Talk to me. I'm desperate to know what's going on with you. Please. Daed will be brokenhearted you left without saying anything to him. He should be back from town soon." She let the tears fall. "I've missed you. Please kumme home. We'll raise the infant together."

Madeline scrutinized Catherine, barely recognizing her. Her red hair curled in ringlets beneath her hat decorated with flowers and a yellow ribbon. She studied Catherine's unbuttoned black velvet cloak, then she gazed at Caroline's dress with long ribbon trim, buttons at the bodice, and a high-necked collar, the waist impossibly tight. How could she breathe wearing it? Her leather shoes had whimsical buttons adorning the sides. The buggy had cushioned velvet seats and a fancier harness than Madeline had ever seen. Where would Catherine get this kind of money? "What are you doing for work? How are you supporting yourself? Please, Catherine, we're worried about you."

Her schweschder squinted, raised her head, and gave Madeline an indignant grin. "I work in the saloon. Rich men have been generous with their money when I've agreed to accompany them to supper and dancing. I have a good singing voice, and I earn a decent wage with it. Oh, Madeline, the piano is a wonderful thing. It was the best decision I've ever made leaving this boring Amish life."

Madeline hugged the child to her chest. A shiver ran through her. Cold, she wouldn't leave her schweschder. This was her only chance to find out any information from her. She didn't like Catherine keeping company with men. And a saloon? None of what her schweschder had told her was good. It was as if she were talking to a stranger. "Catherine, you can't be safe entertaining men in a saloon."

A smug smile crossed her schweschder's face.

"Oh, but I am. I'm much happier than I was living here and wearing those plain, ugly dresses and hoeing the garden. Kumme with me, Madeline. We'll find someone else to raise the baby. Surely you know someone. What about Addie?"

Madeline frowned. Why would Catherine attempt to sway her? She'd never given Catherine reason to think she wasn't serious about maintaining an Amish lifestyle. Catherine really didn't know her at all.

"I'm not like you. I have no interest in leaving Daed or my friends. I'm getting married to Joshua Stutzman in June. He's building a haus for us. I plan to have kinner and look forward to a life with him."

"Before you commit to Joshua, let me show you what the outside world has to offer. I love the music, dancing, singing, and money. The fancy food, clothes, and buggies. I've traveled by boat and by train. Both were thrilling. You're missing out on so much, Madeline. We can enjoy all of these things together."

Her schweschder was way beyond the point of no return. Her jubilation over becoming a part of the outside world shocked Madeline. Defeated, she stared at Catherine, a woman with whom she'd shared a childhood. A woman she no longer knew. She looked at the boppli's precious face. "How can you leave your little one?"

Catherine rolled her eyes. "I have no interest

in having children. You were the responsible one. If you don't want her, give her to Addie. If not Addie, I have no doubt you can find someone to take her."

"Of course I'll keep her. She's a part of us. Who is her daed?"

Waving a dismissive hand, Catherine avoided eye contact. "I don't know who her father is, so you don't have to worry about a man showing up to claim her. Most of the men I meet are passing through town. I've traveled and worked in a number of places in Ohio and Kentucky."

Madeline's heart sank. Catherine was proud of herself. She'd chosen a dangerous path in keeping company with strange men. "Please be careful. I'm afraid for your safety. Catherine, none of this makes sense to me. Why would you live this way?"

Fire in her eyes, Catherine glared at her. "Don't judge me. You'll marry Joshua, have a houseful of children, and work all day and half the night in this boring community, obeying its laws and praying to God. Growing old before your time. My life is lively and fun."

"God loves you, but He wouldn't approve of what you're doing."

She hung her head. "You're right. He wouldn't approve. That's the only struggle I have in life, but I'm not willing to change to please Him." She avoided Madeline's gaze. "How's Daed?"

"He's healthy and working hard. He misses Mamm, but he's coping well. Please stay long enough to speak to him. He loves you." She wondered if it was a good idea for Catherine and Daed to reunite. His heart would break to learn the truth about Catherine's way of life. She was sick, herself, about her schweschder's boasting of working in a saloon and accepting money from men for her time. Was she with these men for just supper and dancing? One look at the boppli told her she was fooling herself.

"Nothing good can kumme from facing Daed. He'd ask the same questions, and his sad eyes would match yours when I told him the same answers. It's best if I leave." Catherine kissed her cheek. "I do love you, Madeline." She didn't acknowledge the child. "Tell Daed I love him too." She wiped a tear, untied the horse from the hitching post, and coaxed the horse into a fast gallop.

Shock rooted Madeline's feet to the ground. Her foreboding warned her she'd never lay eyes on Catherine again. Their parting seemed final, as if Catherine couldn't wait to put as much distance as possible between herself and her Amish life, her family, and her own precious boppli.

She went back to the crate and found Catherine's note. *"Dearest Madeline, you and I both know I have no patience for children. I don't have the desire or the time. She was quite a surprise and not a pleasant one. I don't know who her father is, so you don't need to worry a man will kumme to claim her. She was born December second. I won't be back. I do love you, and I hope giving you this child will help make up for leaving you. Best wishes. Catherine."*

Madeline held the boppli in her arms, threw the note in the crate, pushed the crate with her foot to the side of the porch, and stepped inside the house. She held the boppli close. Catherine's coldness and disregard for her dochder horrified her. Madeline would never abandon her dochder. She couldn't understand how any mamm could do such a thing. What would Daed and Joshua say? Joshua wanted kinner, but would he agree to raise Catherine's boppli? His family would be appalled Madeline would even ask Joshua to include this little one in their new life together. Catherine hadn't cared how this would alter her life.

As she pulled back the blanket, big blue eyes stared back at her. She smoothed the boppli's wispy red hair. The infant's skin was soft and pale. Would she keep Catherine's identity a secret from her, or would she tell the little one when she was older all about her mamm? She wasn't sure what would be best for her niece, now dochder. She'd pray to God for guidance.

She'd feed her goat's milk and use the cotton fabric she'd bought for a long skirt to make nappies instead. She didn't mind a bit. In love with the wee one already, she would do her best to give her a good life.

She glanced out the window. The barn doors were wide open. Daed had returned. She carried the boppli outside and approached him. "Daed, did you find everything in town we needed?"

He smiled. "I found everything." He put his finger in the boppli's hand. "Girl or boy?"

"Girl."

"She's a beauty. Are you watching her for a friend? I don't recognize her."

He'd had a difficult time getting over Mamm's passing, and telling him about Catherine would hurt him deeply. She rolled her tense shoulders. "Meet Catherine's dochder."

"What? Catherine? Where is she?" His expression brightened, hopeful and questioning.

"Catherine is no longer here, and she gave me her dochder to raise. She's enthusiastic about living in the world, and she wants nothing to do with her boppli. I asked her to stay and speak to you, but she thought it best to depart before you returned. She claims she's happy. There's no talking her into staying in Lancaster."

He threw his hat on a haystack and raked a hand through his hair. "I don't understand her. How did your mamm and I fail her? I'm frustrated, angry, and sad all at the same time. Part of me would have wanted to talk to her one more time, but another part of me says she's right. It's best she left if there was no way to reason with her." His eyes pooled with tears. "How could she walk away from her own boppli?"

Watching her daed suffer extreme anguish over Catherine filled her with anger at her schweschder's flagrant disregard for those who loved her. He'd been a faithful and loving daed who didn't deserve such disrespect and disappointment from his dochder. "I don't have an answer to your question. Talking to her was as if I had just met her for the first time. I'm still in shock at the way she talked with joy about her new life."

Her daed gazed at the child. "What's her name?"

"She doesn't have a name. Catherine wanted to remain detached from her."

"The more you tell me about her, the more frustrated I am with her. How can she be so insensitive?"

She closed her eyes for a moment. The weight of the world pressed on her shoulders with Catherine's appearance, holding her niece, now dochder, and observing the agony in Daed's face. It was all too much. Tears streamed onto her cheeks.

Daed gently wrapped his arm around her waist and pulled her to his side. He rested his head on hers. "I'm sorry, Madeline. This must be trampling your heart like a herd of cattle. Don't worry. We'll figure this out together."

She stared at him. "What should we name her?"

He didn't hesitate. "Ruthie, after your mamm."

"What a wonderful idea." Her eyes filled with tears. "Ruthie it is."

"When was she born?" He took the boppli in his arms.

"December second." How much should she tell him? Everything Catherine divulged to her would upset him.

"Where was she headed?"

"I didn't have much time to ask questions. She didn't say where she was off to."

"How does she earn a living?"

Madeline cringed. She didn't want him to ask this question. She had to divert his attention. "The little angel has fallen asleep. Let's take her inside. I'm glad you milked the goats early this morning. We'll need it for her instead of using it for my baking recipes."

"Wait a moment." He walked over to the corner of the barn and uncovered a beautiful maple cradle with a few scratches on the sides. "You and Catherine slept in this, now we'll use it for Ruthie." He carried the cradle inside and put it in Madeline's bedroom, grabbed a blanket, and arranged a soft bed for the boppli.

Madeline gently lowered her into the cradle. She tiptoed out of the room, leaving the door open so she could keep an eye on her. "Let's go to the front room."

Daed settled back on the settee across from Madeline's favorite oak chair. "You avoided my question. Why?"

Her daed had just begun to heal from Mamm's death. He had gotten the sparkle back in his eyes, and he'd walked straighter and laughed more in the last six months. She didn't want Catherine's ill-mannered behavior to destroy his resolve to be joyful. "I'd rather not say."

"Please tell me, Madeline."

She gripped her apron and stared at her white knuckles. He wasn't going to leave this alone. She'd have to tell him the truth. "She works in saloons. She loves dancing and music. I don't know much more."

"A saloon? Has she lost her mind?" He paced the floor. "You said she didn't tell you *much more?* Tell me all of what she said. Don't hold anything back."

The ache in the pit of her stomach got worse. Catherine's declaration about entertaining men had been difficult for her to swallow. For Daed, she couldn't imagine the pain it would cause him. What should she do? What she'd shared already had him pressing a hand to his heart in anguish. She'd never lied to him. She wouldn't start now. "Catherine told me she meets men traveling through the towns where she works. She dines and dances with them. In exchange for her time, they pay her." She stole a glance at him.

His body shook with his pitiful sobs. His agony broke her heart.

She knelt before him and gently held his arm. Tears pooled in her eyes. "I didn't want to tell you. I can't bear to watch you suffer. Please, Daed, don't cry."

He caressed her cheek. "My dear Madeline. Your heart is compassionate. I'm blessed to call you my dochder." He heaved a ragged breath. "Catherine has chosen her road to destruction. We can't do anything for her. She has to want to change. All we can do is pray for God to protect her from harm and to bring her to her senses."

A knock at the door startled them. She answered the door. "Joshua, kumme in."

"You've been crying. What's happened?"

Daed rose. "Joshua, would you like water or lemonade?"

"Don't worry about me. Please tell me what's wrong, Mr. Lehman."

"Madeline, you talk to Joshua. I'll fetch some water." He dragged his feet to the kitchen.

"Please sit." She gestured to the chair. "Catherine came here."

He darted a glance around the property. "Is she inside?"

"She left." She folded her hands in her lap. "She abandoned her boppli on the porch in the cold and headed back to her buggy without knocking on the door. I heard a cry, opened the door, found the boppli, and ran after Catherine. She stopped and talked to me for a few moments. I told her Daed was in town and asked would she please wait and speak to him before she left. She refused."

Bewildered, he said, "She left her boppli with you? Is she kumming back? I don't understand."

Madeline told him the disheartening story. She waited for him to ask more questions.

"I've never known a woman who would leave her child for such selfish reasons. It's appalling. Everything Catherine told you is inexcusable."

She hadn't had time to let Catherine's words sink in. The story she'd shared with Joshua and her daed was kumming out of her mouth, but the immoral life her schweschder was leading hadn't fully registered in her mind until this moment. Madeline had become an instant mamm who wasn't married yet. Her life had changed forever. The bishop and friends would ask questions. Gossip about Catherine and the boppli would start all over again, just when it had quieted down.

Joshua held her hands in his. "Your raising Ruthie doesn't change anything. We'll get married as planned, and we'll treat her as if she's our own. She'll need tender loving care, and you and I will give her all the love we can muster. If God blesses us with kinner, she'll have siblings."

Daed hadn't returned with the water. She

suspected he'd been listening from the kitchen and trying to figure out the best time to make an appearance. "Daed, you can join us. I've told Joshua everything."

He came in and handed them each a glass of water. "Joshua, I overheard most of your conversation. You're a good man to take on Catherine's child as your own. I'm sorry she's put you both in this predicament."

Joshua smiled at Madeline and her daed. "Madeline's problems are mine. We solve them together. There's nothing I wouldn't do for her."

Ruthie cried.

Madeline headed to the bedroom. "I'll bring her in to meet you, Joshua. She's precious."

Daed returned to the kitchen. "I poured goat's milk in a pan to warm. I thought she might wake soon and be hungry."

"Mamm kept our old bottles in a box." She glanced over her shoulder before rounding the corner. Stepping into the bedroom, she searched for the box and called to him. "Found them." She grinned at wide-awake Ruthie. "I'll be right back, little one."

She carried the box to the kitchen. "Ruthie's awake. I'll wash one of these out for her goat's milk. Do you mind taking her to Joshua?"

"I'll wash the bottle for you. This is a big moment for you and Ruthie. You should take her to him."

"Danki, Daed." She kissed his cheek. She re-entered the bedroom and lifted the precious bundle from the cradle and brought her to Joshua. "Would you like to hold her?"

He uncovered the boppli. "She's beautiful." He touched her tiny nose and cuddled her in his strong arms.

Madeline relaxed for the first time since Catherine's appearance. She watched Joshua croon over Ruthie. He had fallen in love with the angel in an instant. He hadn't taken his eyes off her, and he hadn't stopped talking to her.

"Oh, Ruthie, you are adorable. Soon, I'll be your daed. We're going to get along just fine. You already have your own room in a new haus." Joshua kissed her tiny cheek. "I don't know if I can part with her, but I must get home and let you tend to this dear boppli."

"I'm thankful for your understanding. We have more to talk about with how your parents and the community will react to Ruthie once they find out she's Catherine's."

Madeline darted her gaze from his.

"Don't worry about them for now. You've been through enough emotional upheaval today. Enjoy Ruthie and don't lose sleep over worrying about what people will say. We'll take it one step at a time."

Daed held a bottle of warm milk. "Do you want me to feed her while you walk Joshua out?"

Joshua squeezed Madeline's hand. "You stay. I'll show myself out. Again, don't worry. I'm confident our friends will love Ruthie and support our choice to raise her. As for all the others, we'll ignore them."

"You make it sound so easy." Her heart swelled at the fine man she'd promised to marry. Her mind swirled with trepidation.

"No, not easy, but we'll face whatever kummes our way together." He smiled, passed Ruthie to her, and left. She settled into a chair.

Daed handed her the bottle and plopped into the chair next to her. "Joshua didn't hesitate to accept Ruthie. He won't let anything stand in his way of your marriage. You're blessed to have him in your life. I am too. I already think of him as my son."

"He's a wonderful man."

Ruthie had half her bottle gone.

The little one must've been ravenous. Madeline stared at the innocent face and wondered what life had in store for them. She didn't want to imagine the Stutzmans' reaction to Ruthie. Exhausted, she would feed her unexpected dochder, fix some-thing quick for her and her daed for supper, and head to bed early tonight. She doubted she'd sleep. She'd probably toss and turn, wondering what she would encounter from the Stutzmans. She had more than herself to consider. Her future looked very uncertain.

Joshua had put on a good front for Madeline, but he dreaded his family's reaction to finding out about Ruthie. He didn't want Madeline to slip away from him based on their opinion. They'd badger him even more to reconsider his plans to wed Madeline. Would they refuse to speak to him again when they found out he and Madeline were going to accept Ruthie as their dochder? The gossipers in the community would spread Catherine's reappearance and abhorrent behavior like wildfire. He arrived home, fixed and ate a sandwich, and stared out the window as darkness fell. He and Madeline had more turmoil to kumme.

He met Elijah outside early the next day. "Good morning."

"I'm on way to town and thought I'd stop by for a few minutes. Are you enjoying the haus?"

"I am, and you are responsible for a lot of the work. Danki." He pointed and grinned. "I put some finishing touches on the outhaus. Now, I have a cook-stove and a dry sink in the kitchen. I have a bed, furniture for the front room, and a table and chairs for the kitchen. Mr. Lapp offered me a good deal on everything from his store." He gestured to the door. "I'll show it to you."

Elijah went in and ran his hand along the back of a smooth maple chair. "Looks nice."

"I really like it." He leaned against the back of

the chair. "I've got some shocking news to tell you." Joshua told Elijah the heartbreaking story.

Elijah clapped a hand to his chest. "What about her husband? Is she married?"

He shook his head. "She doesn't even know who fathered the boppli."

"Joshua, Joshua, Joshua. Your parents will be outraged when you tell them." He stared at him. "You are going to tell them, right? You don't want them finding out from someone else."

He had planned on putting off talking to them about Catherine and Ruthie, but Elijah had a point. Someone might've already seen Catherine in town. The gossip might have started. He groaned. "I considered waiting to tell them but after talking with you, I don't think I have any choice but to tell them right away."

"Today, Joshua. You can't delay. You want to improve your relationship with them, not make it worse. If they learn about Catherine's return and Ruthie from someone else, they'll be hurt and frustrated you didn't tell them."

He grimaced. "I'm doomed either way. They're never going to wilkom Ruthie into their lives because of Catherine's betrayal of Nathaniel. And her abandonment of her dochder gives them more reasons to justify their closed-mindedness toward the Lehmans. I'm afraid Madeline will shy away from me and from them."

"If you need to talk, I'm here for you, my friend.

This will be a tough road for you to travel. Do you mind if I share your story with Addie?"

"Jah, tell her. She'll offer the encouragement and support Madeline will need."

"Would you like to pray together?"

"Please." Joshua bowed his head.

Elijah put his hand on Joshua's shoulder, and they closed their eyes. "Dear Heavenly Father, we lift Your name on high. Please give Joshua the words to tell his story to his parents. Please help them to accept Madeline and Ruthie and support the union of their son to this lovely woman. We love You. Amen."

"Danki, Elijah."

"God doesn't always answer our prayers right away."

"I know, but I trust God will help me remain calm and give me the words to say amidst the storm I'm facing with them and maybe others in the community. I worry more about Madeline. She's suffered enough criticism from my parents for Catherine's selfish decisions."

"We'll stand by her, and she'll be fine."

"I want to believe you're right. I can't imagine not having her in my life. I don't want anything to change her mind about marrying me. I suppose many women wouldn't put up with what she has from my parents' rejection of her."

"Take it one day at a time, friend."

Joshua bid Elijah farewell and sat on the porch

step. Why put off going to his parents'? He might as well tell them sooner than later. He secured his horse to the harness and buggy and guided the animal to his childhood home. He went home, and his Mamm was outside.

Carrying a basket of eggs on her way to the front door, Mamm stopped, her eyebrows raised. "Joshua, would you like some breakfast?"

She wore a smile and was pleasant. His announcement would ruin her day. Dread washed over him. "Are Daed and Nathaniel inside?"

"Jah, in the kitchen. Neither cared for breakfast earlier this morning, so they did some chores and then came back in. Join us."

He secured his horse, went inside, and hung his coat on a hook. He sat next to Nathaniel at the round maple table. "Good morning."

"Are you finished with your haus?" Daed moved his fork and knife to the side.

"I have to build cabinets and put finishing touches here and there, but jah, it's finished. I'm satisfied with the way it turned out. You're wilkom to stop by."

Nathaniel grinned. "I would like to have a look. Maybe I'll stop by this afternoon."

Mamm served eggs, bacon, and grits with gravy and joined them.

Joshua's lips parted. *I can't believe it.* The conversation was enjoyable. Something he hadn't experienced for a while, without their badgering him about marrying Madeline. He didn't want to dampen their mood, but he must. "Catherine came to the Lehmans' yesterday."

His family's faces paled. They gasped.

Joshua swallowed around the lump in his throat. "She had a boppli out of wedlock, and she left her dochder, Ruthie, named after their mamm, with Madeline. Nothing has altered our plans. We'll marry in June and bring up Ruthie together. I wanted you to hear this from me and not some-one else. The news will travel throughout the community after Madeline takes Ruthie to town and introduces her to friends."

Mamm bristled. "You are not going to rear this horrible woman's child as your own! You must separate yourself from the Lehmans. Now, Joshua. They are nothing but trouble."

Nathaniel narrowed his eyes. "Who fathered the child?"

"I don't know." He wouldn't tell them Catherine had no idea. The less said about his bruder's former love interest, the better. He wouldn't inflict more pain on Nathaniel.

Daed sipped his water and set the glass down with a bang. "The daed could kumme for the boppli at any time."

"She assured Madeline this wouldn't happen."

"She has no control over the daed."

His mamm crossed her arms. "Catherine doesn't know who the daed is, does she?"

The hairs on the back of Joshua's neck prickled, and he shrugged. He had planned to avoid revealing this information.

Nathaniel pushed his plate aside, stood, grabbed his coat, and went outside.

Joshua shrugged into his coat and went after him. "Nathaniel, I can't imagine your pain at this moment. Please talk to me."

"I love her, and I abhor her at the same time. She scared me with her interest in the world. But I put aside my fears she'd leave one day, hoping and praying I was enough for her and she'd stay here for me. Never would I have believed she would give herself to strange men. I thought I meant something to her. How could I have been so wrong and foolish?"

He hoped his parents wouldn't kumme and interfere. He and his bruder were discussing a problem the way they used to. "You're not foolish, Nathaniel. There's nothing wrong with falling in love with her. She chose to leave. Please put the pain of her betrayal behind you. Search and open your heart to another woman."

"Joshua, Catherine's boppli drives another wedge between us. If you marry Madeline, this boppli will remind us of the anguish her schweschder caused every time we look at her dochder."

"You'll kumme to accept the boppli as belonging to Madeline and me."

His mamm and daed stepped outside. "You're wrong. We'll never accept the boppli."

She turned and went inside.

Daed and Nathaniel glared at him in stony silence.

He put his chin to his chest, got in his buggy, and went to town. He needed a new saw blade, and the ride would clear his head. It would take a miracle from God to soften their hearts. He dreaded telling Madeline about this conversation with them. How could they reject this innocent little girl?

The gray clouds matched his dismal mood. The damp, cold air added to the weight of what was to kumme when gossip passed from person to person about Catherine leaving her boppli behind. There was nothing to say in Catherine's defense. From what Madeline had told him, she had no remorse for her actions. Shocked at her abandonment of Ruthie, he would never have guessed she was capable of such a thing.

Tying his horse to the hitching post, he held his hat against the wind. This weather had changed in a hurry. A newspaper blew against his legs. He picked it up and glanced at the page. It was from March third. BIG NEWS! AMERICAN TELEPHONE AND TELEGRAPH INCORPORATED IN NEW YORK CITY AS A SUBSIDIARY OF AMERICAN BELL TELEPHONE COMPANY. He walked in and handed the paper to the boy behind the counter. "I found this outside and thought I'd return it."

"Thank you, Mister. The wind must've knocked over the burn barrel out back. I found this in the back room earlier and threw it in there with some others. I'll go check and make sure we don't have papers scattering."

He'd read the first few lines. Telephones would be convenient for communicating, but he lived by the Amish Ordnung, the agreed-upon rules forbidding any type of modern conveniences in their community. They wanted to keep their lives simple and not get caught up in the types of things the outside world had to offer.

Two men conversed outside the general store. He overheard them talking about President Grover Cleveland. Amish didn't pay any mind to politics, and he was glad. Just hearing what little he did gave him the start of a headache. He had enough problems.

The hardware store was crowded. He maneuvered his way to the tools section. He found the saw blade he wanted, walked to the front, and stood in the long line of customers waiting to pay for their purchases.

Mr. Chupp spoke to Mr. Beachy way ahead of him. "I passed a woman who looked like Catherine Lehman driving a fancy buggy with velvet seats. She wore a fancy Englischer wool coat and hat."

"I thought she and Nathaniel Stutzman would marry, but she left to live in the outside world. I'd be surprised if the woman you passed on the road was her. She's been gone for a while now."

"I'm sure you're right." He crossed his arms. "My fraa told me Joshua Stutzman has eyes for Madeline Lehman, Catherine's schweschder. The man better reconsider. She might leave him in the dust with a bunch of kinner to raise on his own if he marries her."

"If he's smart, he'll change his mind." The men stepped up to the counter together to pay for their purchases.

Joshua winced. He ducked behind the tall man in front of him. He didn't want his friends to know he was in the store. Their comparison of Catherine and Madeline angered him. He had half a mind to confront them, but this wasn't the place, in front of customers. It wasn't the first time he'd over-heard disparaging remarks about Catherine. The gossipers assumed Madeline was the same by association. He ached at the unjust way she was being judged.

The men walked out the door. He paid for his saw blade and went to Madeline's.

She opened the door with Ruthie in her arms and waved him in, putting a finger to her lips. "She's been fussy, and she just fell asleep. I'll lay her in the cradle, and we can talk."

"I'll wait here for you." He smiled at Madeline.

She glowed with the sweet boppli in her arms. His news would stir up the turmoil within her again. The last thing he wanted to do, but keeping each other informed was best. How much more was she willing to put up with from his parents now that Ruthie would be a part of their intolerance? Worry circled in him.

Chapter 4

Madeline joined Joshua in the front room. "This is an odd time for you to visit. You're usually very busy during this time of day."

"Elijah came over early this morning, and he advised me not to wait to tell my parents about Catherine and Ruthie." He grinned. "He knows how I like to avoid unpleasant conversations. I told them earlier today."

"What did they say, and please don't hold back anything."

"Catherine leaving her child for you to care for substantiates why I should stay away from your family, according to them. They don't understand why I would agree to accept your niece after what Catherine did to Nathaniel."

"I'd be lying if I said I was surprised." She hurt each time they treated her like a leper. Madeline knew what she had to do, as much as it would bring anguish to her very soul.

His parents loved Joshua and, in their own way, they thought they were protecting him. She didn't agree with them, but she understood their love for Joshua. She'd pray for God's intervention, but until then, she had to do what was best.

Madeline took a deep breath. "Joshua, I'm convinced God wouldn't want us to marry and go against your parents' wishes. A black cloud would hang over us, and I'd blame myself for tearing your family apart. You've been close with them. Your marriage should bring your family joy, not heartache."

Joshua put a finger to her lips. "Are you saying you won't ever marry me?"

"Your family may never accept Ruthie and me into their fold. I can't ask you to wait indefinitely."

"This is my family's problem, not ours. Madeline, I love you and Ruthie, and I'm not giving up so easily. I have faith God will fix this." He turned and left.

She couldn't bear the agony on his face. Her body ached, and she was certain she'd never love anyone again like she loved Joshua, the perfect man for her. She hoped he wouldn't pursue her. She'd weaken, and she mustn't, for she truly believed she was doing the right thing. She slumped in a chair, buried her head in her hands, wept, and prayed.

Daed entered the room and sat beside her. "Madeline, I talked to Joshua at his wagon. The man is shattered. He loves you. Work this out together. Please."

She raised her head and dabbed her wet cheeks with her sleeve. "Our families should be uniting and not causing strife over our impending marriage. I don't believe God would bless our union if it means destroying Joshua's relationship with his family."

Her daed sighed. "I'm sorry our family problems have caused so much heartache for you and Joshua. I understand why the Stutzmans are skeptical of you, since they haven't gotten to know you. Your schweschder, unwed and abandoning her boppli, disgusts me. I can imagine how they must feel. I'm sure they're afraid that you do not have a true commitment to Joshua after what Catherine has done to their family. They just need to know you to realize they can trust you. I understand waiting to marry, but don't give up. Have faith, like Joshua, this will all work out."

"It will take a miracle to change the Stutzmans' minds. God tells us to honor our daed and mamm. If I marry Joshua against his family's wishes, and our marriage hurts his relationship with them, the blame will rest on me."

"You're hurt and frustrated. I'm here for you. Together, we'll get through this. Pray and ask God for His guidance and His purpose for our families." He kissed her forehead.

She had never been more heartsick in her life than now. Joshua, the love of her life, had been the only man she'd wanted to spend her life with besides her daed. The thought his parents would forever oppose their marriage, and the idea he might propose to another woman someday, sent a ripple of pain through her heart. She couldn't concentrate on what might be. She had to think of what she believed God would have her do for now. She loved the Bible story of how Ruth left her family and country and clung to her husband's mamm, Naomi. Ruth and Naomi had such a close relationship. She wished she could have the same relationship with Mrs. Stutzman someday, but she and Joshua's mamm having this same bond didn't seem possible.

Madeline dressed Ruthie and grinned at the clear sky through the window Friday morning. "Ruthie, we're going to Addie's today. She'll be delighted to meet you." She said good-bye to her daed and carried Ruthie to the buggy in a crate lined with blankets. She roped and secured it to the bench and headed to Addie's haus.

Addie opened the door and gasped. "What a wilkom surprise to have you here. Elijah told me about Catherine and Ruthie. I want you to tell me what happened."

"Oh, Addie, I was shocked." Madeline shared her story.

Addie reached for Ruthie. "She's beautiful. I don't understand how Catherine could leave this beloved little girl." Her lips quivered. "I wish I could talk you into marrying Joshua, but I understand. I love Elijah's family. I'm not sure I could've married him if they had objected to our future together. I wouldn't have wanted him to have to choose me over them. We socialize and help each other a lot. I'd be crushed his parents weren't a part of our lives. I don't think God would honor such a marriage. I will pray God convinces them they are wrong about you."

"I knew you'd understand. Danki." Madeline covered her friend's hand.

"Let's take your mind off this." She pointed to a stack of folded clothes. "Beth Troyer brought over dresses and kapps her dochder has outgrown. She said if I don't have a girl, to pass them onto a mamm who does. You can have them for Ruthie. I'm sure some of our other friends who have had girls will offer me more clothes if I have a dochder. There are also glass bottles."

"Danki, I'll need them. Catherine left dresses with her, but not Amish ones. I'll put them to good use." She hugged her friend. "I'll need you to lean on. Danki." She stayed an hour, bid her friend farewell, and drove home.

Daed approached her. "I'll take the horse and put him in the barn. You tend to Ruthie." He untied the crate and lifted it out of the buggy.

He kissed Ruthie's forehead. "Did you enjoy your visit at Addie's?"

"Jah, she lifted my mood and offered her unwavering support. I'm fortunate to have her loyal friendship. I trust her to keep anything I tell in her confidence, and she accepts me unconditionally."

"True friends like Addie aren't easy to find."

Madeline gazed into his wise eyes. Addie had provided additional strength and encouragement throughout her troublesome relationship with Joshua's parents after Catherine's abrupt departure. She enjoyed sharing a laugh, a secret, or everyday conversation with her best friend. They gave each other advice and hugs. She'd look forward to the birth of Addie's boppli, and she hoped Ruthie and Addie's little one would become close friends.

Madeline wished Catherine had loved her as a schweschder and best friend the way Addie did. She resented Catherine for turning her world upside down. How could she and Catherine have been raised by the same parents? The woman lived a sinful life Madeline could never understand. Catherine didn't get her curious and rebellious nature from their parents. She really didn't know Catherine at all. She rolled her shoulders. God had a plan for her and Ruthie. She had to quit dwelling on her schweschder and get on with life for Ruthie and her daed's sake.

Ruthie had fallen asleep on the ride home and soiled her dress. Madeline changed Ruthie into a fresh nappy and selected one of the dresses Addie had given her.

The boppli woke for a few moments and fell asleep again in her arms as she entered the front room. Madeline jerked to a stop and gasped. *Joshua.* Her heart skipped a beat. She met his gaze and held it.

Daed pushed the door open and headed outside. "I'll be in the barn." He glanced over his shoulder.

Joshua rushed to her. "Madeline, I can't lose you. Please reconsider." He caressed Ruthie's cheek. "She needs a daed, and it should be me."

She gave him an endearing glance. "Let me put her in her cradle. She just fell back to sleep." She left the room and lowered Ruthie into the cradle. Shaking, she returned to Joshua. She had missed his face and his hand in hers. But she saw no hope for a future for them. Not as long as it meant going against his parents' wishes.

She faced him. "Joshua, your parents don't want you to suffer the ridicule we are going to get from others about Catherine and Ruthie. They don't trust me not to run away like Catherine and take the kinner we have together. I understand their position, even if I don't like it. Can you honestly say you think God would honor our marriage under the present circumstances?"

He reached for her hands. "I believe God will turn this around for us. Is there anything I can say to sway your decision?"

"Please understand I will always love you, but I feel I'm right." She stared at their hands. "I wish it weren't so."

Daed walked in and put a hand on Joshua's shoulder. "I'm sorry you and Madeline are suffering. Please know I am confident you and my dochder will be together someday."

"Danki. I should go finish working on the haus. I just had to stop by."

"Good day, son." Her daed left them alone.

Joshua opened the door for her.

Madeline stepped outside and accompanied him to his buggy.

"I love you, Madeline." He pulled her to him and kissed her on the lips.

Warmth filled her. She couldn't breathe. A thrill ignited her very soul. She gazed into his soulful eyes. "Joshua, I'll remember this kiss for the rest of my life." She let the tears fall onto her cheeks.

Ruthie cried.

"I must go to her. I'm sorry, Joshua." She ran inside.

Joshua watched her go in the haus. He touched his mouth. The softness of her lips lingered. He shouldn't have given her such a passionate kiss, but he had to hold her. It might be his last chance to kiss her. Why couldn't he make her understand they weren't responsible for his parents' implacable judgments?

Dressed for church and in his warm coat, Joshua breathed in the cool, crisp air on this first Sunday in April as he headed to the Yosts' haus for the service. A little over a week had passed since Madeline had told him she wouldn't marry him because of his parents' disapproval. Church service wasn't held last week, and he would've spent the day with her family, but he'd thought it best not to pressure her for now. The Yosts were hosting church today. She would probably be in attendance. He was anxious to talk to her.

He tied his horse to the big oak tree. He went inside and sat next to Elijah.

Elijah patted his knee. "Addie and I have been praying for you and Madeline. How are you holding up?"

"Not good. I'm at a loss as to what to say or do to convince her we should marry. As her daed said, it's in God's hands."

"The Lehmans arrived early, and the bishop met Ruthie. He stated Ruthie is fortunate to have Madeline and her daed to take her in. He'll announce her addition to their family after the service."

"Madeline must be pleased to have the bishop's blessing. His support will encourage the congregation to accept Ruthie with joyful hearts. I've overheard gossip in our community from friends and neighbors expressing their distaste for Catherine abandoning her boppli. They don't approve of Madeline raising Ruthie and think she should've insisted Catherine live up to her responsibility. My parents are feeling justified in their position on this matter. I'm disheartened she won't allow me to share this difficult time with her."

Joshua scanned the women's side for Madeline and caught her gaze. They exchanged an endearing glance. He listened to the bishop's message about trusting God's ways and supporting and loving our friends going through difficult times. He gazed at his parents and yearned for the bishop's words to penetrate their hearts.

Bishop Kauffman opened his Bible and read First Corinthians, Chapter Thirteen, Verses Four through Eight: " 'Love is patient, love is kind. It does not envy, it does not boast, it is not proud. It does not dishonor others, it is not self-seeking, it is not easily angered, it keeps no record of wrongs. Love does not delight in evil but rejoices with the truth. It always protects, always trusts, always hopes, always perseveres. Love never fails. But where there are prophecies, they will cease; where there are tongues, they will be stilled; where there is knowledge, it will pass away.' "

Joshua believed God wanted him and Madeline to build a future together. After the after-service meal, he watched friends approach his love and Ruthie with smiles and kind words, and a few shy away from them.

He waited until the crowd thinned to go to her. "Would you step aside with me for a moment?"

"Of course." She strolled with him to the bench under a cluster of maple trees. "How are you? I'm sure you've heard the talk about Catherine and our family."

"Jah, I'm worried about you." He smiled. "The bishop and community gave Ruthie a warm wilkom. His message was pertinent to our situation. Maybe his words will change some hearts."

Madeline bounced Ruthie on her hip. "Jah, I'm grateful he is doing his best to support our family."

"I wish you'd agree to marry me and show everyone we are united going through this." His family had left early, probably to avoid approaching Madeline and Ruthie. She was most likely aware of it, and their quick exit was no surprise. Their actions today provided a perfect sample of what life would be like if he married her. Did they have any idea what sadness filled him over their rejection of her?

She smiled. "It's easier for you right now. Your parents and you can enjoy time together without our wedding hanging over their heads. I don't want to tear you apart from them."

"*Easier* isn't a word I'd use. I'm devastated without you. I'm working on the haus as if you and Ruthie will be joining me someday soon, because I have faith it will happen." He brushed her fingers with his and walked away.

For four weeks, he worked alongside Mr. Lehman, doing chores on the man's property, and Mr. Lehman lent a hand helping him with repairs on his haus and barn. Madeline's daed invited him to supper for his labor, and they, along with the woman he loved, would laugh and talk about life and Ruthie. He didn't bring up his parents or marriage. He just made his presence a reminder he wasn't going away from her. She'd tell him about her day, and he played with Ruthie. He loved every minute of it and held out hope she'd change her mind.

He woke and lay in bed in his parents' haus Tuesday morning. He'd worked until nightfall with his daed and bruder, then stayed late talking with them. His mamm insisted he stay overnight. He'd gone home before supper to tend to the animals and returned. He sensed she missed him living there, and he was exhausted and didn't mind. He glanced at the calendar. *May fifth.* Where had the time gone? Ruthie was changing right before his eyes. She'd gotten more active and was rolling over. He'd built her a bigger bed. She'd outgrown the cradle. He'd bitten his tongue a few times this past month to keep from discussing his future with Madeline during his visits with his family. He'd laughed and gone down memory lane with them like old times.

A hard rap sounded. He shrugged into his pants and shirt and went to the door. His family beat him there.

Elijah waved him out. "Joshua, go fetch the doctor. I'm on my way to get Madeline. Addie and the boppli are in trouble. Her parents are out of town visiting a sick aunt."

Mrs. Stutzman ran to her son. "I'll go with you."

Joshua didn't want Madeline and his mamm in the same room. "Please stay home. The doctor will need room to work."

"What's the holdup? We need to be on our way." She climbed into the spring wagon.

There was no time to argue. He didn't answer her and stared straight ahead. The horses were at a full gallop on the trip to town and he only slowed when they approached the doctor's office. He hurried to tie the reins around the hitching post, then ran to the office. *Good.* There were no patients waiting, and the gray-haired man was just reading a medical journal. The doctor would be more apt to leave right away to help Addie.

"Dr. Livingston, please kumme with me to Elijah Mast's haus. His fraa, Addie, is with child. It's too soon for her to give birth. She and the boppli need your assistance. I'll take you in my wagon."

The doctor grabbed his bag. "I have my buggy parked out front. I was planning to call on a few patients in a short while. You caught me in time. I'll follow you and make my visits after I tend to Mrs. Mast." He untied his horse and followed Joshua.

Joshua and his mamm didn't speak until they pulled up in front of Elijah and Addie's haus. "Mamm, go in, but please be kind to Madeline."

His mamm bristled and, without a word, went inside.

He jumped down, held his reins, and accepted those of the portly doctor. "I'll take care of the horses."

Dr. Livingston nodded and darted after Mrs. Stutzman.

Joshua tied the animals under the shade of the oak trees and fetched enough water for them. He hurried through the door and found Elijah holding his head in his hands at the kitchen table, and he wrapped his arm around the worried man's broad shoulders. "I'm here for whatever you need, friend. How's Addie?"

Tears streamed down Elijah's face. "I rushed back here and heated pots of water for when the doctor arrived. They haven't asked for more. Maybe that's a good sign. I didn't know what else to do. I've never felt more helpless. I'm afraid, Joshua. We've waited a long time for this boppli."

Joshua dragged a chair right next to Elijah and sat. "Pray with me. Dear Heavenly Father, please give Elijah the strength to handle whatever is to kumme. We pray You bring Addie and her boppli through this day with good health and the boppli to stay in her womb and be born at the right time. We don't know why these things happen, but we trust You and we love You. Amen."

Elijah raised his watery eyes. "Danki, friend." He sighed. "Your mamm and Madeline are with Dr. Livingston. I was surprised you brought your mamm here with you."

"She was adamant. I had no choice."

"Times like these can bring people closer. The more help for Addie and our unborn child the better." He scratched his chin. "I wonder what's happening." He got up and paced.

Mrs. Stutzman joined them. "Dr. Livingston said he thinks Addie and the child will be all right. The bleeding wasn't severe and has stopped. He found a heartbeat for the boppli." She sneezed. "Excuse me. Madeline's helping her change into a gown. She managed to put clean sheets on the bed by having her roll from one side to the other. Give them a few minutes." She washed her hands, then touched the pan on the cook-stove. "I sat and turned my head most of the time. The sight of blood makes me woozy. Would you like coffee?"

"Please, Mamm. Give us each a cup."

She served them. "Elijah, is there anything I can do for you?"

He shook his head. "Danki for being here."

Joshua pulled her aside. "Is Madeline doing all right?"

"Dr. Livingston is treating her as his nurse, and she's good at it." She caressed her son's cheek and reentered Addie's bedroom and shut the door behind her.

Joshua was baffled. Should he get his hopes up? She'd complimented Madeline, something he never expected to happen.

Dr. Livingston entered the kitchen, wiping his hands.

Elijah stood ramrod straight. "How are my fraa and boppli?"

"Addie's weak and tired, but she'll be fine with rest. The baby has a strong heartbeat. She's farther along than I'd thought. She should stay in bed until we're sure the bleeding has stopped. At least a week. I suspect the pain may've been caused by something she ate this morning that didn't agree with her, and it scared her into thinking it was from her being with child. I've had many patients bleed now and then while carrying their little ones and the births went without a hitch."

"Danki, Dr. Livingston. What good news." Elijah's eyes pooled with tears.

"Don't hesitate to call me again. Hopefully, you won't need to until your baby is ready for you to hold him or her." Dr. Livingston placed a reassuring hand on Elijah's arm, picked up his bag, bid them farewell, and departed.

"Kumme with me, Joshua. Let's go see Addie." He went to his fraa.

Joshua followed Elijah. His mamm sat quietly in the corner of the room. His eyes fell on Madeline seated in a chair next to Addie.

Addie managed a half-smile. Her face flushed and eyelids drooped, fighting sleep. She held out her hand to Elijah. "Our boppli is strong. I was scared. I love our little one so much already, I can't imagine not having him or her in our lives." A sob escaped her throat.

Madeline got up and offered Elijah the chair. She moved to the doorframe, next to Joshua.

He stood with his arm touching hers. "What a day this has been for them. I'm relieved Addie and the boppli are all right. They gave us quite a fright. It won't be easy for Elijah having Addie on bed rest."

She didn't move her arm away from his. "Addie's parents return from visiting her aunt, and her in-laws return late tomorrow from their short trip. They'll gladly pitch in."

Mrs. Stutzman stood and walked over to Addie and Elijah. "I'm glad you're better. Take it easy. If you need anything, please let me know." She paused in front of Madeline and Joshua. "I'll be in the wagon."

Addie and Elijah thanked Joshua's mamm and bid her farewell.

Joshua stood next to Madeline and his body rippled with delight. He'd give anything to have a lifetime with this woman. She brought out the best in him and made him feel like he could conquer the world. Why couldn't his parents give him the one thing he wanted most? To put their feelings aside and let him and Madeline marry?

Surely, his mamm had observed Madeline's compassion toward her friend. She jumped in to take instructions from Dr. Livingston to aid Addie. What more did his mamm need to understand the differences between Catherine and Madeline? Their traits were as far apart as the east was from the west. Had his mamm learned anything about Madeline today?

He caressed her cheek and pulled her aside. "This has been a long day for you. I'm proud of you for assisting the doctor. You amaze me. May I fetch you a glass of water? Or there's coffee on the stove in the kitchen."

"I'm fine. I enjoy helping the doctor. To me, medical care is interesting. It's rewarding to take part in helping the injured or sick. I admire nurses." She sighed. "Of course, loving Addie, I'm pleased to support and comfort her. I'm glad the doctor agreed to let me help. It breaks my heart they're afraid for their boppli. They have such a close relationship, I know they'll be strong together and get through this worrisome time before the birth."

Joshua struggled not to spill out his emotions. Addie and Elijah clung to their faith in God and to each other during this frightening time. He and Madeline had a similar bond. If they married, he suspected they would behave the same way when faced with hardship. He would discuss his woes, joys, problems, and plans with her, take her advice into consideration, and hold her when she needed his strength. If only she would listen to him. Today wasn't the day to push her. She was worn out.

"I'll visit Elijah tomorrow to help him with chores."

"Between the both of us, we'll keep a close watch on them. Tomorrow, Addie's parents will be back from visiting an aunt and her in-laws will also return from their trip. They'll be home late tomorrow."

"Both sets of parents have a close friendship aside from being thrilled their kinner married each other." She gave him a forlorn look.

He knew she wished for the same type of family closeness. He opened his mouth to speak but remained silent.

Mamm came back inside. "I've been waiting in the wagon long enough. I'm getting chilled. Addie and Elijah are doing well. We should let them rest." She gave Madeline a curt nod.

"Jah, we should go. I left Daed with Ruthie. Hopefully, she took a long nap today." Madeline went and hugged her friend. "I love you, Addie."

"Madeline, danki for being here with me, for changing my sheets and gown, and for your support and encouragement. I'm blessed to call you a friend."

"I'm glad I could help. Take it easy." Madeline squeezed Addie's hand.

Joshua said, "Elijah, if you need anything, kumme and get me."

"Danki, I will."

Joshua, Madeline, and his mamm bid the relieved couple good-bye and left. "I'll take you home first."

He helped Madeline into the back of the wagon. Mamm sat on the bench seat next to him. They stayed silent on the way to Madeline's. He wished he could read their minds. The women didn't seem tense with each other but rather depleted of energy. Maybe this experience had given his mamm pause about her opinion of Madeline.

He walked her to the door. "I'll pick you and Ruthie up at eight tomorrow if you would like to stay with Addie while I'm there."

"I'll be ready. Danki."

He wanted to kiss those sweet lips, but he wouldn't dare with his mamm looking on. He wouldn't dishonor Madeline this way.

"It's going to take time, but I believe my family will accept you. Just be patient."

"You've always been my rock. You still are. I wish I could agree with you." She glanced at his mamm and distress played on her lovely features.

"Don't worry. I've got enough faith for the both of us." He grinned and left.

On the way home, he didn't hurry the horse. "Mamm, did you talk to Madeline while you worked with her today?"

"Madeline was busy following the doctor's instructions as if she were a trained nurse. I'm squeamish around blood, so I turned my head. I'm embarrassed to admit I wasn't much help. Madeline doesn't flinch."

Was she praising Madeline or was it a mere observance? "Has your opinion of her improved?"

"No, son, it has not. She's still a Lehman and Catherine's schweschder. She can't be trusted. Find a woman from a respectable family."

He tightened his grip on the reins and clenched his teeth. She wasn't giving Madeline a chance. He wouldn't get anywhere arguing with her, and what would he accomplish? He was silent. Minutes later, he said, "I'm going to Elijah and Addie's tomorrow. I'll be gone most of the morning."

"Very good, son. Maybe I should go sit with Addie. Her parents may be late returning home."

"I'm picking Madeline up and taking her there at Elijah's request."

She sighed. "Very well. I'll cook a dish of food for you to take to the Masts' tomorrow. I left you a surprise on the counter. I baked your favorite apple pie."

He kissed her cheek. "Danki, Mamm." *What? No argument about him taking Madeline to Addie's and not her?* He shrugged. Something had weakened Mamm's resolve about Madeline, even if she didn't admit it. Any other time, she'd scold him for spending time with her or, at the least, suggest Madeline drive herself to Addie's.

Chapter 5

Madeline carried Ruthie outside. She loved planting season. It brought their friends and neighbors together to help each other. Soon, the weather would get warmer, and she'd enjoy her favorite season of summer. She waved to Joshua, who was halting his horse. "I'm ready."

He stepped out of the buggy and offered his hand to help her in. "My two favorite girls look lovely as always."

She shouldn't be spending time with him, but she couldn't help herself. It was wrong to encourage him after canceling their wedding, but she didn't have the strength to turn him away. Nor did she want to. "I hope Addie is doing well."

"You and Ruthie will cheer her. You both cheer me."

They chatted about the weather and their friends on the way.

Joshua halted the horse, jumped down, and helped Madeline and Ruthie out of the wagon. "Enjoy your time with Addie. I'll take care of the horse and find Elijah."

Madeline nodded, went to the door, and opened it. "Addie, is it all right to kumme in?"

"Of course. Join me in the kitchen."

"What are you doing up? You should be resting." She gestured. "Kumme with me. You're going back to bed."

Addie padded in front of her to the bedroom. "I feel good. No more pain or bleeding. I'm being careful. But I'll obey." She took off her shoes and crawled into bed. She smiled at Ruthie. "She's the best boppli with her cheerful disposition."

Madeline dragged a chair close to Addie's bedside. "She only cries if she needs food or sleep."

Madeline heard a woman's voice outside. She peeked out the window. Mrs. Stutzman was kumming toward the haus. "Mrs. Stutzman is here."

Addie chuckled. "The woman is a mystery. She's so against you and Joshua. She's outspoken and won't budge when she thinks she's right. Kind and generous with her time to help the widows and ill in our community, she has a good heart. She puzzles me."

Madeline sighed. "She's shielding her sons. Her allegiance is to Nathaniel and Joshua. It's just that she's holding the wrong person responsible for hurting her son. I pray someday she'll realize I'm not the enemy."

"I understand your reasoning in not marrying Joshua. Elijah and I are grateful our parents get along well. They enjoy each other's company and love kumming here together to work or chat with us. A dark shadow would be cast over us if either side didn't approve of our marriage. Their refusal to accept us would've been a nightmare for our future. I pray God will intervene on your and Joshua's behalf and solve this problem for you."

"I accept His will for both our lives, and I believe it's not for us to marry. He'll provide. I'm heartbroken and don't understand why this is happening, but I trust He'll give me guidance."

A rap on the door interrupted their conversation.

Madeline raised her eyebrows. "I'll let her in." She left Addie's bedroom and went to the front room. "Good morning." She opened the door. "Addie's in the bedroom."

"I brought venison and boiled potatoes for their supper. I can find my way to Addie's room. I'll put the dish in the kitchen."

Madeline watched her go to the kitchen then to Addie's bedroom. She wrinkled her nose and listened. *Nathaniel?* She recognized his voice. He was upset and talking to the men on the porch. She threw open the door. "What's the matter?"

Nathaniel stepped inside.

Joshua and Elijah joined Madeline and Nathaniel. Joshua removed his hat and scratched his head. "Nathaniel, I was puzzled your wagon is here. Is everything all right?"

Before Nathaniel could answer his bruder, Mrs. Stutzman approached them. "Nathaniel, I recognized your voice. What brings you here?"

Nathaniel pressed his hat to his chest. "Daed fell and bumped his head. He said he got dizzy and stumbled on the porch steps. His arm is swollen. I'm going to get the doctor."

"Can he speak?" Madeline pressed a hand to her heart.

"Jah, he is fine to talk, but he's in pain. I asked Mr. Yoder, our neighbor, to stay with him. He's pressing a towel to Daed's head to slow the bleeding. I'm scared, Joshua. What made him dizzy?"

"I have no idea. Maybe the doctor will provide answers after he's examined him." Joshua patted his bruder's arm.

Mrs. Stutzman pushed open the door. "We must go." She headed to her wagon.

Nathaniel nodded and ran off the porch to his buck wagon.

"I'm kumming too. I want to help. I'll fetch Ruthie." Madeline darted to the bedroom before Joshua could respond. "Addie, Nathaniel came and told us Mr. Stutzman is injured. I'm going to go with them to check on him. Will you be all right?"

Addie wrung her hands. "I insist you go. I'll be fine. Please let me know how he is when you have a chance."

Madeline left the bedroom.

Elijah shrugged. "I'm sorry I'm not much help, Joshua. I need to stay with Addie."

"Of course. We can take care of Daed."

Madeline grabbed her shawl, wrapped Ruthie in a blanket, and headed for the door. She followed Joshua to the wagon and got in. She wanted to show the Stutzmans she cared about them. "I need to let Daed know where I am. He'll be worried."

Joshua flicked the reins and urged the horses to a gallop. "We pass your haus on the way. We'll stop there and tell him." He came alongside his mamm's wagon. "We're stopping at the Lehmans' to let Madeline's daed know what has happened."

His mamm nodded with pinched lips.

Madeline nodded to her.

Joshua passed her and hurried to the Lehmans'.

Mr. Lehman ran to them. "You all have worried faces. What's wrong?"

Madeline explained.

"I'll follow you over there. Maybe I can be of assistance."

Joshua nodded. "Danki. We'll see you there." He guided the horses to his family's haus.

Nathaniel and Dr. Livingston arrived at the haus at the same time as Joshua and the others.

Mr. Lehman halted his horse and jumped down to secure his animal to the hitching post. "I'll take care of the horses."

Madeline passed Ruthie to Nathaniel. "Would you watch her while I help Dr. Livingston?"

Joshua's bruder stared at her, then took Ruthie. "I'll do anything so you can help Daed."

Madeline followed Mrs. Stutzman inside the haus.

Mrs. Stutzman directed Dr. Livingston to the bedroom.

Mr. Yoder stood and addressed Mr. Stutzman. "You've been able to hold the cloth to your head instead of me for the past few minutes. I'll get out of the way. If you need anything, send Nathaniel to fetch me."

Mrs. Stutzman said, "Danki you for help. Please give Mrs. Yoder my best."

"Will do." Mr. Yoder tipped his hat and left.

Madeline stepped closer to the doctor. "Do you need me to assist?"

He removed the cloth Joshua's daed had pressed to his head and took a quick look. "Yes. Mr. Stutzman has taken quite a blow to his head. We'll need to clean and stitch the wound. Do you mind getting my scissors, a needle, and thread out of my medical bag?"

"Not at all." Madeline dug inside the doctor's bag and found what he needed.

Mrs. Stutzman sat next to her husband. "Where did you fall?"

The man winced. "I walked outside and got a little dizzy as I lifted my foot to take the first step. I fell on top of my arm and hit my head on a sharp stick as I hit the hard ground. I'm not usually so clumsy."

Joshua stood next to his mamm. "Is there anything I can do?"

"I'm in good hands, son. You, your mamm, and Nathaniel cringe at the sight of blood. You comfort them and let Madeline and Dr. Livingston take care of me."

Joshua smiled. "Danki for kumming to help Daed, Madeline. We really appreciate it." He escorted Mamm out of the room and joined Nathaniel in the kitchen.

"I'll go fetch some clean water." Madeline left to wash her hands, returned with a clean pot of water, and handed the doctor each item as he requested it. She swallowed the fear of rejection from the Stutzmans in her throat. They'd not objected to her being there. Nathaniel was still holding Ruthie, and his smile hinted he was enjoying her. A miracle for sure. For the first time in a while, hope sprang within her.

Dr. Livingston cleaned, stitched, and bandaged the patient's head wound. He washed his hands and examined his patient's arm. "I don't know what caused this. You are alert and oriented. Can you walk a few steps for me?"

Mr. Stutzman stood and walked gingerly, holding his injured arm. "The dizziness is gone. I don't have trouble walking."

"I don't know what caused your dizziness. You seem fine now. If you experience any lightheaded-ness again, come and see me. Please sit and hold out your arm." The doctor pressed on his arm in several places.

"Ouch!" Mr. Stutzman looked at the ceiling.

"I'm sorry. I had to check the bones. Please turn your arm from side to side."

Mr. Stutzman grimaced and moved his arm slowly as the doctor had instructed him.

"I don't believe you've broken any bones. You'll need to baby it for a few weeks. No lifting anything heavy."

"I don't believe I could even if I wanted to." Mr. Stutzman held his arm tenderly with the other one.

"I suggest you take a strip of cloth and make a sling to hold your injured arm to your chest until it starts to feel better."

"I have property to maintain. What will I do?"

"You've got friends and family to help you. You'll need to let them take over until you recover."

Madeline knelt beside him. "My daed will be happy to lend a hand. He and Joshua work well together. Please let him kumme and work with your sons." She smiled. "I would be happy to make you a sling. I'll ask Mrs. Stutzman for some material."

Dr. Livingston stood. "You'll need to clean your wound and put a fresh bandage on daily for the next two weeks." He put a roll of gauze on the small table next to him.

"My sons and fraa turn away at the sight of blood. With my injured arm, I'll need someone to change the bandage for me." He looked at Dr. Livingston. "Would you mind?"

"I'm sorry. I'm too busy, but maybe Madeline would have the time. She's been a big help to me with Addie, and now you."

Madeline met Mr. Stutzman's gaze. "I'd be happy to."

Joshua's daed gazed at her with sad eyes. "I'd be grateful to you."

Tears stained her cheeks. "I'll kumme at ten in the morning right after I do chores. Does the time work for you?"

"Jah, I appreciate it."

Madeline felt as if she'd grown wings and could

fly. Joshua's parents had given her a glimmer of hope. Would Nathaniel? And what about Ruthie? Would they wilkom her into their home too? She'd bring her to their home each day, and she hoped they'd kumme to love her. At least they were headed in the right direction. She and Dr. Livingston went to the kitchen. Her daed, Mrs. Stutzman, Joshua, and Nathaniel, holding Ruthie, were sitting around the table. They said good-bye and thanked Dr. Livingston for his help.

Joshua said, "Let's all go join Daed in the bedroom." He led the way, and they followed. He pulled up chairs for Madeline, Mr. Lehman, Nathaniel, and himself.

Mr. Stutzman moved over in the bed to make room for his fraa. "Gather around the bed. I wouldn't mind some company." He smiled at Madeline. "Madeline will be kumming by the haus to change my bandages each day."

Joshua's mamm sat on the bed next to her husband. "Sounds good to me. I and your sons can't stand the sight of wounds and stitches. I'm thankful you're willing to do so, Madeline."

Madeline pressed a hand to her heart. She wanted to shout with joy. "I'm pleased to do it."

Joshua motioned toward the front door. "Madeline, kumme outside with me for a few minutes." He waited until they were on the porch. "My heart is beating fast. You're generous to kumme and help Daed. I'm shocked Daed and

Mamm agreed to Dr. Livingston's suggestion it be you."

"I am grateful." Madeline smiled wide. "Daed and your family were laughing when I entered the room, and your bruder is still cradling Ruthie in his arms."

"He hasn't stopped smiling since he began holding her."

"I'm happy your family is finally giving me a chance. Oh, Joshua, this is a miracle!" She gave him a reluctant glance. "I don't want to go, but I must get Ruthie home and feed her."

He kissed her cheek. "I'll open the door for you." They went back to the bedroom. Madeline reached for Ruthie. "Danki, Nathaniel, for watching over Ruthie."

"My pleasure." He gave her a sheepish grin. "She loves it when I tickle her. She kept your daed, Mamm, and me in stitches with her giggles."

Madeline's heart warmed. Nathaniel had succumbed to Ruthie's sweet nature. She'd won him over, something she'd never imagined would happen. Joshua had never given up faith God would work a miracle in their lives. Shame on her. She shouldn't have either. She'd do her best to show them her motives with their son were honorable. "We'd best be on our way."

Mrs. Stutzman smiled. "Danki, both for your time and kindness."

Madeline and her daed waved and went to their wagon.

On the way home, Daed patted her knee. "Your smile is making my day. I'm surprised you'll be the one to change Mr. Lehman's bandages. I see God's hand in this."

"Me too." She took a deep breath and grinned.

Joshua grinned at Nathaniel. "Ruthie was comfortable with you."

Chin to his chest, Nathaniel shrugged. "She's a beauty." He walked away before Joshua could say anything else.

His bruder had softened. What would he find with his parents? He went inside and returned to his parents' bedroom. "Daed, how are you doing?"

"My head hurts, but I'm more worried about my arm."

Mrs. Stutzman held her husband's hand. "Let your sons take care of our property. I can help them too. You need to do as the doctor told you and let your arm heal."

Joshua pulled a chair close to his mamm's. "I'm glad you both accepted Madeline's offer to change your bandages."

His parents exchanged a guilty glance.

His daed said, "It's very kind of her."

His mamm nodded.

Not the reaction he was hoping for, but maybe it was premature at this point. He'd be patient.

"I'll be by tomorrow to check on you. If you need me, please don't hesitate to send Nathaniel. I love you both." He headed out the door.

On his way home, he said, "Dear Heavenly Father, please heal Daed. Danki for Your hand in my family's willingness to allow Madeline into their home in the kumming days, and please open their eyes to realize what a kind and loving woman I long to have as my fraa. How I want to marry her. Please, Heavenly Father, bring our families together. Amen." He would marry Madeline Lehman one day. He was sure of it. He just had to convince her to have faith and believe it too.

Chapter 6

The next morning, Madeline arrived with Ruthie.

"Daed, danki for dropping me off."

"I'm going to stay. I'm sure Nathaniel can use some help."

"You'll be behind on your chores. I'm sure Nathaniel and Joshua can handle things for Mr. Stutzman."

"Joshua has helped me without hesitation on many occasions. I can handle our place, and I'd like to help."

"You're a wonderful man, Daed. I don't know what I'd do without you."

"You go on in. I'll take care of the horse."

Nathaniel met her at the door. "I'm glad you brought Ruthie. Do you mind if I take her?" He reached for the boppli.

Stunned, Madeline passed her to him. "Danki." She chuckled. "Ruthie is certainly comfortable with you."

The boppli cooed and patted Nathaniel's cheek.

"We've become fast friends." Joshua's bruder beamed.

Joshua waved her over. "If you need anything, please fetch me. I'm going to be mending the corral fence. My family seems receptive to you kumming today. I think you'll find them very appreciative you're willing to help Daed." He beamed. "Are you comfortable going inside alone?"

"Jah, I'd prefer it. I want them to know I'm sincere and it will give me time alone with your parents to allow them to say anything they would like without you there. Yesterday, things went well. I'm hoping today will be even better."

Joshua squeezed her hand. "I'm proud of you."

Her daed approached them. "Joshua, can I help you with anything?"

"I could use a second pair of hands."

Mr. Lehman rubbed his hands. "Lead the way. I'm ready."

She grinned at the men and walked to Nathaniel, who was sitting on the porch rocking Ruthie.

Should she talk to him about Catherine and ask him to find it in his heart not to hold her schweschder's wrongdoing against her? *No.* She wouldn't ruin their happy moment. "Daed is going to stay and help with chores."

He nodded. "Your daed is quite a gentleman. I'll go out and join him and Joshua." He handed Ruthie to her.

Madeline carried Ruthie inside.

Mrs. Stutzman greeted her. "I've got coffee. Would you like a cup?"

"Please." She followed her to the kitchen. "How is the patient?"

Mrs. Stutzman sat across from her at the kitchen table and passed her a cup. "He slept like a bear in hibernation last night, and he devoured his oatmeal this morning. I helped him get dressed."

Madeline stifled her surprise. Mrs. Stutzman spoke to her as if they were friends. The tight-lipped woman she had encountered on numerous occasions at church had disappeared. Her relaxed and amiable manner was unusual. She couldn't believe her eyes.

"I'm glad he's on the mend. I'm sure it will take time, but I'm happy to assist in any way I can."

Joshua's mamm snapped her fingers. "I forgot to find fabric for you to rip and make a sling." She jumped up and retrieved it from a chair in the corner. "I left my basket of assorted fabric on the chair last night to remind me. Little good that did." She held up the material. "What do you think? Will this do?" She held up a long piece of material.

She stared in wonder. Mrs. Stutzman had asked for her opinion. Her heart skipped. She'd take all the kindness the woman was willing to bestow. "The size is perfect."

"Would you make the sling and fit it to him? He might take it better from you than me. He says I'm bossy sometimes."

Madeline swallowed her chuckle. Bossy. Jah, she'd have to agree with Mr. Stutzman. "I'd be glad to." She glanced at Mrs. Stutzman. "Do you mind holding Ruthie while I tend to Mr. Stutzman?"

"I'd love to. I dragged out the cradle Joshua and Nathaniel both slept in for her."

Ruthie cooed.

"She's in a cheerful mood."

"She really likes Nathaniel."

Mrs. Stutzman rocked Ruthie in her arms. "He couldn't stop gushing about her after you left. She's a pretty little boppli."

Madeline swallowed the surprise in her throat. The reception she and Ruthie had received this morning was a far cry from what they were used to from Mrs. Stutzman. She was elated. "I have to warn you, she'll charm you with her cheerful disposition."

Mrs. Stutzman chuckled. "I'll take my chances." She snatched up a small box and tossed it to

Madeline. "The doctor left some gauze for changing his dressing."

Madeline caught it and headed to the bedroom.

Mr. Stutzman smiled. "Good morning, Madeline. How's Ruthie today?"

"She's entertaining your fraa. She's a happy boppli." Madeline washed her hands in the bowl of clean water on a corner table and dried them, then she changed Joshua's daed's dressing. "Your wound doesn't ooze or seep, I'm pleased to report." She washed her hands again, then reached for the fabric. She tore it, satisfied with the length, and tied it in a knot, making a large loop. "May I place this over your head to your neck? You can place your arm in it, and we'll adjust it as necessary."

Joshua's daed held still while she put the loop in place. He grunted and put his arm in the sling. "It's a perfect fit. Danki."

"I hope it helps." Mrs. Stutzman came in with Ruthie and rubbed his arm.

The couple shared a good relationship. Their love was evident in the way they held each other's gazes, Mrs. Stutzman's touch to her husband's arm, and her words of encouragement. Madeline longed for her and Joshua to share this type of love into their old age one day. She stayed and chatted with them for a couple of hours.

Daed, Joshua, and Nathaniel joined them.

Mr. Stutzman turned to her daed. "Mr. Lehman,

danki for taking time out of your day to do chores here for us."

"Joshua has done a great deal of work for me. It's the least I can do."

"Your dochder's been a big help to me already. I don't want to impose on you too."

Mr. Lehman grinned. "Madeline enjoys helping people. You're not imposing on either of us. We're happy to do whatever you need."

She and Daed chatted with the Stutzmans for about an hour. Ruthie entertained them with her giggles and undecipherable chatter. Mrs. Stutzman and Nathaniel took turns holding her. Madeline had relaxed, laughed, and had a good time with the Stutzmans. Her daed and the Stutzmans laughed and enjoyed each other's company. She and her daed bid them good-bye, and they drove home with Ruthie in her arms, fast asleep. Mrs. Stutzman had sent home her honey sugar cookies. Madeline broke off a piece of one and put it in her mouth. They really could use a tad more sugar, but Madeline would never mention it.

They arrived home. Alone after supper, she knelt by her bed. "Dear Heavenly Father, please forgive me for being of little faith that You would work a miracle in the Stutzmans' hearts to ever wilkom me in their home. I'm ashamed. I prayed but did not trust You as Joshua has done. Danki for the happiness You've brought to our families today. Please allow our families' relationships to grow. You know how much I love Joshua. Please give us the acceptance we need from the Stutzmans to marry if it is Your will. I love You. Amen."

Two weeks later, Dr. Livingston arrived to remove Mr. Stutzman's stitches on the beautiful spring day of May twenty-first. "You don't need a dressing any longer. Your wound has healed enough to go without it." He examined his arm. "You're moving your arm better. The swelling has decreased. How's the pain?"

"Much better."

Joshua and Nathaniel stood by Madeline and her daed and their mamm, both beaming.

Glad Mr. Stutzman's arm strength and wound were healing nicely, she would miss her time with them. They'd had pleasant conversations and gotten better acquainted. She hadn't broached her canceled wedding with Joshua and neither had they. She didn't want to spoil their newfound camaraderie. She and Joshua had relaxed around them, and confidence had grown in both their hearts for the possibility his family was warming to her.

Her daed had talked to Mr. Stutzman each day after helping Joshua and Nathaniel. The two men had laughed and formed a tentative bond. Madeline's heart burst with pride for her daed. He had, no doubt, done it for her and Joshua, and he'd benefited from Mr. Stutzman's friendship at the same time.

Dr. Livingston bid them farewell and departed.

Madeline and her daed stood.

"We should go, but I've enjoyed our visits. Please kumme and visit us."

Mr. Stutzman gestured. "Please, sit down. While we have both our families in attendance, we all have something to say, and I'll say it for us. We apologize for our rude behavior toward you, Madeline and Ruthie. We don't condone Catherine's betrayal of Nathaniel or her abandonment of Ruthie. We were wrong to allow her bad decisions to cloud our opinion of your family. It would be our humble desire for you, Madeline, to reconsider becoming our dochder-in-law."

Joshua had tears in his eyes. "Mamm, Daed, danki." He crossed the room to Madeline. "Please say you'll marry me."

She faced him. "Jah! Jah! Jah!"

He picked her up and swung her around. "I'm so happy!" He lowered her until her feet touched the floor, then went to his daed. "I'm grateful to all of you. You won't be sorry. As you've learned, Madeline is nothing like Catherine. She's everything you'd want in a dochder-in-law."

Nathaniel had been quiet. He stood and hugged Joshua. "I've been selfish, and I've wallowed in my hurt from Catherine long enough. It would be an honor and a privilege to have Madeline and Ruthie join our family. I couldn't ask for a better schweschder-in-law and sweet little Ruthie as a niece."

Mrs. Stutzman circled her arm around Madeline's waist, holding Ruthie with her other arm. "I have grown to love you during these weeks. I've learned a lesson in humility watching you. In spite of our rude behavior, you stepped in and showed us you are a compassionate and selfless woman."

Nathaniel lifted Ruthie from his mamm. "I'll be your uncle soon."

Madeline's knees buckled with her emotion. She wrapped her arms around Mrs. Stutzman, and they held each other and wept tears of joy. They parted, and she said, "I'm not satisfied with my stitching in dresses. Addie usually helps me, but I don't want to add to her workload. Would you mind sewing my new dress for the wedding?"

"I'd be delighted." She gestured them out of the room. "Off with the two of you. You've got much to plan. We'll entertain Ruthie, or rather, she'll entertain us." She chuckled.

Mrs. Stutzman watched Ruthie and smiled at the boppli's expressions. What a blessing to behold.

Joshua shook Mr. Lehman's hand. "Finally, I'll be your son soon."

"I'm honored." Mr. Lehman's eyes watered with emotion.

Joshua motioned to the door. "Madeline, let's go for a walk."

They stepped outside, and he took her behind the workshop and planted a big kiss on her lips.

She tingled with joy.

He pulled her close. "I love you, Madeline, and I can't wait to call you Mrs. Stutzman."

She hugged him. "I asked God to forgive me for not believing He would work a miracle in our lives. I'd given up. You didn't. You taught me a valuable lesson, Joshua. I'm blessed you're such a faithful and loyal man of God."

"Let's pray." He bowed his head, and she did too. "Dear Heavenly Father, danki for answering our prayers and changing the hearts of my family to wilkom Madeline and Ruthie into their lives. For their joy at anticipating our upcoming marriage. We ask You to heal my daed and give him patience to get through this difficult time. Amen."

Madeline raised her head. "You had faith when mine wavered. Another example of the type of family leader you'll be for Ruthie and me. I admire your fortitude, Joshua."

"You put others first. You didn't have to get in my buggy and pitch in to help Daed, but you didn't hesitate. I love you for your giving nature and abundant capacity to pour out your empathy for others." He kissed her again.

Her heart beat fast with happiness. "You give

me too much credit. You have more patience than I do." She tilted her head. "What date should we choose for the wedding?"

He tapped his finger to his lip in thought. "June eighteenth. I'll stop by the bishop's haus and ask if his calendar is still open for the date."

"We'll only have a little over a month to prepare and notify our friends. Do we have enough time?"

"I'm not waiting another moment to marry you. We'll enlist the help of our friends and, together, we'll enjoy a wonderful day."

He kissed her hard on the lips. "I love you and Ruthie, Madeline. Our haus will be in good shape by the time you move in. I just need to buy more furniture."

She and Joshua went inside.

Mrs. Stutzman used a strip of long cloth and took Madeline's measurements, penciling them on a sheet of paper. "I'll start on your dress tonight. I'll send Joshua to get the fabric from you."

"Danki." Madeline and her daed waved good-bye and took Ruthie home. Joshua followed them to obtain the material.

Her daed flicked the reins. "I'm thrilled for you and Joshua, Madeline. God answered all our prayers and performed a miracle. This is one of the happiest days of my life, and I didn't think I would ever speak those words again after your mamm passed."

"You are, in part, responsible for making this

day happen. You cultivated a relationship with the Stutzmans on behalf of Joshua and me. You're a wise man, Daed, and a patient one. You could've had a hardened heart toward Joshua's family, but instead, you turned the other cheek and forged ahead. Danki doesn't begin to express my gratitude."

"We've been through rough patches in our lives, but together, we've persevered with God's help. He taught me a lesson through all of this to trust Him in the midst of a storm. To love others the way He loves us. At times, I had a notion to turn away from the Stutzmans, but God convinced my heart to do the opposite. And He was right. Everything has turned out wonderfully."

"I couldn't get out of my own way, thinking I had determined God's will without giving Him a chance to work a miracle in the Stutzmans' attitude toward me. Joshua never wavered in his faithfulness to God about us."

"He's a wise young man. I'm blessed he's marrying my dochder. When's the wedding? Have you picked a date?"

"June eighteenth, the same one we picked the first time. Joshua will ask the bishop today or tomorrow."

Her daed chuckled. "He won't waste any time. He's been champing at the bit to marry you for a long time now. I don't blame him."

She laughed. "I'm anxious to wed him too."

She kissed Ruthie's cheek. "She's not budged since we left the Stutzmans'. She's worn out."

"I am too." Her daed grinned.

Joshua halted his horse, held the reins, and jumped down. "Sweetheart, I'll not stay. We've had a big day. A day we'll never forget. I love you, Madeline Lehman. I wish we could have our ceremony tomorrow."

Madeline beamed. "God has been very good to us." She glanced at the front door. "I'll fetch the fabric and be right out." She went inside, put Ruthie in her cradle, and brought the unfinished dress to Joshua. "I never thought I'd be sending it with you for your mamm to stitch."

"Mamm is stubborn, but she's got a big heart. Now she's accepted you, she'll pour out her love on you and Ruthie. A true answer to prayer." He kissed her hard on the lips, then got in his wagon and tipped his hat.

Chapter 7

Joshua whistled on his way to Bishop Kauffman's haus. The birds were chirping in the trees, and squirrels ran through the yard. He enjoyed them, and his day couldn't have been better. Madeline would be Mrs. Stutzman soon. Bishop Kauffman's long lane and vast corn and hay fields painted a perfect picture with his white dwelling in the center. His barn could use a fresh coat of paint.

He halted the horse and tied him to the hitching post. He rapped on the door and the bishop answered, peering over his spectacles.

"Joshua, what brings you here today?" He motioned him in. "Have a seat. How's your daed?"

"His head and arm are healing better each day."

"Glad to hear it."

"Bishop Kauffman, you scheduled a wedding for me to marry Madeline Lehman on June eighteenth, and we'd like to keep the date. I wasn't sure if you'd heard murmurings our wedding was cancelled for a period of time."

Bishop Kauffman settled back in his big oak chair. "I had been told by several of our mutual friends your wedding had been called off. I've held the date until I was told by you officially."

Joshua held his hat in his lap. "She worried my parents would never accept her, and she insisted we have their blessing. I had faith God would intervene and soften their hearts, and He did. I had hoped to get married on the tenth, but we need the additional time to prepare."

"Some of our congregation are appalled about Catherine's return and abandonment of Ruthie, and they are judging the Lehmans for Catherine's bad behavior. My messages have been on love, forgiveness, and unjust judgment of others to show them their attitudes need to change. I suggest we choose a date in July or August, giving the gossip time to settle down. I'm hoping my messages penetrate their hearts and they'll be glad to attend your wedding, rather than object to it."

He shook his head. "With respect, bishop, I want to marry Madeline as soon as possible and present a united front to the community. Our friends and family who love us will be there, and they're all we need."

The bishop stayed silent a moment. "You're right, and I admire your determination. I'll be honored to marry you and Madeline on June eighteenth. Now Ruthie will have a daed. I'm proud of both of you for giving her a home."

"We'll tell our friends and family to spread our good news, but will you announce it in the next service?"

"Absolutely!"

Joshua shook the bishop's hand and went home. He'd count the days until his marriage to Madeline.

Joshua rose early and milked the cows, fed the chickens, and worked in the garden. No time to make furniture before Madeline and Ruthie moved in. He washed his hands and face and went to town. The post office, general store, and Lancaster Inn had a whirlwind of activity with men and women entering and exiting. The clang of the blacksmith's hammer annoyed him most days, but today, it was delightful.

He stopped in front of Lapp's Furniture and secured his horse. He strolled inside.

Mrs. Yost and Mrs. Weaver admired the maple table and chairs in the corner. The elderly women were two of the worst gossips in their community. He avoided them and scanned the floor for a hope chest and clothespress.

Mrs. Yost had a loud voice. "Madeline Lehman is a sweet woman, but what man in his right mind would marry her? Now she's stuck with her sinful schweschder's boppli to raise alone. She should never have agreed to give the child a home."

Mrs. Weaver nodded. "If Catherine would run off and live a sinful life, what makes you think Madeline won't do the same one day? Their mamm died young, and their daed must not have disciplined them."

"Joshua Stutzman almost married Madeline, until his family forbade him to. Why on earth he'd consider such a thing is beyond me."

"I ran into Mrs. Stutzman earlier this morning." Mrs. Weaver gave her friend a sly smile. "She said the wedding is on, and she's in full support of her son marrying Madeline and accepting the child as his own."

"Has she gone mad?" Mrs. Yost raised her hands

in disgust. "What in the world changed her mind?"

"She went on and on about how Madeline came over every day to change Mr. Stutzman's bandage, and they are convinced she's nothing like Catherine. She adores Catherine's child."

"I would never let my son marry her if I were in the same predicament."

"Me either." She picked up a breadbox. "I'll buy this one. Are you ready to go?"

Joshua approached them. "Mrs. Yost and Mrs. Weaver, I'm glad I ran into you. Madeline Lehman and I would like to invite you to our wedding on June eighteenth. We don't have much time to alert our friends, so if you'll spread the news, we'd appreciate it."

He watched their eyes widen and mouths open. He stifled his chuckle. They'd been caught exchanging nasty gossip. Their red-faced expressions were priceless. His mamm talking to one of the two biggest gossips in their community about her support of Madeline and Ruthie becoming a part of their family surprised and elated him.

He didn't wait for them to speak but tipped his hat. "Good day, ladies."

They turned and bustled to Mrs. Lapp at the checkout counter.

Joshua grinned and approached Mr. Lapp. "Good afternoon. I'll purchase this cedar hope chest and clothespress."

"I heard your conversation with two of my customers. I understand congratulations are in order."

"Jah, I hope you and your family will attend our wedding on June eighteenth. The bishop will announce the time after the next Sunday service."

"We'll be delighted to attend. You know how we Amish find any reason to have a good meal. All kidding aside, I'm happy for you, Joshua. Ruthie needs a daed, and she's blessed you've chosen to take on the responsibility."

"Danki."

"Pay Mrs. Lapp for the chest, and the clothespress will be our wedding gift to you and Madeline."

Joshua stepped back. "You're very generous to offer such a gift. Danki."

He slapped Joshua on the back. "I've known you since you were little. It's my pleasure."

Joshua waited until Mrs. Yost and Mrs. Weaver left, then stepped to the counter and paid for his purchase. "Mrs. Lapp, you're invited to my wedding."

"So I've heard. You should reconsider, son. I wouldn't want you to suffer if this Lehman woman leaves you like her schweschder did to your bruder. There are plenty of eligible young Amish women in our community who would better suit you. An unwed woman with a boppli isn't a proper woman for you to marry."

He sucked in a breath. Not a statement he

expected from Mrs. Lapp. The family had always treated him with kindness and respect. Mr. Lapp didn't share his fraa's opinion. "I trust her, Mrs. Lapp. Once you get to know her, you'll understand why." He raised an eyebrow. "I'm surprised you'd say such a thing. Your husband is in support of my choice."

Mrs. Lapp waved a dismissive hand. "My husband is a good man, but he doesn't understand these things. Marry a respectable woman and have kinner of your own."

"On June eighteenth, I will be taking your advice. I hope you'll join us for the happy occasion."

Mr. Lapp joined him. "She'll be there, along with the rest of my family." He grinned. "I had my two boys load your furniture into your wagon."

"What a kind gesture. I appreciate it." Joshua smiled and, with a lilt in his step, walked out the door. His wedding announcement would spread faster than he thought. The two biggest gossips in town would make sure of it.

He passed his family's haus and noticed Madeline's buggy. "What is she doing here?" Turning around, he drove down the lane, secured his horse, and went inside. The love of his life stood in a new dark blue Amish dress with her arms extended, and his mamm knelt on the floor pinning the hem. What a beautiful picture. "How are my two favorite ladies doing?"

Ruthie cried in Nathaniel's arms. "Ruthie is hurt. I'm sure you meant to say *three* favorite ladies." He laughed.

"You're correct." He kissed Ruthie's fingers. "You are precious, little one."

Madeline smiled. "Your mamm has been so good to stitch my new wedding dress."

"It's very pretty." Joshua grinned and met her beautiful dark blue eyes. Her radiant glow validated that she matched his happiness about their impending marriage.

Mamm removed a straight pin from her lips. "Have you been to the bishop's yet?"

"The date is still June eighteenth, and the community should be aware of our wedding by the end of the day, maybe even noon."

Madeline wrinkled her nose. "I don't understand. What do you mean?"

"I ran into Mrs. Yost and Mrs. Weaver at Lapp's Furniture. I invited them to our wedding."

Madeline, Mamm, and Nathaniel burst into laughter.

Nathaniel bounced Ruthie on his lap. "Smart man. Did they mention if they'd be attending?"

Mamm gave them a sly grin. "Those two whine and complain, but they never miss a social gathering for the food or the gossip. They'll be there."

"I don't want to wish my life away, but I'm anxious for the day to arrive."

"I'm with you, my love." Joshua winked.

Mamm stood and pinned the sleeves. "Did you tell the Lapps your news?"

Joshua frowned. "Mrs. Lapp surprised me. She isn't in favor our union, but Mr. Lapp is very supportive and looks forward to our wedding." Joshua glanced out the window. "Speaking of the Lapps, Eva, their dochder, is here."

Nathaniel stood. "I'll be right back."

Mamm, Joshua, and Madeline raised their eyebrows.

"Let's peek out the window." Madeline hurried to watch them and stood next to Mamm. "They have big smiles, and Nathaniel is showing her Ruthie. He appears very interested in Eva Lapp."

"She's pretty." Joshua grinned.

"You think so?" Madeline smiled and nudged him.

"Not as pretty as you, of course." He chuckled.

She gave him a mischievous expression. "That's better." She smiled. "All kidding aside, Eva is attractive, with her petite frame and sweet heart–shaped face. She has a pleasant voice and quiet way about her."

"Eva is a sweet young woman." Joshua's mamm glanced at him. "Madeline's going to keep you on your toes, Joshua."

"I'm looking forward to it. I doubt there will ever be a dull moment with her or Ruthie."

Nathaniel entered, with Ruthie in his arms and

Eva by his side. She carried two pies. "You all know Eva Lapp. She's brought me a custard pie, and our family a sugar cream pie."

Eva looked at Nathaniel with her big blue eyes, as if he were the only one in the room.

Joshua understood. He felt the same about Madeline. "Did Nathaniel invite you to our wedding?"

"Jah, I'm thrilled for you. Is there anything I can do?"

"You can bake more pies and bring them." Mamm handed her a cloth ball with pins. "Right this minute, you can hold this for me. It will keep me from having to bend so much."

Eva accepted the pin cushion. "I'll bake an assortment of pies and bring them." She beheld Madeline. "Your dress is lovely on you."

"Danki. I can't sew very well. I'm grateful to Mrs. Stutzman for her help. Her stitches are perfect."

"Mamm and I get by, but it's not one of our best talents."

"I'll be happy to teach you, Eva." Mamm lifted a pin from the small ball.

Ruthie clapped her hands and cooed.

"We're done, Madeline."

Madeline left to change and returned. She reached for Ruthie. "Nathaniel, why don't you and Eva play horseshoes or take a walk? It's a beautiful day with the flowers blooming."

He handed Ruthie to her. "Danki."

Joshua watched his bruder and Madeline exchange a conspiratorial look and knew they had formed the bond he had yearned for all along. Eva Lapp would be a good choice for a fraa for Nathaniel. She had beauty and grace. Eva and Madeline had these traits in common. He stole a glance at his bruder before the couple left. "Nathaniel is happier than he's been in a while."

Madeline nodded. "First, Ruthie lit up his world, and now Eva has kumme along to make it even brighter. I hope they form a solid friendship, leading to something serious. She's a kind and sweet woman."

Mamm grinned from ear to ear. "I'm going to have to buy more chairs for my table soon. My family is expanding!"

Weeks had passed, and Madeline was sure they'd invited all their friends. The food been planned, and women had committed to bringing their favorite dishes. Addie's stomach was getting bigger, and her friend glowed, waiting for the day her boppli would make his or her appearance. Everything was going well. She touched the cape of her wedding dress. Mrs. Stutzman was an excellent seamstress. She hugged herself. *Joshua's bride.* She liked the sound of those words.

Knock. Knock.

She ran out to the front room.

Daed opened the door. "Mrs. Stutzman, what a pleasure." He motioned her in.

Madeline wondered why she was here. The woman had cooked and baked for days to prepare for this day. She'd finished Madeline's dress and managed to run her household all at the same time. Madeline wondered when she slept. She'd been a good source of advice for raising Ruthie, and she'd given her tips on how to clean, sew, cook, and bake. They'd become fast friends. Mrs. Stutzman held a package wrapped in white fabric tied with twine.

"I'm surprised you had time to stop by." She hugged her.

Mrs. Stutzman passed her the present. "Here's a surprise for you. I finished it last night."

Madeline untied the twine and peeled back the fabric. Her eyes teared. She put the fabric on the chair and held up the small, dark blue dress. "Oh, Mrs. Stutzman, the dress is beautiful and just like mine. Ruthie will look adorable in it. Danki." She had grown to love Joshua's mamm, and it was a pleasant surprise to discover her soft side.

His mamm had been kind and thoughtful and went out of her way to show she truly cared to know her.

"You can call me Mamm, but I understand if you'd rather call me Isabelle."

"Danki, Mamm. It's perfect."

Swiping a tear from her eye, Isabelle Stutzman hugged her. "I won't keep you. Go get ready for your special day." She kissed Madeline's cheek. "I'm happy to call you my dochder." She turned and went to her buggy.

Daed patted Madeline's back. "Your life has taken a turn for the better. One blessing after another has kumme your way these past weeks. I'm so happy for you and Ruthie to gain a new family."

"You're gaining a new family too."

"I don't mind a bit."

Madeline changed Ruthie into her new dress and then gazed at hers hanging on the door. The dress had perfect stitching and fit her better than any of her other dresses. Mrs. Stutzman and she had bonded when she made adjustments to the dress. She'd treasure the garment because it symbolized Mrs. Stutzman showing her acceptance, friendship, and kindness. She shrugged into it and carried Ruthie to the buggy.

Daed flicked the reins. "I love you, sweetheart. Enjoy this day and make your wedding a beautiful memory. I'll never forget the day I married your mamm. The snow fell and the wind was bone-chilling cold, but we were warm on the inside and didn't notice. She glowed, and I stood tall and proud to call her my fraa. I don't regret a minute of our years together."

"You set a good example of what to look for in a husband. Joshua reminds me of you."

"Danki, dochder. I appreciate the compliment."

Madeline scanned the buggies parked under the trees, the horses, and friends and neighbors outside. Mr. Stutzman had insisted they have the ceremony at their home. It was larger than the haus she and Daed resided in, and he had more ground to host the after-ceremony meal.

Benches in rows lined the front lawn, and tables were off to the side. The air was a bit cool.

Addie waddled to greet the Lehmans, pressing her hands to her stomach. "Mr. Lehman, how are you?"

"I'm doing fine. You look radiant."

Addie blushed. "Danki." She turned to Madeline and kissed Ruthie's hand. "Are you nervous? You look lovely."

"I'm anxious and ready. Joshua and I have been through a lot to get to this day. I can't wait to call him my husband." She hugged her friend. "How are you feeling? Did you and Elijah agree on names for the boppli yet?"

"Really good, and jah, we finally did agree on Miriam for a girl, and Eli for a boy."

"I like the names you chose."

Daed reached for Ruthie. "The horse is secure. Let me carry Ruthie."

Madeline handed her to him.

Ruthie patted his face with her tiny hands.

Her daed gave her a half grin. "Madeline, I'm going to miss having you and Ruthie with me every day. The haus will be too quiet."

Madeline smiled broadly. She did worry about leaving her daed alone. She'd visit and have him for meals often. Joshua would include him in projects and keep him company too.

"We'll be close by. You are wilkom at our haus anytime, and we will visit you often."

He kissed her cheek. "I'm counting on it."

She spotted Joshua with Elijah. "Addie, let's join the men."

Joshua grinned. "You look radiant."

"Danki." Her face heated and she gave him a shy grin. "You look handsome, yourself."

The bishop approached them. "Joshua and Madeline, may I speak to you for a moment?"

They walked away from their friends and joined him.

"Joshua and Madeline, is there any reason why you shouldn't be married today?"

They shook their heads.

"There will be no divorce, so if you have any doubts, now is the time to profess them."

They shook their heads again.

"We're ready, Bishop Kauffman. Right, Madeline?"

"Without a doubt, Joshua."

Bishop Kauffman extended his arm. "I'm happy to marry you today. Follow me, and we'll begin." He waved the crowd to the benches. "Everyone, please take a seat." The women sat on one side, and the men on the other.

Madeline sang the hymns from the Ausbund with joy and thanksgiving. She listened to the bishop's message on wrongful judgment and forgiveness. Attendees included men and women she hadn't expected to show today. Maybe the Stutzmans' change of heart had set a good example and the bishop's previous messages had been effective. She was grateful for whatever the reason. Lancaster was her home, and she planned to live her life with her family until she left this earth.

She'd asked God to give her the grace to forgive Catherine, and He'd granted her request. She had no ill will toward her schweschder any longer. The bishop's messages had worked a miracle in her heart, and she was blessed to have Ruthie in her life. She prayed for Catherine's safety and return to Amish life each day, but she knew Catherine had to want these things for herself.

Bishop Kauffman closed his Bible. "Madeline and Joshua, please join me at the front. Addie and Elijah, you may stand with them."

Addie clasped Madeline's hand. "I'm thrilled for you, dear friend."

Madeline squeezed her friend's fingers. "I treasure you, Addie. You've been there for me through all the bad and good days."

"That's what good friends are for, and we'll share a lifetime of them."

Madeline met Joshua's gaze as she stood facing him. The man who would protect her, love her, and guide her. She swelled with pride and love for him. Not many men would raise another man's boppli, but he hadn't hesitated. She loved him even more for it.

The bishop asked, "Madeline, do you take this man to be your loving husband?

Madeline spoke loud and clear. "Jah, I do."

"Joshua, do you take this woman to be your loving fraa?"

"I most certainly do!"

Madeline grinned as she listened to the chuckles from the congregation.

The bishop performed the rest of the ceremony and then pronounced them married. He directed them in more hymns and then dismissed them for the after-wedding meal.

Joshua stole her away from the crowd and led her behind his daed's workshop. "I promise to love and take the best care of you for the rest of my life, Mrs. Stutzman. How I treasure the sound of your new name." He wrapped his arms around her and planted the biggest kiss on her soft lips. "I love you."

Madeline's heart melted. She wanted to start their life this minute and leave, but she would settle for sharing their wedding day with friends and family. "I love you too, husband."

He held her hand, and they strolled toward the tables filled with dishes of food. Joshua pointed. "Nathaniel and Eva are sitting on a blanket talking. He appears smitten. His mood has improved since they've been socializing."

Mrs. Weaver and Mrs. Yost approached them. Mrs. Yost held out a gift. "The Stutzmans and your daed have spoken with us about you. The bishop has also had a word with us. We owe you both an apology. I'm afraid we misjudged you, Madeline. Please forgive us."

Madeline said, "I accept your apologies. I'm glad you came today. Danki."

Joshua grinned. "Ladies, danki for your honesty."

"We're happy for you both." They walked away to join the women at the food table.

Joshua chuckled. "I consider their apology another miracle." He kissed her hand. "Madeline Stutzman, this has been the perfect day. I don't want to forget a minute of it." He grinned. "I have some gifts for you at our new haus. I'll show them to you later."

"Joshua, tell me. I can't wait!"

"You know I can't keep a secret. I bought you a hope chest and the Lapps gave us a clothes-press."

She hugged his neck. "I can't wait to fill them. Danki so much. They're perfect gifts."

Madeline had never been happier. God had

performed several miracles to make her day extra special. He'd given her a wonderful husband and Ruthie had a loving daed. Their families had blessed their union, along with those who had once been against them. She whispered a prayer of thanks, and Joshua bowed his head. She raised her chin and opened her eyes. "Joshua Stutzman, please take your bride to the wedding table before the food is all gone!"

A Summer
Wedding in
Paradise

Amy Lillard

To Lynne,
So wish you were here to see this!

Chapter 1

Reba Schmucker quickened her footsteps and wished for the umpteenth time that Amish were allowed to wear watches. It would surely help her keep track of the time, and right now she needed that more than ever.

So she had gotten a little bit of a late start this morning. That was normal for her, but from there things just kept happening to put her behind. Her brother Abner had decided to play a joke on her last night and hid the dress she had picked out for today. Which wouldn't have been the end of the world if he hadn't hidden it outside and if it hadn't rained all night. And it surely would have been a sight better if she wasn't behind on her laundry and had a suitable dress clean to wear to work today. But he did hide her dress outside. It had rained all night long, and she was behind on her laundry.

The scent of Spring Meadow wafted from her clothes. She gave a small sneeze. The best she was able to do was spot clean the dress she wore a couple of days ago, spray it down with the fabric deodorizer her *mamm* bought for the furniture, and pray no one noticed.

She looked up at the sun as if it would somehow tell her the time and just how late she was.

Surely she had made up a couple of minutes with her brisk pace. She kept to the side of the road, ducked her head, and kept on walking. No time to lollygag.

Days like today, she wished she had kept her scooter. Or at the very least borrowed Abner's for the trip to school. It wouldn't do for the teacher to be late. It simply wouldn't do.

From behind her she heard the sound of a carriage approaching, and it was coming up quick.

"Whoa," the driver called. "Whoa!"

The clatter of horse hooves grew louder along with the whir of the wheels on the pavement.

Something was wrong. She turned to look at the approaching buggy. Something was very wrong. The hairs on her arms stood up as the driver barreled down on her. "Get out of the way!" the driver yelled.

She couldn't see his face, just the foaming sweat and wild spittle from the raging horse. She didn't have time to think, only to react, as the horse quickly drew closer. A car was coming in the opposite direction. The carriage was coming up behind her. She only had one choice.

Reba dove into the ditch, water surging up her nose as she went headfirst into a large rain puddle.

She sputtered, coughed, and pushed herself to her hands and knees as water dripped into her eyes. The mud sucked at her limbs as she managed to get to her feet. Cold rainwater soaked her dress and her apron. It rained in rivulets down her belly and between her shoulder blades.

She held her hands out and looked down at herself, hardly believing what she saw. She was soaked to the bone. The carriage was long gone. The car honked its horn, but didn't slow. Unbelievable.

She was left to scramble to the top of the shallow ravine where she had fallen and back up to the side of the road.

Water dripped from the hem of her dress and wiggled its way into her shoes. The front of her apron was covered in mud and grass. A trickle of water ran down her scalp and under the collar of her dress. She shivered. She didn't need to see the rest of herself to know that her prayer *kapp* was ruined, her hair caked with mud, and her face a mess as well.

She looked to the heavens. "Really?" she asked no one in particular. God. Then she shook her head in apology. God wasn't at fault. It was the buggy driver. He was the one. If he hadn't lost control of his horse, then none of this would have ever happened. And he didn't even bother to stop. Didn't bother to swing back and see if she was all right. Some people had no manners and that was all there was to it.

With a deep breath to restore what she could of her good nature, Reba took a step toward school.

"Ow!" Her ankle nearly gave way underneath

her. She winced and tried again. She must have bruised it when she fell. She tentatively shifted her weight to that foot once again, but couldn't bear it all. But she had no other way to get to the schoolhouse. She lurched forward, her ankle throbbing and the water in her shoes squishing with each halting step.

What a day this was turning out to be. And all because her brother was getting married. Well, her next-to-oldest brother, Jess.

If any of her brothers deserved a bit of happiness or a second chance at love, it was Jess. His wife had been killed over a year ago in a tragic buggy accident. Linda Grace left Jess with three little girls to raise and a dairy farm to run. But last Christmas Jess had met their new teacher, Bernice Yoder. Reba wouldn't say it was love at first sight. Jess and Bernice got off to a rocky start, since the new teacher had come out to the house to talk with Jess about the way his children were arriving at school. But somehow they had managed to work through their differences and fall in love. Which was the exact reason Reba was on her way to the schoolhouse today. Bernice had wanted a little time off to get ready for the wedding; there were just so many plans to make, even in an off-season wedding. Next year they would have a new teacher, but in the meantime, Reba had offered to fill in.

She was beginning to regret that decision.

No. She shifted her thoughts. It wasn't Jess's fault. Nor Bernice's. The buggy driver. He was to blame. Some people had no sense of community or responsibility. They only thought of themselves and didn't give one care for the people around them. It was a shame, really. That wasn't the Amish way.

Limp. Squish. Limp. Squish. The white-painted, one-room schoolhouse finally came into view. She had never realized how far it was to the school until she had to walk it on a swollen ankle while water dripped into her eyes and mud dried on her face. She stopped in the drive of the school, her feet stuck in the fine gravel. What was she going to do? She couldn't teach school like this.

She looked down at herself one more time just to make sure. *Jah*, her deep rose dress was dripping wet, her black apron smeared with mud. She could only imagine that her prayer *kapp*, hair, and face had suffered a similar fate.

"*Aenti* Reba?" Her eldest niece, Constance, was standing in front of her. The sweet, blond-haired child must have stopped playing with her friends to come meet Reba in the drive. "Are you okay?"

Reba pulled herself out of her thoughts and focused on Constance. "*Jah*. Of course." She forced a bright smile. No sense in letting some big oaf with no manners ruin her entire day.

"What happened?"

Reba waved one hand in the air as if it were no

big thing. "I slipped on the way here, and I fell in a big puddle."

Constance's big gray eyes grew even wider. "Oh."

"But school's about to start, and I can't wear these clothes to teach. Would you mind running to *Mammi*'s house and getting me a clean dress?"

"No. Of course not."

And what clean dress is she supposed to get for you?

Constance moved as if to walk past, but Reba stopped her. "You'll have to have *Mammi* help you," Reba said. "The laundry is sort of backed up these days."

"I will." Constance gave an understanding nod. "Do you want me to get you a clean prayer *kapp* as well?"

So it was as she thought. Her covering was also a mess. It was scandalous.

"Yes, please."

Constance smiled and started toward the road.

Bless that girl. Reba watched her headed down the road. With any luck she would be back in half an hour. Until then, Reba would get everyone to reading at their desks and she could assess the situation. Maybe get the mud from her face. She pressed the back of one hand against her forehead. It came back streaked with mud. And her hair. Don't forget her hair.

"Reba! Reba! Reba!" Johnny Lapp ran toward her, his silky blond hair flying out behind him.

But that was Johnny. The boy never walked anywhere, preferring to get where he was going as quickly as possible. Maybe she should have sent him after her clean clothes.

She pushed that thought away. "*Jah?*"

"The repairman is here. He told me to tell you so."

The repair—"Oh, right." She had momentarily forgotten that the board had wanted to do a couple of repairs around the schoolhouse before it let out for summer. One of which was the leaky roof.

What a fabulous day!

She was wet, covered in mud, and had to deal with a stranger in the classroom as she tried to teach the scholars. As if only two weeks left of school wasn't enough to set their minds to daydreaming.

"*Danki*, Johnny. Can you ring the bell and help me get everyone in their seats?"

He nodded his head, then frowned. "What happened to you?" he asked, just then taking in her untidy appearance.

"I had a little accident on the walk here. That's why I need your help. Are you up for the job?"

"*Jah.*" He gave an important nod, then sped off to ring the bell.

Reba limped up the drive, waving to the children who called out a greeting. Somehow she managed to smile with every step even though her ankle was radiating pain to the ends of her toes and clear up to her knee.

A new-looking buggy was parked to one side, the dark horse tethered to the hitching post. There was something familiar about the beast. Or maybe that was the pain making her thinking cloudy.

Clang! Clang! Clang! Johnny rang the bell. The kids stopped what they were doing and started up the schoolhouse steps. At the sound, a stranger stepped around the side of the carriage. A handsome stranger.

Reba stumbled, and even though her ankle was paining her so badly she was nauseous, she managed to catch herself before she fell face-first at the stranger's feet. Did she mention he was handsome?

"Whoa, there." He snagged her arm before she could stumble again. Something about his voice . . .

"*Danki*," she murmured. She did her best not to stare into his midnight blue eyes. Of course the day a handsome stranger walked into her life, she looked like she had been used as a rug at the annual mud sale.

"Did you have some trouble on the way in?" He took his hand from her arm, and his warmth went with it.

She shivered as another bead of water slid down her spine. Her prayer *kapp* strings dripped down the back of her dress.

"*Jah.* I've had quite a morning."

He smiled, flashing deep dimples in both cheeks. Was it bad of her that she noticed he was clean shaven and unmarried? "So you don't normally come to work soaking wet?"

"No." She laughed. "This big oaf ran me off the road this morning." She shook her head. "His horse got away from him. He didn't even stop."

His smile froze on his face. "That was you?"

She blinked, everything falling into place. "It was you!" She took a step back, only barely aware that the scholars were watching them through the windows. She moved closer to him so she wouldn't have to raise her voice. Though she wanted to. Oh, how she wanted to. "You are the most inconsiderate man I have ever met in my life."

"I apologize."

"That hardly helps me now, does it? I'm covered with mud and gunk and grass."

He gave her a sheepish grin, almost shy. Like that was going to change her mind about what happened. "My horse got away from me. That beast is unreliable, for sure."

"Like others I know."

He stopped and blinked as if he wasn't sure of her meaning, then it became clear. "I think you're being a little harsh. I said I was sorry."

"That doesn't exactly get me clean and dry, now does it?"

Abel blinked once again, trying to figure out what her problem was. Well, he knew what her problem was, but it wasn't like he meant to knock her into a puddle. "What can I do to make it up to you?" It was all he could offer. He couldn't go back in time and do this morning all over again.

Or even back to yesterday when he bought the crazy horse.

When something looks too good to be true, it probably is.

His *dawdi*'s words came back to him. Why hadn't he remembered them yesterday when he'd bought the horse for barely half of its estimated worth? Why hadn't he spent a little time training him instead of immediately taking him out on the road? With all the trouble the horse had caused him, the previous owner should have paid *him* to take the beast.

She looked down at herself. Water dripped from every edge of her clothing. Mud streaked her face, her prayer *kapp*, and her legs. "There's nothing you can do."

"How about lunch?" There had to be something. She looked beyond pitiable, soggy, mud-caked, angry.

"I already have a lu—" She stopped, looked around her, then sighed. "I had a lunch . . . earlier. . . ."

Which meant her lunch cooler had become his

victim as well. Most probably it was floating next to where she had fallen in the gigantic roadside puddle.

"Lunch," he said again. "It's the least I can do."

She opened her mouth, to tell him no, he was certain, but he cut her off before she could speak.

"What are you going to eat?"

"I'll find something."

Just then one of the little girls hurried up carrying a plastic grocery sack. "*Mammi* said this was the only dress she could find for you." She handed the bag to the teacher.

"*Danki*, Constance."

The blond-haired girl smiled and skipped up the steps into the schoolhouse.

"I'll just let you . . ." He flicked a hand toward the bag.

She just nodded, turned on one heel, and limped her way into the schoolhouse, trailing water behind her the entire way.

The dress must have belonged to her *mammi*. Her father's mother had been an ample woman and the dress hung off Reba's shoulders and fell nearly to her ankles. Thankfully, the apron hers and fit, but all that did was make her dress bunch around her waist. Even worse was the color. A muddy gray that did nothing for her pale complexion. Her *mamm* would tell her that she shouldn't worry about such things, but at her age and unmarried? She had to worry about it all.

She used a wet wipe to wash most of the dirt from her arms and legs, but when it came to her ankle . . . ouch! It had already turned a sickly shade of purple and blue. She supposed it would have been a good color for a dress or the sky just after sunset, but when it came to skin, it was a color she didn't want to see. Her ankle was also nearly twice the size it should have been, the swelling stretching as far as her toes. And now that she had taken her shoe off, she didn't think she'd be able to get it back on. It might be a little unusual, but she supposed she could teach today with only one shoe. Wearing a too-big dress, a fitted apron, and a soiled prayer *kapp*, since her *mamm* hadn't included one, while sitting down since she could hardly stand any weight on her ankle. What a day!

She limped out of the storage room and somehow managed to make it to the front of the class. But only barely. She collapsed into her chair and surveyed her eager scholars.

Oh, who was she trying to kid? They weren't eager. They were ready to go fishing and swimming. She remembered when she was in school, even working in the fields was better than sitting in a classroom all day.

"Okay, everyone. I know this is going to be a little different today, but we all have to work together, all right?"

All of the desks had been pushed as close together as possible so the repairman could work. The scholars' attention was split between the strange man on a ladder and their seated teacher.

"Everyone but the first grade, get out your reading books. First grade come up here for math. We're going to do things a little differently today."

Somehow Reba managed to keep everyone's attention for the beginning part of the morning. Especially since the repairman—Abel, she learned his name was sometime during the morning—was pounding away at a spot in the ceiling.

He climbed down his ladder and disappeared a little after eleven, returning just as she had one of the eighth graders ring the bell for lunch.

"I hope you like pizza." But he didn't have pizza for just the two of them. He had pizza for the whole class.

The children cheered. But Reba wasn't willing to completely forgive him. Not just yet.

"Pizza?" he asked, holding out a plate with two slices of pepperoni.

"*Danki*," she murmured as she accepted the food.

"Here's a drink for you, Reba." Hope, another of Jess's girls, handed her a plastic cup full of water. "Constance told me to bring it to you."

Reba smiled at her niece. "Thank you to both of you."

"Does your ankle really hurt?" Hope asked.

It throbbed like the dickens, but there was no sense telling Hope that. "I'll be okay." Once the swelling went down.

"You hurt your ankle?"

Reba reluctantly nodded. She supposed that he had been so busy with the repair that he hadn't noticed that she was seated the entire morning.

"Can I take a look at it?"

She started to tell him no, but swiveled in her chair, holding her foot out for him to see. If she had thought the swelling was bad this morning, it was doubly so now. And sometime during the morning, the purple and blue had been joined by a sickening pink.

"That's broken," Abel said, his words blunt and straight to the point.

Reba shook her head. "It's just sprained. It'll be okay in a day or two."

"No, it won't," he said, with a shake of his head. "And I'm sorry, but that is definitely broken."

Chapter 2

"A broken ankle," Reba groused as she hobbled up the porch steps toward home.

"Can I help you?"

She shook off her father's attention and pulled herself up using the handrails. Reba stopped at the top and turned toward her *dat*. "Sorry," she mumbled.

A broken ankle, and it was all Abel Weaver's fault. Well, his horse's fault, at least. And now she would spend the next eight weeks in a walking boot. She stumped into the house and did her best to reverse her mood. She hated the boot, but she hated hating it even more.

"How'd it go?" *Mamm* came out of the kitchen, tossing a dish towel over one shoulder. The house smelled wonderful, like oven-fried chicken, tomato pie, and green beans.

Reba's stomach growled, reminding her that she hadn't actually eaten lunch. Abel had taken one look at her ankle, and the next thing she knew, she was in a car and on her way to the emergency clinic. He had stayed with her in the waiting room until her father arrived, then Abel had headed out. She supposed he figured he had done enough. *Jah*, right.

"It's broken," Reba and *Dat* answered at the same time.

"Oh, my." *Mamm* shook her head.

"When are we eating?" Reba asked. Her ankle was stabilized, but hurt like crazy. She would definitely need to eat before she took any of the pain medication the doctor had prescribed.

"Jess has someone coming over tonight to talk about doing the repairs on his house."

"Why aren't they eating at his house?"

Mamm frowned. "Jess needed some help, Reba."

"I know," she groused. This whole ordeal had made her cranky.

"Somebody didn't get to eat lunch today," *Dat* said.

Mamm nodded in that understanding way of hers. "Go change your dress, Reba. I'll fix you a snack to hold you over until supper."

After a small plate of cheese and crackers, Reba felt a little more like herself. Abner arrived home, teasing her about the boot. Reba liked to believe he was simply happy she was still alive, but he felt the need to hide his feelings.

She tried to help *Mamm*, but she wouldn't hear of it, waving Reba back into the living room "to rest." Reba was quietly grateful. The boot was heavy and awkward. Aside from the pain, she was plumb worn out from the day.

"Reba! Reba! Reba!" Constance, Hope, and Lilly Ruth skidded into the house, their eyes searching her for any signs that she was injured beyond what they had been told.

"We were so worried," Constance said.

"I'm fine." Reba gave them a smile.

"After you left, Johnny Lapp's mother came to take over the class." Hope made a face.

"She smells funny," Lilly Ruth said.

Constance elbowed her in the side. "You're not supposed to say things like that."

"But it's true," Lilly Ruth returned. "If I said she smelled good, that would be a lie."

"You're not supposed to talk about how people smell."

"Not even if they smell good? Like Abel." She grinned. "He smells good."

"Lilly Ruth." Jess's tone was low with warning.

Constance rolled her eyes, but only where her father couldn't see her.

Reba resisted the urge to join her. "Not even if they smell good," Reba confirmed. The last person, the very last person, she wanted to talk about was Abel Weaver. With any luck and the good Lord's grace, she would never have to lay eyes on him again.

A quick knock sounded on the door.

"That must be him."

Jah, the mysterious guest who was coming to help Jess get his house ready for the wedding.

Jess opened the door, waving in whoever was standing over the threshold. "Come in. Come in."

And Abel Weaver stepped into the house.

"You!" She glared at him.

He jumped, obviously not expecting her to be there. "Reba?" His blue eyes roamed over her, taking in the propped-up foot and the boot covering her leg from the bottom of her knee to the tips of her toes. "So I was right. It is broken."

"How very helpful of you to run women off the road, then diagnose their injuries."

"Reba!" *Mamm* scolded.

The second the words left her mouth she regretted them. "Sorry," she mumbled.

Abel turned a color very close to the dress she had on earlier. The dress draped over the washing machine, now covered in mud.

"You two know each other . . . ?" Jess started, then he obviously put the facts together and came up with the afternoon's events. "Oh."

"When the doctor's bill arrives, be sure to send it over," Abel said.

Dat shook his head. "We'll do no such thing. It was an accident."

Abel started to protest, but *Mamm* stepped in before he could speak. "Everybody come on before the food gets cold."

"I'll get started tomorrow," Abel said as he and Jess walked out to his buggy. The horse he'd bought just yesterday was at home in the barn, and he had borrowed his cousin's mare for the trip over to the Schmuckers'. What were the odds that the woman he accidentally ran off the road this morning was the teacher, and the sister to the man who had hired him for his first job in Paradise? Mighty slim, he was sure. Yet here he was.

"Come by after eight," Jess told him. "The girls will be gone, and the milking will be complete. Then I'll be able to go over everything that needs to be done."

"If you're sure you still want to hire me."

Jess shook his head with a grin. "Don't let Reba bother you. She's a little cranky these days."

And she wasn't cranky before? But he couldn't ask that question. It was entirely too personal. "I understand," he said instead.

"See you at eight," Jess said.

Abel climbed into his buggy and waved goodbye. If he were keeping track, he would have to say today was the strangest day he'd ever had. He could only hope that the rest of his time in Lancaster would settle down a bit. He wasn't sure how much more of this he could take.

Constance Schmucker stepped onto the small ladder and flipped on the water. She loved being at *Mammi*'s house even when there was work to be done. Her *dat* had tried to figure out why she enjoyed chores at her grandmother's more than she did at home, but decided that it was a mystery for the ages. But Constance knew what it was. It was companionship. Oh, not with her sisters. She was with them all the time. But washing dishes with *Mammi* and Reba was so much more fun than washing dishes alone. She could only hope that when Bernice finally came to live with them and be their new *mamm*, she would have that companionship every day. The thought made her heart soar like a bird.

But her aunt was propped up in the living room

on the couch, her broken ankle causing her great pain. Constance hated to see someone she loved hurt that way, even if she understood it was an accident. Still, it had left her aunt, who was normally so happy, as surly as a poked bear.

"Is Reba going to be okay?" Lilly Ruth asked. Of all of the sisters, Lilly Ruth seemed to worry the most. Constance worried, but she considered herself to be a problem-solver. Just like last year, when she had taken it onto herself to match up her *dat* with their new teacher, Bernice Yoder. *Jah*, problem-solver. That was her.

"Of course, dear," *Mammi* said. She stood at the counter next to Constance and scraped the leftovers into plastic tubs. Constance knew that *Mammi* would send the food home with them. She always did.

Mammi stopped long enough to hand the dish towel to Hope, who would help with the dishes. Lilly Ruth sat at the table swinging her feet as she watched her older sisters.

Hope stood next to Constance, waiting for clean dishes to dry.

"It's hard to see her unhappy," Lilly Ruth said.

Mammi nodded. "Having a broken ankle is hard. I tell you what. Why don't you draw her a picture? That should cheer her up."

Lilly Ruth smiled, showing the gap where her front teeth were missing. "I would like that, too."

Mammi moved away to get Lilly Ruth a piece

of paper and some crayons, but Constance couldn't help but think that Reba's unhappiness had to be more than just her injury. Her *dat* had been unhappy last year, but he was happy now. Was it only because he and Bernice were getting married in a couple of weeks? Or could there be more to it than that?

She thought about the other married people she knew. *Mammi* and *Dawdi* were married. They were happy people. And the people at church. Well, most of them seemed happy.

Hope nudged her in the side. "Hurry up."

Constance looked down. She had been washing the same dish for quite some time. She hadn't realized her churning thoughts had slowed her hands. She dipped the dish into the rinse water and handed it off to her sister. "Patience is a virtue, Hope."

"And so is a sister who doesn't daydream."

Constance didn't reply as *Mammi* came back into the room. She set Lilly Ruth to coloring. But Constance couldn't help mulling the problem over in her head, even as they finished their chores, packed up the leftovers, and headed for home.

Lilly Ruth had given Reba the picture she had drawn, and their aunt had smiled, but Constance saw the sheen of tears in her eyes. Reba wanted them to think she was happy, but Constance knew better.

Once they were home, everyone piled out of the buggy. Constance was left to store the food in the refrigerator, then take her sisters upstairs to get ready for bed. And still this problem nagged at her, like when a piece of popcorn got stuck in her teeth. But she didn't think dental floss would fix this. No. Not at all.

Hope poked her in the ribs once more as Constance stood in front of the sink. "What's wrong with you?" her sister asked. "You're hogging the sink. How am I supposed to brush my teeth if you're standing there staring at the mirror?"

Constance bumped her back. "I'm not staring at the mirror. I'm thinking about things."

Hope narrowed her gray eyes, looking more like their mother every day. At times like this Constance missed their *mamm* so much, but God had provided them with a new one. And she could hardly wait for Bernice to come and live with them. "Oh, *jah?*" Hope asked. "What were you thinking about?"

"Boys?" Lilly Ruth chimed in from behind them.

Constance whirled on her sister, ready to deny it, but she couldn't. She had been thinking about boys, in a roundabout way.

"You are thinking about boys," Hope said, in awe.

Constance shook her head. "Not for me, silly. For *Aenti* Reba."

Her sisters stopped.

"Reba?" Lilly Ruth asked.

"You're worried about her, *jah*?"

Lilly Ruth nodded.

"What are you planning?" Hope asked.

Constance shrugged. "Nothing much. But don't you think that Reba would be happier if she had a husband?"

Her sisters seemed to think about it a moment. "I don't know," Lilly Ruth finally said.

"Well, I do." Constance gave a firm nod. "*Dat*'s getting married, and he's happier."

Her sisters nodded. There was no arguing with that.

"*Dat* said not to meddle," Hope reminded them.

"We're not meddling," Constance said.

"What's meddling?" Lilly Ruth looked at each of them in turn, trying to figure out the definition.

"It means messing in things that aren't your business," Hope said.

"Oh." Lilly Ruth looked crestfallen, then her expression lifted. "It's okay then. Reba is our business. She's our *aenti*."

Two against one. Constance pinned Hope with a stare that she hoped was reminiscent of the one their mother gave them when they misbehaved. She wasn't sure exactly how effective it would be, but she had been practicing it in the mirror when no one else was around.

As she crossed her arms, Lilly Ruth came to stand next to her and crossed hers as well. Unity. *Jah*, that was what they needed.

Hope held out for a few minutes more, then threw her hands in the air. "All right," she said. "But when *Dat* gets mad at us, I'm gonna say I told you so."

"*Dat* is never going to know. Because we're not going to tell him. And when Reba gets married, no one will even care anymore."

"If you say so," Hope grumbled.

Constance nodded. "I say so. Now." She rubbed her hands together in excitement. "Who should we get to fall in love with her?"

"Abel," Lilly Ruth chirped. "He smells good."

Reba felt more than a little conspicuous as her *dat* pulled up to the school the following morning.

"*Danki* for the ride, *Dat*."

"Do you need some help getting down?"

"Probably." She had needed help getting into the buggy. She was going to be needing a lot of help for the next eight weeks. The walking boot was heavy and awkward. And she felt like all eyes were on her. Who fell in a puddle and broke their ankle? Only Reba Schmucker, that was for sure.

Her *dat* climbed out of his side of the buggy and came around to help her to the ground. Reba was all too aware of everyone staring. Didn't they have something else to look at? She was going to have to find another way to get to school tomorrow. Maybe if she borrowed Abner's scooter. Or she could get one of those rolly-chair things that people used. She could brace her knee on the bench part and roll her way into school. Then again, that might draw more attention than having her *dat* drop her off.

"Bye, *Dat*." She gave him a small wave as he climbed back into the buggy.

"I'll pick you up this afternoon." He clicked the reins and set the horses into motion once again. Great. Her embarrassment would be complete. Not only was her *dat* dropping her off at school in the morning, he was coming back to get her in the afternoon. That was just beautiful.

She turned toward the schoolhouse, so aware that all eyes were on her. She drew the attention of some of the scholars, who began to run toward her in excitement.

"Reba! Reba!" they called as they ran, smiles on their faces. She supposed she had concerned a few of them, leaving in the middle of the day like she had to go to the emergency clinic and have her ankle x-rayed. But she was back now and was ready for the day to return to normal as quickly as possible.

She hobbled toward the schoolhouse, answering the kids' questions as simply as she could. *Yes, my ankle's broken. No, it doesn't hurt right now. Yes, we're still having class. No, there is no extra recess.*

But the best part of the day? No more Abel Weaver.

He had finished his work yesterday, and there was no reason for him to return today. And considering his and Jess's conversation last night after supper, he was at her brother's house, most likely terrorizing dairy cows and making a mess of her brother's life.

That's not fair, a little voice inside her whispered.

But she wasn't concerned with fairness. Something about that man rubbed her the wrong way.

She stumped up the steps leading to the schoolhouse, then stood on the porch and surveyed the school yard. "Five more minutes, scholars," she called. A few of them groaned, but they knew better than to protest too much. She opened the door to the schoolhouse and stopped just on the other side of the threshold. "What in the world?"

Someone had moved the desks back to their proper places, most likely Abel after he finished up yesterday afternoon. Or Johnny Lapp's mother, who had come to take over for her. But that wasn't what caused her distress. The exact spot where Abel had been working yesterday was now a big, gaping hole in the ceiling. The ceiling pieces were scattered about, and she swore she heard the flapping of wings as if a bird was caught between the ceiling and the roof.

"Didn't Abel fix that yesterday?" Daniel King asked.

"*Jah*, he did." Reba pressed her lips together. Some repair job. Some repairman. He made a bigger mess out of it than they'd had to begin with.

"Daniel, run down to the phone shanty and call my brother, Jess. His number is in the book there. Tell him to bring Abel up here immediately. Tell him it's important. I would call, but . . ." She waved a hand toward her boot.

"*Jah*. Okay, Reba." Daniel took off in a run.

She turned back to the mess. All the desks would have to be moved again, and the debris needed to be swept up.

"What happened?" Constance came into the schoolhouse, her gray eyes wide with shock. Her little mouth formed an O as she surveyed the room.

"Abel Weaver." Reba gritted her teeth. "That's what happened."

Chapter 3

"She wasn't supposed to be angry." Hope sidled up next to Constance at the pencil sharpener.

Once again their desks had been pushed to one side of the room. Abel had shown up just after the bell, looking at the mess as if he'd never seen it before.

Constance supposed he hadn't. She and her sisters had come to school early and undid the repairs he had done the day before. But it was no easy feat. Her arms still ached from holding them over her head as she used the broom to bust through the ceiling. Plaster had gotten everywhere, and they barely had enough time to brush it out of their hair and use a wet wipe to get it off their dresses before the other students started to arrive.

The hardest part had been seeing Reba's face and pretending that she had known nothing about what had gone on in the schoolroom. It was better that her aunt thought the repair had failed so Abel would have to come back and fix it. How else were they going to get together? Abel was supposed to be working to get Constance's house ready for the wedding.

"I told you," Constance started, "she's upset

because she wants to be married. Like *Dat* and Bernice."

"If you say so," Hope grumbled.

"I say so," Constance shot back.

"Girls," Reba said, in her stern teacher voice. "It's time to get back to your seats."

The fact that the two of them had managed to get to the pencil sharpener at the same time was proof positive that *Aenti* Reba wasn't thinking as clearly as she normally did. She would've never let the two of them cluster there together.

Constance would have liked to believe that Abel Weaver was the distraction. She might be acting angry now, but Reba would soon think differently. Plus, it was the only thing Constance could think of to get the two of them together. And she was quite satisfied with the idea. Quite satisfied indeed.

It took Abel the better part of the morning to repair the hole in the ceiling. He had never seen anything like it. It looked as if someone had taken a stick or two-by-four and rammed it into the ceiling, tearing down plaster and Sheetrock. He'd never seen a repair just . . . gone like that before. And he was so aware of Reba Schmucker glaring at him every fifteen minutes or so. It wasn't that she didn't have cause to be upset with him about her ankle, even though he had apologized—several times—for the accident.

This was different. He had fixed this problem yesterday, and she was glaring at him like he was to blame for the mess that she came into today. Well, he wasn't. It looked like vandalism to him. He should talk to Jess about it. He was on the school board. Unfortunately, things like this happened all over. Reba needed to be careful coming into a schoolhouse where someone saw fit to tear things up.

He heard her say something, but he wasn't paying attention. Her voice was nice just to listen to. He didn't have to decipher the words to enjoy the melody they created as she spoke. That was followed by the sound of books slamming shut.

"Lunchtime!" someone called.

Lunchtime? Already? Abel wiped the rest of the plaster from his fingers and climbed down the ladder steps. The repair looked good. Better, even. They would have to wait before he could paint. He should probably get something to eat and head back to Jess's. He could paint tomorrow.

"Abel?"

He turned as Constance Schmucker came toward him. At least he thought it was Constance. Lilly Ruth was the youngest, with lots of red hair, freckles, and blue eyes just like her *dat*. Constance and Hope looked so much alike he had trouble remembering who was who unless they were standing side by side.

"Would you like some lunch?"

He opened his mouth to tell her no, that he was going back to her house to work, but she continued before he could speak.

"I brought some extra today." She shrugged. "The Bible says it's good to share."

It did? He guessed sharing went right along with being neighborly and loving one another, so maybe it did. "That's very nice of you."

She smiled prettily.

"I need to wash my hands first." A dry rag could only do so much.

Constance nodded. "Just meet me out underneath the apple tree."

"*Danki*," he said, and went to the sink to wash his hands.

A few minutes later he stepped out into the warm May sunshine. It wouldn't be long before summer was fully upon them. And after that was fall and Abigail's wedding.

He wished her all the happiness in the world, but he wasn't able to stick around and watch it. That was why he had come to Paradise. To get away, to heal his broken heart. It felt like a coward's way out, but he didn't care. A man could only take so much. And having to watch Abigail with Luther at her side was almost more than he could take. But the pitying looks from his friends, neighbors, even his own family members, completely did him in. It was past time for a fresh start.

Some fresh start, he thought as he walked toward the large tree at the edge of the playground. All he had done so far was upset a beautiful girl, break her ankle, and then somehow destroy her classroom. Okay, maybe *destroy* was too strong a word, but it had definitely made her angry. Which was the exact reason why, when he saw her under the apple tree, he should have turned around and walked in the opposite direction. But he promised Constance he would eat lunch with her. He'd just never dreamed that Constance would also eat lunch with her aunt.

Constance caught sight of him and scooted over, patting the space between her and Reba. "Come sit by me," she said.

Lilly Ruth and Hope sat facing their sister, so there wasn't much room to sit anywhere else.

Containers of food sat in the center of their almost-circle. Reba moved a little more, shifting her weight as she did so. Her injured leg was stuck out to the side, the other one tucked underneath her skirts. Every time he saw her, he wanted to apologize. He'd never had a horse get away from him like that and had never, ever harmed another person as a result.

"I hear my niece has invited you to eat with us." Her blue eyes were guarded.

"That's right," he said as he settled down next to her. "I hope that's okay."

She gave a quick nod.

What was he thinking? That she would tell him no, that she really didn't want him there?

Exactly. He had a feeling that Reba Schmucker said what was on her mind when it was on her mind. He couldn't say that was the most desirable trait in a woman, but it seemed to fit her personality just fine. It wasn't like he was in the market for a new love. He'd had enough problems with his heart as a child, and it had been broken as an adult. It needed more time to heal than it'd had up until this point.

"Would you like a tuna sandwich?" Constance asked. She held a baggie containing a sandwich toward him.

"*Danki*," he said. "It's my favorite."

"It's Reba's recipe," Hope chimed in.

"Ow!" Hope rubbed her arm. If he wasn't mistaken, Constance pinched her, though he couldn't figure out why.

"It's good," he said, around a large bite.

"*Danki*," Reba murmured. But she didn't meet his gaze. Now, why did he get the feeling that it wasn't her tuna recipe at all?

"I like that color on you, Reba," Constance said.

"*Danki*." Reba brushed down the skirt of her lime-green dress.

He wasn't one to criticize, but it did look a little . . . bright. But who was he to say? Every bishop was different, just like every *Ordnung* was different. And if the women in Paradise wanted to wear wild colors, then he wasn't about to say otherwise.

"Would you like another?" Hope held out a plastic container full of carrot sticks.

He shook his head. She offered them to Reba.

"*Danki*," Reba said.

Seriously? Was that the only word she was going to say the entire time they sat there?

Or maybe the question was, why did he care? So she didn't like him. It wasn't like it truly mattered. But somehow it did. Despite every-thing—knocking her in the puddle, making her lose her lunch, causing her to break her ankle—he still wanted her to like him. How was that for schoolboy dreams? Little boys always wanted to be the teacher's favorite.

Reba managed not to look at him or speak to him for the rest the time while they ate lunch.

He had been sitting there the whole time trying to devise ways to get her to talk to him, look at him, like him. Even as he told himself it didn't matter.

Lilly Ruth jumped to her feet and tugged on his hand. "Time to play softball. Come play with us."

"I really should be—"

"Chicken?"

He whirled around, unsure if he'd really heard the word or not. Was Reba talking to him?

His gaze met hers, and he saw a sparkle in those blue eyes. She *was* talking to him, and she was issuing a challenge. Was he going to accept?

Absolutely.

"Are you coming?" Lilly Ruth asked, then her face fell. "You can't play today, Reba."

She gave a small shrug. "It's okay. I'll sit here and keep score."

Hope and Constance got to their feet, and the three of them directed Abel toward the empty field just on the other side of the outhouses.

The starch went out of Reba's demeanor the minute he turned his back. She wanted to have a long talk with Constance about inviting people to eat with them, but how would that look? It was okay to invite people to eat as long as they weren't handsome men who ran her off the road and didn't know how to properly repair a ceiling.

She really was going to have to talk to Jess about the shoddy repair job Abel had done yesterday. It had looked okay when she left to go to the hospital, but it wasn't like she went over and inspected it. How did the man make a living as a handyman if he didn't repair anything correctly? Or maybe that was why he had to move here. He had run out of marks in Punxsutawney or wherever it was he was from.

She sat in the shade of the apple tree as the kids divided up into teams. Not all played softball during their breaks, and others were swinging and playing on the monkey bars. She shifted her attention to them, checking to make sure they were okay before turning back to the game.

Softball was such a fun time. She hated that she was sitting under a tree with her foot in a boot instead of out there playing. Only two more weeks left of school, and she was sidelined for the rest of it. With any luck, by the time she got her foot healed, it wouldn't be too hot to still play.

The kids all wanted Abel on their team, and finally someone flipped a coin to see which team got him. Constance cheered and Lilly Ruth pouted, which meant they were on opposite teams this time.

But if they thought having Abel on their side was going to be an advantage, it quickly became apparent that they were wrong. He struck out twice, then served as a pinch runner for Mary Ebersol, who stubbed her toe the day before. But he couldn't run any faster or better than he could hit the ball.

After he was thrown out at second, he plopped down in the shade next to Reba and grabbed his water bottle from their lunch.

"Have you played softball much?" she asked.

Not bothering to meet her gaze, he simply flipped a hand toward the game. "Oh, I'm letting them win, you know."

Now, why did she have the feeling he was telling her a lie? "That's really great of you. But how about the truth?"

He shook his head. "The truth is not nearly as exciting as you might think."

"Try me."

"I was born with a heart condition. I had to have four surgeries by the time I was six. So I didn't get to play outside much." He scoffed. "I didn't get to play anywhere much. By the time the doctors felt like they had my heart healthy enough to play, those times were gone."

Tears pricked at the backs of her eyes. He might've been the man who tried to kill her yesterday, but no one deserved that sort of childhood. "Those times are gone only if you let them be."

"Is that an invitation to come back and play softball again?"

Reba smiled. "Anytime."

What had gotten into her? Why was she inviting Abel Weaver to come play softball at the school-house whenever he wanted? He was the last person she wanted underfoot. And she would not allow herself to be moved by his story of heart problems and lost childhoods.

She sent Chris Lapp over to ring the school bell and get everyone back in from lunch.

Abel might have been a terrible softball player, but the children loved him. He helped them gather up their equipment and store it in the shed, then they danced around him, begging him to stay for the rest of the afternoon. And the worst part? She couldn't tell him no. Amish schoolhouses were open to visitors, though most times it was a parent or a curious teacher from another district.

"Please, Abel!" the children chanted.

He looked at Reba and gave a helpless shrug.

There were worse things, she told herself. But she couldn't think of one.

Reba did her best not to watch Abel for the rest of the afternoon. But her eyes seemed determined to follow him wherever he went. She tried to tell herself it was because she was stationary, sitting to one side of her desk and having the students come up to her for their lessons, while Abel moved around helping this child and that with different questions they might have. Reba had been concerned at first that it would be distracting, but it actually turned out to be a good thing. The kids worked very hard to get the work done so that he could double check it for them, and she could find no fault in that. But it was when he got to Libby King's desk that his true nature came out.

"I can't do it," Libby said. The poor girl struggled daily in class, and Reba was at a loss for what to do with her. Bernice had done everything she could to help her along, but it seemed the more they tried, the more frustrated Libby became.

Abel nodded sagely. "I understand. Reading was hard for me, too. But I learned a trick." He leaned down closer to her, and Reba only heard the rest of his words because she was so near Libby's row of seats. "Would you like for me to tell you that trick?"

Libby nodded. "Yes, please."

Abel squatted down next to her chair and picked up her book so they both could see it. "When you're reading, close one eye."

"Which eye?" Libby asked.

"It doesn't matter. But when you pick one, that's the one that has to stay closed while you read. Even if you have to put your hand up to cover it, okay?"

Libby nodded, then closed her left eye. She began to read, then switched eyes, opening her left one and closing the right.

"Stay with the same eye the whole time you're reading," Abel coached. "Otherwise you'll get mixed up again, okay?"

Libby nodded.

"It's very important that you do it that way or it might not work, *jah?*"

"*Jah.*" Libby picked up her book, closed her left eye and began again. She read a small passage from *Little House on the Prairie*, not missing even one word.

When she finally stopped, she was bursting with pride and accomplishment. "I did it!"

Abel nodded. "*Jah*, you did."

He moved away as Libby continued to smile.

"How did you manage that?" Reba asked. It was nothing short of a miracle.

Abel gave a casual shrug. "I had trouble when I was about her age. My tutor told me the same trick."

Reba shook her head. "I've never heard of such a thing."

"I'm not even sure if it is a thing," Abel said. "But I think with one eye closed, you must concentrate on keeping the eye closed and reading the words so there's no room for anything else."

Reba shook her head. "If you say so. All I know is it worked. She has never been able to read that much at one time."

"Glad I could help."

At three o'clock, Abel went out to ring the bell. Reba was exhausted. Lugging around a broken ankle all day was no small chore. And as much as she loved the children, she would be more than ready to give up her teaching post, and bow out to whatever new teacher the board chose.

"You want me to erase the blackboard?" Abel asked.

Reba shook her head. "One of the boys will do it in the morning. It gives them something to help release the energy that boys seem to have so much of."

Abel grinned. "I understand."

320

And that was when she knew what she didn't like about the man. It was his grin. He flashed that grin like it was solid gold, winking dimples at everyone around. It was disarming. Unnerving. And downright vain to go around grinning like that at everybody.

Jah, that was what it was.

Abel Weaver's dastardly dimples.

Chapter 4

"Where are we going?" Reba asked her *dat* that afternoon when he picked her up. Definitely tomorrow she was giving the scooter a try. As long as Abel Weaver was off the roads, she should be safe.

But her father had passed the turnoff that led home. "It's your night to go help Jess."

Reba groaned.

"What's the matter? Are you not up to it?" he asked.

How she would like to say no, she wasn't up to it. That she needed to go home and rest. But that would only delay the inevitable. If she didn't go tonight, she would have to go tomorrow. Or the next day. She heaved a great sigh.

"Why do I get the feeling something else is wrong?" *Dat* asked.

"Nothing's wrong."

He shook his head. "Do I need to remind you that lying is a sin?"

"Abel Weaver." They were only two words and yet they held so much weight.

"Are you saying that you don't want to go to Jess's because Abel will be there? What's wrong with Abel?"

"What's *not* wrong with Abel?" Reba asked. Aside from those dimples . . . "He ran me off the road yesterday. Now my ankle's broken. I spent all day yesterday in *Mammi*'s dress, and I'm supposed to like the man?"

Dat tsked. "I think you're being a little hard on him. He did apologize. And he offered to pay the medical bills."

Reba growled. "I don't want anything from him. Except to be left alone."

"I see," *Dat* said. But from the tone of his voice she had a feeling he could see nothing. "I still think you're being too hard on him. He's a good guy, a nice Amish man. He's just trying to make a living like everybody else."

"With a crazy horse and stupid dimples."

Wait . . . what? Who said that?

"Now I really see." *Dat* grinned.

Reba sat for a moment weighing her options. She could deny everything, which would just lead her *dat* to believe even more that she had a thing for Abel Weaver. Or she could remain quiet and her *dat* would still believe that she had a thing for Abel Weaver. Although it was never her strong suit, she decided keeping her mouth shut was probably the best course of action.

She folded her hands in her lap and stared straight ahead, lips pressed firmly together. That was all she had to do: remain still and quiet the rest of the way to her brother's house. Piece of cake. She could totally do this. After all, anything she said would only worsen the situation with her father. That was the last thing she needed, somebody recounting the virtues of Abel Weaver. No, it was better this way. Much better this way.

"There's just something about him I don't like," Reba said. *Whew.* It felt good to get that off her chest.

"You know what they say, don't you?"

She sniffed. "No. I don't believe I do."

"When a woman starts protesting a lot about a man—"

She shut her eyes and held up both hands. "Don't even go there."

Her father chuckled.

Well, that didn't go exactly as planned. That was all she needed, her father thinking she was interested in Abel Weaver. The only thing she was interested in was him staying as far away from her as possible. But helping her brother tonight was not going to make that a reality.

Her *dat* turned down the lane that led to Jess's house.

As expected, Abel Weaver's buggy sat off to one side.

The horse was unhitched, which meant he was in for a long stay. Great. She would probably have to cook supper for him tonight, too.

"Whoa." Her *dat* pulled back on the reins, stopping the buggy in Jess's drive. "Jess said that he would take you to school in the morning." His eyes twinkled. "Or maybe Abel will give you a ride."

Reba groaned. She grabbed her purse and her school bag. She was about to get out of the buggy when she realized she was stuck until someone helped her down.

Her *dat* laid one hand on her arm, stopping her midflight. "Calm down, Reba. I've never seen you this upset over . . . not much."

For a moment there, she was afraid he was going to say *nothing*. And her broken ankle was a lot more than nothing. But the more her *dat* talked to her, the more she realized she was overreacting to Abel's part in yesterday's accident. And the more she realized that was exactly what it was. An accident. So what had her so upset?

She shook her head.

Must be those dastardly dimples.

"Thanks for the ride, *Dat*."

"Hang on," he said. "I'll come around and help you down."

Just as he had that very morning, her father helped her to the ground.

Reba waved good-bye and bobbed her way toward the porch. Maybe that was another cause for her surly attitude. She hated asking for help. Pride might be a sin, but she appreciated the fact that she could do things on her own. She could stand on her own two feet, do practically anything, and hadn't needed anyone. Until now.

"Jess," she called as she let herself into the house.

"Reba!" All three of her nieces ran toward her at the same time.

She held up her hands to stay them off. "You can't jump on me now or you'll knock me down."

They grabbed her hands and led her into the kitchen.

"I'm so glad you're here," Lilly Ruth said.

"Where's your *dat*?"

Constance made a face. "He's in the barn with Abel."

"He smells good," Lilly Ruth said. "Ow."

"Hope, did you just pinch your sister?" Reba asked.

Hope turned wide, innocent gray eyes on her. "No."

But Lilly Ruth rubbed her arm.

"Apologize now."

"But I didn't pinch her."

"Hope." Reba turned her voice into a low warning.

"Sorry," Hope mumbled.

But one look at Constance's face, and Reba wondered if she had chosen the wrong sister. "Constance?"

"Sorry, Lilly Ruth."

Reba turned away, but not before she caught Lilly Ruth sticking her tongue out at her sisters. That one she let slide. She knew Lilly Ruth took a lot of bossing from the two older girls. Sometimes it was good to let her get one in of her own.

"What are you cooking for dinner?" Constance asked.

"You mean what are you helping me cook." Reba stumped over to the refrigerator to see what her mother had laid out the day before.

"*Mammi* put half a chicken out to thaw," Hope said.

"She said Abel's favorite was chicken and noodles," Lilly Ruth added.

"And I'm supposed to make his favorite?"

"It was *Mammi*'s idea," Constance said.

Somehow Reba doubted that.

"How will he ever start to like you if you don't do nice things for him?" Lilly Ruth took one look at her sisters' glowering faces and slapped one hand over her mouth.

"I see." Reba looked at each girl in turn. "You three aren't trying to match-make, are you?"

The three had been instrumental in getting their *dat* and their teacher to fall in love last year. But she didn't want to be a part of any love scheme.

"No."

"Of course not."

"No, no, no."

The three talked over themselves. That alone was enough to confirm their guilt.

Reba studied each of their tiny faces. Only Hope's gave her away. She chewed on her lower lip, her eyes darting from Constance to Lilly Ruth and back again.

"Hope?"

"I didn't want to," Hope cried. "They made me. I told them it was a bad idea."

"Thanks a lot, Hope," Constance said. "You ruined everything."

The two girls started arguing, talking over each other as they bickered.

"Enough!" Reba said. The girls fell quiet, their chins down as if they were embarrassed to meet her gaze. "I appreciate your attention," Reba said. "Really, I do. But it's not necessary."

"We just want you to be happy," Lilly Ruth said. "Like *Dat*."

Was that how people saw her? Unhappy because she didn't have a husband?

She shook her head. "I have the three best nieces in the entire world," she said. "How can I not be happy?"

Constance raised her gaze, her big eyes filled with tears. "And you're not mad?"

She was furious, but how could she tell that to an eight-year-old and her younger sisters, who wanted to see her happy? Who could find fault with that? "Of course not," she said. "I love you all very much. But from here on out, why don't you leave the matchmaking up to God?"

Three smiles spread across three sweet faces. The girls threw their arms around her, hugging her close and nearly knocking her backward. Reba wrapped one arm around them and braced one against the tabletop to keep from toppling over.

"We love you, too, *Aenti*."

"And we promise," Constance added. "No more matchmaking."

"So, Abel," Constance said, just after the last bite of supper. "Was that the best chicken and noodles you've ever eaten?"

He sat back in his chair as the young girl picked up his empty plate. "It was very good, *jah*."

"The best?" she pressed.

"Perhaps." He patted his full belly. The chicken and noodles were good, though he was a little confused as to why Constance would demand that he declare them the best.

"But you did enjoy them, *jah*?" Hope asked.

"Very much," he said, wondering which one of the girls actually made the chicken and noodles.

"*Aenti* Reba made them, you know," Lilly Ruth added.

From across the table, Reba cleared her throat.

All three girls turned in her direction. Her stern look added to Abel's confusion, but he had a feeling this was something of a family issue.

"Go on," Reba said. "Take the dishes to the sink."

The girls did as she asked, then Reba stood to follow behind them, he was sure. Abel was on his feet in a heartbeat. "Allow me to help them tonight."

Reba shook her head. "That's not necessary."

"I'm sure you're tired after being on your ankle all day. It's the least I can do."

"What do you think? That if you do the dishes I'll forgive you?"

"It's worth a shot."

"Really. It's not necessary," Reba said.

Jess pushed back from the table and stood. "How about the men clean up tonight?"

From the kitchen area the girls cheered.

"Only if you let me give them their bath," Reba countered.

Abel watched the play between brother and sister with great interest. It was obvious they loved each other very much, but Abel had a feeling they bickered as much as they got along. He wondered if it had been that way their whole lives or if this was something that started in adulthood. Being an only child, he'd never had such a relationship. But he loved to watch the interactions with his cousins almost as much as he enjoyed watching Reba and Jess.

Jess grinned. "You've got yourself a deal," he said. "It's hair-washing night."

Reba's eyes narrowed playfully. "Oh, you'll pay for that one, brother," she said. "Just when you least expect it." She turned toward the girls. "Come on. Upstairs with you all."

The three girls shuffled toward the staircase.

"What about clearing the table?" Jess asked.

Reba shot him a sly grin. "That's part of the cleanup."

Jess opened his mouth to protest.

"Hup." Reba shook her head. "No excuses. It's hair-washing night." She waved the girls up the stairs.

Jess propped his hands on his hips as he watched his sister disappear. He looked back to the mess on the table and over to Abel.

Abel shrugged. "Is she always like this?"

Jess shook his head. "No. Sometimes she's worse."

Abel laughed. She was a mess, that was for sure. But there was something he enjoyed about sassy Reba Schmucker. He just couldn't put his finger on exactly what it was. The clothes she wore were too bright and she had a tendency to speak her mind. He was certain those traits would get old after a while. So why did she feel the need to constantly prove herself? He supposed with five brothers in the house, that might be the root of some of her behavior, but it was almost as if she dared the world to find fault with her. Or maybe she just liked to push the system.

Abel banished the thoughts about Reba from his mind and turned to help Jess clear the table. Once all the condiments were put away and the dishes stacked next to the sink, Jess handed Abel a towel. "I'll wash; you dry?"

Abel nodded, though he knew the task would allow way too much time to think about Reba.

"You're not mad, right, *Aenti* Reba?"

"Of course not," Reba told Lilly Ruth. How could she stay mad at these precious girls?

She had put them all in the tub, let the older girls wash themselves, and somehow managed to get Lilly Ruth clean herself, even as she fought the big plastic boot on her ankle. Clean, smelling good, and all dressed in their pajamas, the three girls stood before the mirror. Hair-washing day was always a big deal. One time they had tried to rotate and wash each girl's hair a different night, but it seemed as if somehow the rhythm always got off and someone's hair never got washed. Shampooing them all at the same time seemed to be the best plan, even though it took way longer to do it this way.

She sprayed each girl's hair with detangler, then took up a comb and began with Lilly Ruth.

"I think I can do mine tonight," Constance said. She said this every night, and Reba let her try every night. And every night Reba ended up having to comb through the tangles. It was part of the ritual.

Constance struggled with her hair as Reba went on to comb through Hope's. She sent the two girls out of the bathroom and started to help Constance. It didn't help that Constance's hair had a little bit of curl and tended to flip this way and that and tangled at the slightest provocation.

"Ow," Constance said.

"Sorry," Reba murmured. She should've done Constance's hair first, even though Lilly Ruth ran out of patience way before her sisters were done. Maybe then Reba wouldn't be so tired or so ready to go sit down.

Finally, she managed to get most of the tangles out of Constance's hair. She parted it down the middle and was giving her one last comb-through when she noticed something white buried in the strands. Was that . . . ?

"Constance, I thought you washed your hair."

"I did."

"Then what's in it?" Reba tried to grab the pieces of white, only to have them disintegrate between her fingers like wet chalk. Or plaster.

"How did you get white . . ." She looked over

Constance's shoulder and met her gaze in the mirror. "Did you tear up Abel's repair?"

Constance's blush said it all. "I did it for you."

Reba sucked in a deep breath. She wasn't even sure where to begin with it all. She flipped the lid down on the toilet and sat, pulling Constance into the V between her knees. She brushed her hair back from her face. "I love that you tried to help me," Reba said. "But Abel worked very hard on that repair and he had to come fix it again. You made extra work for him."

Constance ducked her head and sniffed.

Reba lifted her chin with one finger. "I think you owe him an apology."

Constance nodded.

"And the other girls?"

Constance shook her head. "They were there, but it was all my idea. I was just trying to help."

As badly as she wanted to be angry, Reba just couldn't manage the emotion. Everyone should be loved by someone as much as these girls loved the people around them. She was well and truly blessed.

"I still think you should take them with you," Reba said.

Constance nodded again. "Right now?"

Reba nodded. "No time like now."

Abel looked out over the cornfield and across the road to the beautiful stars dotting the night sky.

There was a good reason why the town was named Paradise. It might not be Paradise for everyone, but he could see the relation. Beautiful, peaceful, a new home. It was just what he needed.

The door behind him opened. He turned as Reba and the three girls came out onto the porch. They stood next to him.

Reba cleared her throat. "Abel, the girls have something they need to say."

Constance sniffed but took a step forward. "I hope you're not angry."

He wasn't sure what to say to that, so he simply waited for her to continue.

"I tore up your repair so you would have to come back and fix it." Twin tears escaped her big gray eyes and slid down her cheeks.

Her sisters stood one on each side of her, their heads bowed as if praying for their sister to have strength.

"Why . . . why would you do that?" He kept his voice low and soft. He'd never had to deal with such a situation, and he wasn't sure how to proceed.

"We wanted you to spend more time with Reba."

"More time with Reba?" He looked up and caught Reba's gaze. She gave a small nod. "Oh."

"Please forgive us," Lilly Ruth added.

"It wasn't even my idea," Hope added.

"Hope," Reba warned.

"I mean, I'm sorry," Hope backpedaled.

"I know you shouldn't have had to fix it twice," Constance said.

Abel gave a quick nod. That was true. But the day he'd spent at the schoolhouse had been one of the best ones he'd had in a long time, maybe since Abigail chose another.

"Do you forgive us?" Lilly Ruth asked.

Abel cleared his throat. Somehow emotion had settled there, clogging it and making it hard to talk. "Of course," he said. "Of course, I forgive you."

Suddenly he was bombarded with hugs. Three sets of little arms wrapped themselves around him. Tears wet the sides of his shirt as they held him close. Murmurs of *we're sorry* and *thank you* were threaded throughout, and it was all Abel could do to keep his own tears at bay. When had he turned into such a softy? Then again, it would take a hard heart to deny these girls anything.

"Go on to bed now," Reba said.

The girls released him and, with watery smiles, said good night and headed back into the house.

"That was very gracious of you," Reba said.

Grace had nothing to do with it. "They are precious little girls."

Reba laughed. "They're a mess. Each one of them."

Abel chuckled. There was no arguing with that. "But why would they tear up the repair so I

335

would come back?" He had a feeling, but he wanted to hear her say it.

"Last year they did a little matchmaking between their teacher and Jess."

"Bernice?" Abel asked.

"The very same."

"And what does this have to do with me?" he asked.

Reba gave a small cough. "It seems they thought you and I might make a good pair."

"So they were matchmaking?"

Reba laughed, the sound a bit choked and mostly humorless. "I know, right? But yes, they consider themselves accomplished matchmakers since their *dat* and their teacher are getting married in two weeks."

Abel shook his head. "So they did all this to get the two of us to fall in love?"

Reba clasped her hands in front of her. She spread them to each side, then clasped them again as if she had no idea what to do with her own hands. "I'm afraid so."

Abel shifted his weight to one leg. "I see." He seemed to think about it a moment. "And would that be so bad?"

Those were evidently not the words Reba expected to hear. A frown marred her brow as she eyed him across the darkened porch. "Would what be so bad?"

"Falling in love with me."

Chapter 5

Reba's good leg nearly gave out from underneath her. "What—what?"

"Would that be so bad?" he asked again.

Jah, that was what she was afraid he said. "Define *bad*."

He shook his head. "Never mind."

Something in his expression tugged at her heart. She took a step closer and laid one hand on his arm as he turned back to stare at the nighttime sky.

"No," she finally admitted. "It wouldn't be bad at all. But . . ."

He shifted to face her once again. "But what?"

"I'm not in the market for a husband." She'd given up that dream a long time ago.

He gave a quick nod. "What about a friend?"

"I beg your pardon?" She was really going to have to try harder to keep up with this conversation, but she did not expect the things he was saying.

"How about a friend? Could we be friends?"

"Friends?" *Keep up, Reba!*

"I'm really not in the market for a wife."

He wasn't? "You're not?"

"But I could use a friend."

Reba gave her head a small shake to clear her thoughts. It didn't help.

"I know . . . I mean, I know you're upset with me because of your ankle, and you have every right to be mad. I am truly sorry."

"And you want to be my friend?"

"*Jah.* Of course."

Friends. That sounded safe enough. "Okay. We can be friends."

He flashed her a smile, which included those dastardly dimples. But this time she was immune to them. They were friendly dimples, not nearly as dastardly as when he had sent them her way earlier. And now that all the misunderstanding surrounding Constance, Hope, and Lilly Ruth's matchmaking attempts was cleared up, being friends sounded like a fine idea.

"So what are you doing Saturday?" Abel asked.

"Saturday?" Great. She had resorted back to repeating everything he said.

Abel nodded. "I need to find a horse. The one I have is not reliable."

"I'll say."

"I'd like somebody to give me a second opinion. And since my horse-picking-out skills are lacking these days . . ."

"Saturday. Yes, I think I can swing that."

"Good." His smile deepened, along with those not-so-dastardly dimples. "I'm looking forward to it."

The rest of the week went by like a breeze. If *like a breeze* included being in a hard plastic boot for a broken ankle, but Reba was becoming used to lugging the apparatus around. Now if the break would just stop itching.

Abel pulled up in front of her parents' house just after nine.

Reba was watching out the window, but trying not to let him see. She wouldn't want him to think she was anxious to go with him to look for horses. After all, it wasn't a date. They were just friends. But she needed to tell her heart that. It was flip-flopping in her chest like she had a real date or something.

"*Mamm*," she called. "I'm going now."

Her *mamm* replied from another part of the house, and Reba hobbled out to the waiting carriage.

Abel met her on the passenger's side of the buggy. "Do you need help getting in?"

As much as she would have liked to tell him no, the truth was she did need help. That was the hardest part of having a broken ankle. She had to rely on others for help. That didn't set right with her. Not one bit.

"*Jah*, if you don't mind, please."

"Not at all."

The trickiest part was stepping up onto the running board and into the buggy. Mainly because her booted foot wasn't stable. Abel had one hand on her waist and the other on her arm, holding her steady as she balanced her weight to climb in. He was strong and sure, and she knew she wasn't about to fall, so why did her heart flutter in her chest as if she were about to go down any minute? Maybe because she didn't know him very well. He could actually turn her loose and walk away. Though she had no doubt he would never do that.

She willed her heart back to its normal rhythm as he walked around the carriage and got in the other side.

"So, where are we going?" That was a safe enough question, right?

Abel clicked the horse into motion, the sway of the carriage bumping her against him as they rode along. "There's an auction today over in Bird-in-Hand. I thought we would start there."

She gave a quick nod. "So, whose horse is that?"

"My cousin's."

"I didn't realize you had family here."

He gave a small shrug. "I have family all over."

"Any brothers and sisters?" It wasn't like she was prying. Friends had to know stuff about one another, didn't they?

He shook his head. "I'm an only child. But I've got a lot of cousins."

She couldn't imagine what it was like to be an only child. Their house had always been full of love and noise, but she wouldn't have had it any other way. True, her brothers were more annoying than most, but they made life interesting, if nothing else.

"And that's why you moved here? Because of your cousin?"

He kept his eyes trained on the road as he answered. *"Jah."*

Now, why did she have the feeling he wasn't telling her the whole truth?

"Is that the only reason?" And why was she bound and determined to find out the rest of the story?

"People have all kinds of reasons for doing all kinds of things," he said. "One reason is as good as any."

But somehow she didn't think that was entirely true. Whatever brought him to Paradise, it wasn't something he wanted to share.

Side by side, Reba and Abel walked by the pen holding the horses.

"What are you looking for?" she asked.

"I don't know."

"How am I supposed to know what you want if you don't even know what you want?"

"I don't think you can do any worse than I did with the last horse." He shot her a sheepish grin.

Dimples.

She shook her head. "Where did you get that beast?"

Abel stopped and propped one foot on the bottom rung of the fence. He looked out over the pen of horses milling around. "A friend of my cousin. He was supposed to be a good horse."

"I guess *good* is relative."

He chuckled. "I guess. I think he was an old racehorse. But I'm not sure how, since he was so jumpy."

She nodded. "What spooked him, anyway?"

"A grocery sack."

Reba couldn't stop her bark of laughter. "A grocery sack?"

"Trust me, I know. The grocery sack got caught in the wind and blew between his legs. He completely lost his composure." He paused for a second, looking out over the horses. "I really am sorry about your ankle."

She smiled and shook her head. "I'm sorry I was so . . . grumpy about it."

"Who told you that you were grumpy?"

She gave a one-armed shrug. "Oh, everybody. My nieces, my mother, my brothers, my *dat*."

"Ouch."

"Sometimes the truth hurts."

"And sometimes people expect too much of others. I think I would be grumpy if I were knocked into a puddle and broke my ankle when I was simply trying to walk to work."

Her grin widened. "If some big oaf couldn't control his horse?"

"You got it."

He pointed to a rusty mare toward the center of the pen. She had a white blaze on her forehead and a silky white nose. Even from this distance Reba could see a gentleness in her eyes. She was calm and collected while the other horses milled around her. "What about her?"

"I'm no expert," Reba said. "But I would buy her in a minute."

Abel gave her another one of those heart-stopping grins. "Done deal."

"How about some lunch?" Abel asked, just after twelve. He had won the bid on the horse and even managed to get her under his budget. Now if he could just get rid of the other beast, he would be set. Even better if he could talk the pretty woman at his side into sharing a meal with him.

"I really should get back to the house," Reba said. She didn't look at him when she said the words, and he wondered if there was a little more to that statement.

"I still owe you a meal, remember?"

"You bought pizza," she said.

He shook his head. "And you didn't get to eat any of it."

"So I didn't." She had eaten two bites of one slice before she left for the hospital, but her ankle was hurting her so badly she couldn't eat any more. "You don't have to buy me lunch."

"But I want to." He gave her his best smile. "Please."

Something he couldn't identify flashed in her eyes, but it was gone in a heartbeat. "Okay," she said.

"Don't sound so excited about it."

She crossed her arms and gave him a look. "It's just a lunch between friends, right? Nothing to get excited about at all."

He gave a nod. "That's right." But he wanted her to get excited about it, even enjoy herself a little bit. And he had the perfect plan.

He might not have grown up around these parts, but he had heard people talking about the cute little petting zoo across the street from the Hayloft Candles. How fun it would be to grab something to eat and go sit at one of the benches he had heard others talk about? Maybe they could even feed the animals. Just get away for a little while.

He dashed into Amos' Place next to Stoltzfus Meats and grabbed them a couple of wraps, then back out and down the road.

A small frown puckered her brow as he pulled into the parking lot. "What are we doing here?"

"It's a beautiful day. Maybe we should have a picnic."

"Picnic?" She said the word as if she'd never heard it before.

"*Jah*. That's when you sit at a table outside and eat."

"And friends go on picnics?"

He gave a quick nod. "Now they do."

They took their food around the pond to the wooden bench on the far side.

"So, what do you think?" Abel asked as he settled down next to her. They faced the pond so they could watch the fountain as well as the ducks, geese, and swans that floated in the water.

"I love it here." Reba smiled. "I like to bring the girls here so they can feed the animals. Susie, the red Highland, is their favorite by far."

"Oh." He looked somewhat crestfallen. "Of course you've been here."

She set down her turkey wrap and turned to face him. "Did you think I had never been here?" she asked. "I did grow up in the area."

"I know. It was dumb of me. But I wanted to take you someplace special. Someplace you had never been before."

She shook her head with a small laugh. "This place is special. And I love it here. Thanks for bringing me."

"Thanks for coming with me."

The moment snagged as if caught in the branches of a tree. All of a sudden, everything just . . . stopped.

She stared into his eyes. He stared back into hers.

Something was happening here, and she wasn't sure what. But if she had to guess, Abel Weaver wanted to kiss her.

Yet they were in public, surrounded by *Englischers* and Amish alike. Children ran past, and the moment was gone.

Abel cleared his throat. "So, after we finish eating, do you want to go feed Susie the Highlander?"

Reba gave an awkward nod. "Scottish Highlander," she corrected. "And I don't like to feed her."

"Why not?" He picked up his wrap and started to eat once more.

Reba pulled a face. "She has a sticky tongue."

"A sticky tongue?"

"You'll see."

Sticky was not the word. Or maybe it was just one word. He held his cupped hands in front of him, offering Susie the feed he'd purchased from the machine closest to them.

"It's not so bad," he said, while inwardly he cringed. Susie had a tendency to lick whatever was close as she scooped up the food with her tongue.

"If you say so." Reba did not look convinced.

"I say so," he said. After all, he really couldn't tell her how gross it was. He surely didn't want her to think that he couldn't handle something like a sticky tongue of a Scottish Highland cow. What kind of man would that make him?

And of course, concentrating on not shuddering at the feel of Susie's sticky tongue against the palm of his hand gave him something to think about other than almost kissing Reba Schmucker in front of all these good people.

He could only thank heaven above for the strength to keep his wits about him as he stared into her sky-blue eyes.

"Can we feed the ducks now?" Reba pointed toward the pond.

"I thought you'd never ask." He dug a quarter out of his pocket and passed it to her.

She laughed and plugged the coin into the machine.

By the time they were done, Abel was certain they had fed every animal in the place, including the goats, the peacock, and the potbellied pig.

He snatched some hand sanitizer from the dispenser on the way out, wondering how long it would be before his hands felt clean again.

But the worst part was he had no reason to delay Reba any longer. He should have come up with another activity, but he hadn't quite expected to enjoy himself this much. And that was because the Reba Schmucker he had today was so different than the Reba Schmucker from a few days ago, the woman who was mad as a wet hen and bound and determined to blame him for all the problems in the world. This Reba was fun to be with. She smiled a lot. She laughed a lot. And it was just what his heart needed.

It was better this way, he told himself. He wasn't in the market for anything more serious than casual friends.

"I guess I should be getting you back home," he said, steering her toward his buggy.

"Do you mind if we make one little stop?" she asked as he helped her into the buggy.

He hoisted himself up beside her. "Not at all." That would only prolong his time with her, even if for just a little bit.

He started the horse toward the main road. "Where to?"

"I need to go by Leon King's place."

"Doesn't he farm goats?"

"That's him."

"Left? Right?"

"Right," she said.

At the road he started to turn the buggy to the right.

"No, left," she said. "Right as in left is right."

"What?" he asked, with a chuckle.

She laughed. "Turn left."

"Got it." He pulled out onto the road, and they were on their way once again. "What are you going to Leon King for?"

"I need to get some more goat's milk."

"More?" he asked. "You've bought it before?"

"I've been making soaps for Bernice and Jess's wedding. You know, for the favors."

"Of course." He nodded. "But you don't have time to make that many soaps." He had no idea how long it would take, but he was fairly certain that if she worked every day between now and the wedding, she still wouldn't be able to make four hundred bars of soap to include in the wedding favors.

"I've got most of them done already," she assured him. "We just need a few more, so I'm making another batch."

Abel shook his head as they pulled into Leon King's drive. Was there anything Reba Schmucker couldn't do?

"What about you?" he asked as they walked next to the pen containing the goats.

"What about me?"

"Do you have any plans to get married?" She had said she wasn't in the market for a husband. But somehow he needed to hear her say it again.

"No." She shook her head, her expression unreadable. "What about you?"

He should've stopped this conversation when he had the chance. "No. But there was a time . . ."

She turned as Leon King marched out of the barn. He seemed to know exactly what Reba was after, and they were on the road back home in minutes.

"You were engaged?"

And he had thought the conversation was over. He gave a small cough, then cleared his throat. "*Jah*. I was engaged."

"What happened?" She shook her head. "If you don't mind me asking. You don't have to answer. That's too personal."

It was too personal, but he'd started this conversation and he needed to see it through. "She chose another." There. He said it. And it didn't tear his heart in two. In fact, for the first time in months his heart managed to keep its normal rhythm when Abigail was brought up.

"And they got married last season?"

"This October. She's supposed to get married at the end of October."

He could almost see the wheels turning in Reba's mind. No, Abigail wasn't married yet. But he wasn't about to fight for the woman's affections. Love shouldn't be a competition. Abigail chose another, and it was as simple as that. She went with Luther, and Abel moved to Paradise.

"Do you want me to take you to your parents' house? Or Jess's?"

"My parents', please." She folded her hands in her lap, and he felt as if he had made a mistake. Though he wasn't sure how. He chanced one last look in her direction, then trained his gaze to the road ahead. What did it matter, after all? They were just friends.

Of course he had been engaged. He was strong and handsome, and aside from knocking women into puddles and playing a small part in broken ankles, he was a great guy to be around. But that love for another, that was what she saw in his eyes when she looked closely.

Not that it mattered. They had agreed to just be friends.

But she had allowed herself to daydream just a bit. She knew she was loud. She knew she wore her dresses in too-bright colors and that she was what some men considered a "handful." Anyone who had ever shown any interest in her during her *rumspringa* days had either been scared off by her strong personality or unwilling to try to change her. Not that she would've changed. She was the way God made her, and that was all there was to it.

So even despite her nieces' admirable intentions of helping her find a husband, Reba knew she was destined to be an old maid. After all, who wanted a sassy-mouth wife?

But there had been a small time when she felt that maybe, despite their agreement to only be friends, she and Abel could possibly have a chance at having something more. But now that hope was dashed away like the seeds of a dandelion.

They remained silent for the rest of the way to

her parents' house. Reba wasn't sure what was on his mind, but she used the time to rearrange her thoughts, get everything back in order, and put Abel firmly back into the friend category. Despite everything, he would make a wonderful friend. And if that was to be their relationship, so be it.

He stopped his carriage in front of the house, and like the gentleman he was, he hopped down and came around to help her from the buggy.

The last thing she wanted was Abel's strong hands on her waist, lifting her safely to the ground. But what else could she do?

His touch sent tingles through her. Even the thought of his touch made her tingly. But she shoved him firmly back into the friend box and gave him a quick smile as her feet touched the ground. She stepped away, needing to put some distance between her and all that tingling.

"Thanks for going with me today," he said.

Reba nodded, her prayer *kapp* strings brushing against her neck with the motion. She shivered, despite the warm sun surrounding them.

It seemed like forever since they had been looking at horses and picking one out for Abel's buggy. But all in all, it had been a beautiful day. And even if things had changed—or rather they had shifted back to their original agreement—she'd had fun.

"My pleasure," she said.

She should go back to the house now, up the

back porch steps, through the door. Shut it behind her and not think about Abel Weaver again for a long, long time.

He nodded, then took one step backward as if headed to the other side of the buggy. "I really did have a good time."

She nodded dumbly.

"Oh," he said. "Don't forget your goat's milk." He reached into the buggy and brought out the container she'd gotten from Leon King. He handed it to her, and their fingers brushed. There went those tingles again.

He smiled.

Dastardly dimples.

What was wrong with her? Never before had any man affected her so. Why now? And why this man, who had no interest in weddings or marriage, other than getting her brother's house ready for his upcoming nuptials?

"Well, I guess I better go make the soap. You know . . . for the wedding." She nodded again, feeling like one of those bobblehead statues she'd seen in the souvenir shops.

"Right," he said. "Making soap. Right."

"Would you like to go to church with us tomorrow?"

He took another step backward and bumped into the carriage wheel. One hand reached out to steady himself. "Church?"

"*Jah*. Church. Unless you have church in your

353

district tomorrow. Then you should go to church with your church." Why was she rambling?

"I would love to," he said. "We don't have church tomorrow, and I would like that very much."

"Just as friends," she hastily clarified.

Abel nodded. "As friends. *Jah*. Of course."

He straightened and hustled around to the driver's side of the buggy. He got in and shut the door in record time.

"Do you want us to come by and get you?" Reba asked.

"How about I come get you?" he said. "They're supposed to bring my horse by this afternoon. I sure would like to try her out."

Reba narrowed her gaze. "What if she ends up not being a very good horse?" Images of the two of them careening down the road being pulled by a wild, rusty-colored mare flashed through her mind.

"Don't you trust your horse-picking-out skills?" he asked.

"I suppose."

He grinned. "I'll pick you up tomorrow at seven."

"Is that what you're wearing?" *Mamm*'s eyes were wide and her mouth hung open.

Reba looked down at her dress. "What's wrong with it?"

"Isn't that the dress from Jess and Linda Grace's

wedding?" She turned back to the frying pan on the stove.

Reba offered a quick, one-shoulder shrug. "Maybe."

They both knew full well that it was. There was nothing else like it in Reba's closet. She ran her hands over her apron, smoothing out imaginary wrinkles. The dress underneath was a very conservative, very somber gray. The color had looked beautiful on Linda Grace, with her gray eyes and blond hair. And as her attendant, Reba was required to wear the same thing. It was a miracle it still fit. It had been almost ten years ago. But that was the beauty of pinning dresses. One could let them out when they needed it. Like today.

"Maybe nothing," Abner said, with a laugh. "Why are you wearing that?"

As the youngest of the Schmucker children, Abner had taken it upon himself to be the orneriest. Or maybe it was that the rest of them made him feel like he needed to tease and cajole his way through life.

"There's nothing wrong with this dress," Reba said, with a sniff.

Mamm slipped the eggs onto a plate and handed it to Reba. "Not a thing. Except it just doesn't . . ." She frowned, as if unable to find the words.

"It's boring." Abner laughed.

"It's a fine color." She almost choked when she

said the words. Abner was right. It was a boring color, but today she felt the need to be a little . . . less.

"Sit down. It's almost time for breakfast, Reba." *Mamm* turned back to the stove, cracking two more eggs into the skillet.

Reba's father stomped down the stairs, followed closely by Henry, second to the youngest of the Schmucker children.

"Wow. What happened to you?" Henry asked. "Are you sick?"

Reba slid into her place at the table. "No, I'm not sick. Why would anything be wrong?"

Henry shook his head. "That dress."

"What's wrong with my dress?" She immediately regretted that question.

"It just doesn't look like you," Henry added.

"I'll say," Abner put in.

"Boys." It was a church Sunday, and *Dat* was not in the mood for any shenanigans. *Mamm* had finished cooking and sat down in her own place at the table. Everyone bowed their heads for prayer. A few moments later they lifted their heads and began to eat breakfast.

Reba shifted uncomfortably in her seat. She couldn't say that the material of the dress was actually itchy, but it seemed to rub her skin all wrong. Which was ridiculous. It wasn't made out of anything different than any of her other dresses, so why did she feel so conspicuous? The whole point was to wear something less noticeable.

"What time did Abel say he was coming again?" *Mamm* asked.

"He said he'd be here about seven," Reba answered.

Henry and Abner started elbowing each other in the ribs.

"What's that for?" Reba asked. Another question she would come to regret.

"That's why you're wearing such an ugly dress. You want to impress a boy."

Reba sniffed. "Abel Weaver is hardly a boy, and we are only friends."

Abner and Henry snickered.

"Boys," *Dat* said. He didn't bother to look at them as he spoke.

She had endured such ribbing her entire life. If it wasn't the older brothers, it was the younger ones.

A knock sounded on the door, and Reba was on her feet in an instant. "I'll get it." She waited only long enough for *Dat* to nod before she hustled over to the door. She paused, brushed her hands over her dress and apron once more, then wrenched open the door. As expected, handsome-with-dastardly-dimples Abel Weaver stood on the other side.

"Good morning," he said, with a quick nod. She thought she saw a flash of shock chase across his

357

expression, then it was gone, in its place a look of quiet acceptance. Had it really been there at all?

"Hi," she said. "We're just finishing breakfast, would you like something?"

Abel stepped into the house and took his hat from his head, twirling it in his hands as he shifted his weight from one foot to the other. "No. But *danki*. I've already eaten."

"I shouldn't be much longer," Reba said. "Would you like to wait in the living room?"

Abel gave a quick smile of relief. "That would be great. Thanks."

She escorted him to the couch, then hustled back to the dining area to finish her breakfast. She had been toying with the idea of changing her dress before going to church. Maybe everybody was right and the color was too somber for her. Or maybe she was just trying to be something she wasn't. But Abel was here and now she was stuck wearing it for the rest of the day. She looked down at herself before sliding back into her seat. It wasn't so bad.

Was it?

Church in a new district was always an adventure. A person never knew exactly what they were going to get. But it was also nice to hear someone else preach. Sometimes it was easier to pay attention to the sermon if he wasn't accustomed to the man speaking, or distracted by the people around him. And though the bishop was a fine preacher, Abel did find himself distracted. But not in the way he would have anticipated.

He cut his gaze toward the other side of the room, where the women sat. Just a couple of rows up and two spaces in sat Reba Schmucker, and in a plain gray dress that he would never have imagined she owned. Or maybe he had read her wrong. Could it be that she wasn't the person he thought she was? He shook his head. He really didn't know. But bossy Reba in her loud clothing might not be the only Reba there was.

Not that it mattered to him. They were just friends. And that was exactly the way he wanted it.

"Can you believe she rode to church with him?"

"Can you believe he rode to church with *her?*"

Reba ducked around the corner of the house, out of sight from the women on the porch. She wanted to believe that they were talking about someone else, but she knew. They were talking about her and Abel.

"And that dress," the first woman continued. Reba wasn't positive, but she thought it was Mae Ellen Bontranger. They had run around together years ago. But Mae Ellen had changed once she got married. "Who does she think she's fooling in that?"

"Him?"

The pair started to laugh, and Reba recognized the second woman to be Fran Allgyer. Both were married, doing well, and looking down their noses at those who weren't.

So Reba wasn't married. So she had no prospects. That didn't mean she wasn't doing well. She had three beautiful nieces, a loving family, and a wonderful new friend in Abel Weaver. That should be enough for anyone.

She cleared her throat and ran her hands down her front. Chin up, she stepped around the corner. If they wanted to talk about her, let them say it to her face.

"Reba!" Fran exclaimed. "There you are." She implied that she had been searching for Reba instead of lounging about on the porch and gossiping about her.

"Here I am."

"That man you came with, is he a friend of the family?" Mae Ellen asked.

Reba forced a smile. "Something like that. He's helping Jess get his house ready for the wedding."

"He's handsome, *jah*?" Fran asked.

Reba gave a small shrug. "I suppose." *If you like sweet smiles with even sweeter dimples*. Not that she was going to tell Fran and Mae Ellen that.

"Is there a romance brewing?" Mae Ellen asked.

Like Reba would tell her if there were. "No."

Fran gave a small pout. "Too bad."

Definitely.

"Reba!" She turned as Abel waved. "Time to go."

Reba gave Fran and Mae Ellen a flash of a smile. "My ride." She jerked a thumb over one shoulder, then made her way across the yard to Abel's side. She did so as gracefully as she could, considering the boot on her ankle. Funny how they wanted to talk about Abel, but no one had asked her about her broken bones.

Let them think what they would. If they thought Abel was available, they might try to set him up with their sisters, cousins, and friends. She knew from their trip yesterday that he was not ready to be bombarded with single women. Letting them believe that she and Abel might have a budding romance would save him the trouble of fending them off himself. It was the least she could do, really.

"Are you ready to go?" he asked as she drew closer. He grinned, and she nearly tripped over her own feet. *Handsome* really wasn't the word.

"When you are."

He nodded. "Your parents invited me over for the afternoon. I hope you don't mind."

She smiled in return. "Of course not. But don't feel obligated to come if you would rather spend time with your cousins."

"Just between you and me? Your *mamm* makes much better pie than my cousin."

• • •

She wasn't going to get overly excited, just because he was coming over for the afternoon. Just because he was sitting next to her. Just because they had allowed themselves to become friends.

"Can we stop by Jess's on the way?" Abel asked. "I want to check on a couple of things."

"*Jah*, sure," she said. "But no working, right?"

"Right."

Constance hopped down from the buggy and looked up just as another carriage came down the drive. The sun was shining behind it and it was hard to see, but the carriage shifted and the driver came into clear view.

"Hope, look." She tugged on her sister's arm and nodded toward the approaching buggy.

"Is that Reba and Abel?"

"*Jah*." Constance couldn't stop her smile. Maybe they had been successful after all. It had been a lot harder trying to get Reba and Abel together than it had their father and Bernice.

"Do you think . . . ?"

"What's going on?" Lilly Ruth climbed down from the buggy and shaded her eyes.

"Here comes Reba and Abel." Constance couldn't keep the ring of pride from her words. She would add her slip to her evening prayers. But she couldn't have asked for a better response.

Reba and Abel going to church together was fantastic, but them going visiting after church? It was almost more than she could have hoped for. And now that she had the two of them together . . .

"What are you thinking?" Hope asked.

Constance gave a small shrug. "Nothing. Just, isn't it great to have the two of them here . . . together?"

Hope shook her head. "We promised not to meddle."

Constance grinned, the plan already forming in her head. "We're not meddling. We're match-making, and that's something entirely different."

Chapter 6

"Reba, did you know we have some new puppies in the barn?" Lilly Ruth sidled up next to her, her fingers trailing in the strings of Reba's prayer *kapp*.

"I didn't."

Jess and Abel had gone out to go over the list of chores that needed to be finished. Since Jess was headed to an auction tomorrow, he wouldn't be around when Abel started to work. She supposed that technically what they were doing this afternoon wasn't work, but it pushed the boundaries for sure.

"Will you go out to the barn with me to look at them?"

"Sure." Reba set the seed catalog to one side and stood. "Where are your sisters?"

Lilly Ruth shrugged and pulled on her arm. "I don't know. But I want to see the puppies, and *Dat* said I couldn't go out there by myself."

Reba frowned and nearly dug in her heels. Jess wouldn't let Lilly Ruth go to the barn? She had grown up toddling into the barn. Something was up, but Reba pushed her questions aside and allowed herself to be tugged to the door.

"*Dat* said we could keep one." Lilly Ruth skipped ahead a bit once she realized that Reba wasn't going back on her word to visit the puppies.

"That's good."

"*Jah*," Lilly Ruth said. "We can't decide which one, though. *Dat* said to give it some time. They're too small now to have gotten their personalities. Once their eyes are open, they'll have that and we can decide then."

Reba wasn't entirely sure that was what Jess had told his daughters, but it was close enough for her to understand.

"In here." Lilly Ruth led the way, only slowing down when she stepped foot into the barn.

Reba ducked in behind her. She could hear the tiny grunts of the pups before they ever got to the stall. "Which dog is that?" she asked.

Lilly Ruth shrugged. "She's a stray. Just came up a couple of days ago."

Which would explain why Reba was just now hearing about the puppies.

"They're in here."

Reba turned at the sound of Constance's voice. Her oldest niece tugged on Abel's hand, dragging him through the barn.

He stumbled a bit when he saw Reba standing there. "Hi," he said.

She gave a small wave in return.

"Aren't they sweet?" Constance asked.

"They are fine pups," Abel dutifully replied.

"*Dat* will let you have one. I know he will," Lilly Ruth said.

"When they're ready to go," Constance added. "Hi, *Aenti* Reba."

"Seems to be a busy place," Abel commented, lowering his voice so only Reba could hear him.

"*Jah.* It does," Reba returned.

"Did you hear that?" Constance asked. She looked at each one of them in turn.

"I didn't hear anything," Abel said, his brows merging to make one handsome frown.

"I did." Lilly Ruth gave an exaggerated nod. "*Dat*'s calling us."

"But—" Reba started. Yet, surprise, the girls weren't listening.

"We better go see what he needs," Constance said.

"Bye." Lilly Ruth waved and took off out the barn door, Constance right on her heels.

Reba watched them go with a shake of her head.

"I think we've been set up," Abel said, with a chuckle.

She flashed him a grim smile. "I know we have."

Abel looked down at the wriggling black and white puppies, then up to the woman standing next to him. "You're pretty calm about it."

"That's all you can be where Constance, Hope, and Lilly Ruth are concerned. They're just trying to help."

He murmured something unintelligible, but it seemed to satisfy her.

"I'm sorry," she said. "I know this must be uncomfortable for you."

"It's all right," he said. "Are you ready to go?"

She nodded. "If you're finished here."

They walked out of the barn together as a buggy pulled into the drive.

"Busy place," Abel murmured.

"That's Bernice."

The bride returns.

They waited as she got out of the buggy. Abel could understand how Jess had fallen for her. Bernice Yoder was a beautiful and poised woman.

"Bernice!" Constance, Hope, and Lilly Ruth rushed out of the house in a flurry of color. They surrounded her, jumping up and down in excitement.

"Are you staying?" Constance asked.

"For a bit." Bernice shifted her attention to Reba. For a moment he thought Bernice drew back in shock, but it happened so fast that he knew he was mistaken. "Hi."

"I'm glad you're back," Reba said.

Bernice smiled, and her whole face lit up. "Me, too." She turned to Abel. "I don't believe we've met. I'm Bernice Yoder."

"Abel Weaver. I'm helping Jess get the house ready for the wedding."

"So I've heard."

"I hate to rush off," Abel said. "But I need to get Reba home."

One slim, dark brow shot upward as Bernice centered her attention on Reba. "Oh?"

As he turned, he thought he saw Reba shake her head. But he must've been mistaken about that, too.

"Abel went with us to church today," Reba said. Her words seemed stilted. "I only rode with him to make sure he didn't get lost."

Bernice nodded. "Oh, I see."

Somehow he didn't think she meant those words. Or perhaps her tone indicated something more. He looked back to Reba. But she only stared at him, eyes wide and innocent.

"Surely you can stay a bit longer." Bernice turned to each one of them. "I thought we might have a piece of pie." She smiled. "Get to know each other better."

"I'm always up for pie," Abel said. He looked to Reba. "Do you need to get home?"

She clasped her hands in front of her and opened her mouth to speak. It took her so long to find the words he wondered if she was trying to find a nice way to turn down Bernice's offer. "No," she finally said. "That sounds nice."

"Do you have a dress I can borrow?" Reba latched onto Bernice the moment they got out of Jess and Abel's sight.

"Perhaps something like you're wearing?" Bernice folded her arms and leaned her back end against the kitchen counter. "Would you like to explain to me what's going on here?"

Reba shook her head. "Don't get all teachery on me. Do you have a dress or not?"

"Nope. It doesn't work like that," Bernice said. "Tell me what's going on, then I'll see if I have a dress."

A hundred different ways to explain why she needed her dress ran through Reba's mind all at once. But they were slippery thoughts and slid away before she could grab ahold of one. That left her standing with only the truth to share. "I like him."

Wow. That didn't hurt nearly as bad as she thought it was going to. But the next part might. "He's such a nice man. And he's been hurt before."

"So you're pretending to be something that you're not?" Bernice asked. "How's that a good idea?"

"That's not it at all. I'm just trying to be what everyone expects from an Amish woman. That's not wrong, right? I mean, we have these rules in place for a reason."

Bernice shook her head. "I'm not buying it for a minute. You have hated those rules your whole life. In fact, I think you've probably broken every rule in the *Ordnung*."

"Not true." It was so far from the truth it was laughable. So she wore her dresses a little bright and sometimes she didn't twist her hair. And *jah*, she would like to cut her prayer *kapp* strings completely off. What good were they anyway? But were those rules really that important? She didn't think so. But someone like Abel . . . he would.

"Maybe I just want to wear dresses that aren't so bright."

Bernice seemed to think about it a moment. "Okay. So you don't want to wear a bright dress. I can understand that."

"So you have a dress I can borrow?"

"Come by the house tomorrow, and I'll see what I can find."

Reba shook her head. "I'll stop by tonight, okay?"

Bernice laughed. "You have got it bad."

369

• • •

Just friends, Reba reminded herself as they drove home. She and Abel were just friends. But their friendship was young, still budding. And she didn't want him to think that his new friend was a troublemaker. That was the only reason she wanted to borrow a dress from Bernice. That, and she was certain the gray one she had on now was about to cut her circulation off. Underneath her arms was the worst spot. It hadn't been so bad sitting at the table during breakfast, but spending all day in the small garment was about to take its toll.

"Abel?" she started as they swayed with the stride of the horse.

"Hmmm?"

"I was wondering . . ." She folded her fingers into her apron, trying to find something to do with her hands except let them flutter about the air like crazy butterflies. "This is the last week of school, you know."

"*Jah.*"

"Well, the children had such a good time with you the other day, I was thinking that maybe you could come to the end-of-school picnic on Friday."

"Friday?" he repeated.

"*Jah.* Friday. That will still give you plenty of time to get the work done at Jess's, right? Then you could play softball and eat with us. It'll be a fun time. I mean, if you like that sort of thing."

And he seemed to. At least, he seemed to have a good time the other day.

"*Danki*," he said. "I would like that very much." He grinned, flashing those dimples once more.

Just friends, she reminded herself. Just friends.

"You want to tell me what's going on?" Bernice asked, a couple of hours later.

Once Abel had dropped her off at the house, Reba had hitched up her buggy and rode over to the *dawdi haus* Bernice shared with her cousin, Sarah.

"I just need to borrow a dress."

Bernice stood in front of her closet, arms folded. She was a smart woman, and there was no fooling her. "The truth, please."

"I think I like him," Reba said, with a wince. It was the second time she had admitted as much, and it hadn't gotten any easier with repetition.

"Like him? Or like him–like him?"

Reba shook her head. "We've agreed to be friends. He just broke up with his fiancée."

"That really didn't answer my question, you know."

"We're friends," Reba said. "That's all."

"Then why are you pretending to be something you're not?"

"Who said that?" She said the words, but the pang in her stomach stretched its tentacles to the ends of her fingers.

371

"Nobody needs to say anything. You're not acting quite like yourself. You didn't try to scare Jess even one time this afternoon. *And* you're wearing gray."

"Maybe I feel it's time to grow up. Stop pushing the envelope."

"Or maybe you think he'll like you more if you conform."

Reba sighed. "I just don't want him to think I'm a troublemaker."

"He won't."

"His old district is so much more conservative than we tend to be." And she liked to push all the rules as far as possible. It wasn't a good combination. Not if she didn't change something, and fast.

"So this isn't to snag his attention as a man."

"*Pbfbth* . . ." Reba blew out a breath and dismissed the thought with a flick of her hand. "No. Of course not."

Bernice studied her for just a moment, then she gestured toward her closet. "Take your pick."

Reba took a step back and surveyed the contents of her closet. Every color in the rainbow was represented there, even yellow, the color of sunflowers. She had made them all, much to the chagrin of her family, and none of them were appropriate. At least her laundry was all caught up. Except now she didn't want to wear any of them.

She hung the dress she had borrowed from Bernice in the middle of her color wheel. The *frack* was blue, still pretty, but not nearly as bright as her own blue selections. With any luck, it would make her eyes appear bluer and her hair darker. Not that she wanted Abel to notice that. They were just friends, after all.

"What are you doing?" *Mamm* came into her room carrying a stack of laundry.

"Nothing." She did her best to pull her face into an innocent expression.

Mamm set the clothes on Reba's bed. "Where'd you get that dress?"

"That?" She waved a hand toward her closet. "I borrowed it from Bernice."

Her mother looked into the closet at the row of dresses hanging there, all clean and bright. "*Jah?*"

"I wanted to see if I liked her . . . pattern . . . uh, better."

"Reba." *Mamm* propped her hands on her hips.

"Okay. I wanted something a little less . . . obvious to wear."

"For?"

"Clothing?" The word came out as a question.

Mamm scooted the clothes back, took a seat on the bed, and patted the space next to her.

Reba hesitated for only a second, then joined her mother on the bed.

"Would you like to tell me what's going on?"

Reba gave a quick shrug. "Nothing, really. I'm

just thinking about changing my look. You know, toning it down a bit."

"This wouldn't have anything to do with Abel Weaver, would it?"

"No—maybe."

"Which is it?"

"I invited him to the last-day-of-school picnic. I wanted something more . . . appropriate to wear."

"Because . . . ?"

"I like him. And we've agreed to be friends. I just think that . . . that . . ."

"That he would like you better if you were someone else?"

"No." She sucked in a deep breath. "I think it's time to reinvent myself."

"Reinvent yourself?" *Mamm* frowned.

"How many times have you told me to behave myself? Be a proper Amish woman so I can get a proper Amish husband?"

"Is that what all this is about? Getting married?"

Reba shrugged. "I've been thinking about it, *jah*. I mean, isn't every Amish girl raised to get married?"

"I suppose." *Mamm* studied her with patient blue eyes. "But you shouldn't compromise who you are."

"But . . ." There were a hundred things she could say to finish the thought, but none of them would come.

Mamm patted her hand and stood. "But nothing.

If it's in God's plan for you to get married, then He will send you someone. Someone who will not expect you to be anything other than who you are."

Reba stared after her as her mother left the room.

"But what if Abel Weaver is my someone, and I've already blown it?"

Chapter 7

Really, what choice did he have?

Abel had worked most of Monday morning painting the house and touching up his previous paint job on the carriage house and the barn.

But there, sitting on the bench just to the right of the front door, were three red and white insulated coolers. Constance, Hope, and Lilly Ruth had left their lunches behind. What could he do but hook up his new horse and run them to the school-house? Jess was at the auction. Abel couldn't let the girls go hungry.

Of course, it didn't hurt that he would see Reba again. The weekend had been the best time he'd had in a long while. He had been wondering all morning if he would see her again before the end-of-school picnic.

Now that Bernice was home, he was sure she would be the one taking care of Jess and the girls in the evening. He was even a little surprised that Bernice wasn't there right then, cleaning on the house with five or six of her closest friends. But if he had learned anything from his cousins, it was that Amish women sometimes started cleaning two months before an event. Most likely, Bernice had been cleaning house since March.

"Come on, girl," he told the mare. "Let's go deliver lunch and see what's happening at the schoolhouse."

The playground was empty when he pulled into the packed gravel drive. The scholars must have still been inside finishing their lessons. He tethered his horse and hustled up the steps.

"Abel!" The kids cried his name as he entered.

"Scholars." The one word from their teacher was heavy with warning.

They all turned around and faced front again.

"Reba, we should sing to him," one of the girls said. Abel thought she was a fifth grader, but he wasn't sure.

It was a tradition to sing for visitors, but he had interrupted enough. "No, no, that's all right. I just came to bring the Schmucker girls their lunches. They accidentally left them on the porch."

Constance and Lilly Ruth shared a look that had Abel wondering if he had fallen into their trap once again.

"You can leave them on the table by the door." Reba seemed all business today. Sort of no-nonsense despite the watermelon-colored dress she wore.

He frowned, surprised at himself for even noticing. But he noticed a lot of things where Reba was concerned. The first time he had seen her it had been hard to tell anything about her dress, seeing as how it had been covered with mud and grass. Then she'd put on a too-large dress of a somber gray. When they went to the auction, she'd had on bright green. Then gray, now bright pink. It was as if she couldn't make up her mind who she was. The dark gray looked like something a still-grieving widow might wear, while he knew for a fact her bright dresses would have been a problem for his conservative bishop in Punxsutawney. So who was the real Reba Schmucker?

He set the lunch coolers on the table, then started for the door.

"Abel, stay," Constance said.

Her words were followed by a chorus of "Stay, Abel."

One stern word from their teacher, and the scholars fell silent once more, though he could hear a bit of rumbling underneath the quiet.

"I'm sure Abel has more to do than hang out with us. And if we're going to get our lessons finished on time, we need to stay on task."

A few *aws* went up, but they didn't last long.

As much as Abel would have liked to say that

he didn't have anything better to do than have lunch with the scholars and join in their game of softball once again, he needed to get back to the house and finish the last coat of paint.

With a quick wave to the kids, he loped down the porch steps and into his waiting carriage.

That settled it. After the last scholar left that afternoon, Reba locked the schoolhouse and stomped down the stairs. It hadn't even been two weeks, and she was already tired of the walking boot on her broken ankle. But even worse? Abel Weaver showing up in the middle of the day unexpectedly. How was she going to convince him she was different if he continually took her off guard?

Thankfully, she had managed to convince her father she could drive her own buggy to school and back home again. That would surely save her having to explain to him why she wanted to go to the fabric store on a Monday afternoon. She might have borrowed a dress for Friday's festivities, but if Abel was going to drop in willy-nilly, she had to have more than one appropriate dress in her closet. She had already told her mother that she was looking at a new pattern. What better way to try it out than to make a new dress? Tonight.

An hour later Reba grabbed the sack of fabric from behind the seat and hurried toward the house.

Her mare was in the barn and the carriage put away; now all she had to do was sew a dress. She skipped up the steps and through the front door.

"Reba," her mother called. "There you are."

"I, uh . . . *jah*."

"I was beginning to get worried about you."

Reba slipped off her shoe and held up the sack. "I had to stop by Zook's and get some fabric."

Her mother used a dish towel to brush the flour off her apron. "You bought fabric? Today?"

Reba nodded. "I thought I'd make myself a new dress tonight." She waited for her mother to find fault with the idea.

But *Mamm* just smiled. "A new dress would be very nice. Let me see."

Why was she so reluctant to hand the sack to her mother?

Mamm peeked inside, then held up the fabric. "Oh."

Reba knew better than to ask if she liked the color. It was somewhere between a brown and burgundy. To Reba it was similar to a raisin and had about as much appeal. But at least it was more color than gray.

"Did you pick this out yourself?"

"Of course. It'll look good with the black, *jah*?"

It would be dark and drab, and her mother knew it.

Mamm almost nodded. "*Jah*," she said slowly. "Black would be okay on top of that."

"But it's not a bad color? Right?"

Her mother placed the fabric back in the sack and handed it back to Reba "No. It's not a bad color. It just seems . . . different than what I would have expected you to buy."

"I'm reinventing myself, remember?"

Her mother nodded. "I know that's what you say. But perhaps you should give that some more thought."

"It's time, don't you think?" She couldn't go around forever pushing the envelope to see how far she could go before she got into trouble. Everybody had to grow up some time or another.

"I suppose," *Mamm* said. "I just didn't think you would go this far this fast."

Reba clutched the fabric to her chest and raised her chin in the air. "Well, I think it's a magnificent color." But the lie tasted bitter on her tongue.

"Give us a ride home?" Constance asked, the following afternoon.

Reba had waited all day for a surprise visit from Abel Weaver. But he hadn't come by.

He didn't have a reason to.

Constance, Hope, and Lilly Ruth were brought to school by their *dawdi*. There were no forgotten lunches today. No appearance needed to be made at the schoolhouse. No last-day-of-school picnic. And then there was the little matter of him working at Jess's house to get it ready for the wedding. Abel didn't have time to just run into town and say hi to her. She should've realized that last night when she stayed up late sewing her new dress. But it was made now, and it didn't look half bad. At least, she didn't cringe when she looked at it.

"If you take us by the house, you might get to see Abel," Lilly Ruth said.

Constance elbowed her in the ribs.

"Ow," Lilly Ruth said.

"Girls." Reba looked at each one of them in turn.

Constance and Lilly Ruth had eager, expectant looks on their faces as they waited for their aunt to decide about taking them home in the buggy.

Hope, on the other hand, stood off to one side, arms crossed and a frown on her face. "We always walk home. We don't need to go home in a buggy."

"Hush," Constance said. "Why shouldn't Reba take us home?"

"You might get to see Abel," Lilly Ruth said. This time she was quicker than Constance and stepped back as Constance sent her elbow sideways.

Lilly Ruth stuck out her tongue. "And he smells good."

"Girls," Reba said once again, but this time her tone didn't have quite the bite it had earlier.

Seeing Abel didn't sound like such a bad idea

after all. Especially since she had made this dress with him in mind. But there was a very good chance that he had already left Jess's house, and he wouldn't be there if she took the girls home. And really, how could she turn down those sweet faces?

She hooked one arm toward her buggy. "Let's go."

Constance and Lilly Ruth climbed into the back while Reba, after two attempts, managed to pull herself into the buggy and settled in the front with Hope.

Reba was getting better. This morning it had taken four tries before she managed to push herself inside without help.

She clicked the horses into motion and pointed the buggy toward her brother's house.

"I told them not to meddle," Hope said. "But they're doing it anyway."

"Hope," Reba started gently. "It's not nice to tattle."

"I know." Hope's frown deepened. "But they're breaking their promise. Isn't that worse?"

"Some promises are easier than others to keep." Boy, were they. Like the one where she promised herself not to worry about finding a husband? And she said she was going to trust God? So why couldn't she just let God's will be? Why did she have to make this new dress?

Abel Weaver's handsome face flashed in her

mind. It was those dimples. She was sure of it. Dimples like that made girls do crazy things.

"If you say so." Hope did not look convinced.

"I do," Reba assured her.

Hope continued to frown all the way to her house. Reba decided it was best to let her work through whatever was between her and her sisters. She might have told the girls not to meddle, but honestly, she felt as if she could use all the help she could get.

She pulled the buggy into Jess's drive, and her heart gave a hard pound at the sight of Abel Weaver's buggy still parked there.

"Are you coming in?" Constance asked, after Reba stopped the buggy.

"Of course."

"I think Bernice has finished sewing our dresses. You can come look at them," Lilly Ruth said.

Reba would have rather gone to the barn to see what Abel was doing out there. She had a feeling he was done with his tasks inside the house.

"That's a fine idea." She tethered the horse and followed the girls into the house.

What a difference just a few months made. Jess's place had never looked better. Not since Linda Grace had died. His first wife was a wonderful Amish woman and a very good mother. But after her passing, Jess had fallen onto hard times, doing his best to keep up with all of his farm chores and three little girls who missed their mother terribly. Housework became the last thing on his mind, until the house itself was close to a certifiable disaster.

Now it fairly sparkled with cleanliness and love. Reba was happy for her brother and the joy he found with the beautiful schoolteacher. No one deserved such happiness more than he. But if she was being honest with herself, she was just a tiny bit jealous. Jess had managed to find two women to love. Why couldn't she even find one man for herself?

Bernice was nowhere to be found, and Reba could only imagine all the last-minute wedding preparations she was out making. Second marriages might happen off-season, but that didn't mean they were any less of an affair. Amish families were big, their weddings even larger, and a happy union of two people was more than enough reason to celebrate.

Lilly Ruth grabbed Reba's hand and directed her toward the back bedroom. "Our dresses are back here."

Bernice had chosen a beautiful sea blue color for the wedding. The fabric was the same shade as the water off some exotic island in some faraway land that Reba had trouble even believing existed. But the color really was nothing short of beautiful, not too bright and definitely not the ugly color she had on.

Reba felt more drab than ever as she looked at

the beautiful dresses hanging around the room. There was one for Bernice, of course. And ones that matched for the girls. And one for Reba herself.

Since Bernice's sister was married and her cousin Sarah a widow, Reba had figured Bernice would choose another female cousin to serve as her attendant. But she'd been happily surprised when Bernice asked her.

And next Tuesday she would wear that beautiful dress that matched Bernice, Constance, Hope, and Lilly Ruth and witness her brother's second happy marriage. The thought brought tears to her eyes.

Lilly Ruth tugged on her hand. "Are you okay?"

Reba nodded and swallowed back her tears. "I'm fine."

Hope sidled up to her other side and took hold of her hand. "Then why are you crying?"

Reba shook her head. "Sometimes we cry happy tears, *jah*?"

Lilly Ruth's freckled forehead puckered into a frown. Her blue eyes sparkled behind her clear-framed glasses even as she shook her head. "I've never heard of happy tears."

"It's a big girl thing," Constance said. "You'll understand when you're older."

"You're not that much older than I am."

Constance sniffed. "Old enough."

"How about let's stop bickering and go get a

snack," Reba suggested. She had a feeling Jess was out in the barn. And since neither he nor Bernice was around, Reba didn't have reason to hang out much longer. She would have to leave soon before it became painfully obvious she was waiting to catch a glimpse of their handsome repairman.

Not ones to turn down cookies and milk, the girls ran to the kitchen without waiting for Reba to follow behind. She set them all up with a snack and grabbed a cookie of her own for the road. "I guess I need to be getting home now."

Constance took a bite of her cookie, then looked to the door. "Are you sure you can't stay longer?" She looked back to Reba.

It was pathetic, really, how she was waiting to see him. The worst part of all was she knew Constance was thinking the same thing. She really needed to get out of here before she lost every bit of her dignity. "*Jah*, I'm sure I can't stay any longer. I'm supposed to help *Mamm* today. I'll see you all tomorrow." She smiled and started for the door.

Her steps slowed as she walked across the porch and down the stairs. She could always blame it on her ankle boot; a person couldn't be too careful while wearing something like that. But really, her steps slowed to a snail's pace.

Where could he be?

Why do you care?

Pathetic was not even the word. She needed to leave this to God. Wasn't that what her mom told her she should do?

She grabbed a hold of the sides of her buggy and started to hoist herself inside.

"Reba," Abel called. She stopped, her breath leaving her in an audible *whoosh*.

"Abel." She tempered her smile so it just went from ear to ear. She was so happy to see him she was afraid it would slide right off her face.

She waited by the buggy as he drew near.

"Just the person I wanted to see."

"Oh, *jah*?" she asked. Friends, she told herself. They had agreed to just be friends. That was all she wanted from him. Friendship. She wanted to be a good friend. But it was just friendship. So why was her heart thumping wildly in her chest at the sight of his blue eyes and those dimples?

"My cousin is having a get-together Thursday night. I was wondering if you wanted to go with me?"

"Get-together?"

Abel nodded. "They like to have a welcome summer kind of party. I guess there'll be a lot of family and a few friends and cupcakes. You like cupcakes, right?"

She laughed. "I absolutely love cupcakes."

"Then it's your kind of party. Will you come?"

Reba could scarcely believe this was happening. "Of course I will. I would love to."

• • •

Maybe she should have made more than one new dress. What if Abel came by the schoolhouse on Wednesday? What would she wear then? She paced in front of her closet. She had the dress she had borrowed from Bernice, but that was what she was going to wear on Friday. Though it was brighter than the gray she had worn to church and the new dress she had just taken off, she knew she couldn't wear it Thursday night to the party and again on Friday. And she didn't have time to make a new dress tonight. She might be able to tomorrow night, but it was still pushing it. She had barely gotten the one made on Monday. She shook her head. Reinventing herself was turning out to be harder than she ever imagined.

Her only choice was to wear one of her pre-reinvention dresses tomorrow, the dress she borrowed from Bernice on Thursday, and her new dress, the raisin-colored one, on Friday to the picnic. The way things were shaping up, she was spending all day Saturday tied to the sewing machine. It was the only way to make this reinvention work.

Abel had thought he'd been set up on Monday with the three little lunch coolers all lined up on the bench outside the door of Jess's house. But today, seeing those same three little lunch boxes neatly in a row on the bench outside of Jess

Schmucker's front door, he knew. He *had* been set up. As much as he would have liked to teach three little girls a lesson, he knew he couldn't let them go hungry.

He hitched up his horse and headed to town. Yet he didn't want Reba to get the wrong impression. He would have to explain to her that he felt that Constance, Hope, and Lilly Ruth were doing their thing again, trying to get the two of them together. And he knew she would believe him after all the things that the three girls had already put them through. He could only hope it didn't come across as prideful. *Jah*, he would make a good husband. Someday. Maybe to even someone like Reba. If he could ever figure out exactly who she was.

He had been surprised to see her yesterday in that drab brownish-colored dress. It looked like something his great *grossmammi* would wear. But whoever she was, Abel knew he wanted to get to know her better. And maybe, once he healed his broken heart, they might have a chance at even more.

Just before lunch, the school door opened, and Reba's greatest fear walked in.

"Abel!" the children called.

Lilly Ruth actually jumped up from her seat without permission and raced toward him. She threw her arms around him, hugging his legs as she craned her head back to see him better. "Did you bring our lunches?"

Reba started to tell Lilly Ruth to return to her seat when her words hit home. How did she know why he had come? He didn't have a lunch cooler in his hands.

She didn't need to ask the question in order to get an answer. She already knew. "Lilly Ruth, sit down," Reba finally said.

Lilly Ruth gave Abel one last squeeze, then returned to her seat.

Abel turned his attention to Reba. Why, oh, why hadn't she worn the gray dress today? It was too small and horribly uncomfortable, but at least she would have been her reinvented self.

Abel frowned. Was he looking at her dress?

He couldn't be. Men didn't notice such things. *Mamm* barely noticed. And tomorrow she would have another chance to show him the new and improved Reba Schmucker. And for a lot longer than it took to drop off lunch then drive away.

Just as they had on Monday, the children wanted to sing to Abel. They wanted him to stay and eat lunch, play softball with them, and help them with the remainder of their work. But he politely declined, promising to come back on Friday and spend the entire day with them.

"Everyone, get out your readers. I'll be right back." Reba stood and followed Abel out the door. "I'm sorry," she said as the door closed behind them.

"For what?"

"I think the girls are at it again. You know, trying to get us together."

He chuckled. "Whew! I'm glad you noticed it, too. I was trying to figure out how to talk to you about it without seeming . . . arrogant."

"They are definitely up to something."

He loped down the steps and made his way over to his buggy. "They mean well."

"You're not upset?"

He gave her that heart-stopping smile. "How can I be? I'm flattered they think enough of me to want to add me to the family."

"They're pretty smart kids."

He climbed into his buggy and touched the brim of his hat in farewell. "See you tomorrow night, Reba Schmucker."

She stood on the small stoop watching him drive away. Tomorrow night. Her and Abel on what could only be described as a date. "Looking forward to it," she whispered. More than she had anything in a long, long time.

Chapter 8

"No no no no no!" Reba stripped the ponytail holder from her hair, released the clip barrettes, and grabbed her brush. She had spent so much time worried about her dress, she hadn't given a second thought to her hair.

Never in her life had she wanted her hair to look just right. But the sides weren't rolling evenly, and the last bob she had created at the nape of her neck felt heavy and unnatural.

She braced her hands on the bathroom counter and stared at herself in the mirror. She sucked in a deep breath, but didn't feel any better.

"Reba?" *Mamm* rapped lightly on the bathroom's open door. "Is something wrong?"

She took in another breath, preparing to answer, but what was she going to say? That her hair wouldn't cooperate and tonight might end up being the most important night of her life?

She couldn't say either of those things. A man was supposed to look below the surface, not at a woman's hair, dress, or figure, but to her heart underneath.

She picked up her brush once again and ran it through her hair.

"You're not worried about your appearance, are you?"

"Of course n—*jah*, maybe a little."

Mamm took her by the shoulders and spun her around. "Sit." She closed the toilet lid and urged Reba to sit down. "You never worried about such things before," *Mamm* said, and she began to fix Reba's hair.

Reba shrugged. "It's no big deal."

"It shouldn't be," *Mamm* agreed as she made two perfect rolls on each side of her head. "But sometimes it can be hard not to worry about how we look and how others see us."

Reba met her mother's gaze in the mirror in front of them. "How do you keep from worrying about it?"

Mamm smiled as she scooped Reba's hair into a quick ponytail. "Head down," she instructed.

Reba leaned forward and braced her forehead on her outstretched arms. A few well-placed bobby pins later, *Mamm* touched her shoulder. "All done."

She lifted her head to perfect rolls with a perfect bob. Reba turned her head from side to side, studying her mother's handiwork. "Thanks, *Mamm*." She stood and gave her mother a hug.

"You're welcome." *Mamm* hugged her in return.

"So, how?" Reba asked. "How does a person quit worrying about things like hair and appearance?"

"Prayer," her mother said. "Prayer and the good Lord's grace."

"Did you have a good time?" Abel asked as they made their way back to her parents' house. She seemed to have enjoyed herself, but he was never sure of anything where Reba Schmucker was concerned.

"I did, *jah*. And the cupcakes were delicious."

"I told you. My cousin Johanna makes the best cupcakes."

Reba nodded. "She should open her own business."

"Everyone keeps telling her the same thing, but it would be really hard for her considering the children." Johanna was only thirty and already had six kids, three boys and three girls. She had her hands full with the family, too full to be making cupcakes for anything other than family parties. Thankfully, the Weavers liked to have parties. Otherwise, they would never get their fill of her delicious creations.

"Speaking of kids," Reba started. She shifted in her seat, half turning to face him as she spoke. "Are you sure you're not upset about the girls? I mean, they made you make two unnecessary trips to the school."

"I wouldn't call them unnecessary. They had to eat."

"And they would have been able to, if they weren't trying to play matchmaker."

"There's only two more days of school, and one of those is the picnic."

"What are you saying?" she asked.

He gave a quick shrug. "There's only one more day, and they won't have forgetting their lunch as an excuse to bring us together."

"I suppose not," she murmured.

The thought made Abel's stomach sink, just a bit. As confusing as he found Reba Schmucker, he enjoyed her company twice as much. Her no-nonsense ways and fresh attitude made him smile. And smiling wasn't something he'd done a lot lately. Well, not the real thing. He forced smiles for months after he and Abigail broke up. Then living in Punxsutawney became harder and harder. The only choice he had was to move to Lancaster. And given the people he'd met so far, Jess and Bernice and the woman at his side, this move might turn out to be the best thing for him.

Whoa, slow down. No need to go that fast. But the more time he spent with Reba, the more he wondered why some man hadn't snatched her up already. True, the very first time he met her, he wondered how any man could possibly stand her bossy ways. She wasn't bossy. She was unique. He found he liked that about her.

They rode side by side, her shoulder brushing against his every so often as the carriage tilted with the lay of the road. He wanted to say something clever, but the words failed him. He wanted to say something charming, but nothing came. So he remained quiet, the only sounds the click of the horse's trappings and the soft whir of the wheels on the road.

"Thank you for inviting me," Reba said. He could see her driveway up ahead. Their date was nearing an end.

Was it a date? He had to think about it a moment. He said he wasn't ready to date. He said he was taking this slow. He wasn't in the market for a new love. Yet somehow he seemed inexplicably drawn to Reba Schmucker.

Or maybe that was just Constance, Hope, and Lilly Ruth putting them together every chance they got. He wondered how he would feel if their interference hadn't been . . . well, interfering.

He turned down Reba's drive and bit back a sigh. There was no going back. There was no way to find out if things would be different if she didn't have three little matchmaking nieces. She did, and they had tried to make a match. And just because he and Reba had been thrust together, just because they were in such close proximity, didn't mean there was more to their relationship than what was on the surface. Was there?

He shook his head. All these thoughts were going in circles and confusing him even more.

He pulled to a stop and sat there for a moment, debating whether to get out. Would she invite him in? Did he *want* her to invite him in? Even more importantly, did she need help getting down?

"I'm glad you came with me tonight."

In the darkness, Reba nodded. The only thing casting the glow around them was the soft porch light.

"*Danki* for inviting me."

He nodded, then stopped. "You've already said that."

She gave him a trembling smile. "*Jah*, well, I meant it twice."

She seemed nervous. What did she have to be nervous about?

"I had a good time," he said. He kept saying things, purposely trying to detain her. He wanted to spend more time with her, *jah*. That was true. He wanted to find out more about her. Who was Reba Schmucker?

Tonight, with his family, she had seemed relaxed and natural. Now, at his side, she seemed anxious and a little uncomfortable. Could she be feeling the same thing he was? Or maybe she didn't feel anything at all and was ready to get out of the carriage and run to her house, and he kept talking to her like some crazed suitor.

"Do you still want me to come to the school tomorrow?" Now why had he asked that? Because he was worried. He was worried that she regretted that invitation. And he didn't know why.

"*Jah*, of course."

Say something to keep her from leaving.

He took her hands into his own, running them over her knuckles in a small caress. He wanted to keep talking to her, he wanted to keep touching her, he wanted to keep being with her. But if he didn't come up with something clever to say, there would be nothing left between them. She would have to get out of the carriage and go into the house. They couldn't sit there all night.

"Reba," he started. He really didn't have anything to say after that, but knew that if he spoke her name, it was one sure way of stalling the inevitable.

She tilted her head back and stared at him. Her eyes, bright blue, shining despite the dim interior of his buggy.

Say something.

But he had no words. So he did the only thing he could. He lowered his head and pressed his lips to hers.

Whoa, Nelly.

Reba resisted the urge to put a hand on the back of her prayer *kapp* to hold it in place. With her head tilted back and Abel's lips on hers, she was surprised it didn't fly off in shock and sweet, sweet passion.

He was kissing her! Really kissing her! And until this moment, she hadn't realized that she had been thinking about this moment ever since the time she decided not to blame him for a broken ankle. That long. His kiss was sweet and sassy, teasing, and gentle. And she wanted it to last forever and ever. Because she had a feeling once he discovered who she truly was, there would be no more kissing. There would be nothing left for either one of them. And she wanted it to last just a bit longer.

All too soon, he lifted his head. His expression was unreadable. His gaze darted about. In the dim interior, she couldn't discern one emotion from another. Was he moved? Surprised? What if he was disgusted? It wasn't like she'd done a lot of kissing in her days. Okay, so there was one boy way back when, but his kiss was nothing like Abel Weaver's.

"I shouldn't have done that." Abel's words dropped like a dead duck between them.

Reba scooted back from him just a bit. If he was already regretting the decision to kiss her, then she definitely needed to put as much distance between them as she could. Because that kiss was not on her list of regrets.

"What?" No! She should've asked why? She heard what he said. But why did he say it?

Abel shook his head. "Do you need help getting down?"

"No." This was not happening at all the way she thought. But she should've realized. Abel Weaver had a broken heart. It might have been born with problems, but now it was broken by a woman. Who knew when it would be whole again? She'd gone into this knowing that was the truth. She couldn't blame anybody but herself. Not even him.

She slid open the door and started to get down. But in her haste it seemed she caught the side of the boot on something and couldn't find her way out of it.

"Wait," he said. "I'll help you." He got out of the buggy and came around.

Reba blinked back her tears. This was the last thing she wanted. She didn't want help from him. She didn't want help from anyone, and she had allowed herself to need him. Or maybe she had just been pretending, but she had wanted to be with him. She had wanted to have his help. She had wanted that kiss. But he said it was a mistake.

"I've got it," she lied as she continued to try to pull herself free.

"It looks that way."

Stubborn man. She had told him she was fine and he insisted on coming around and wrapping his hands around her waist. Somehow he hoisted her to the ground, freeing her when she wasn't able to release herself.

"Thanks," she said. "For nothing."

She started to turn away, but he grabbed her wrist, whirling her back around. "What does that mean?"

She shook her head. "If you don't know, then I'm not going to tell you."

He stared at her for a second, his fingers still wrapped around her wrist, preventing her from a dramatic exit. If he would only let her go, she would stomp up the stairs, slam the door, and make a big production to let him know just how unhappy she was. And what then? How was that going to solve anything?

He released her and folded his arms. "I'm sorry, okay?"

"No. It's not okay." Couldn't he see that? But she had embarrassed herself enough for one night.

A strange light dawned in his eyes. She was unsure how she even saw it, considering hers were filled with tears. "I'm not sorry for kissing you," he said. "I'm sorry for kissing you now."

The entire world seemed to stop. The crickets stopped chirping and the frogs stopped croaking and the wind stopped blowing. Everything was still. Had she heard him correctly?

"Would you explain that, please?" Her heart stilled in her chest, somehow taking a lesson from the frogs and the wind.

"I told you about Abigail."

Abigail. So that was her name.

"She's supposed to marry another this fall. I moved here because I couldn't stand watching the two of them together. I needed a fresh start. I never dreamed that I would meet someone like you my second day here. And I never imagined that you might be the one to make me forget her. But I think we're moving way too fast. I'm not sure my heart is ready for a new love. So as badly as I wanted to kiss you, I should've waited. I can't give you false hope."

Reba was certain she'd never heard sweeter words. "I don't have false hope."

"You sure about that?"

She bit her lip and gave a quick nod. "I've waited a long time to meet someone like you, Abel Weaver. And I'll wait as long as I need to for you to get your heart back right."

"It took years to repair my heart physically. The defect I was born with. I don't know how long it takes to heal a broken one."

Reba trailed fingers down his cheek, quickly imagining what he would look like once he started growing his marriage beard. What a handsome man Abel Weaver would make. Handsome enough, gentle enough, and stubborn enough that she would wait on him as long as she needed to. "However long it takes," she said. "I'll be here."

Reba floated into the house, dream-walked to bed, then had beautiful nighttime dreams of a bearded Abel Weaver wearing brightly colored shirts while she sewed raisin-colored dresses for their daughters. It was a strange dream, but she knew: It was God's way of telling her that all things happened the way they were supposed to. She couldn't ask for more assurance than that.

"You're looking chipper today," *Mamm* said as Reba came down for breakfast the following morning.

As planned, she donned her raisin-colored dress, though she was half-tempted to wear the borrowed blue dress that she had worn the night before. Somehow she felt that the in-between color had given her good luck of sorts. But she wouldn't want Abel to think she wasn't wearing clean clothes, so the brownish dress it was.

"I am feeling chipper." She smiled. "It is the last day of school, after all."

"Are you thinking about teaching again next year?" *Mamm* asked.

Reba grabbed a glass of orange juice and shrugged one shoulder. "I don't know." It wasn't like she knew her plans. It wasn't like she and Abel would be married this fall, but maybe she should let the teaching position go to one of the younger members of the community. That would allow her to possibly get ready for her own wedding.

Mamm handed her a plate with two eggs and toast. "If you're feeling so chipper, are you sure you want to wear that dress?"

So it wasn't the prettiest color. Oh, who was she trying to kid? The color was downright ugly. But it was conservative and subdued and everything she was reinventing herself to be. And she would be spending the balance of the day with Abel Weaver. It was better this way for sure.

"Of course," she said, with more confidence than she felt. It wasn't about the dress. Hadn't *Mamm* said that very thing the night before? So what difference did it make what color she wore? What difference did it make if she wore a bright color or somber color? She was still the same Reba Schmucker if she wore bright pink or the dullest gray. She didn't have to constantly battle the system. She could conform from time to time. What was wrong with that?

"If you say so." *Mamm* turned back to the stove.

Reba ate breakfast as quickly as possible, gathered up her treats for the picnic, and hitched up her horse. Today was a beautiful day. She couldn't ask for a better day for the last-day-of-school picnic. It made the sun shine a little brighter and the sky a little bluer, since Abel was coming to spend the day with them. He might not be ready for a new relationship; she could understand that. But she would be here when he was. Being his friend, going places with him, and enjoying his company.

Wearing ugly, puce-colored dresses.

She pushed that thought away as she pulled into the schoolhouse drive. A few of the students had already gathered, playing in the yard until time for school to begin. Except for today. They wouldn't go into the schoolhouse. They would remain outside, playing games like jump rope and softball and eating until they couldn't hold another bite.

"Reba! Reba! Reba!" The kids gathered around as she managed to hoist herself out of the buggy. She couldn't say she was the most graceful with her walking boot on, but she was getting better at it. By the time she got it off she would be able to hop down like nothing had ever happened to her ankle at all.

"Is everybody ready for the picnic?" She held up her sacks of goodies. The kids cheered.

"Is Abel coming?" Constance asked.

"He said he was." She handed off the sacks to a couple of the older students, then hitched her horse to the post. There were still a few more minutes before school officially started. And it wasn't like he told her he would be arriving in time for the first bell. In fact, they had never really talked about when he was coming to join the festivities. He might not come until the afternoon. As far as she knew, he'd gotten most everything done at Jess's house. Good thing, seeing as how the wedding was Tuesday. But that didn't mean he didn't have another job to go to this morning and he would only be able to come by later, after the softball game had started.

"But he is coming." This from Lilly Ruth.

The other kids dispersed, and Reba was left with her three nieces. "He said he would come," she said. Something in their voices made her stomach uneasy. Did they expect him not to come, or was this just another part of their matchmaking efforts?

"You didn't do anything, did you?" She looked at each of her nieces in turn.

Hope took a giant step forward. "I just want to say that I haven't done anything since you told us not to, Reba. Unlike some other people I know." She cut her gaze toward each side, pinning her sisters individually with an accusing stare.

"Maybe you should have," Lilly Ruth said. She stuck out her tongue.

"Girls." But the warning was only halfhearted. She kept glancing down the road, wishing the corn weren't quite so tall so she could see farther. But there was no sign of Abel's buggy. Was he even coming at all? Only time would tell.

At eight o'clock she rang the bell, gathering all the kids into the classroom one last time. She was really hoping he would be here before now, but she wasn't about to let herself get worried. He said he would come. Now he had a reliable horse. It wasn't like the rusty-colored mare he bought last week at the auction was as crazy as the stallion he had given up. She just needed to be patient. He would get there in his own time.

She went through the day's festivities with the kids and turned them loose outside. The seventh and eighth graders helped with the games and got everyone organized for a softball game later. Reba knew that parents would be stopping by all day, and yet she still checked the roads for Abel.

It was almost ten o'clock when he pulled his buggy to a stop in front of the schoolhouse.

By the end, she had stopped watching and only knew that it was him for the chorus of "Abel's here!" that went up around the playground.

He got down from the buggy and immediately Reba knew something was wrong. Or maybe *wrong* was the incorrect word. But he didn't seem like the same carefree Abel of yesterday. Her gaze swung from him to the passenger seat in his buggy. A petite young woman sat there.

Please let that be one of his cousins.

Reba pasted on a friendly smile and followed the sea of children toward Abel Weaver.

"I was beginning to think you weren't coming." She injected as much teasing into her voice as she could muster, but it seemed as if it fell short regardless of her efforts.

He pressed his lips together and gave a quick nod. "I didn't know what to do with . . ." He gestured back toward his buggy.

"Is that your cousin?" Reba asked. *Please let it be his cousin.* "She needs to go to the doctor or something?" She'd never wanted someone to be sick more in her life. But deep down she knew what he was about to say next.

"That's Abigail."

Chapter 9

Somehow Reba managed to tell Abel that it was fine. That she understood. That no, the kids wouldn't be disappointed if he didn't stay and play softball. They would understand that he needed to go work out this problem from his past. Now she just had to convince herself.

But it wasn't fine. And she wanted to rail toward the heavens. Abigail whatever her last name was had given up Abel Weaver, and Reba had found him. It wasn't fair that she could waltz back in and snatch him away. It just wasn't fair. But Reba could tell from the look in his eyes what his decision would be. He had all but told her the night before that he was still in love with Abigail. And if she had come back to claim her love for him again . . .

What was she saying? Of course Abigail was coming back for that. Why else would she drive all the way from Punxsutawney to Lancaster, if not to reclaim the love she'd thrown over once before?

The saddest part of all for Reba was that they both knew that he would forget her. He would take Abigail back. He would move back to Punxsutawney. At least he would save Reba the heartbreak of having to see him day after day or even accidentally run into him in town. It was the only consolation she could offer her heart.

The second miracle of the day was that she somehow managed to smile, conduct the last-day-of-school picnic, referee the softball game, and drive home without one tear. But by the time she pulled into her drive that afternoon, she knew that her time for breaking down was near. That was all she needed. One good evening to cry, pound her fists against the bed, and wonder at the unfairness of it all. Then tomorrow she would get up and . . .

Well, she didn't know what she would do. She would start to move on. She would start to live her life again. She would be Reba without Abel. She'd been Reba without Abel before; she could do it again.

"Reba, is that you?" *Mamm* asked as she came in the front door.

"Yes, *Mamm*."

"Do you want to—"

But Reba didn't wait around for the rest of the sentence. She headed up the stairs as quickly as possible and threw herself into her room. She collapsed onto the bed, the weight of trying to keep herself together all day finally taking its toll.

Sobs racked her body as she gave in to her grief.

"Reba?" *Mamm* pushed the door the rest of the way open and came in. Reba sat up, wiping her cheeks and pretending she hadn't been crying her eyes out.

"Child, what's wrong?"

Reba shook her head. "I just—I mean—Abel," was all she could say.

Mamm sat on the bed next to her and wrapped her arms around Reba's shoulders. She laid her head in the crook of her *mamm*'s neck and sighed. For a moment she wished she were little again. She would crawl into her *mamm*'s lap and sit there completely surrounded by her mother's love. But she was too big for that. And she would have to go on. She pulled back and wiped her tears once more.

"His fiancée came today."

Mamm blinked. "He has a fiancée?"

Reba shook her head. "She's an ex, but he still loves her. And she wants him back."

"Don't you think you should find out for sure before you completely give up hope?"

"It's not necessary," Reba said. "We talked about her last night. About how we would take things slow because he wasn't quite over their relationship yet. And now that she's back . . ." Tears welled in her eyes once more.

"Why? Why? Why?" she asked her mother, but she didn't need to finish the rest of those questions. Why, after all this time, did she find love only to lose it? Why did love have to hurt so badly? And why was she never allowed a turn at love?

Mamm wrapped her arms around Reba once more and rocked her back and forth. Sunday was a church day. Monday was the last day before the wedding, and Tuesday was Jess and Bernice's big day. But for right now, Reba was going to cry.

It was nothing short of a miracle and a loving family that kept Abel at bay. She knew he'd come by the house a couple of times since that Friday, but her family had sent him away both times. She knew she would have to face him at some point. But she couldn't face him now. Not yet. She still needed a little more time to mourn the loss of the relationship before she could pick herself back up and begin again. Only then would she be able to face Abel Weaver, hold her chin high, and tell him that it didn't matter. That she wished for him to have the utmost happiness in the world. And if that happiness was with Abigail, then she wished him all the best. One day she would be able to tell him that. But today was not that day.

Reba ran her hands over her apron and sea-colored dress. Sort of like the one Bernice had loaned her, this dress was not as bright as Reba's old stuff, but definitely not as boring as the raisin hue of the dress she had made last week. What a fool she had been to think she should change for a man only to lose him to the very thing she was trying to become.

No, today was not that day, because today was Jess and Bernice's wedding day. The first day of June, so bright and pretty, a beautiful day to start a new life.

There been that split second when Reba had thought that love would be for her, but now she knew it was not meant to be. Always an attendant but never a bride.

"I don't understand," Lilly Ruth said. "Why isn't Abel here?"

Reba smoothed a hand over the young girl's bob, making sure all the beautiful red hair was in place. "He's not . . ."

What could she say? He wasn't really their friend? He surely acted like it. He wasn't part of the family? He wasn't invited to the wedding? But that didn't seem to make sense, either. Maybe she should just tell Lilly Ruth that Abel didn't love them after all. But that sounded harsh and bitter. And she didn't want to be either.

"Well?" Constance crossed her arms and calmly eyed her aunt.

"I, uh . . ." Reba stuttered.

"This is why you shouldn't meddle." Hope pointed a chastising finger at both of her sisters. By the way she was acting, a stranger would think that she was the oldest and not the middle child who normally tried to keep the peace.

"He was our friend," Lilly Ruth countered.

Reba knelt down so she could look at her sweet niece straight ahead. "He was. And he probably still is." She shook her head. "And he still is, but that doesn't mean he will come to every family function we have." What a disaster that would be! But the girls didn't need to know that now. They didn't need to know that once he was officially back with Abigail, he would more than likely move back to Punxsutawney and never set foot in Lancaster again. All that could wait for another day. Maybe when that time came, Constance, Hope, and Lilly Ruth wouldn't be so enamored with Abel Weaver.

"But we thought he liked you," Constance protested.

"Just because he's not here doesn't mean he doesn't like me." Reba did her best to explain.

Lilly Ruth stomped one foot. "But we thought he *liked* you."

"You're too young to worry about such things." Reba had to push the words past the huge lump in her throat. She might not have Abel Weaver any longer, but she had three little girls who loved her beyond reason. She had a wonderful family, annoying brothers, and loving parents. She truly was blessed. Even if she ended up being an old maid, it wouldn't matter. She had lived her life well-loved, even if she wasn't loved by Abel.

"If you say so," Lilly Ruth grumbled.

Reba kissed each one of them on the cheek, counting her blessings as she went. "I say so."

Half an hour later everything was in place.

The bishop stood in the living room ready for Jess and Bernice to come down together to be

413

married. Reba stood to his right, waiting there in front of all the friends and family. This was Jess and Bernice's big day. A day that, a year ago, no one would've dreamed was coming. And her brother deserved all the happiness he could get.

She looked to her mother and father sitting there, their pride shielded but not dimmed. And next to them, Hope, Constance, and Lilly Ruth . . . should've been sitting. But the bench was empty. She had told them to sit there. So where were they?

Hands trembling, Reba scanned the crowd looking for the three little girls. They couldn't be far. Not in a house full of guests. But considering the fact that they were only as high as most people's waists, they could be anywhere.

Somehow she caught her *mamm*'s attention. She nodded toward the empty bench, raising her eyebrows, hoping her mother understood.

Where are the girls? she mouthed.

Mamm looked at the empty bench, then back to Reba. The fear in her mother's eyes made Reba's stomach sink all the lower. Something was wrong. Where were the girls?

Mamm leaned in and said something to *Dat*. He shook his head. Something was terribly wrong. Her father got up and headed to the back of the house.

Reba turned to the bishop. "I'll be right back."

"What?" he asked, but Reba was already gone.

She had to find the girls, and she had to find them now.

Of all the things Abel thought he'd be doing on the first Tuesday in June, crashing a wedding was the last thing on his mind. But what else was he to do, really? He had tried four separate times to go visit with Reba, and she was never around. After the second time, he got the feeling her family was telling him lies about where she was. But it took another visit and another denial for him to realize it was Abigail. Reba had misunderstood what was happening between him and Abigail. And now he had to find Reba and tell her the truth before everything was ruined.

He pulled his buggy to a stop, not even bothering to unhitch his horse. There were enough horses in the pasture that he would have to worry about finding his when the dust cleared. And he was just late enough there were no more attendants to take his buggy and give him a number. It didn't matter. He had to find Reba as quickly as possible. But the way his luck was going, the wedding would have already started and she would be up in front with the bishop and unavailable to Abel until after the service. He started up the steps to the Schmucker house only to have the front door open. Reba barreled into him.

He staggered backward, grabbing ahold of her arms to steady them both.

415

"Abel? What are you doing here?"

"I've come to talk to you. I need to tell you something."

She shook her head. "It will have to wait. The girls are missing."

After two hours of searching the farm, one thing became abundantly clear. Constance, Hope, and Lilly Ruth were nowhere around. They checked the hayloft, the basement, the attic, every stall in the barn, and every one of the buggies belonging to the wedding guests. And the longer they looked, the more worried Reba became. "Where could they be?" She looked from Abel, to Bernice, to Jess. And she knew all of their expressions were mirrors of her own. Worry mixed with worry and accented with worry.

Jess held up his hands, the picture of calm, so unlike his redheaded nature. "We're not going to panic. If they're not on the farm, then they're off the farm. Where could they have gone?"

Members of the family and the immediate wedding guests standing around started tossing out ideas on where the girls could've gone.

"Where were they last seen?" Bernice asked.

"I had them in the back sewing room," Reba said. "We were getting changed into our dresses. They were talking to me about . . ." She turned. "About you, Abel."

"Me?"

"No time to explain."

"Why were you talking about me?"

Reba closed her eyes and tried to remember the exact conversation they'd had and if that had anything to do with their disappearance. "I think I know where they've gone."

Jess gave a quick nod. "Lead the way."

"I'm not sure this is the best idea."

Reba shook her head at Abel's words. It was the best idea they had. And since Abel's buggy was still hitched to a horse, they had taken off down the road. Bernice and Jess were walking the cornfield along the side, but Reba had another idea.

"It's simple, really. I think they were going to your house to invite you to the wedding."

He frowned. "O-kay."

"I know. They don't know where you live. But if they went to the schoolhouse, they might be able to figure it out which direction to go."

He gave a quick nod. "And they might still be there."

It was all they could do. And hope and pray.

"There!" Reba pointed to the edge of the cornfield. In the shade of the tall stalks, three little girls lay in the cool grass. They looked to be asleep. "Please let them be asleep." Not hurt or worse.

Abel pulled the buggy into the packed gravel

drive as three mischievous, sweet, beautiful little girls sat up and rubbed their eyes.

Reba stumbled down out of the buggy, somehow managing to catch herself even with her booted foot before she hit the ground face-first.

"Girls! Girls!" She ran to them as fast as she could, falling onto her knees and scooping them up into her arms. She kissed their hands, their faces, their noses, anyplace she could reach. She was so happy to see them unharmed and well.

Lilly Ruth frowned and pushed her away. "What's wrong?"

Reba laughed through her tears. "What's wrong? You've been missing for hours."

Constance's eyes grew wide. "Oh, no. We just stopped to rest for a minute to try to figure out where Abel lived."

Reba tossed a look over her shoulder. Abel skidded to a stop next to her.

"You had everyone worried sick," he said.

"Abel!" The girls jumped to their feet and threw their arms around him.

Reba tried not to be hurt. She had been searching for them, looking for them, worried about them, and they were happier to see Abel than they were to see her. Must be those dimples.

"We're sorry," the girls said.

Reba pushed to her feet. "Why would you run off like that?"

"We were trying to find Abel. We wanted him to come to the wedding, too."

"I told them not to meddle," Hope said.

Constance pinched her sister, and Reba let it go. She would let them have a pinching brawl if they wanted to, as long as they were okay.

"No fighting," Abel said. "Why were you coming to my house?"

"How can you fall in love with *Aenti* Reba if you're not at the wedding?"

Reba ran her hand over Constance's sweet blond hair. "Oh, honey, love doesn't always work like that."

"It worked like that for *Dat* and Bernice," Constance said.

"You should call her *Mamm*," Hope corrected.

"I'll call her *Mamm* after they marry. Right now she's Bernice."

"I want to call her *Mamm*," Lilly Ruth said.

"Girls."

The world didn't work like that. Love didn't work like that. And that was something Reba knew firsthand. Just because she was falling in love with Abel Weaver didn't mean he was falling for her in return. Maybe if they had a little more time. Maybe if Abigail hadn't come back and claimed his heart for her own.

Abel cleared his throat. "That's right. Sometimes people want you to love them, but it doesn't work that way."

Reba closed her eyes as her heart leapt into her throat. It was one thing to know it to be the truth and another to hear it from his lips.

"But I thought you and Reba liked each other." Lilly Ruth bounced on her toes.

"We do," they said together. They stopped. Reba looked at Abel. Abel looked at Reba. They both turned back to the girls.

"But if you like each other, why can't you fall in love?" Constance asked.

"It takes more than that to fall in love," Reba said. At the same time, Abel asked, "Who said we weren't in love?"

They stopped. Abel looked at Reba. Reba looked at Abel.

"What do you mean?"

"Who said we aren't in love?"

She shook her head.

"How much more does it take to fall in love?" he countered.

Reba closed her eyes and held up her hands. "Okay, everybody, stop."

She opened her eyes and trained her gaze on Abel. "I saw you with Abigail." There. She said it. Right out loud for everybody to hear.

"Me too," Lilly Ruth chirped.

Abel shook his head. "It's not what you think."

Reba knew what it looked like. But if it wasn't what she thought . . . "Then tell me what it was."

Abel sucked in a deep breath and propped his hands on his hips. He stared out over the cornfield as if the words were somehow hidden there. Then he turned back to Reba. "Before I tell you what Abigail was doing here, I need to tell you this."

Reba's breath hitched as she waited for him to continue.

"When I came here, I wanted to heal my broken heart."

She nodded. That much she'd known from the start.

"And that night, when we were talking and . . ." He cleared his throat. Reba blushed. Thankfully the girls didn't notice. Or they didn't say anything if they did. "I told you that I couldn't fall in love until my heart was healed. And that might take some time, *jah*?"

Reba nodded again.

"Abigail came to tell me that she thought she'd made a mistake."

Reba swallowed hard. Why was she even listening to this? Every word was chipping off another little piece of her already broken heart.

"Once I saw her again I knew. My heart is already healed."

"It is?"

"Well, it's further along than I thought."

Reba shook her head. Was he saying what she thought he was saying? "What are you saying?"

"I'm saying, Reba Schmucker, that it might

not take quite as long as I thought to be ready to love again. Except." He paused.

"Except what?"

He shook his head. "You're confusing."

She stared at him, mouth agape. "I'm confusing you? How about you with a broken heart, that may or may not be *badly* broken. Or maybe it is? Or maybe not. Or maybe it won't ever heal?"

He laughed. "Okay, I'll give you that one. But I don't know who the real Reba Schmucker is. One day you're wearing bright green, the next day you're in gray. After that, you're wearing a watermelon-colored dress, the next after that you're in some brownish-burgundy color."

"It's puce."

"Puce?"

She nodded. "I had to ask the clerk, but that's what color it is."

Abel shook his head. "What's wrong with what you have on right now?"

She looked down at the dress that Bernice had picked out for the wedding colors. "Nothing."

"What's wrong with that bright green? I like the green."

"Most of those colors are a little bright for the bishop."

"What about something like what you have on now? Why does it have to be one or the other? Why does it have to be gray or bright pink?"

Why did it have to be?

"Are you saying that you would love me even if I never were puce again?"

"I'm saying I hope you never wear puce again." The girls cheered. "So, we get to have another wedding?" Lilly Ruth asked.

"Not yet," Reba said.

"Maybe soon," Abel said at the same time. They stopped. Abel looked at Reba. Reba looked at Abel. They both shrugged.

"We can figure it out all out later," Abel said. "Right now we have a wedding to get these girls back to."

Reba stood next to Bernice and across from her brother, so proud for him in this moment. No one deserved happiness more than Bernice and Jess. No one except for maybe her and Abel. She glanced out to the crowd where Abel sat in the front row. He wasn't exactly dressed for a wedding. But no one had the heart to tell him that he had to go home. Not that Reba would have stood for it if they had. Next to him were three little mischievous girls who somehow knew that love could be found in the most special places. He smiled, showing her those wonderful dimples. And she wondered then if she would have an opportunity to look at them for the rest of her life. She had often wondered why God never sent someone just for her. And then she realized He did. And that someone was Abel Weaver.

Center Point Large Print
600 Brooks Road / PO Box 1
Thorndike, ME 04986-0001 USA

(207) 568-3717

US & Canada:
1 800 929-9108
www.centerpointlargeprint.com